The Notekeeper

Hannah Treave is the pseudonym for Fiona Ford, an experienced freelance journalist and prolific novelist. She has written for weekly women's magazines for the past fifteen years and is the author of six novels – two under the penname Fiona Harrison, *A Pug Like Percy* and *A Puppy Called Hugo* (HQ, 2017), two WWII sagas for Orion (*The Spark Girl* and *A Wartime Promise*) and a series set during the Second World War, the first of which, *Christmas at Liberty's* (Penguin Random House), was a bestseller in 2018.

The Notekeeper

HANNAH TREAVE

CANELO

First published in the United Kingdom in 2023 by

Canelo
Unit 9, 5th Floor
Cargo Works, 1-2 Hatfields
London SE1 9PG
United Kingdom

A CIP catalogue record for this book is available from the British Library.

Print ISBN 978 1 80436 129 0
Ebook ISBN 978 1 80436 128 3

Printed and bound in Great Britain by Clays Ltd, Elcograf S.p.A.

1

For Chris – thank you for telling me to write from my heart

Prologue

The lights of the runway dazzled up ahead. It was as though the twinkling blue and white lights had been arranged especially for her – a reminder that she had made the right choice. As the twin engines roared into life, she took a deep breath. The rumble of power beneath her would carry her thousands of miles away. This was it. No going back.

As the aircraft accelerated, she fixed her gaze on the lights. They flashed past so quickly they looked like one great line rather than individual dots. And then they were up, the plane soaring into the Australian night sky with all the grace and elegance of a leaping ballet dancer. She let out a loud gasp, the realisation of what she had done hitting her with such force she disturbed the sleeping passenger beside her. Hastily muttering an apology, she turned back to the window, her eyes drinking in the dark shapes of her homeland, knowing she would never return.

When she woke that morning, she hadn't expected to find herself on an international flight. In fact, her day had begun like any other. She hadn't slept, but sleep was something that belonged in her old life. A life that had once been filled with happiness, work, school runs, movie nights, beach walks, early mornings and love.

And so, after her husband had left for work that morning, she had made her usual coffee and nibbled on a slice of toast. Then she had started on the ironing, picking up one of her husband's work shirts and her nurse's uniform. But, as she had reached for her son's navy blue T-shirt, she crumbled. The sight of it lying innocuously in the basket had sent her crashing to the floor, ironing board, iron and T-shirt swiftly following suit. And she had lain face down on the cold, tiled floor, sobbing her heart out for the life she had once known, the life that had been lost and the life she no longer had.

When she could cry no more, she looked around the home she had lived in almost all her married life. She felt suffocated – she had to get out. She raced to her nightstand then reached into her drawer and pulled out the pristine blue passport that hadn't been used in years. Next, she put on her shoes and coat, pausing only to grab her bag, then she stepped out of the house.

-

It was only when she went to shut the door that she realised she had forgotten the most important thing of all. Running back up the stairs, she reached into the drawer of her nightstand again and pulled out a folded piece of lined paper. Just the feel of it in her hands gave her strength. Pressing the paper to her lips, she gently kissed it, slipped it into her bag and ran down the stairs. She went straight out of the front door, not even bothering to check she had locked up properly. All she wanted was to get away.

And she had. She had taken the bus to the airport and, like a scene from a movie, had bought a ticket for the first flight to London, not caring about the cost.

Now, as the cabin crew began pushing the drinks trolley along the aisle, she leaned forward in her seat and reached for her bag. Pulling out the paper that meant so much, she savoured the scant few words, treasuring every one.

I just want to be a cowboy.

As she read, she felt a surge of strength. This scrap of paper had given her something she thought had gone forever – hope.

Chapter One

Two years later

The sound of heavy, laboured breathing was the only noise in the room as Zoe Evans reread the few lines on the notepad that rested on her lap. It was the fourth time she had read the note and she still hated almost every word. She looked up sharply, causing a greying blonde tendril to fall from the bun pinned at the nape of her neck.

'Arthur, are you sure this is what you want to say?' she queried, gazing at the man responsible for the note.

The breathing grew more laboured as the elderly man in the wheelchair nodded, his rheumy eyes steely with determination. 'I am. I've spent too long in denial; it's time the truth came out.'

Zoe ignored the urge to groan in despair. She had been a nurse for over twenty years and learned long ago that nagging patients was not the most effective way of getting them to do what was best.

'Okay.' She gave Arthur a reassuring smile. 'But don't you think telling your wife of sixty years that you never loved her and death will be a sweet release from her never-ending nagging, sharp tongue and' – Zoe paused to peer down at her notepad – 'constant smell of gas, is a bit cruel?'

Arthur nodded. 'I'm sure. I've never held with lies.'

Zoe put the pad down and shoved the pen in the pocket of her uniform. She disliked lies too, but equally didn't think giving people the unvarnished truth was always right.

'Is there anything else? Something *nice*?' she asked. 'Audrey's your wife. She's been bringing you to this hospice as a day patient for the last six weeks. You've shared a life together; you've built a world around each other.'

Arthur's expression softened. 'Course I love Audrey, but this bloody cancer's given me a kick up the backside. I don't want to meet my maker knowing I haven't been honest. I'm grateful for all Audrey has done. She and I have rubbed along together all right but I've never got over my first love – Deirdre Hamilton.'

At the mention of Deirdre, a dreamy expression crept across Arthur's face. Zoe could see he was somewhere far away from this Victorian villa that was now a hospice on the outskirts of Bath. As the late April sunshine streamed through the windows of the day room, she patted his leg, bringing him back to the present.

'I'm not sure Audrey needs to know that.' Zoe tried again. 'Surely there's something else you could say? Soften the blow.'

Wrinkling his nose, Arthur thought for a moment, then said, 'All right, tell her to buy carrots. She doesn't eat enough veg but she does like carrots.'

Zoe stifled a laugh but, seeing Arthur was serious, swiftly rearranged her face. Taking the pen from her pocket, she scribbled down his words and looked up at him expectantly.

'You get that?' he asked.

'I did,' she promised. 'Are you sure you want Audrey to have this?'

'I am,' Arthur replied in a tone that was weak but firm.

Zoe didn't press the point. She could see the trip to the day room had drained him. The colour in Arthur's cheeks was fading and his breathing becoming even more strained.

Getting to her feet, Zoe began wheeling Arthur back to his bed. She noticed he didn't gaze out of the window to admire the pair of oak trees that gave the hospice its name of The Oaks, as he usually did. Experience told Zoe it wouldn't be long before her patient met his end.

The truth was, Arthur wouldn't be the first of her patients to want to leave a note telling his family and friends what he really thought and Zoe knew he wouldn't be the last. Taking the last words of the dying, or recording messages for those left behind, was something Zoe had done since she started nursing at the hospice two years earlier. She knew how powerful a final note could be and how cathartic it was for those facing the end.

'Hey, Zoe!' A loud Antipodean voice from behind interrupted her thoughts.

Stopping to turn around, she came face to face with her colleague Miles Anderson. Still wearing a heavy coat and stuffing the remnants of a bacon sandwich in his mouth, Miles looked as though he'd just finished a shift on the bins rather than a nurse about to start work.

Zoe felt her hackles rise. 'Thought you started half an hour ago?'

Miles shrugged, brushing crumbs from his thick dark beard, seemingly unbothered by Zoe's rebuke. 'You know how it is. Late night last night, couldn't get up.'

Zoe frowned. She did know how it was, but she didn't approve. Like her, Miles was a native Australian, but unlike her, he was five years younger at thirty-nine, and doing his best to live every moment as if it were his last, or as he put it, hitting forty and knocking on death's door.

'You might want to try,' Zoe said, through gritted teeth. 'You only live around the corner. It's not fair on the patients, or the rest of us, if you're late.'

'Yeah, yeah.'

Arching a blonde, straggly eyebrow, Zoe drew herself up to her full five foot five inches and gave Miles what she hoped was a withering stare.

It seemed to do the trick. Miles hastily removed his coat and shoved his bacon sandwich wrapper into his pocket.

'Sorry, boss.' He seemed genuinely contrite.

Zoe shrugged. 'Only for another twenty-four hours, then this new troubleshooter starts.'

'Temporary troubleshooter,' Miles corrected, wiping his greasy hands on his scrubs-covered legs. 'How long is he here for?'

'Until the Harper family are happy The Oaks is doing well now they've taken it over,' Zoe replied.

'And merged it with St Mary's,' Miles said glumly, referencing the shiny, newer hospice on the other side of Bristol that outperformed The Oaks in almost every survey.

As a scowl flooded Miles's face, Zoe giggled. Ever since Miles had slept with one of the nurses from St Mary's, who had the audacity to break his heart, Miles had had a bee in his bonnet about the rival hospice.

'I don't see why we even need a troubleshooter,' Miles growled. 'We're doing all right.'

'Not right enough,' Zoe said, fixing her baby-blue eyes on the junior nurse. 'The only bright spark is that this new troubleshooter man will also be the new nurse manager so all this responsibility is off my hands for good.'

Miles laughed. 'I hope you're right. Word on the street is the guy's a bit full-on.'

'Good!' Zoe exclaimed. 'That means he can have a go at you when you're late or ringing in saying you're crook on Saturday mornings.'

'It's not every Saturday morning,' Miles protested.

'It's enough for me to notice,' Zoe said with a sigh before she brightened. 'Anyway, not my problem now; it's all down to Ben Tasker.'

'Yeah well, might be nice to have a bloke in charge instead of all these women,' Miles grumbled, his expression full of misery once more.

'I don't care.' Zoe grinned. 'Soon I'll be able to get back to what I love most.'

Miles rolled his eyes. 'I'd say it's personal grooming but given your beauty regime is barely soap and water, I can't think what it is.'

To anyone else the slur might have hurt but Zoe was nonplussed. 'Just because I'm not vain about my appearance doesn't mean I don't have a life.'

'You don't have to be vain to run a brush through your hair or tidy up those eyebrows that look like you've got a pair of slugs stuck to your face,' Miles said, then, sensing he may have gone too far, looked at her apologetically from beneath his own manicured brows. 'Sorry, Zoe, didn't mean it. We just worry. All us nurses here do. As far as we can tell, your life revolves around the hospice.'

'So what?' Zoe protested, feeling her pale cheeks flame with indignation. Having a go at her appearance was one thing, but calling into question her professionalism was another. 'There are worse ways to spend your time than helping the dying.'

'True,' Miles said carefully, shoving his hands in his pockets. 'But life's all about balance. You work way beyond your shifts, and all those notes, Zoe! They're so old-fashioned. It's like you're patron saint of the dying.'

'I am not patron saint of the dying and giving notes is not old-fashioned. It's a very personal form of communication,' Zoe said, glancing down at Arthur, who by now had nodded off in his wheelchair.

'Well, I reckon you're the only one keeping stationery shops in business any more,' Miles teased.

Zoe said nothing. She wasn't unique; many of the nurses and paramedics she worked with wrote to patients with terminal illnesses as a way of lifting their spirits. Many believed, as she did, that in this digital age there was something special about a note, a physical record filled with cheer that patients could touch and connect with in a way a text or email couldn't hope to replicate.

Yet Zoe also knew that nobody went out of their way quite like she did. She was diligent in asking each hospice patient if there was any last message. Sometimes she did it as they took their last breath; sometimes it was in the days or hours before they passed away. Zoe knew how it gave them something to hold on to during those dark moments of grieving ahead.

'You're an amazing nurse, Zoe,' Miles continued. 'I just don't know why you don't have more fun.'

'Working here is fun,' she said evenly.

Miles shook his head, as though he were looking at a lost cause. 'Zoe, working here is nothing but hard yakka. You never book a holiday, you never take a day off—'

'Yes I do!'

'To do your *laundry*,' he said, giving her a withering stare. 'Your housemate, Sarah, told me.'

'Well, she shouldn't have,' Zoe protested hotly. 'What I do with my time off is my business.'

'All right,' Miles exclaimed, backing away as if in fear she might explode. 'I'm only saying.'

'Well, don't. Anyway, who knows what might happen when Ben Tasker starts tomorrow.'

Miles smiled. 'Yeah, who knows. Maybe you'll have time for the odd beer in the pub or start wearing clothes that aren't navy scrubs.'

At the last remark, Zoe ran out of patience and began wheeling Arthur back to his room. As she did so she caught a glimpse of her appearance in the single-pane windows. Miles was right, she looked like an old woman with her un-ironed clothes, wan skin and blonde-grey hair so unkempt it could have its own personality. But what did it matter? Helping patients have a good death was what counted, something Zoe was sure that she and the new troubleshooter would agree on.

Chapter Two

Miles wasn't the only one late for work that day. By the time Zoe's shift was over she had counted two more nurses and one member of the support team that were late for their shifts. Boarding the bus home, she found herself feeling relieved, yet again, that her days of being in charge were almost over. When she had first joined The Oaks, the hospice had been independently run for more than thirty years, welcoming patients young and old. Zoe had loved the place from the moment she walked through the doors, yet recently it had become obvious funds were drying up.

Cutbacks were constantly being made, and Zoe often saw board members hovering in corridors, talking in hushed tones about saving money. The place had always bustled with positivity but in recent months as corners were cut and jobs slashed, Zoe knew the death knell had sounded. It hadn't been that surprising when a few weeks ago the Harper family, who owned several other hospices across the country, announced they would be adding The Oaks to their portfolio. Naturally, there had been mixed feelings but the board had done its best to convince everyone the Harpers knew how to turn things around, so the deal was done.

Last week Zoe had discovered Ben Tasker would be taking over her role for a few months. Something of a wonder nurse, Mr Tasker had been working with the Harper family for several years as a troubleshooter, ensuring each of their hospices was profitable, with patient care at the heart of every facility. Whilst everyone around her grumbled at the changes, Zoe was delighted. All she wanted was to be a nurse; the arrival of Ben Tasker was a good thing.

Before long, the bus neared Bath city centre and Zoe looked out of the grime-smeared window as they neared the Guildhall. Further up ahead was the creamy stone of the abbey, then the weir at Pulteney Bridge with rushing water so loud you had to shout to make yourself heard.

The ancient city of Bath had captured Zoe's heart two months after she arrived in the UK. She and a nursing friend had taken a day trip from London and been enraptured from the moment they stepped off the bus. Together they marvelled at the elegant townhouses of the Royal Crescent and Circus, and walked into the centre to drink in the view of the abbey and the Pump Rooms. Sadly, their funds hadn't stretched to admission to the Roman Baths, so instead they munched on sandwiches in Queen's Square. As they watched the pétanque players, Zoe felt at peace for the first time since arriving in the UK.

And so, on the bus back to her grotty flatshare in Earl's Court, Zoe had written to her landlord and the nursing temp agency that employed her, giving them both the required notice. A month later she had moved into a house in Bath and found a job at The Oaks. The rest was history.

Now, after disembarking the bus, she walked through the city's stone streets, the spring evening sunshine gently warming her skin. Zoe was home within minutes.

'Hello?' she called, unlocking the heavy wooden door and stepping inside the tiny entrance hall.

'We're in here,' came a voice from the other end of the cramped terrace.

Zoe smiled at the sound of her housemate, Sarah Rokeby, home from her social worker job early for once. She made her way towards the kitchen and had only taken a couple of steps when Sarah's daughter barrelled towards her, hurtling straight into her shins.

'How are you going, Lottie?' Zoe asked, her voice full of warmth, as the little girl threw her stubby arms around Zoe's legs.

'Good. Mummy did finger-painting with me and I had ham sandwiches at school,' the six-year-old said, her face buried in Zoe's scrubs.

'Sounds like a great day.' Zoe beamed and picked up the little girl, balancing her on her hip. Together they walked into the kitchen where Sarah was at the sink filling the shiny Dualit kettle with water. It had cost an eye-watering amount but Sarah had claimed it made the best tea in the world and she didn't begrudge a penny. Zoe had said nothing. She might have got used to life in the UK but she still couldn't understand the obsession with tea. It was dishwater at best.

'Good day?' Zoe asked, setting Lottie down.

'Not bad,' Sarah replied, her brown bob skimming her shoulders as she tipped her head and smiled. 'I managed to get some casework done while Lottie had a nap.'

Zoe nodded approvingly. 'Well done. How long until you get someone else into your office?'

'We've a new starter in a month,' Sarah said, stifling a yawn. 'Let's just hope they last longer than a couple of weeks. I might get a day off then.'

Sarah handed Zoe a coffee; she took the cup gratefully and smiled.

With her open face, warm brown eyes that brimmed with kindness and infectious smile, her friend and housemate was known for her compassion. When Zoe arrived in Bath, Sarah had welcomed Zoe into her home with open arms. At the time Sarah was a social worker attached to The Oaks. She had recently split with Lottie's father and, feeling lonely as a single parent of a six-year-old, had offered Zoe a room, insisting there was no need to pay any deposit. Zoe had been grateful as money had been tight but had assured Sarah she would lodge with her for just a few weeks until she got herself sorted. Now, two years later, the three of them had become an unlikely family.

Just then, Zoe felt her phone vibrate in her pocket. Pulling it out, she felt a stab of irritation as she saw a message bearing the name David flash across the screen.

Sarah frowned. 'That who I think it is?'

Zoe nodded as she shoved the phone back in her pocket without reading the text.

'Came right on time,' Sarah said evenly, taking a seat at the round table in the kitchen.

Pulling up a chair opposite her friend, Zoe sighed. 'His text messages are like clockwork. Every birthday, Christmas, first of every month, and Sean... always when Sean...'

The words hung in the air, Zoe unable to finish the sentence and Sarah not needing her to.

'Do you read any of them?' Sarah asked, hauling Lottie onto her knee.

'Occasionally,' Zoe said. 'But they're always the same. He loves me, he misses me, he can't wait for me to come home. It's as though I'm on holiday and will be back any day.'

Sarah shook her head and Lottie joined suit, making Zoe laugh at the serious expression that didn't belong on the little girl's face.

'Why don't you just put your ex out of his misery and tell him to sod off and leave you alone?' Sarah suggested, as she had a thousand times before.

'It's not that simple.' Zoe pulled her hair free from its bun and shook her locks free, mentally preparing herself for the usual argument she had with Sarah whenever David contacted her.

'But it should be,' Sarah reasoned. 'All these messages. They can't be good for him *or* you.'

At that statement, Zoe felt a sadness pass through her. This wasn't how she had envisaged married life. She had never thought she and David would end up living separate lives on opposite sides of the world when they married just after her twenty-first birthday.

'Seriously, Zoe, why don't you just divorce him?' Sarah asked carefully. She leaned across the battered pine table and reached for Zoe's hand. 'That way you could be free once and for all without having one foot in Oz and the other here.'

'It's not like that,' Zoe muttered.

'It's exactly like that,' Sarah said firmly.

There was a silence as Zoe digested her friend's wisdom.

'It seems too final to divorce him. We were together for over twenty years.'

'You haven't been together for the past two,' Sarah said bluntly. She took her hand from Zoe's and helped herself to a biscuit from the plate of chocolate-covered digestives that sat in the centre of the table.

Zoe waited for Sarah to finish chewing. 'Even so, the idea of it is just too painful. I'd feel as if I was letting Sean down.'

'Even if I agreed that you were letting Sean down, which I don't by the way,' Sarah said through a second mouthful of biscuit, 'it's not right you're stuck in limbo. You can't let go of the past and you can't move forward. If you decided to make a clean break you might be more interested in management.'

'None of that is true,' Zoe said hotly. 'Besides, I don't want to be a manager; I like the day-to-day of nursing.'

'If you say so,' Sarah said, looking unconvinced. 'Anyway, have you thought that this troubleshooter—'

'Ben Tasker,' Zoe interrupted.

'Yes, all right, *Ben Tasker*, might have other ideas for you,' Sarah put in, reaching for another biscuit. She offered the plate to Zoe, only for the nurse to shake her head. 'He might want you to take on more responsibility with you having so much experience.'

Horror flashed across Zoe's face, making Sarah giggle.

'Come on, it's not that bad,' she said encouragingly.

'It bloody is!' Zoe changed her mind about a single biscuit and helped herself to two. 'When the Harpers came in for a meeting before the takeover, I was asked by their human resources person twice if I'd take on more responsibility and I refused. This Ben Tasker better not look to me. I like drug rounds, rotas and bed pans, thank you.'

'And notes,' Sarah put in. 'Don't forget the notes.'

'I hope you're not being sarky,' Zoe barked, sending a mouthful of crumbs everywhere, making Lottie laugh.

'As if.' Sarah gave her a butter-wouldn't-melt look and Zoe drank the last of her coffee.

That was the brilliant thing about their friendship, Zoe thought. They each knew just how far to push the other and when to back off.

'Speaking of which, I've got a note to deliver now,' Zoe said. 'Do you and Lottie fancy coming with me?'

'But you've only just got home,' Sarah wailed. 'I thought we could watch something crap on Netflix and drink cheap wine after I've got Lottie to bed.'

'Not fair!' Lottie protested, not wanting to miss out on any fun. 'I want cheap wine too.'

At the statement, the girls giggled while Lottie's face was a perfect picture of six-year-old vexation.

'It's not far,' Zoe said. 'You can both come; it'll be fun.'

Sarah looked doubtful. 'The last time I came with you, you gave a woman a note on bright pink paper that said her sister had stolen all her jewellery but she wanted to tell the truth on her deathbed. To say it was awkward was an understatement.'

Zoe laughed. In fairness, it had been a bad delivery but she had no idea that the woman's sister would be elderly and unforgiving, or that the jewellery had contained a couple of De Beers diamonds.

'This will be different, I promise.'

Sarah still looked doubtful. 'All right. But if it's as bad as last time, I want chips and a bottle of plonk after.'

'Me too!' Lottie added as she slid off Sarah's knee and slipped her hand into Zoe's. Looking down at the little girl, Zoe felt a surge of affection. She had always adored children and Lottie had taken up a special place in her heart, right next to a hole that could never be filled.

Chapter Three

Thankfully, the note to the son of a former naval officer had gone well. There had been no surprises contained within the envelope, just a few loving words from father to son – the perfect goodbye.

Despite the success of the visit, which meant no need for cheap wine, Zoe woke the following morning tired and foggy-headed. David's unread message had played heavily on her mind and she had spent much of the night tossing and turning, images of her ex-husband invading what little sleep she had managed.

Now, she sat upright in the double bed narrowly squeezed into Sarah's spare room. Steadying her breath, Zoe reached for the glass of water on her nightstand and took a sip. Everything in her dreams had felt so real. She had been reading a book on the beach, then David and her mother, Ruth, had arrived. They said they had a surprise. After a lot of clapping and cheering, Sean had appeared, beaming at Zoe as he always did. He hadn't changed a bit, she thought, as her eyes roamed across his face, taking in his golden hair and freckled nose. She had scrambled to her feet, desperate to hold him in her arms. Only as she stood, Sean had backed away, disappearing into the sea. She had cried out, begging him to come back, only to wake up with sweat dripping down her forehead and her body entangled in uncomfortable, damp sheets.

She breathed in slowly through her nose and back out again, just as the counsellor had taught her. Then when she felt calm, Zoe got dressed and filled her flask with coffee. As an afterthought, she reached for her car keys, grateful that arriving at work this early meant she was guaranteed a parking space.

Zoe arrived just as dawn began to break and took a moment to appreciate the view. The Oaks stood in acres of parkland with wide walkways strewn with cherry blossoms. Cosy dells and hideaways gave an air of intimacy and the large hedges that lined the garden drowned out the sound of any road noise, making the hospice feel like a peaceful home from home. This had been her first view of The Oaks and she had loved it. As her eyes roamed across the Victorian villa, she could only hope Ben Tasker would feel the same when he arrived later that day.

Getting out of the car, she realised she was nervous. Despite the fact that her days as team leader were over, this takeover would undoubtedly mean change. Nodding a hello at the security guard as she walked inside, Zoe ignored the smell of bleach that filled her nostrils thanks to the early morning cleaners, and heard someone call her name. Whirling around, she came face to face with hospice director Karen Lowell. The hospice was largely digitised, but Karen was old-fashioned and preferred paper. Her arms were full of files, and her glasses were falling down her nose, cardigan buttoned up wrongly. Zoe relaxed. Karen was down to earth, responsible and kind and, much like her, she adored the personal touch of paper. It was no surprise she always felt happy in the older woman's company.

'You're finally off the hook,' Karen said, with a grin.

'Finally,' Zoe said, enjoying the feeling of relief as she said it.

'I'll get you to do a full hand-over with Ben but we've a fairly busy day set up for him upstairs with compliance videos and the like,' Karen explained, as she walked briskly along the corridor.

Zoe did her best to keep pace with the director. 'I remember only too well.'

'Quite,' Karen said, in an accent Zoe had come to recognise as pure posh Bath. 'So, until he settles in, if you could oversee the day-to-day?'

Zoe nodded as Karen paused.

'There is one more thing, however,' the director began. 'We've rather a special admission coming in this morning. You know Simon Harper of course, the new owner. He's bringing his mother in to us and has asked that you personally oversee the process.'

'Me?' Zoe gasped. 'Why?'

'I imagine your reputation rather precedes you,' Karen replied with a smile. 'It's common knowledge you're the best nurse we have and it's also common knowledge you won't take the mantle of responsibility any further.'

'I've always been about patient care.'

'We all know that and we're grateful,' Karen said smoothly. 'It's just something to bear in mind when people ask for you to look after their dying mothers. If you do that, then people will naturally see you as a leader.'

'I know.' Zoe sighed. She knew she ought to be flattered but the truth was she was too tired and her head was all over the place thanks to the dreams that had seemed more real than imaginary. 'When is Simon's mother arriving?'

'Later this morning.' Karen handed a file to Zoe. 'Here are all her details. She'll be a day patient initially.'

'Madeleine Harper, seventy-four with a brain tumour,' Zoe said, flicking through the file. 'Crikey. Not that old in this day and age.'

'Quite,' Karen replied brusquely. 'She's expected at nine – can I leave her with you?'

Zoe had barely finished nodding before Karen walked away.

'And Zoe,' Karen said, stopping abruptly in the corridor. Zoe looked up. 'Do please ensure you and the staff make Mr Tasker feel welcome.'

'Of course,' Zoe said. 'I'm sure Ben will want what the rest of us wants, to do the best for our patients.'

Karen let out a bark of laughter. 'That may be so, but bear in mind Mr Tasker has some rather visionary ideas for the department. As I'm part of the team that has to oversee this damned takeover, it would mean an awful lot to me if you gave him and his ideas your full support.'

Karen not only had a way about her that made it impossible to do anything but agree, she had also battled on the front lines as a nurse for more than thirty years. Consequently, Zoe held her in high regard and she nodded dutifully.

'Knew I could rely on you,' Karen said with a smile. 'There are some forms underneath Mrs Harper's file for you to fill out. If you could complete them and pop them in Mr Tasker's pigeonhole as soon as you can, that would be appreciated.'

Zoe leafed through the papers. There was a questionnaire about what you wanted from your nursing role, a management style quiz and a form to fill in listing any extra-curricular hobbies and what you thought you could do for the hospice. Zoe's mind boggled at the sight of it all. How did the new troubleshooter have time for stuff like this? She was about to say as much when she realised Karen was still talking.

'Equally, do keep May the fourteenth free, won't you?'

'Sorry?' Zoe looked at the director blankly.

'The fourteenth,' Karen said impatiently. 'It's a Thursday. We're hosting a small gathering at the hospice for staff and friends to welcome our new owners. Bring your flatmate.'

It was more of an order than a question.

'Oh, right.'

'Excellent.' Karen beamed. 'Wonderful to see you, Zoe.'

With that, Karen stalked off along the corridor towards her office, leaving Zoe with Mrs Harper's file. Making her way into the empty day room, Zoe perched on the edge of one of the wing-backed chairs. Reaching into her overstuffed rucksack, she sifted through the usual debris of hand gel, face masks, her Kindle, phone and a clean T-shirt, until her hand rested on what she was looking for. Pulling out a fistful of brightly coloured notecards, she chose one with an image of a cheerful seascape. Unfolding the card, black fountain pen hovering above it, Zoe thought for a moment and began to write.

Dear Mrs Harper,

Welcome to The Oaks. I know what lies ahead will be a challenge but we are all here for you, whatever you need and whenever you need us.

Respectfully yours,

Zoe Evans, Senior Staff Nurse

Zoe stuffed the card inside the envelope and found her way to Mrs Harper's bed. Placing the note carefully on the pillow, she straightened the already pristine sheets and smiled. The note may not improve Mrs Harper's diagnosis but Zoe hoped that this small touch would help her realise there was still hope to cling to.

Chapter Four

Despite Zoe's promises, she didn't get to meet Ben Tasker during her shift. In fact, the moment she stepped behind the nurses' desk she was set upon by Karen's deputy, Indira, who had a worryingly large amount of paperwork clutched to her chest.

'Can you go through these?' she asked, her devilish grin spreading large across her light-brown features.

'What are they?' Zoe asked, peering dubiously at the sheets of A4 hanging from Indira's grasp.

'Budget statements you've been a part of, orders and inventories. Karen wants Ben to have a clean slate.'

Zoe looked aghast. 'You're kidding?'

Indira, a woman slightly older than Zoe, gave her a sheepish smile. 'It won't take long. If you could make a start after you get Mrs Harper settled?'

'Mrs Harper's here?' Zoe asked. As she followed Indira's gaze, she noticed an older woman with rich dark hair, flecked with grey, and immediately beside her saw The Oaks' new owner, Simon Harper. For a moment Zoe felt startled. She had only met Mr Harper once, but had thought of him as powerful and unyielding, with his broad frame and strong jawline. Here, though, as he tried to cajole his mother into a wheelchair, he looked like a lost little boy and Zoe felt for both of them.

'I'm not an invalid yet, dear.' Mrs Harper's smooth, firm voice rang out across the corridor as Zoe neared them. 'Please don't treat me like one.'

'I'm only trying to help,' Mr Harper pleaded. 'I'm doing this for you.'

'No, Simon,' Mrs Harper cut in sharply. 'You're doing this for yourself. Don't rewrite history by pretending otherwise.'

Zoe smiled in welcome, keen to dispel the altercation.

'Mrs Harper, Mr Harper,' she said, extending her right hand for each of them to shake. 'It's a pleasure to welcome you. I'm Zoe, one of the nurses who will be looking after you today.'

The older woman turned to Zoe and offered her a smile that didn't reach her pale grey eyes. 'Thank you, dear. I too would like to say it's a pleasure but honestly, who wants to end up in a hospice at the end of their life?'

Zoe choked back a giggle as the woman gazed around the hospice in distaste, her eyes lingering on the magnolia walls, which were in dire need of repainting. She secretly enjoyed the more outspoken patients; they made life more interesting.

'Mother, please,' Mr Harper said again, and Zoe guessed he had heard this argument before.

Mrs Harper raised her hands in surrender. 'Fine, I'm only joking. It's just a day. I'm sure Zoe and I will get along famously.'

Recognising that was her cue to smile reassuringly, Zoe lifted the corners of her mouth and turned to her new boss. 'Of course we will. Mrs Harper, let me show you around.'

A look of relief passed across Mr Harper's face. 'I'll pick you up later, Mother.'

He bent down to kiss his mother's cheek, then walked swiftly along the corridor.

Mrs Harper let out a sigh. 'I know he means well, but since my diagnosis he's fussed around me like an old woman. I swear it's one of the reasons he wanted to buy this place.'

Zoe walked around to the back of the wheelchair and breathed in a cloud of Chanel No. 5. Mrs Harper clearly still had her pride, Zoe thought, as she pushed her latest charge towards the day room.

'Why would that make him want to buy the hospice?' the nurse asked.

'Because before it was a hospice it was also *my* family home,' the older woman said with a touch of vehemence. 'The thing my son has conveniently forgotten, however, is the fact I hated it here.' She turned around to look Zoe as they entered the brightly lit room filled with patients talking, reading and playing cards. 'This was the dining room. My mother used to host fabulous parties, only for my father to get drunk and make a fool of himself. They were not happy times. I left as soon as I could.'

Pushing the wheelchair towards the window, Zoe patted Mrs Harper on the shoulder and made her a cup of tea from the urn on the other side of the room. Pressing it into the older woman's hands, Zoe sat on the chair opposite. 'Why did your son want you here then, as you begin your final journey?'

Mrs Harper rolled her eyes as she set the cup on the wooden coffee table that stood between them. 'Because he thinks that by bringing me here it will be like coming home. He doesn't remember how I rarely brought him here to see his grandparents. And when I did I was always keen to rush off.'

'I'm sorry,' Zoe said. 'Do you want me to talk to him?'

Another snort of laugher escaped Mrs Harper's lips. 'My son, listen to someone else? I don't think so, dear, though it's kind of you to offer. Do you have children?'

Zoe was about to shake her head as she always did but something in Mrs Harper's manner made her want to tell the truth.

'Yes, a boy.'

'Well, if you want my advice, don't let them grow up,' Mrs Harper said sagely. 'It's when they grow up they become men you barely recognise.'

Mrs Harper turned her bright eyes towards the window and Zoe tried to steady herself. She took a deep breath, her heartbeat racing as she did her best to force the image of Sean from her mind. She couldn't allow her past to take over her work. Her job was the only thing that kept her going.

With so much to do, she passed the care of Mrs Harper on to Miles for the rest of the day and by the time her shift finished at six o'clock, she was more than ready to call it a day. Walking out of the hospice doors, she rounded the corner of the grounds. Once she was sure she was out of sight, she leaned against one of the large oak trees and groaned loudly.

'Sounds like your day was almost as bad as mine,' came a deep voice.

She jumped at the sound, feeling annoyed and embarrassed at being caught out in a private moment. Peering around the tree, she caught sight of a tall, dark-skinned man, dressed in a grey suit with a tie hanging loosely around his neck. As he leaned against the trunk, legs crossed at the ankle, she saw he was smoking what looked like a very expensive cigar.

'You can't smoke that here,' she snapped.

'Why?' the man said, pursing his lips into a large 'O' and blowing a perfect smoke ring. 'Last time I checked you could smoke outside.'

'Yes, but this is a hospice,' Zoe hissed, making a point of waving the smoke away from her face. 'It's not right.'

'Why? Because everyone's dying?' The man laughed, his smile reaching his brown eyes. 'I don't think it will make a difference.'

'No, because it's disrespectful,' Zoe countered.

She hated this argument. Sometimes visitors to The Oaks brought in whisky, wine and even on occasion drugs for their loved ones to help ease their final moments, all because 'it hardly mattered any more'. It was an attitude Zoe struggled to understand. It wasn't that the drugs and booze were going to kill them; it was a matter of respect. She offered the man her best scowl, and Zoe felt a flash of pleasure as he threw the cigar to the ground, then stubbed it out with his foot.

'You're right, sorry,' he said, his face contrite. 'Tough day.'

'Yeah, me too.'

'I take it you mean as a nurse rather than a resident?' the man said, gesturing towards her scrubs.

'What gave it away?' she said in a sarcastic tone, her feathers still ruffled from their exchange.

'Are you in charge then?' he asked.

She shook her head, feeling impatient. She was tired and wanted to go home for a glass of wine. 'No.'

'You sure?' the man said, raising an eyebrow. 'You seem naffed off and the way you had a go at me for smoking definitely had a whiff of bossiness about it.'

'I hardly had a go at you,' Zoe countered. 'I just asked you to stop smoking on hospice grounds. Who am I to stop you killing yourself?'

'Quite.' The man grinned. 'Even though that cigar was a one-off, you wouldn't mind if I lit up another one in a few minutes?'

'Anything you do out there,' Zoe said, jerking her head towards the road, 'I couldn't give a monkey's about.'

'You must be a hit with the patients,' the man said with a smirk. 'Your bedside manner's a charm.'

Rolling her eyes, Zoe stuffed her hands in her pockets and walked towards the car park. She was in no mood.

'Not even going to say goodbye?' he called as she walked away.

Zoe swallowed her feelings of annoyance and as she reached the car, almost threw herself inside. Today had started badly and only got worse following her conversation with Mrs Harper. Resting her head against the steering wheel, she closed her eyes and finally allowed herself to think about her son. Images of him building sandcastles on the beach, grinning whenever he watched *Toy Story* and sleeping, safe and sound in his bed, flooded her mind like a movie on fast forward. It was then Zoe gave in to the threat of tears that had been brewing since she woke. The only saving grace was that the smoking man wasn't around to see it.

Chapter Five

Arriving at work the following morning, Zoe stole past the nurses' desk, eager to avoid interruption. There was something she wanted to do before she officially clocked on.

Padding towards Arthur's room, she gently pushed open the door and saw he was lying in bed, gently snoring, his wife Audrey asleep in the chair beside him. Zoe looked closely at the couple and saw Arthur had his fingers wrapped tightly around Audrey's. Despite all his bluster, it was clear Arthur adored his wife.

Taking care not to disturb the sleeping couple, Zoe moved Arthur's water pitcher and set the two envelopes down on the bedside table. For Arthur she had chosen one of her favourite seascapes, with a few words inside, thanking him for the joy he always brought to her day. Her letter for Audrey had been written on a sheet of hand-dyed pale blue notepaper. She had bought it from a craft shop. The moment Zoe saw the silver shooting star embossed on top of the page, she knew it was perfect for someone needing a kind word to get through the day.

With the notes safely delivered, Zoe returned to the nurses' desk and saw Indira perched on a chair, her eyes glued to Instagram.

'What are you doing here?' Zoe said.

Indira looked up and smiled. 'Ben asked me to try and bring our Instagram account up to date. I've been uploading pictures, ready to capture any appropriate moments as we get rooms ready for new admissions.'

Zoe frowned as she peered over Indira's shoulder. 'I didn't know we were taking in any new patients today.'

'Couple of transfers from St Mary's,' Indira replied. 'They were day patients but Ben has arranged for them to come here. Oh, and Mrs Kennington died last night.'

'Oh no.' Zoe set her rucksack on the floor. 'Did she get her affairs in order?'

'If you mean did anyone take her last words down, the answer is no,' Indira said with an eye-roll.

Zoe bit back a feeling of irritation. Mrs Kennington had only been admitted yesterday and she had been so busy dealing with Mrs Harper and getting everything ready for Ben, she hadn't had time to talk to her about any last words or even write a welcome card.

'Look, don't worry, she had a good end,' Indira said kindly, seeing Zoe's expression. 'She went very peacefully and her daughter was with her.'

'Oh, that's good,' Zoe said with a sigh. 'I wish I'd had a chance to welcome her at least, though.'

'You can't do everything.'

'No, but I hope now we have a new boss I might be free of paperwork.'

Indira said nothing as she looked out across the hospice. Zoe followed her gaze. As usual at seven in the morning, the place was busy with doctors making rounds, patients sitting up in bed, hanging on their every word. Others were in the day room, clinging to old routines like listening to breakfast radio, reading the newspaper or scrolling through their phones. It all seemed very much business as usual. Yet there was a man in the corner wearing the same navy scrubs as hers that Zoe didn't recognise.

'Who's that talking to Mrs Taylor?' she asked, as the man let out a belly laugh that reverberated across the day room.

'That's Ben Tasker. Didn't you meet him yesterday?'

Zoe shook her head. 'I didn't get a chance.'

'He's lovely,' Indira said warmly. 'Go and introduce yourself.'

As Ben laughed again, Zoe found herself smiling too. There was something very comforting about the sound. It was a genuine laugh that came from the soul. Nodding at Indira, Zoe walked towards him, but as she did so Ben turned around, causing Zoe to stop abruptly. Ben Tasker was none other than the man she had shouted at for smoking last night.

As their eyes met, she felt her cheeks flame red and the blood pump too hard around her veins. She had been rude. Ben was a newcomer and also her boss. She would have to apologise. Urging herself to walk towards him, Zoe tried to ignore the dread building in the pit of her stomach.

As she drew closer, Zoe looked at him properly. With his bald head, dark skin and eyes that crinkled when he smiled, he seemed different to the man she had rowed with yesterday. More relaxed, friendlier even.

'Zoe Evans,' she said nervously, extending her hand. 'I think we might have got off on the wrong foot.'

Ben didn't speak straight away. Instead, he looked her up and down and took her hand.

'You mean when you had a go at me for smoking a celebratory cigar after the first day in my new job?' he said, eyes twinkling with mischief.

'Something like that,' Zoe replied, feeling awkward as she dropped his hand. 'I didn't know who you were.'

'Ah.' Ben's mouth twitched at the corners. 'You only shout at people who aren't your boss?'

'It wasn't like that,' Zoe tried again.

Ben smiled. 'No worries. Let's forget it.'

At the suggestion, Zoe felt relieved. 'How are you settling in?'

Ben surveyed the day room. 'All right. Everyone seems nice but it's different from my last place.'

'How so?' Zoe asked.

'Bigger, more patients,' Ben explained. 'This will be more of a challenge and the Harpers have got lots of plans.'

'You've got a lot on your plate.'

'Trouble is, I'm never in these roles for long, usually six months to a year, so by the time I've made any changes I don't get to reap the rewards.'

'That sounds hard, but I like the idea of a fresh start every so often.'

'Yeah, it's not bad,' Ben replied. As he fell silent, Zoe saw his eyes land on the door leading to the children's ward. 'I think you have more children here than at my last place,' he said in a low voice. 'There, we had one every few months. I've already overseen two children's admissions since I've been here. The parents looked bereft.'

'I expect they were,' Zoe replied. 'It's always tough for the littlies, but remarkably they're always the chirpiest.'

Ben narrowed his eyes. 'Littlies? Thought I detected an Antipodean twang. Where are you from?'

Zoe smiled, ready to repeat the answer to the question she was routinely asked. 'Australia. Sydney actually. I keep thinking I've got rid of my Aussie accent, then I trip up.'

'You shouldn't want to get rid of it,' Ben pointed out. 'Accents are important. They ensure we're not the same.'

'And you of course are pure posh Bath,' she teased good-naturedly.

'I, my lover, am from the mean streets of this city,' he said, dropping the neutral tones and striking up a very convincing West Country accent.

Zoe balked in surprise. 'You're either a very good mimic or telling the truth.'

'I'm telling the truth.' Ben's eyes crinkled with genuine delight. 'For the first twenty years of my life that's how I sounded.'

'What changed?'

'I left Bath, went to Oxford to study biomedical sciences, then moved to London.' Ben shrugged.

'Ah,' Zoe said knowingly. 'If you're from the mean streets of Bath, how come they let you in?'

'I was the "minority did good",' Ben replied, a little wearily Zoe thought, as he shoved his hands in the pockets of his scrubs. 'Black kid, clever, had encouragement from my single-parent mother and a neighbour who was good at maths. Got me excited about learning, enough for me to go to uni, the first in my family.'

'I was the first to go to uni in my family too.'

'What did you study?' Ben asked.

'Nursing,' Zoe replied, as if it were obvious. 'It was all I ever wanted to do.'

'That must have been nice, having it all worked out from a young age?' Ben mused.

'I've never thought of it that way,' Zoe said, rubbing her chin. 'I suppose it was. I take it you didn't dream of being a nurse?'

Ben laughed. 'No way! I wanted to be a rapper.'

Zoe giggled with him. 'And you studied biomedical sciences for that? What happened?'

'I realised I was shit at rapping,' he admitted. 'Still, Drake's loss is nursing's gain.'

Zoe stared at him for a moment, realisation dawning. 'Are you the Ben Tasker that won that Dying Concerns award a couple of years ago?'

Now it was Ben's turn to look embarrassed. 'Well, I was part of a very large team. I accepted that award for everyone.'

'You wrote that book,' Zoe continued, as if he hadn't spoken. 'You were in all the papers. It was all about the final stages of dying, with interviews from the patients. All the money went to charity, and you were called a hero for confronting the unconfrontable.'

'The book was my idea. But it was my whole team that worked on it,' he explained, looking embarrassed. He paused for a moment then changed the subject. 'Listen, Zoe, I wonder if we could have a quick chat.'

'Okay.'

Ben cupped her elbow with his palm and steered her out of the day room and into the nook of the stairwell. He looked around to check they were alone. 'I wanted a quick word about your notes. They concern me.'

'They concern you?' Zoe echoed.

'Yes.' Ben nodded. 'I need you to stop.'

Zoe felt as if the air had been sucked out of her lungs. For a moment she couldn't think of anything to say.

'Why?' Zoe gasped.

Ben rubbed the back of his neck, a flicker of awkwardness passing across his features. 'I think they could cause problems and you're exposing yourself and the hospice unnecessarily.'

At the suggestion, Zoe felt a wave of anger. 'You can't be serious!'

'I'm very serious. I'm sorry, Zoe, I've been told how important they are to you—'

'And to the patients,' Zoe interrupted. 'They enjoy knowing that their last wishes will be passed on to loved ones, and the notes I give them when they stay with us brighten up their time here. Think how lovely it is to receive something handwritten these days. And for our patients, knowing someone has taken the time and trouble to write to them, to think about them as a human rather than someone facing the end of the line… I don't think you have any idea how much of a difference it makes.'

'I don't doubt it, but the risks outweigh the benefits.'

'What does Karen say about this?' Zoe demanded.

Ben's expression hardened. 'I'm in charge and have the full support of senior management regarding this and any other decision. I've been brought in to troubleshoot the hospice's problems and to me your notes are a problem.'

Zoe said nothing, not trusting herself to speak as she took in what Ben's order would mean for her and her future. The notes were a lifeline, not just for the patients, but for her.

'I'm sure you can find other ways to show the patients how much you care, Zoe,' Ben said, with a final nod before he walked away.

As Zoe watched him return to the day room, she felt a fresh stab of fury. Her notes weren't just whimsy. As far as she was concerned, the last few words of the dying helped save the lives of those left behind.

Chapter Six

By the time Zoe got home she had worked herself into such a frenzied state she was incapable of speech, something that wasn't lost on Sarah.

'Zoe, sweetheart, what the hell has happened?' she gasped, watching Zoe walk into the living room like a possessed zombie.

'I'm fine,' Zoe growled, throwing herself on the sofa.

'You don't look fine,' Sarah said, pressing a large glass of red wine into Zoe's hands. 'In fact, you look bloody awful. What's happened?'

Zoe stared dolefully into her drink. 'I don't even know where to start.'

'The beginning,' Sarah encouraged. 'Come on, out with it.'

Zoe told her friend everything. From her first awkward encounter with Ben to how she had discovered he was her boss, and then his latest missive to stop Zoe from giving and taking the notes she loved.

'You're joking! What an arsehole! I'm sorry, Zoe, how dare he do this?!'

'Oh, he dares all right.' Zoe let out a hollow laugh. 'Says I'm putting myself and the hospital at risk.'

'Bollocks!' Sarah snapped. 'What does Karen say?'

'I haven't spoken to her about it,' Zoe admitted. 'I know she's given Ben her full support. He as much as reminded me of that when he told me to stop my notes.'

'Arsehole,' Sarah snarled again.

Zoe smiled at her friend and Sarah squeezed Zoe's knee, fully understanding the notes weren't just about helping her patients. They gave Zoe a lasting link to Sean.

'What are you going to do about it?' Sarah asked. She reached for the bowl of crisps that stood on the table and took a handful.

'Besides fantasising about sticking pins in Tasker's eyes?'

'Yeah, besides that.' Sarah fixed her gaze on Zoe as she reached for another handful of crisps. 'You can't accept this.'

Zoe shrugged. 'What choice do I have? He's the new boss.'

'Yeah, who'll be gone in six months or so.' Sarah reached for her wine and took a large gulp. 'If it were me, I'd carry on.'

'You would not!' Zoe gasped.

'Yes, I bloody would,' Sarah said, with spirit. 'He hasn't even had the good manners to discuss the matter with you. To get a bit East London, it's bang out of order.'

Despite her sadness, Zoe laughed at Sarah's dreadful cockney accent.

'I can't do that.'

'Why?' Sarah asked, draining her glass.

'Because I'll get the sack.'

'You will not.' Sarah waved her hand, batting Zoe's concerns away as if they were an irritating fly. 'And if you did, you could go to the papers and tell them how you were sacked for taking down the last wishes of the dying. I'm sure that would do Mr Tasker's reputation the world of good.'

'Blimey!' Zoe gaped at her friend in wonder. 'Remind me never to cross you.'

'Keep my glass topped up and you won't.' Sarah nudged her almost empty glass towards the wine bottle beside Zoe.

Taking the less than subtle hint, Zoe refilled Sarah's glass and topped up her own.

'Seriously, Zoe, it's not like you're trying to fiddle dying people out of their pensions. If it were me, I'd perhaps be a bit more discreet with the notes but this Tasker bloke will be gone soon.'

Biting her lip, Zoe thought for a moment. Sarah had a point; even Ben had said how he never stayed long enough to see the results of his work. And nobody had ever once complained about her letters. In fact, according to patient satisfaction surveys, families and patients appreciated the thoughtful service she offered.

Tucking her legs beneath her, Zoe rested her head on Sarah's shoulder. 'Thank you.'

'You're welcome.'

'Tell me about your day,' Zoe said, aware she hadn't asked her friend anything about herself yet.

'Much the same as any other,' Sarah said with a yawn. 'Tiring.'

'I take it Lottie's in bed?' Zoe asked.

Sarah grimaced. 'She saw her father today and she's exhausted. He took her to the park and let her go down the slides that are far too big for her.'

'Ah.' Zoe nodded knowingly, helping herself to some crisps, enjoying the way they crunched noisily in her mouth. 'Still, every kid needs a dad.'

'Yup,' Sarah agreed. 'I know he tries with her but why do I get all the boring stuff, and he gets all the fun stuff? It's not fair.'

'The joys of being a mum,' Zoe said, reaching out for another fistful of crisps and earning a smack on the hand from Sarah in the process.

'Get your own!' she admonished.

Grumbling, Zoe went into the kitchen and nabbed two bags of salt and vinegar and a Twix for afters. Clutching the chocolate, she felt a sudden pang of longing for home. Right now, she would give anything for a good old Aussie Tim Tam, which healed all wounds. Still, any port in a storm, she thought, ripping open the chocolate wrapper and leaning against the worktop. As she took a large bite, her eyes roamed the kitchen.

For a small terrace, Sarah had kitted the galley kitchen out well, with navy walls, white-gloss kitchen units and smart posters of New York. She'd even done a good job on the tiny balcony that stood outside the kitchen, making enough room for a small table and chairs where you could enjoy a coffee and the early morning sunshine away from the bustle of the city.

Bringing her attention back inside, Zoe's eyes landed on a thick white A4 envelope propped up against the money tree on the windowsill. It was addressed to her in a bold black typeface; she gave a start as she took in the familiar Australia Registered Post logo.

'When did this letter come?' Zoe called.

'This morning. I had to sign for it before I left for work,' Sarah said, walking into the kitchen. 'I thought it might be important. David's never done that before, has he?'

Shaking her head, Zoe stared at the letter as if it were a bomb. She really didn't want to open it. Even so, Zoe was curious. Was the letter from David? He wouldn't have had time to go to the post office. He always joked he was a mechanic not a secretary. Could it be from her mother? But Zoe dismissed the thought. She still talked to her mum occasionally on the phone and they emailed. Ruth hated the way Zoe had left Australia and why, but unlike her sister, Jemma, who lived in Melbourne, she at least understood, always insisting Zoe would return home when she was ready.

'Maybe it's tax stuff or something?' Sarah suggested.

Zoe shook her head. 'It hasn't got a tax office stamp.'

'Could it be something to do with Sean?' Sarah asked gently.

Zoe felt the usual pain that washed over her whenever his name was mentioned.

'I don't know,' Zoe whispered. 'But I do know I'm too afraid to find out.'

'Time to be brave,' Sarah said determinedly. 'It's obviously important.'

Zoe looked at Sarah. Her friend was right and before she could change her mind, Zoe snatched up the letter from the windowsill and ripped the creamy white envelope open. Pulling out a sheaf of papers, she read the top sheet and felt her stomach turn over.

Dear Zoe,

I've written to you many times over the years and I know why you rarely ever reply. You haven't forgiven me. I knew that when I came home and found you gone all those years ago. I don't blame you because I have never forgiven myself. For the past two years, Zoe, I've been hoping you'll come back, but I'm beginning to realise that's not going to happen and I know we both need to move on.

That's why I think we should separate officially. As you will see from the documents enclosed, I have been to Family Court and filed for divorce. If you want to contest it, you'll need to contact the court and file a response, but we've been apart so long now I can't think you'll want to. My solicitor will be in touch to talk about the settlement of our assets, otherwise our divorce should be settled in about three to four months. I'm sorry, Zoe. I love you but we can't carry on like this any more.

With love,
David

Hands shaking, Zoe put the note down, dashed to the sink and threw up. When she had finished, she stared at the contents of her stomach in the bowl. What else was life going to throw at her?

Chapter Seven

David's petition for a divorce combined with Ben's insistence that Zoe stop taking notes left her feeling overwhelmed. As a result, over the next fortnight, Zoe coped by doing what she always did whenever she felt upset and threw herself into work.

And so, Zoe volunteered for overtime, attended to drug rounds, admin, dressings, blood transfusions, discharge planning and of course patient care. Despite Sarah's suggestion she carry on taking notes anyway, Zoe had put her stationery away – at least temporarily. Although she considered the notes she gave and received an essential part of caring for her patients, Zoe knew her head was in too much of a mess to consider breaking the rules.

The truth was, David's idea of a divorce had rocked her more than she liked to admit. Although she and David had been separated for more than two years, a divorce was something Zoe didn't want. It would break her last link to Sean. She had assumed that, like her, David would be happy not accepting the past or embracing the future. But he hadn't been. And now Zoe was hiding in the drug supply room hoping to find salvation.

'Can you go and see Mrs Timpson?' Miles boomed, poking his head around the door.

Zoe held up her hand as she finished counting syringes. 'Why?'

'She's asking for you,' Miles said. 'Think you made an impression on her yesterday. I tried telling her I was the handsome Aussie one but she insists it's you she wants.'

'I've a feeling she wants to complain,' Zoe said awkwardly. 'She spent all day telling me her friend Ada Roberts had a much more organised death at St Mary's.'

'Did she really say that?'

Nodding, Zoe followed Miles out into the corridor. 'Yes. She also said I'd only gone into nursing for the money.'

Miles cackled with laughter. 'Tell her you'll give her a lift in your Lambo later if she's still upset.'

Smiling at the joke, Zoe followed Miles into the day room and was surprised to see the older woman sitting beside the French doors, playing cards with Ben Tasker.

Zoe looked to Miles for an explanation, but he shrugged his shoulders and made a shooing motion for Zoe to go and see what she wanted. Zoe knew why Miles was in such a rush for her to see the cancer patient. Mrs Timpson was a former headteacher and made no secret of the fact she thought she knew best. She had been admitted to The Oaks in the past as a day patient but with her bowel cancer battle almost at an end, she had moved in permanently to see out her final days.

'How are you, Mrs Timpson?' Zoe perched next to the older woman on the armchair.

Mrs Timpson turned away from her cards and looked at Zoe. 'This young man has been trying to take all my money.'

Wondering if that was what Mrs Timpson wanted to complain about, she glowered at Ben, who was grinning behind his cards.

'You keep playing bad hands. Not my fault you've lost your touch, Mrs Timpson.'

As the older woman opened her mouth, Zoe could see she was tired, the act of trying to find the right words beyond her reach.

'Shall we get you back to your bed?' she asked kindly.

Suddenly Zoe's patient found her fire. 'Not until I've at least won my bar of chocolate back.'

Zoe glared at Ben. He might be her boss but she wasn't going to let Ben's behaviour go unchecked. Wasn't gambling with a patient as potentially damaging as her notes? Her warning look seemed to bear authority as Ben put down his cards, and slipped the bar of Dairy Milk across the table towards Mrs Timpson.

Satisfied, Zoe turned to the former headteacher. 'Nurse Anderson said you wanted to talk to me?'

For a moment Mrs Timpson looked blank. 'Yes. I've heard about you. My friend Ada told me you're the one that takes notes from people before they die.'

'Well, yes,' Zoe replied hesitantly.

'Are you still doing that now you've been demoted?' she asked bluntly. 'Only I don't want to be missing out because you've suffered a humiliation.'

There was a snort of laughter. 'You tell her, Mrs T,' Ben agreed, avoiding Zoe's gaze.

'I'm afraid that's not something I do any longer,' Zoe said smoothly.

Mrs Timpson looked at her, bemused. 'What do you mean?'

'We're under new management and the notes aren't something I can offer any more.'

'What rot!' Mrs Timpson snapped. 'It's a note I want, not open-heart surgery.'

Zoe smiled sympathetically, doing her best to remain diplomatic even though she was aching to reveal that the nurse who had nearly nicked Mrs Timpson's bar of chocolate had stopped Zoe doing her job.

'I'm so sorry,' Zoe managed. 'Perhaps a relative could take the note instead.'

'That won't work!' Ms Timpson exclaimed, her rheumy eyes filled with frustration. 'I need to *leave* a note for a relative.'

'I'm sorry,' Zoe said again. 'I really am. If there's anything else I can do for you…'

The short burst of fire that had powered the older lady disappeared as she gave a forlorn shake of her head. 'Can you take me back to my room, please?'

'Of course.'

As Zoe helped Mrs Timpson back to her room, Zoe's eyes met Ben's. Given Mrs Timpson's disappointment, Zoe half expected to find a hint of apology, but there was nothing in his gaze but a blank stare. Zoe was stung by her new manager's indifference and in that moment realised she had been right all along. When Zoe first met Ben Tasker, she had wondered if she had stumbled across a tosser. The only difference between then and now was that she knew she had.

–

Returning to the day room twenty minutes later, Zoe saw Miles checking the hand sanitiser stations were full. At the sound of someone behind him, he spun around and gave Zoe a bright smile.

'You all right?'

'Why wouldn't I be?'

'Because the looks you were giving our boss earlier made me wonder if you were about to tip Mrs Timpson out of her wheelchair and use it to batter him around the head.'

At the image of her swinging a wheelchair in the day room, Zoe laughed. It would make a change from the usual sudoku puzzles and afternoon tea that passed as entertainment for the residents.

'Yeah, I'm fine,' she said.

Miles nodded. 'Just thought there was a bit of tension, plus you always duck out of the staff meetings he calls—'

'I've been busy,' Zoe protested.

'If you say so.' Miles wiped down the chairs with antibacterial spray. 'But whenever his name comes up you don't say a word.'

'It's called being professional.'

'And the rest.' Miles shot her a knowing look. 'Seriously, Zoe, you can talk to me if there's anything bothering you.'

For a moment Zoe was about to make a joke but, seeing the look of sincerity on Miles's face, she thought better of it. There were times he truly meant well.

'Everything's fine,' she said, with a sigh. 'I'm struggling to adjust, that's all.'

'In what way?'

Zoe shrugged. 'I dunno, change is hard and it doesn't help that our new boss has forbidden me from taking notes or delivering them.'

Miles's broad lips twisted in disbelief. He opened his mouth, about to say something, then she saw him look past her shoulder and alter his expression. 'G'day, Ben, how are you going?'

'All right thanks. You?'

Zoe whirled around and looked at the troubleshooter standing in the doorway. Was it her imagination or did he look sheepish?

'Can't complain,' Miles replied evenly. 'Anything you need?'

Ben swung his arms back and forth, avoiding Zoe's gaze. 'I've been trying to find the staffing files. Human Resources said you kept them down here.'

'We used to,' Zoe replied. 'Karen moved them up to her office when you started. She's old-fashioned, likes to ensure records are at hand on paper.'

'Isn't it all done by computer?' Ben asked, looking troubled.

'Yes, but Karen likes a physical back-up.'

Another frown crossed Ben's features. 'I didn't realise. I'll have to talk to her about that; there could be compliance issues, not to mention GDPR.'

Zoe didn't dare look at Miles; she was sure she would burst out laughing if their eyes met.

'Karen's on a course and not back until Friday,' Zoe explained.

Ben scratched his head. 'Thanks. Although she'll be at the party tomorrow. Perhaps I'll talk to her then.'

At the mention of the staff event, Zoe felt a surge of dread. She hated socialising at the best of times and had hoped to find an excuse to get out of it by now.

'Maybe leave it, eh?' Miles suggested good-naturedly. 'It's a party. Karen'll want a few stubbies and to let her hair down.'

'Will she?' Ben looked astonished. 'She seems so serious.'

'Not all the time. She's professional, but knows how to have a laugh,' Miles offered.

Zoe wondered if Miles was making a pointed remark, but there was no time to dwell as Ben nodded his thanks and turned to leave.

'How are you finding the job, by the way?' Miles called.

Ben smiled as he paused at the door. 'Thanks, I appreciate that. This job is turning out to be tougher than I expected.'

Miles raised an eyebrow. 'Any reason?'

'Not really,' Ben replied. 'Bit more pressure perhaps. This place was on its last legs before the Harpers took it over.'

'It wasn't that bad,' Zoe protested. She knew The Oaks had problems but she and the rest of the staff worked tirelessly to ensure patients were happy. Who did this corporate little idiot think he was? Some sort of nursing saviour?

'Maybe not,' Ben said, eventually. 'But did you know The Oaks used to belong to the Harper family – the house I mean, long before it became a hospice.'

'Mrs Harper mentioned it. Said she hated the place.'

Now it was Ben's turn to look surprised. 'I hope not. Simon went to a lot of trouble to buy it for her.'

'I don't think she wants it.' Zoe laughed. 'But so often people don't take the time to find out what's best and act without thinking.'

The barb wasn't lost on Ben and he glowered at Zoe. She turned her head and looked out of the French doors. As the spring sunshine flooded through the glass, the beams of golden light gave the room a bright warm glow, and Zoe saw the villa from a different angle. Gone were the wing-backed chairs and tattered magazines. In its place she saw a glorious family home, complete with children running on the lawns while adults watched, cocktails in hand, records playing in the corner. It seemed idyllic.

'Not a bad place to end up in, though, during your last days,' Miles said, breaking the silence.

'I can definitely think of worse,' Ben said, checking his watch. 'Well, I'd better get on.'

With that Ben walked away, leaving Miles and Zoe alone once more.

'Tosser,' Miles mumbled once Ben was safely out of earshot.

They laughed and Zoe felt as if a weight had been lifted.

'Thanks for that,' she said as she brought her giggles under control.

'No worries,' Miles said, giving her a playful nudge with his shoulder.

A thought struck Zoe. 'Did you used to laugh at me like that?'

At the look of worry on Zoe's face, Miles chuckled wryly. 'No, well not often anyway.'

Narrowing her eyes, Zoe pretended to be horrified. The reality was that letting off a bit of steam was good for morale, and she didn't mind being the butt of the joke if it made people feel better about their working day. It was natural to want to make fun of the boss.

'What are you going to do about this note stuff?' Miles asked.

'What can I do?' Zoe shrugged.

'Keep taking the notes,' Miles said firmly. 'You heard the bloke. Tasker's mind's fixed on making sure the Harpers are happy. He's not worrying about what you're up to.'

'You sound like Sarah,' Zoe mused, turning her gaze back towards the parkland. Indira was sitting on a bench chatting to one of the patients while her companion lifted her face towards the sun, grateful for a break. It was the little things nurses did that made a big difference, Zoe thought proudly. And Zoe very much counted the letters she wrote and took as one of those things.

Ben Tasker didn't have a clue. All he cared about was sucking up to the Harpers and ensuring his tick boxes and surveys were filled out. That wasn't nursing, that was form-filling and one of the many reasons Zoe had no desire to be in charge.

'You know what?' Zoe said, a smile spreading across her face. 'You're right. I will keep going with the notes and if Ben Tasker doesn't like it, he can shove it where the sun don't shine.'

Chapter Eight

Zoe arrived early for work the next day, armed not only with her party dress, but her notepaper and pen. As she passed the day room, she saw Miles refilling the tea urn and waved.

Miles looked her up and down with interest. 'You doing what I think you're doing?'

Zoe gestured to the paper and pen stuffed in the outer pocket of her backpack. 'I am.'

'You little ripper!' Miles's emerald-green eyes sparkled with delight. 'Do you want me to keep Ben out the way if I see him?'

'Probably best,' she said with a glance at her watch. 'Though he's not due in for an hour. I was hoping I had plenty of time.'

'Go on, girl,' Miles said encouragingly.

With Miles's words of support ringing in her ears, Zoe retreated back into the corridor and made her way to Mrs Timpson's room. Gingerly she pushed the door open and peeked inside, only to be greeted with a cry of, 'Don't loiter.'

Feeling like a naughty schoolgirl, Zoe stood at the foot of Mrs Timpson's bed. She looked pale, Zoe thought, and her large round eyes seemed small and pin-like against her grey flesh.

'I thought I could help with that note after all. That is, if you still want to?'

Mrs Timpson's eyes came alive. 'Why the change of heart?'

Zoe thought about lying but there was something in the woman's expression that stopped her. 'I think it's the right thing to do even though I'm not supposed to take notes any more.

We've had a change in management and it's thought the notes could be a liability.'

'What a load of rubbish,' Mrs Timpson exclaimed. 'I never held with bureaucracy when I was a teacher, and still don't. It gets in the way of what's important.'

'Couldn't agree more,' Zoe replied earnestly.

Mrs Timpson said nothing for a moment as she observed Zoe from the comfort of her bed. 'I suppose if I take you up on your offer, you'll want me to keep my mouth shut?'

When Zoe nodded, the former headteacher's eyes sparkled with merriment. 'I always had a soft spot for the rule-breakers. They had a bit of fire.'

Zoe giggled, all tension in the room gone. 'Would you like me to take a few words down or come back another time?'

'Neither,' Mrs Timpson replied abruptly. 'I've already written my letter. It's in my bedside drawer; could you get it for me?'

Zoe reached into the small cabinet beside the bed. Amongst a couple of paperbacks, she found the letter. Turning the white Basildon Bond envelope over in her hands, she saw it was addressed to a Mrs V. Smith.

'Do you mind delivering it personally? The contents are delicate and my sister might be shocked. If someone is with her when she reads it, it might help.'

Zoe understood immediately, murmuring a soft, 'Of course.'

'It's for my sister's eyes only,' Mrs Timpson said sternly, before her expression softened, 'but let her know I mean every word, won't you?'

'I will,' Zoe said reassuringly.

-

Zoe spent the rest of the day dreading the party, and by the time it rolled around all she wanted was to go home. She knew, however, that her housemate or Karen would never allow it.

'Blimey, look at all this!' Sarah exclaimed, walking into the day room.

Looking around her, Zoe took in the sight through her housemate's eyes. A violinist played something she suspected was Beethoven while guests mingled politely. Trays of canapés and glasses of champagne were being circulated by uniformed nursing students smartly dressed in black and white.

'This isn't usually what the hospice looks like,' Zoe explained.

'I gathered,' Sarah said, smiling as she caught the eye of a waiter with a full tray of champagne. Reaching for two flutes, she handed one to Zoe. 'Remind me what this is for?'

'To welcome the Harpers and the staff they brought with them, which I think is pretty much Ben and a bunch of office staff,' Zoe said, already feeling out of place amongst the glitterati.

She wasn't one to pay attention to her appearance and had settled on simply having a shower, running a brush through her hair and donning an old floral dress with a pair of flats. She thought it would do, but everyone else looked far more polished, dressed in fitted couture and accessorising with Brazilian blowouts.

Out of the corner of her eye, she saw Miles together with Ben and a woman she assumed was her boss's date walk into the room.

Sarah waved her hand. 'Miles, hello.'

'Sarah, haven't seen you for ages,' Miles replied, ignoring Zoe as he leaned forward to kiss her on the cheek. 'You look great.'

Zoe rolled her eyes. Though she had to admit that the teal body-con dress Sarah was wearing, which she had perfectly accessorised with gold earrings made her look incredible.

'Thank you,' Sarah said, her cheeks flushing slightly at the compliment, 'you look pretty good yourself.'

'Well, pain of death otherwise,' Miles said, straightening the blazer he wore over a tight-fitting white shirt. 'Mind you, Zoe, would it kill you to at least try?'

'Oi—' Zoe began, only for Ben to interrupt.

'Don't be so bloody rude, Miles,' he said sharply. 'I think you look lovely, Zoe; that red print is very flattering on you.'

Zoe smiled self-consciously. 'He was just teasing, Ben. Miles is like a very irritating little brother.'

Ben looked wrong-footed. 'Right,' he said, turning to the woman beside him. 'This is Candice.'

Zoe took the woman's extended hand. 'Lovely to meet you. Are you Ben's girlfriend?'

Candice laughed, a loud cackle that broke through the polite murmuring of the other guests. The woman was certainly glamorous, dressed in a bright green silk dress, matching skyscraper heels and red scarf wrapped tightly around her head. She was gorgeous – just Ben's type, Zoe guessed.

'No.' Candice giggled, shooting Ben a look. 'He really is my extremely irritating little brother.'

Ben rolled his eyes. 'By two minutes, C, two minutes.'

'You're twins?' Miles remarked.

'We certainly are,' Candice replied, smiling at her brother. 'We live together.'

'Wow!' Sarah exclaimed. 'I couldn't stand living with my sister.'

'Believe me, I have moments I feel like that myself,' Ben quipped.

'Ha! You'd be lost without me,' Candice said good-naturedly.

'In your dreams,' he replied. 'I'm only doing it so I can afford a place in Camden Crescent – aka one of the poshest parts of the city.'

'It's lucky for you my big fat banker's salary supports your lazy lifestyle,' Candice fired back, helping herself to two mini cheeseburgers from a waiter.

Zoe liked this woman's warmth. 'You're in one of those lovely Georgian flats? I'd kill to live in one of those.'

'I'd have to if it weren't for C,' Ben joked again. 'On a nursing salary I'd barely afford a box.'

'Which is pretty much what I rent,' Miles said with a sigh.

Sarah gave him a playful shove with her elbow. 'I bet it's a nice box.'

Miles looked embarrassed. 'It's all right; you'll have to come round sometime and see for yourself.'

'That an invitation?' Sarah asked, smiling as she took a sip of her drink.

Zoe felt a flash of irritation and took a large gulp of her champagne She might be fond of her colleague but his reputation as a player was legendary, with many at the hospice wondering if he'd run out of room on his bedpost to carve any more notches on it.

'You're from Australia?' Candice observed, interrupting Zoe's thoughts.

'Me and Zoe both are,' Miles said with a grin. 'Though I'm from Darwin and Zoe's a Sydney girl. Unlike Zoe, though, I can't wait to get back.'

'I don't think Australia feels the same way,' Zoe teased. The forced conversation outside of work hours was beginning to get to her, as was her proximity to Ben, and she was suddenly feeling exhausted.

Spotting a passing waiter with a tray of champagne, Zoe decided to follow Candice's lead and, putting her empty glass on the tray, helped herself to two glasses. She smiled at Candice, who winked and did the same.

'How long are you both here for?' Candice asked, taking a large slug from one of her glasses.

'I've got a two-year sponsorship visa,' Miles said. 'It runs out next year, though.'

'And you can't be tempted to stay?' Candice pressed.

'Never in a million years!' Miles said firmly. 'This place is so cold.'

Sarah laughed. 'Spoken like a typical Aussie.'

'I don't think I've ever said that,' Zoe protested.

'You're not planning on leaving, though,' Sarah pointed out.

Candice turned to Zoe. 'What made you decide to settle here permanently?'

'I didn't feel right in Australia,' Zoe explained, reaching for the explanation she always gave to strangers. 'I was born before 1983 so qualified for a right to abode visa, which means I can stay as long as I like.'

'You must miss your family, though?' Miles asked, his eyes full of incredulity.

Zoe shrugged. 'We keep in touch.'

'And you've really never been back?' Candice asked through a mouthful of mini burger. 'My mama would have tanned my hide good and proper if I left and never returned. Your family must be very understanding.'

'They're all right,' Zoe said, feeling uncomfortable. 'I take it your mum's round the corner?'

'She is if you count the crematorium as an address,' Candice said.

'She died four years ago,' Ben explained.

'I'm sorry,' Zoe said.

'Don't be,' Candice said kindly. 'She had a wonderful life. We miss her but she was the one that taught us to live every day as if it were our last and we do.'

'It's why I'm driving an Aston Martin around Silverstone on Saturday,' Ben said with an excited grin.

Candice laughed. 'Don't blame Mum for that. You're doing that because you want to pretend to be James Bond!'

'Who doesn't?' Miles pointed out in mock seriousness.

'Me,' Zoe put in.

'Yeah, but you're no fun,' Miles groaned. 'The highlight of your week is washing your knickers!'

'Oi!' Zoe said, ready to remonstrate Miles again. 'If you want to talk about fun, shall we get started on how many nurses across the south west you've shagged?'

Miles reddened as Ben said, 'That's enough, both of you. You're representing the hospice. And, Zoe, don't take two drinks again; it's not seemly at a work function.'

At the put-down, Zoe felt a rush of fury and was about to say something when she caught sight of Miles, who very subtly mouthed the word 'wanker'. She smirked just as Simon Harper joined them.

'Having a good time?' he asked.

Zoe nodded, running her eye over the hospice owner, who was dressed in a navy suit that had clearly been made to measure rather than bought off the peg. She took a step back to let him into their circle.

'I hear your mother used to live here, sir?' Miles said.

'Yes. I thought it would be right for the old place to come back to the family. My grandfather lost it in a game of cards.' Mr Harper smiled ruefully at the admission. 'Not sure Mum's keen, though.'

'I'm sure that's not true,' Ben said diplomatically.

Zoe rolled her eyes. 'People don't always want to go back.'

'That's enough, Zoe,' Ben said sharply.

At the rebuke, Zoe felt a fresh wave of irritation. She was about to say something else when she caught Candice's eye and saw she looked embarrassed. The last thing she wanted was to upset his sister.

Mr Harper gave them a clipped smile. 'Well, lovely to see you all, have a good evening.'

As the hospice owner walked away, she felt Ben's eyes boring into her.

'Nurse Evans, I think it's time you and I had a little chat tomorrow. My office, first thing.'

Chapter Nine

The following morning, Zoe sat at the nurses' desk, cradling a mug of coffee that had long gone cold as she flicked through her emails. She was tired after last night's party, having drunk far too much fizz following her run-in with Ben and Mr Harper. Then when sleep had found her, Zoe had slept so deeply she missed her alarm. Not daring to be late on top of everything else, she had run a comb through her hair, slapped some water on her face and shoved on yesterday's scrubs, vowing to change and shower at work, something that so far hadn't happened yet.

Instead, she had stared at the computer screen, cursing herself for her unprofessional behaviour. Ben would be gone in a few months; all she had to do was ride it out until then.

Continuing to flick through her inbox, she sifted through the usual notifications – invitations to meetings and reminders about locking up after hours – before finding an email Ben had sent earlier that morning. Clicking it open, she found a formal reminder to come to his office at nine. Her stomach turned over and for a moment Zoe thought her coffee might make a reappearance as she wondered if he was going to sack her. This job was all she had.

'You look like you're wishing you were back on Bondi Beach,' came a loud voice.

Setting the mug down, Zoe looked up and saw Miles standing beside her and felt her nerves settle as he gave her a cheery grin. Taking the seat next to hers, Miles handed her a takeaway cup of coffee from the cafe across the road.

She looked at Miles then the coffee with suspicion. 'Why have you got me a decent coffee instead of the muck from the canteen upstairs? What do you want? Have you got one of the nurses pregnant?' Zoe gasped theatrically, setting the coffee cup down and backing away from it as it were a live grenade.

Miles rolled his eyes and pressed the cup back into Zoe's hands. 'Don't be stupid. I might like the ladies, Zoe, but even I don't shit where I eat.' He looked sheepish for a moment and said, 'At least not any more. Anyway, thought you might be in need of a caffeine boost. Last night was tough.'

Grimacing at the memory, she took a grateful sip of the flat white. 'Don't remind me.'

'Nah, you were all right.' Miles gave her a playful nudge in the ribs. 'You only said what needed to be said. Mrs Harper's telling anyone that will listen she hates it here. Not your fault her son didn't listen.'

'Thanks,' she said, setting the cup down.

As she did so, she looked at the paper cup more closely and to her surprise saw there was a note written in thick black pen on the side.

You're amazing, never forget! Miles xx

Laughing, she stuck her tongue out at her colleague.

'Thank you,' she said. 'I needed to hear that this morning.'

'You worried about this meeting with Ben?'

'A bit,' Zoe admitted. 'He might sack me.'

'He's not going to sack you,' Miles said with an eye-roll, as Karen walked past.

Seeing the two of them, the director smiled. 'You both looked as if you were having a good time last night.'

'It was all right,' Miles said with a shrug. 'Head hurts a bit this morning.'

At the admission, Karen laughed. 'How do you think I feel? At least you don't have to give a presentation this morning with a hangover.'

Zoe wrinkled her nose sympathetically. 'Can't you keep it short? If there was anyone else at the party, they might be grateful for the chance to close their eyes for a second.'

'Funny you should say that.' Karen leaned across the desk. 'I've got a video in my office I thought I might show them; that ought to give me forty minutes to sit down and have a coffee.'

Zoe laughed. It was so unlike Karen, who was a consummate professional at all times.

'I need to talk to you about Mrs Timpson while I've got you here,' Karen said, catching Zoe's eye.

At the mention of her name, Zoe steeled herself. 'Yes?'

'I'm afraid she died last night.'

'I'm so sorry to hear that.' Zoe had hoped to have a bit more time with the former head after discovering her mischievous side.

'What are you sorry about?' Ben asked, appearing at the desk. At the sight of him, Zoe scowled. He looked clean and professional with his freshly ironed scrubs and neatly groomed beard. She even detected a subtle scent of Acqua di Parma. No doubt he had even showered at home that morning.

'Mrs Timpson died last night,' Miles put in.

'Oh, the teacher? What a shame,' Ben said. 'She wasn't with us for very long.'

'That's the way it goes sometimes. I think we made her comfortable,' Miles said.

'I'm sure we did. Indira was with her at the end,' Karen explained.

'No family?' Ben asked, looking surprised.

Karen shook her head. 'I believe not. Although she was quite insistent about a note for her sister. Zoe, do you know anything about that?'

And there it was, the reason she had steeled herself. Zoe was about to answer when the phone rang. Picking up the receiver, she mouthed a polite 'excuse me' to Ben and Karen.

As Zoe answered questions about visiting hours from a patient's relative, she was aware that Ben and Karen had walked off down the corridor and felt relief course through her. By the time she hung up, she felt almost euphoric, a feeling that was quickly dashed by Miles looking at her in surprise.

'You were lucky, mate.'

'It's only a reprieve for so long. He'll ask me about that note during our meeting, then what am I going to do?'

'Oh, forget him,' Miles said, with a frown. 'What were you supposed to do, ignore the wishes of a patient?'

'Probably, yes.' Groaning, Zoe lowered her head against the desk and banged it gently. 'I should have called in sick this morning.'

Miles nudged her playfully. 'You'll be all right. Tasker knows he's onto a good thing with you. He's not going to blow it.'

Lifting her head, she looked at Miles in despair. 'You think?'

'I know,' Miles said gently. 'Everyone here is fond of you, me especially. We won't let anything happen, and if it did, I'm fairly sure Sarah would have my balls on a plate.'

At the image, Zoe chuckled. 'Sarah, huh?'

Miles coloured. 'Yeah, she's all right. For a Brit.'

'She is all right, but don't go after her, okay? She's not one of your usual nurses you can sleep with and forget about. She's been through a lot and she's got a kid.'

'That you warning me off?' Miles said awkwardly.

'That's me saying very nicely, move on. Sarah's not for you,' Zoe said.

'Thing is, Zoe, I really like her. She's different.'

'Yeah, yeah.' Zoe rolled her eyes and turned back to her computer screen.

'I mean it,' Miles insisted. 'But she's not interested in me. She's too busy with work and her daughter.'

'Life's complicated for Sarah,' Zoe said seriously. 'It is for any parent. When she's ready, she'll want a proper relationship and if you're really serious about her that's something you need to understand.'

'I'm not a total moron, Zoe!' Miles growled. 'I do get that.'

Miles walked towards the day room. Zoe watched him go. Miles could be very sweet but he wasn't a parent and would never understand the complications in Sarah's life and how a child would always come first. Inevitably Sean came to mind and even now Zoe knew he would always be her first choice, and that was the way it would always be.

–

An hour later and Zoe rapped lightly on Ben's office door. Within seconds she heard footsteps from the other side, then it swung wide open and she was greeted by a non-smiling troubleshooter.

'Zoe. Come in,' Ben said, beckoning her inside. 'How's the head?'

At the question, she felt a flash of guilt. 'Fine.'

'Good.' Ben moved a pile of books from a chair so she could sit down. 'Sorry about the mess; I haven't had chance to settle in yet.'

'It's fine,' Zoe said, taking the hard plastic chair Ben offered.

As she did so, she took in the tiny office that until very recently had been hers. Piles of books lay on the floor. Staff rotas, files, two plants and a diary lined the desk, while three large bottles of indigestion medicine took centre stage. The only thing that seemed to have been properly unpacked and consciously positioned was a framed photo of him wearing a black graduation cap, Candice smiling by his side.

'Can I get you a coffee? I've got one of those fancy machines,' he asked, gesturing towards the Nespresso perched on the edge of his desk.

Zoe let out an admiring whistle. 'That wasn't here when this office was mine. Yes please.'

While Ben made coffees for each of them, Zoe took a deep breath; she was a bag of jangling nerves.

'I've been doing some thinking,' Ben said, handing her a mug filled with dark liquid. 'You and I have got off to a bad start. I've been here almost three weeks and things seem to be going from bad to worse. It feels as though you have no respect for me.'

Zoe set her cup on a corner of the desk that wasn't cluttered and sat upright in her chair. 'Respect has to be earned.'

'Maybe,' Ben replied, leaning against the window frame, 'but professionalism doesn't. From the moment I met you, you have been antagonistic, rude and unhelpful. It's got to stop.'

Zoe gasped. 'I have never been called unprofessional in my life.'

Ben put his cup on the windowsill and folded his arms. 'So I've been led to believe, but that's not what I've seen. What I see is a nurse who's pissed off she hasn't got her own way and is taking it out on me, the rest of the nursing team and the patients as well. You're like a spoiled child.'

At the insult, Zoe let out a hollow laugh. 'And you call that professional, do you? I'm sure Human Resources would have a field day if they could hear the way you've just spoken to me.'

'You're impossible,' Ben snapped, rubbing a hand over his head in aggravation.

'I might be impossible, but I'm also right.' Zoe leaned forward in her chair, the bit firmly between her teeth. 'I used to do your job, remember?'

'And you left the place in such a state the hospice needed a troubleshooter to put your mistakes right,' Ben fired back.

The two of them glared at each other, but, in the end, it was Ben who broke the silence first.

'I'm sorry, I shouldn't have said that,' he said with a sigh. '*That* was unprofessional.'

'I think it was more than unprofessional,' Zoe said evenly, 'but I appreciate the apology.'

'Do you see where I'm coming from, though?' Ben asked, his tone weary. 'We can't go on like this. I'm sorry you're unhappy with my decision about your note-taking but it stands.'

'Have I said otherwise?'

'No, but you've taken Mrs Timpson's note, haven't you?' Ben reasoned.

Zoe nodded. She was proud of the service she offered patients and wasn't going to lie.

'Where is it?' Ben asked, his eyes cold and unyielding.

Reaching into her trouser pocket, she produced the letter she had been given yesterday.

'Give it to me,' he ordered.

'No.'

Ben narrowed his eyes. 'Give me the letter.'

Zoe shook her head. 'Mrs Timpson asked me to deliver this note personally and I shall do so whether you like it or not.'

'Nurse Evans, you are skating on extremely thin ice. I already told you not to take any more notes—'

'And technically I didn't. Mrs Timpson merely asked me to deliver one,' Zoe said with an air of triumph.

Running his tongue across his teeth, Ben shook his head. 'I saw how you avoided the question when Karen asked you outright if you had a letter from her.'

'And the fact she asked me about it would suggest that Karen doesn't know you've asked me to stop note-taking,' Zoe countered.

'No, she doesn't, but Karen would agree with me,' Ben said sagely. 'She told you I had ideas for the hospice and asked you to get on board. Well guess what, Nurse Evans? Your notes don't fit in at the hospice any longer and neither does your attitude.'

'You might not have liked the way I was doing things before, but don't tell me patient satisfaction scores weren't high because they were certainly a darned sight higher than they have been since you took over. You haven't an ounce of compassion for the patients at the heart of what we do.'

Zoe looked mutinously at her boss. They were at a stalemate and the silence between them seemed to stretch on forever.

'Nurse Evans, I am giving you a verbal warning,' Ben said in a low voice. 'This warning will stay in your employment file for six months. If your actions within the workplace don't change or improve, I will issue you with a written warning. Do I make myself clear?'

Zoe felt sick. She had never had an official warning before. But she wouldn't break down in front of this man; she wouldn't give him the satisfaction.

'Yes, sir.'

'Good,' Ben said at last. 'I will be keeping a close eye on you and your work. If I find you have been involved in writing or delivering any more notes within this hospice, I will take further disciplinary action against you. Is that understood?'

'Yes, sir,' Zoe said again.

Her heart was banging so loudly she was sure Ben could hear it. All she wanted was for this meeting to be over.

'With regards to the letter you have just taken from Mrs Timpson, you will deliver it but I will go with you so there is no issue of impropriety,' Ben said.

'What?' Zoe gasped. 'That's not necessary.'

'Oh, believe me, Nurse Evans, it's very necessary,' Ben said gruffly. 'There will be no argument about it. Any questions?'

'No,' Zoe said, her body so tense she wasn't sure she could say anything else.

'Right, then get out.'

Wordlessly, Zoe left, slamming the door on her way out and finding the nearest ladies' toilets. Safely locked inside a cubicle, Zoe allowed the hot angry tears to spill down her face and sank to the floor in despair.

Chapter Ten

Since her warning from Ben a fortnight earlier, Zoe had worked night shifts wherever possible, something that hadn't gone unnoticed by Karen. Finding Zoe in the empty staff room the following Friday morning, Karen hadn't wasted any time in making her feelings known.

'Zoe, this is ridiculous,' she had said, hands on hips. 'I relied on you to make the takeover easier; instead you've made my job ten times harder. Don't think I haven't noticed how you've swapped your shifts to work almost every night possible and avoid Ben.'

'Sorry,' Zoe said.

Guilt coursed through her. As a boss, Karen had been good to her and Zoe had enormous respect for the woman. Whilst she was pleased to have avoided Ben, she didn't want to make life difficult for Karen.

'I don't want you to be sorry. I need you on the floor. You're the best nurse we have,' Karen barked, before looking at her sympathetically. 'I hadn't realised Ben had asked you to stop your notes. I know how much that means to you and it must be hard.'

At Karen's compassion, Zoe felt fresh hope. Was there a chance Karen might let her continue writing the notes she loved?

'I'm not getting into that now,' she warned, reading Zoe's mind. 'I merely wanted to say I wish to speak with you and Ben in my office at five before you start your next shift. Be prompt; I want this matter resolved immediately.'

And so later that day Zoe had found herself walking into Karen's office, where she and Ben were sitting on the easy chairs at the back.

'Zoe, glad you're here,' the director said, gesturing for Zoe to sit on the sofa underneath the window.

'Sorry I'm late.' Zoe sat down and gave Karen an apologetic smile.

'You're not. I asked Ben to arrive early,' Karen replied bluntly.

Zoe chanced a look at Ben. He seemed laid-back, legs wide open in the man-spreading way some men liked to adopt.

'I wanted to see if we could resolve the issue that has crept up within the department,' Karen said, getting to the point. 'I'm sure none of us are comfortable with the way things are.'

'That would be difficult for me to say, Karen,' Ben began, 'because I've barely seen Zoe since I gave her a formal warning.'

'Precisely my point.' Karen turned to Zoe. 'Why have you put yourself on night shifts?'

'You know why,' Zoe muttered.

'I do know why but I would like to hear you say it,' Karen pressed.

For a moment Zoe had a feeling she had gone back in time and was sitting in her old high school principal's office. For a second, she allowed herself to be transported back to her schooldays. Everything had seemed so simple, the biggest concern being whether she'd have fairy bread or Vegemite when she got home.

'I felt it best for everyone if Mr Tasker and I had some space,' Zoe said.

Karen nodded and turned to Ben. 'Do you agree?'

'If that's what Nurse Evans thinks, who am I to argue?' Ben said, stony-faced.

Karen banged her fist on the coffee table that stood between them, and Zoe jumped as Karen glared at her and Ben.

'You two are behaving like children and I won't have it. This is not only a place of business, it is a place where people bring their loved ones to see out their final days. I will *not* have it turned into a playground because you two can't get along like adults.'

Ben leaned forward in his seat. 'Excuse me, Karen, I think you will find Nurse Evans's conduct is the issue—'

'No, you are both the issue!' Karen roared, not taking kindly to being interrupted. 'I do not have time for this nonsense so let me tell you how things are going to be from now on. Zoe,' she said, looking at the nurse. 'We all recognise how wonderful you are, how much care and respect you put into the work you do. You are the finest nurse we have and I consider your verbal warning unnecessary.'

Zoe felt relief pass through her but the feeling was short-lived as Karen continued. 'But make no mistake, Ben is in charge, and if he has assessed the situation regarding your notes and deemed the right course of action for the hospice is that you stop, he has my support and the full support of the hospice. Is that clear?'

Nodding in reluctant agreement, Zoe watched Karen turn to Ben. 'As for you, Mr Tasker, I am shocked you have caused such stress to one of our best nurses. Zoe's work is exemplary and she has precisely the kind of dedication we want at the hospice. You two need to learn to work together and settle your differences. If you won't do it willingly, I shall force you. Ben, I understand you have a meeting at St Mary's next week?'

'It's more of a presentation,' Ben said, looking as fed up as she felt, Zoe noticed, with a flush of satisfaction.

'Even better. I assume you'll have plenty of files and equipment?' Karen asked.

Ben murmured his assent.

'Wonderful.' Karen beamed. 'In that case, Zoe, I should like you to give Mr Tasker a lift to St Mary's.'

'What?' Both Ben and Zoe gasped in unison.

At the outburst, Karen laughed. 'You see? Something you agree on already. I have arranged for our newest nurse, Abby, to cover your shift, Zoe, and I sincerely hope you will return able to work together. Do I make myself clear?'

Ben and Zoe nodded and Karen smiled.

'Excellent,' she said, gesturing for them both to leave. 'I look forward to you both returning to the floor with fresh attitudes. In the meantime,' she said, looking pointedly at Ben, 'I want you to consider why you asked Zoe to stop writing her letters and whether it was entirely just.'

-

The bank holiday weekend passed in a blur, with Zoe constantly worrying about Tuesday, strongly suspecting this forced trip to Bristol would only make matters worse. On top of that, of course, there was the issue of David; she still hadn't heard from him or his solicitor about the divorce settlement.

In need of comfort, Zoe had indulged in her favourite hobby – rereading the note she kept in a wooden box beside her bed. The note, with the simple phrase *I just want to be a cowboy*, gave her the strength it always did when she was in a challenging situation.

But on Tuesday morning, the power of her treasured note still couldn't stop her worrying about the day ahead. On the drive to work, she tried to push all that lay ahead from her mind and instead concentrate on Mrs Timpson. The former head had passed away a couple of weeks ago and Zoe still hadn't given the note to her sister.

Ben might have insisted on coming with her to deliver the note but the last thing Zoe needed was him involved. Still, she wanted to make sure the note got to its rightful owner as soon as possible. The question was when; she never seemed to have any time to herself.

Ten minutes later and Zoe was still no closer to an answer as she sat at the nurses' desk, leafing through the diary. Despite everything being computerised, the nursing staff still wrote most things down. Nobody had forgotten when the systems went down a couple of years ago, causing chaos for days. Consequently, an old-fashioned back-up had been devised, which unfortunately meant the desk was always littered with notes.

To her surprise, she saw one addressed to her from Ben.

Dear Zoe,

Just to let you know Mrs Harper stayed last night. Simon was away at a conference and he didn't want her left alone. She was in good spirits but asked for you. I told her you would be in to see her when you started your shift so make her your first priority please?

Thanks so much,

B

The informal use of his name gave Zoe a jolt. As she stared at the single initial on the page, his swirly, left-leaning handwriting carving out the letter to denote his name, she felt hopeful this trip to Bristol wouldn't be as bad as she expected.

Making her way to Mrs Harper's room, Zoe was surprised to find the older lady was not only out of bed but sitting in an armchair, cup of tea in hand, gazing out of the window at the lake beyond.

'Good morning,' Zoe said brightly.

Mrs Harper turned. 'Ah, Nurse Evans. How are you? I'd been hoping to see you again soon. I wanted to thank you for the kind note you left.'

Zoe waved her thanks away. 'It was nothing,' she said, taking a seat opposite the older woman. 'Didn't expect to see you as an overnight guest quite so soon, though.'

Mrs Harper gave her a rueful smile. 'Didn't expect to find myself here. Simon thought it best. He was in London until late and worried about me being alone.'

'That's nice.'

'There is nothing nice about becoming an elderly burden to your family,' Mrs Harper said sharply.

'True, but a brain tumour could happen at any age. Being old has nothing to do with that,' Zoe countered.

'You're right,' Ms Harper agreed reluctantly. 'But this isn't how I pictured my life. I always thought I'd leave this place far behind – now I'm back where I started.'

'I understand that,' Zoe said. 'I left Australia a couple of years ago but I'll never go back.'

Mrs Harper looked at her curiously. 'Why?'

'Family stuff mainly,' Zoe said, unsure how best to sum up the truth in a few sentences.

'That *I* understand,' Mrs Harper replied. 'That was why I hated it here. And now look at me.'

'Now look at you, bravely doing battle with a brain tumour,' Zoe offered.

'And losing, which is why I'm here.' She looked around and shivered. 'This place always did suck the life out of you.'

Zoe frowned, wanting to ask more but sensing Mrs Harper didn't want to say any more. Instead, she let her patient drink her tea and Zoe slowly filtered out of the room.

–

The morning flew by, and it was soon time to give Ben a lift to Bristol.

'Despite Karen insisting that we spend time together, I do appreciate this,' Ben said solemnly as they strode across the car park. 'I'd been intending to get a taxi.'

Zoe shrugged. 'It's no problem.'

They descended into an awkward silence. Reaching the Yaris, Zoe unlocked her car and opened the boot for Ben to put his presentation gear inside.

'Nice wheels,' Ben commented, as he sat in the passenger seat.

'Yeah, we're not all on troubleshooter salaries,' Zoe quipped, taking her place behind the wheel. 'Anyway, I like this car. It's nippy and stylish.'

Ben raised an eyebrow, opened his mouth, then shut it again. Zoe was grateful. She didn't want to start the journey with a row. As she edged out of the car park and onto the main road, she glanced at Ben, who was pulling a book out of the messenger bag by his feet. She noticed it was the latest Robert Galbraith and smiled in surprise; she didn't have him down as a lover of fiction. Ben opened the book at a midway point and Zoe turned back to the road, figuring it was probably for the best if they didn't talk. If they could survive this short journey, there was a chance they might be able to work together without screaming at each other.

'Mind if I put the radio on?' she asked, ten minutes into the trip.

Ben shook his head. 'As long as you don't make me listen to Crowded House and INXS on repeat.'

Zoe giggled. 'Because I'm Australian I can only like Aussie music? Expect me to just listen to Kylie and Natalie Imbruglia?'

Ben scratched his head. 'I do love that song, "Torn".'

'I'm more of a Smiths fan.'

'Ouch. Depressing,' Ben said with a wince. 'I'm a Rolling Stones man.'

'Why doesn't that surprise me? I bet your favourite song is "I Can't Get No Satisfaction".'

'Should be, shouldn't it?' Ben joked. 'What with all the stroppy nurses I have to deal with.'

There was a pause and Zoe wondered for a moment if things had thawed between the two of them or if they were on the verge of another row. It seemed Ben was thinking the same as he let out a loud chuckle.

'Sorry. Listen, I've thought about what Karen said. It's possible I did overreact…'

Zoe was so startled, she took her eyes off the road for a second to check if Ben was serious. The solemn look on his face, together with the fact he had shoved his book onto the dashboard, told her he was. She turned her gaze back to the road and thought for a second. If he was offering an olive branch, she supposed she ought to do the same.

'I appreciate that. And it's possible I may not have handled your instruction to stop writing notes as well as I could.'

'I'd like to apologise, Zoe,' Ben said gently, 'and try to put our relationship on an even keel.'

Zoe pulled into St Mary's and found a parking space near the entrance. 'I'd like that too.'

As she turned off the engine, she saw Ben looking at her with sincerity in his eyes.

'I've been doing some thinking and perhaps I was hasty, getting you to stop letter-writing entirely.'

Zoe's eyes widened at the statement.

'I would like to observe your notes and deliveries and see how you handle them. If I think it's effective and of benefit to the patients, I'll look into you continuing with them.'

'Do you really mean that?' Zoe gasped.

'I mean it.' Ben gave her a tight smile. 'I've been a dick, Zoe, I'm sorry. To make matters right, I thought we could start after my meeting. Do you have the letter for Mrs Timpson's sister on you?'

'Yes, it's in my bag, why?'

'I checked earlier on and Mrs Smith lives nearby. We could go and see her afterwards and I can see how it goes.'

'Are you asking to come with me to see Mrs Smith?' Zoe's heart sank.

'I'm not asking, I'm telling,' Ben said firmly, opening the passenger door. 'Wait until my meeting's finished and we can go then. No arguments.'

Chapter Eleven

By the time Ben returned to the car two hours later, Zoe was so engrossed in his novel she barely noticed him open the passenger door and sit beside her.

'Enjoying it?' he asked.

Holding up her left hand to stop Ben talking, her face remained buried within the pages. He had made her wait two hours; the least he could do was wait two minutes.

'Just finishing this chapter.'

And without even looking at him, she continued reading, unaware of Ben's amusement.

'Right, finished,' she said a moment later, closing the book and placing it on her back seat.

'That's mine,' Ben exclaimed.

'Not any more it's not.' She grinned, starting the engine. 'Call it payment for having to drive and wait so long for you.'

'It wasn't my decision,' Ben grumbled, folding his arms. 'I don't think that should cost me a book.'

'Well, it has. I'll give it back to you when I've finished it,' she said, turning left out of the car park and back onto the main road.

There was a silence for a bit, before Zoe asked, 'Good meeting?'

Ben laughed. 'I think you know the answer to that.'

'Let's just say there were many reasons I didn't want to be in nursing management,' Zoe said.

'After that meeting, I can see why.' Ben sighed, leaning his head back against the rest. 'I hate all that compliance and budgetary stuff.'

'I thought you loved it,' Zoe exclaimed. 'Why be a troubleshooter then?'

'It's the best way to make change,' Ben said earnestly. 'If you don't push yourself and others, you can't bring about positivity in your work, so that means doing things you don't like, including meetings.'

'For me the only paperwork I was interested in was patient letters.'

For a moment there was a pause and Zoe had a horrible feeling she had gone too far, until Ben spoke, his tone gentle.

'You know, back when I was a nurse rather than a paper-pusher, I used to write down the last wishes of the dying occasionally.'

Pulling up at a red traffic light, Zoe glanced at Ben. 'You?'

Ben shook his head at the disbelief on Zoe's face. 'Yes, me. I used to be a surgical nurse. When a patient was admitted to the ward I'd see if anyone had anything they wanted to say just in case… you know.'

'Wasn't that a bit morbid if they were going into theatre?' Zoe asked, aghast.

'Isn't what you do morbid?' Ben countered.

'I work in a hospice. What I do helps chivvy people along. The notes help people come to terms with the dying process. It gives them a good death,' Zoe pointed out, putting the car into first as the light turned green. 'You as a surgical nurse asking me that just before the anaesthetist turned up would make me very worried about the operation.'

Ben let out a bark of laughter. It suited him, Zoe realised, as she looked at him for a second. The smile that reached his eyes transformed his entire face, making him appear handsome and relaxed.

'No wonder my patients always looked terrified when they saw me. But I liked taking the notes and delivering them to their loved ones if the patient didn't survive.'

'So why stop?'

At the question, a flash of guilt passed across his face. 'When Karen asked me the other day to be honest about why I'd stopped you writing notes she knew I wasn't being entirely truthful about my reasons.'

'Meaning?'

'Meaning the reason I asked you to stop was because I was once threatened with legal action over a note,' Ben admitted.

From nowhere, the skies darkened and the sudden burst of rain against the windscreen was so loud Zoe had to shout her next question.

'You were sued?' she asked, flicking on her headlights to better see the road ahead.

'Not sued. It was something and nothing really. I gave a note to a relative and the relative took whatever was inside so badly we ended up in a fist fight in the hospital corridors.'

'Oh my God!' Zoe exclaimed. 'What happened?'

'I was suspended, given a written warning and told not to get too involved in patients' lives. Not only could I cause problems for myself but also the hospital.'

'Wow,' Zoe said over the rain, struggling to picture the always-put-together Ben in a fist fight.

'After that I pursued management, vowing never to do anything that would put my career in jeopardy again.'

'That's why you became a paper-pusher?'

'Pretty much,' Ben said. 'Doesn't mean I've forgotten how to be sensitive or how to be a good nurse.'

Zoe felt blindsided by Ben's confession. Could it really be true that he had taken notes as she had? She glanced at him, seeing him in a new light somehow. As she did, the rain stopped as suddenly as it had started and a rainbow formed in the sky above the windscreen.

'Look at that,' she marvelled, as she brought the car to a stop in the road she knew to be Mrs Smith's.

'Perhaps it's a good omen,' Ben said with a brief smile.

'Let's hope so.' As she stepped out of the car, she felt oddly nervous.

'Zoe, I'm not here to catch you out,' Ben said, correctly interpreting the look on her face as he got out of the car. 'I'm here to help. I want this to be a success as much as you do.'

'Okay,' she said, not sure she wholly believed him, walking with Ben towards Mrs Smith's house. It was a lovely street, Zoe thought. All red-brick houses, gravel paths, big gates and cherry blossoms lining the wide pavement.

Moments later, Zoe rang the bell of the smart Victorian home and a man who looked to be a few years younger than Mrs Timpson came to the door.

'Can I help you?' he asked, his smile welcoming as he stood inside his bright hallway.

'We're looking for Mrs Smith,' Zoe said.

'I'm Mr Smith. Can I help?' the man replied.

Zoe exchanged an awkward glance with Ben. Mrs Timpson had said her sister lived alone.

'It's Mrs Smith I need,' Zoe said cautiously.

Mr Smith looked guarded. 'Who wants to know?'

'We do, sir,' Ben said warmly. 'We're from The Oaks, the hospice just outside Bath. We're hoping to find Mrs Smith as we've been taking care of Mrs Timpson, her sister.'

'Hilda?' Mr Smith gasped, clutching his hands to his chest. 'Is she all right?'

'Could we come in?' Zoe said, spotting the neighbours peering through the curtains.

Wordlessly, Mr Smith showed them into a small front room and gestured for them to sit on a sofa under the bay window.

'Is Mrs Smith around?' Ben asked as Mr Smith returned moments later bearing a tea tray.

Mr Smith put the tray down, sat in the chair opposite and took a deep breath. 'I'm Mrs Smith.'

Zoe let out an involuntary gasp.

Leaning forward, she drank in the essence of the man before her. Despite the wrinkles around his forehead and eyes, she could see a resemblance to Mrs Timpson.

'I transitioned ten years ago,' Mr Smith explained. 'I saw Hilda at the time, and tried to explain…'

'And not since?' Ben ventured.

'No, never again,' Mr Smith said with a hint of sadness. 'She couldn't understand what I was doing. Said I was destroying my body.'

'But instead, you were just putting the pieces of the jigsaw together,' Ben offered.

'Exactly,' Mr Smith said, nodding, the relief that they understood obvious in the way his shoulders dropped from his ears. 'What does Hilda want? I can't imagine she's in a good way if she's in a hospice.'

Zoe looked at the floor before raising her eyes to meet Mr Smith's. 'I'm so sorry, sir,' she began. 'She passed away last week.'

Mr Smith's face crumpled. 'No. Not Hilda. She's as strong as firewater.'

'Even firewater has an expiry date,' Ben said, earning himself a glare from Zoe.

'She asked me to give this note to you.' Zoe felt around in her pocket for the letter she had promised to deliver and pressed it into Mr Smith's hand.

He held the paper at arm's length as if terrified it might burn him. 'Do you know what she wanted to say?'

Zoe shook her head. 'Often, when people are dying or facing death, they don't know what they're saying…'

Her voice trailed off as she saw that Mr Smith had already ripped open the letter and was staring at the folded sheet of lined notepaper.

'I hope she was of sound mind when she wrote this,' Mr Smith said, handing the note back to Zoe and Ben to read.

Taking it from his hand, Zoe saw two words. *I'm sorry.*

Zoe turned to Mr Smith and saw the note had devastated him. He was hunched over his knees, arms wrapped around himself as he rocked back and forth, weeping for his sister like a baby.

For the next hour Mr Smith sat in his chair, eyes scrunched up like tissues as he sobbed his heart out. Both Ben and Zoe remained silent, offering a hand or a tissue whenever they thought it appropriate.

'I waited years for my sister to accept me. Why couldn't she have done that when she was alive?' Mr Smith wailed, his blue eyes looking even more piercing against the redness of the skin that surrounded them.

'I think everything happens just when it should. If she had tried to say this to you before she died, Hilda might have ruined what little was left of your relationship, and this letter,' Ben said, gesturing to the note crumpled between Mr Smith's fingers, 'may not have had the effect it was intended to have. You might have been too angry to forgive her. This way, you can preserve the good memories of your sister.'

'I suppose,' Mr Smith said reluctantly. 'But I wish things had been different. So much time wasted.'

Ben and Zoe left shortly afterwards and drove back in near silence. As they arrived back at the hospice, she realised she had been worried about what Ben was thinking.

'Thank you for bringing me to see Mr Smith,' Ben said cautiously as they got out of Zoe's car. 'It was lovely. I think I needed reminding just how powerful notes can be and how they can be such a comfort for the living. After the incident with my own letter, I worried too much about what I could control so I threw myself into my work, never wanting to let the same mistakes happen again. It became my world and I think that's why I never stayed married or had kids.'

'You were married?' Zoe exclaimed.

Ben laughed at the look of disbelief on Zoe's face. 'Funnily enough I did find a woman to marry me! We only lasted two years before we got divorced, though. I realised I loved my job more than her.'

'That's honest.'

'I didn't waste any tears over it,' Ben mused. 'I missed her. But it wasn't like I ever wanted kids. Jess, my wife, always hoped I'd change my mind when we married but I didn't. Family life wasn't for me and when she asked for a divorce, I felt relieved. Being without her meant I could give more of myself to the job I loved.'

'I get that,' Zoe replied. 'I'm getting divorced myself.'

The moment the words were out there, Zoe wondered why she was telling her boss her secrets.

'Is that what you want?' Ben asked gently.

'I don't know,' Zoe said in a small voice. 'We've been separated a couple of years; he's back in Australia. It feels like the end of everything.'

'Or it could be the start of something. Maybe life is pushing you forward because you haven't been doing it yourself.'

'What gives you that idea?' she asked.

'I don't know.' Ben shrugged. 'Just a feeling. It's as if you're in limbo.'

There was that word again, Zoe thought. The one Sarah had used to describe her life. Part of her wondered what was wrong with that.

'I spoke to Legal last night about your notes,' Ben said, bringing her back to the present. 'They suggested we draw up a document that says you're acting under your own steam rather than that of the hospice. If you're happy to keep going with the notes on that basis, I don't have a problem with you continuing.'

'Are you serious?' She gasped.

Ben smiled. 'I should have done it this way all along. I'm sorry.'

'And I'm sorry,' Zoe said, giving her boss a small smile. 'It should never have come to this.'

'Let's put it behind us,' Ben suggested, extending his right hand for Zoe to shake.

Zoe took it. Standing in the car park, she couldn't help noticing how big his hands were, and how her own palm was half the size of his.

'And, Zoe,' Ben said, loosening his grip. 'If you could get Miles to stop calling me a wanker every time I see him, I'd appreciate it.'

Zoe laughed. 'I'll see what I can do.'

Chapter Twelve

The morning after she and Ben had called a truce, Zoe walked into the staff room and found Indira and Miles hunched over the table by the window, gossiping like a pair of old women.

'Hope I'm not interrupting,' Zoe called.

At the sound of her voice, the pair turned around and Miles grinned expectantly. 'Just the person. How did it go with the wanker?'

Zoe grinned. 'Well. Better than expected.'

'Karen's plan worked?' Indira clapped her hands together in delight.

Only Miles looked disappointed. 'When you say well, how well do you mean?'

'I mean he apologised, came with me to deliver Mrs Timpson's letter to her brother and has said I can keep taking the notes if I want,' Zoe explained.

Now Indira's eyes were out on stalks as she digested the news. 'You're kidding! This is more than Karen could have hoped for. I'm off to tell her right now; she'll be over the moon.'

With that, Indira pushed past them both in a flurry of excitement, leaving Miles glaring at her, arms folded. 'Does this mean we have to start being nice to Ben?'

At the sight of Miles's forlorn face, she squeezed his shoulder sympathetically. 'I think we might have to try. I'm sorry.'

Shaking his head, Miles muttered what sounded like a torrent of filthy swear words and followed Indira out of the door. She laughed at his reaction. He was such an old stirrer.

Shucking off her coat, she shoved it in her locker with her bag and, as she went to shut the door, noticed something fall to the floor. Stooping to pick it up, she was surprised to see a white envelope addressed to her in what looked like Ben's writing.

Dear Zoe,

In the spirit of our new start (and because I wanted to show you how much I support your notes) I wondered if you could come to my office this afternoon for a quick chat? About three if you can?

Thanks,

B

Zoe wondered what he wanted. However, there wasn't long to ponder Ben's request because, the moment Zoe stepped onto the ward, she discovered Arthur was nearly at the end. She checked his vitals and realised if she was quick there would be time to wake Audrey, who had been napping in the day room. Before she did, there was one final thing she wanted to check.

'Arthur, sweetheart,' she whispered. 'It's Zoe.'

'Zoe?' Arthur rasped. 'Am I going?'

Zoe stroked Arthur's face. 'I wanted to ask you about the note you asked me to give Audrey. Do you remember?'

There was a silence before Arthur spoke.

'Yes,' he rasped again.

'Do you want me to give it to her as we talked about, or do you want me to change it?'

Arthur's breathing became shallower. She was worried he wouldn't be able to give her an answer, leaving her in the unenviable position of having to decide whether Arthur really wanted the note delivered.

'Just tell her about the carrots,' he whispered, every word more difficult to say than the last. 'I want her to look… after… her… herself.'

At the final word, Zoe felt a stab of affection for Arthur. She knew he was merely trying to be like many of her patients, full of good humour, wit and spark until he couldn't do it any longer.

'I'll tell her. You can relax.'

There was a movement out of the corner of her eye and Zoe saw Audrey standing hesitantly in the doorway. Smiling, the nurse beckoned her in and gestured to the empty chair beside Arthur's bed.

Arthur's wife turned to Zoe with fear in her eyes. 'What do I do?'

'Just be here,' Zoe whispered. 'Take in your final moments together. I'll be outside if you need me.'

Arthur's wife had timed her arrival perfectly and Zoe knew she would be able to stay strong enough to say her good-byes without allowing herself to become swept away with the outpouring of grief that would come afterwards.

Sure enough, twenty minutes later, doctors pronounced Arthur dead and Zoe led Audrey to the relatives' room, where she pressed a cup of hot, sweet tea into her hands. Zoe could only imagine the pain Audrey was in. She had lost her best friend, her partner and a life she had known for over fifty years in one cruel moment.

'I never said thank you,' Audrey said eventually, her West Country burr punctuating the silence.

Zoe looked at her in surprise. 'For what?'

'That lovely letter you wrote. That morning when you left us each a letter, I was feeling so broken at what Arthur and I were both going through and what we would have to face individually. I knew the end was in sight and I didn't want to leave Arthur,' Audrey explained. 'I had no idea where or how I was going to find the strength to carry on. And then there was that lovely letter of yours with the star on it, encouraging me to keep going, insisting I would get through all that lay ahead and one day even find joy again.'

A flush of embarrassment rose through Zoe at the praise. She liked to try to deliver her notes furtively so she could avoid conversations like this. It wasn't that she didn't want to talk about the letters she wrote, more that she didn't feel it was worthy of commendation. The idea was to make the recipient feel better, not her.

'You're very welcome,' she said at last. 'I thought you might be in need of a boost. It's tough being left behind.'

Audrey's eyes clouded with tears. 'Yes. Nothing prepares you.'

Zoe sat next to Audrey and held her hand. 'Is your son here?'

'He's out in the car. This will be difficult for him; he was very close to his father. He couldn't face saying goodbye.'

Zoe nodded. This wasn't uncommon. 'Is there anything I can get you?' she asked softly.

Audrey wiped the tears from her eyes. 'You're very kind, dear. Arthur was very fond of you.'

'And I was fond of him,' Zoe said. She had come to look forward to seeing Arthur each morning, his blunt honesty always a refreshing start to any day. 'Actually, I have another note for you. From Arthur this time.'

Handing the folded purple notepaper across to Audrey, Zoe couldn't miss the flash of hope in her eyes. Zoe knew what it meant. There was still some last connection to her husband, some last trace of the life they had shared together.

Audrey unfolded the paper, and Zoe watched as she read through the few words, tipped her head back and let out a great belly laugh.

'Always buy carrots,' she managed through gasps of laughter. 'Those were his final words to me? Always buy carrots.'

'He said you didn't eat enough veg,' Zoe said kindly. 'He wanted you to take care of yourself.'

Audrey nodded, her eyes still crinkled with a mix of delight and disbelief. 'I know that, dear. He always nagged me. Said he'd be no good if I went before him.' Zoe said nothing; she just watched Audrey clutch the notepaper to her heart. 'And here I am, alone. What bloody good will carrots do me now?'

The new widow gave in to the grief that had never been far away, her body convulsing with great, violent sobs. Immediately, Zoe wrapped an arm around Audrey's shoulders.

'They'll do you no good at all now,' Zoe said over Audrey's tears. 'But I promise you one day you'll find yourself in the supermarket staring at a bag of carrots and it won't hurt so much. You'll even want to eat them, because you'll find the love you and Arthur shared is still there and that's something that never goes away.'

Chapter Thirteen

Arthur's widow didn't leave the hospice for several hours, which meant Zoe was ten minutes late for her meeting with Ben. Knocking on the door, Zoe felt a pang of relief that this time Ben was smiling as he welcomed her inside.

'Zoe! Come in. How are you?'

'Fine, sorry I'm late. Arthur died and I was helping his widow.'

Ben waved her apology away and gestured to the seat opposite his desk. She glanced around and saw he had cleaned the place up since she was last here. Paperwork was neatly filed away, books lined the shelving unit in the corner and staff rotas hung on clipboards by the window. The three bottles of indigestion remedy still had pride of place at the front of his desk, however, and Zoe couldn't help noticing that every bottle was nearly empty.

'Don't worry about it,' said Ben. 'Though I'm sorry to hear about Arthur. He was a lovely man.'

Zoe smiled. 'He was. I shall miss him.'

'I've been doing some thinking.' Ben switched on the Nespresso machine perched on the windowsill.

'About my notes?'

Ben nodded and when the machine finished whirring and grinding, he handed her a black coffee before slipping in another pod to make himself one. 'And a few other things. Let me say again how impressed I was with the way you handled Mr Smith yesterday.'

Zoe felt her cheeks flame with colour. 'Thank you.'

The troubleshooter took a seat on the other side of the desk, drink in hand and faced Zoe. 'I should have said it earlier. You've made me realise how important these notes are, and actually, I could do with your help.'

'Well, of course I will if I can,' Zoe said cautiously as she cradled her drink.

'Good.' Ben ran a hand over his shiny bald head. 'Because you know how I told you I also used to take down notes for my patients?'

Zoe nodded.

'Since our visit to Mr Smith yesterday, I've been thinking about some of my old patients.'

Ben reached into his desk drawer and pulled out four envelopes, fanning them out on the desk.

'What are these?' Zoe picked one up and turned it over in her hands, spotting the name Irene on the front.

'These are the notes I couldn't deliver,' Ben admitted.

'You failed to deliver them?' Zoe echoed in dismay, her eyes never leaving the envelopes.

A look of discomfort passed across Ben's face. 'Yeah. I'm not proud of myself. After I was officially reprimanded, these notes ended up shoved in the back of my locker. You know what it's like.'

'I don't,' Zoe gasped, shaking her head. 'I've always delivered every note to every intended recipient and I would have done it regardless of the warning you placed on my HR record.'

'Well, aren't you a bloody good nurse and all-round brilliant human being,' Ben snapped before relenting. 'Sorry.'

'No, I'm sorry,' Zoe said with a sigh. 'I'm being a cow. And I do get it. I mean, you were once a surgical nurse. It's a miracle you took notes at all, never mind delivered any.'

Ben laughed. 'I was also a hedge fund manager before I got into nursing but I think there's a compliment somewhere.'

'There is.' Zoe smiled. 'Just not a very big one.'

'Touché,' Ben remarked.

'So how can I help you?' Zoe asked, her tone softer.

'I want to make things right,' Ben replied, his large brown eyes filled with earnestness. 'I want these letters to go where they were meant to.'

'Some are a good five years old,' Zoe said, looking at the date written on the back of one of the envelopes. 'Whoever these were meant for might not even be with us any longer.'

'I know,' Ben said quietly. 'But these letters have been playing on my mind since our visit to Mr Smith. I was hoping you might help me deliver them. You're a professional, and with some of these notes being old, it might take a professional to smooth the waters.'

Zoe laughed as the penny dropped. 'You want someone to get shouted at with you.'

'If you put it like that, yes.' Ben chuckled. 'What do you think? Will you help?'

'Wouldn't it be easier to post them, with a covering note explaining you're sorry and a bit crap?' Zoe said with a sigh.

'I've thought about it but I think these notes deserve the personal touch, don't you? Would you post any of your notes?'

'God, no!' Zoe shuddered at the idea. 'But I would have delivered them in the first place.'

Ben looked at Zoe pleadingly. 'Please help me, Zoe.'

Running her eye across the envelopes still fanned out on the desk, Zoe thought about all the hopes and dreams contained within these notes. Loved ones never knowing the most important thing their dying friend or family member needed them to hear. The thought made Zoe feel ill.

'Go on,' she said.

Ben clapped his hands together and smiled in delight. 'You won't regret this. How about Saturday for the first delivery?'

'Great. Shall I pick you up?'

'Lovely, thanks, Zoe. I really appreciate this.'

'I want to say you're welcome but I'm not sure I had a great deal of choice,' Zoe said with a grin as she got up to leave. 'How about eleven?'

'Eleven is perfect.' Ben fixed his gaze on her. 'Is it weird if I say I'm looking forward to it?'

Zoe shook her head. In a funny way she was looking forward to it too.

-

As Saturday dawned, Zoe got out of bed and her eyes fell on the wooden box that stood on her bedside table. Opening it up, she reached for the note that lay inside and briefly pressed it to her heart. On today of all days, the note seemed more poignant than it usually did. She placed it in her bag, sure it would act as a good luck talisman for whatever lay ahead.

And when Zoe watched Ben clamber into her car a short while later, she felt she would need that talisman as she realised she felt oddly nervous.

'Who are we going to see first?' she asked, trying to ignore her feelings.

'Mr Myerson,' Ben said. 'His wife died from motor neurone disease. She asked me to pass on a note several weeks before she died.'

'Crikey.' Zoe blanched. 'Motor neurone disease is cruel.'

'It is.' Ben sighed as he clipped in his seatbelt. 'She refused a tracheostomy to help her breathing in the end. Said she wanted to go home and die naturally.'

'And is that when she gave you the note?' Zoe asked, starting the engine and slipping the car into first gear.

'Yes,' Ben said, a guilty look passing across his face. 'She could still communicate with her eyes and a computer, like Stephen Hawking used to.'

'I remember.' Zoe carried on up the road and signalled right.

'Of all of them, this is perhaps the one I feel most guilty about,' Ben admitted. 'Mrs Myerson was a brilliant scientist; she had so much to offer.'

Zoe said nothing, recognising Ben needed to gather his thoughts before they reached the address. Twenty minutes later they pulled up outside a large white house set back from the road. Zoe switched off the engine, looking up to marvel at the gravel drive and fancy turrets. This house felt like paradise but in fact was a reminder that death touched everyone.

'Shall we?' Ben asked, unclipping his seatbelt.

'Course.'

Together they reached the house and Zoe pressed the video bell.

'Here goes,' she said encouragingly.

It seemed ages before the door swung open, and as it did Zoe found herself smiling into the face of a woman roughly her own age.

'Can I help you?' she asked, with the hint of a South African accent.

'Oh, hi,' Ben said warmly. 'We're looking for Mr Myerson.'

The woman frowned. 'I'm sorry, nobody of that name lives here.'

'This is fifty-three, right?' Ben asked, leaning back slightly to check the door number.

'It is,' the woman confirmed. 'But it's just me and my husband. We bought this house from Mr Myerson three years ago.'

Ben gasped. 'Three years?'

'Do you have a forwarding address for him?' Zoe asked.

The woman shook her head. 'We never met. Is there anything I can help with?'

'No,' Zoe said, giving the woman an apologetic smile. 'It was Mr Myerson we needed. We'll try and find him another way. Thanks for your time.'

Looking relieved they weren't going to prolong the conversation, the woman nodded. 'Sorry not to be more help.'

As she shut the door, Zoe looked at Ben and saw the disappointment on his face. 'Hey, it was always possible he wouldn't be here. We can still try and find him.' Ben looked blankly at the ground and Zoe nudged him gently with her elbow. 'This is only the first letter.'

'Yeah, and a stark reminder of how I've let people down,' he said gruffly. 'I always prided myself on being a good nurse, but when it comes down to it, I can't manage the most basic thing, delivering a bloody note to its intended recipient.'

'Come on, enough with the self-pity. We tried; sometimes that's all you can do in life.'

Ben lifted his gaze and shook his head. 'In my book, Zoe, trying's not good enough.'

Chapter Fourteen

The steam from the scalding hot cup of coffee in front of her flew up Zoe's nostrils. Pushing the cup away, Zoe glanced at Ben, who was sitting across the table of the dimly lit cafe. He was staring at the table but she could see the frustration in his eyes.

'Who's next?' she asked above the din of chatter. This was a setback but there was no need for it to throw them off course. 'My next day off is Friday – we can get on with the next letter then if you like.'

Ben shook his head, Mrs Myerson's letter still in his hands. 'I dunno. All this is beginning to feel like a waste of time.'

'How can you say that? We've only tried one person so far.'

'Yeah, and I think it's a pretty good indicator of how the rest are going to go,' Ben replied glumly.

Zoe felt a flash of annoyance. Honestly, what did he think was going to happen? That everyone would be where he left them because the great Ben Tasker had suddenly decided to get his act together? Life didn't work like that.

'Thought you weren't a quitter,' she ventured.

Ben said nothing and stared at the ground, looking moody.

'You're wearing a look I see in my patients when they've had enough,' Zoe pointed out. 'Look, things didn't go to plan. That doesn't mean you give up.'

'I don't back losing battles and this feels like a losing battle,' Ben protested hotly.

'No, it's a cock-up,' Zoe said, running out of patience. 'It won't be easy just because you want it to be. If you'd really wanted to do something about these letters, you'd have done it before now. You didn't need me or my notes to jolt you into action, I just made you feel guilty, but you'd managed to live with that guilt for some time.'

'Ouch.' Ben shrank back in his seat.

Zoe didn't care. She was tired and didn't feel like sugar-coating things for her boss. 'Things change, people move on, you have to deal with that.'

'Sounds as if you're talking from experience.' Ben reached for one of the two Chelsea buns that stood on the table and took a large bite.

'You could say I'm the queen of experience,' Zoe said with a sigh. 'But if there's one thing I've realised, it's that life keeps moving. People will hurt you, people die, things will go wrong, things will go right and all you can do is keep breathing, keep going and keep trying.'

'What's the point?' Ben asked through a mouthful of bun. 'We all die anyway.'

'There is no point,' Zoe said slowly. 'Not really. But the way I see it, if we don't try that's so much worse. That's writing off the human race and saying all life is pointless. We're this weird science experiment, and whoever's collecting the data is probably going to be really cheesed off if we all give up.'

'Basically, because of science I have to keep going with this plan to deliver these notes?' Ben looked dubious as he finished his bun.

'I reckon.' Zoe shrugged as she helped herself to the remaining Chelsea bun. 'Anyway, I thought you were a gladiator that liked a challenge. The way you're carrying on at the moment you're more like bloody Eeyore.'

Ben threw his head back and howled with laughter. His belly laugh was so loud, other people looked around and joined in with Ben's giggles, even though they didn't know what the joke was. Zoe found herself doing the same, and together she and Ben laughed until their sides hurt.

'You're blunt,' he said, in between gasps of laughter. 'You're the most direct nurse I've ever met.'

Zoe tried to stop laughing, her cheek muscles beginning to hurt. 'I just tell it like it is.'

'You do that all right,' Ben said, bringing his breathing back to normal. 'I like it.'

For a moment, Zoe felt a sense of relief. She was beginning to like Ben, and didn't want to offend him. 'Happy to be of service.'

'I forgot how blunt you Aussies are,' Ben continued. 'I travelled around the country for a year when I was twenty-two and, like you, settled in Sydney after working in Darwin and Perth for a bit. The people were brilliant. Direct and no bullshit.'

'I'm actually from Melbourne,' Zoe said.

A look of confusion passed across Ben's face. 'I thought you were from Sydney?'

'I am, sort of. I was born in Melbourne but I moved to Sydney when I was eighteen after my dad died.'

A flicker of regret passed across Ben's face. 'I'm sorry.'

Zoe pursed her lips in the way she always did when anyone mentioned her dad. Losing him had been tough. She still missed him, still wanted his advice. She had often wondered what he would have thought of her leaving David and Australia without a word. He wouldn't have been pleased but she was confident he would have understood.

'Don't you ever go back and see your family?' Ben asked.

'No. You know what it's like working in healthcare. Time off isn't always easy.'

'True,' Ben conceded. 'But there are things you make time for. Why did you really leave Australia?'

Zoe had known the question was coming. She had known since telling Ben about her divorce. He would ask questions and perhaps that was what she wanted. To tell someone everything that had happened.

'Someone close to me was killed in a hit-and-run,' Zoe said at last. 'I didn't want to stay in Australia after that so I left.'

Ben's eyes widened. 'Just like that?'

'Just like that,' Zoe confirmed.

There was silence for a minute before Ben spoke. 'And it seems as though you didn't just run from your husband, you ran from your life too.'

'I don't know what you mean,' she said, feeling awkward.

Ben looked at her, his eyes brimming with kindness. 'Yeah, you do. From what I hear, you don't do anything apart from work and I can't help wondering why that is.'

There was a pause. Zoe felt panic rise within her. She didn't talk about her past – it was too painful – but maybe it was time. She reached down for her bag, which was resting on the floor. Opening the zip, she pulled out the letter. She had known she would need it today but hadn't expected this. Rubbing her thumb across the well-worn folds, she passed the note across the table to Ben.

'What's this?' he asked, taking the paper.

'Open it,' she instructed.

Frowning, Ben did so and read aloud. '*I just want to be a cowboy.* What does this mean?'

Zoe closed her eyes. 'The person who died was my seven-year-old son. He was killed in the hit-and-run while my husband was watching him. I left Australia because I couldn't stand the reminders of all I had lost.'

'Zoe, I'm sorry,' Ben whispered.

Blinking back tears, Zoe fixed her gaze on Ben, wanting him to understand why the letters she took meant so much. 'That note you're holding contains my son's last few words before he died. That note has been the one thing that has kept me going since he passed away and it's why I fought tooth and nail to keep note-taking. Those last few words don't just help the dying; they can help save the lives of those left behind.'

Chapter Fifteen

Ben gazed at her, unsure what to say. Zoe was desperate to break the silence. She needed things to be normal. Work had been her lifeline since Sean died; that couldn't change now.

'Please don't ask me if I want to talk about it,' she said eventually.

Ben held his hands up in an apologetic gesture. 'I'm not going to force you to do anything.'

'And don't treat me differently, either; I don't want your pity,' she said mutinously.

'I'm not here to give it,' he replied softly. 'I am here if you change your mind and want to talk, though.'

In that moment, much to her surprise, Zoe found she did want to unburden herself. She had only ever told Sarah the full story about Sean's death. People at work knew she had a son who had died and Karen was aware of more specific details but nobody else. Yet there was something about Ben that made her feel as though she could open up.

'It had been a normal day,' Zoe began, remembering how she had stood in their large sunny kitchen, finishing the last mouthful of her breakfast and gazing out at the blue pool in their garden, glistening in the morning light. It needed cleaning, she'd thought, resolving to ask David to sort it out that week.

'Things were quiet at the garage David managed. He had some holiday owing so he took a few days off. He said he would do some odd jobs and take Sean to school. He'd also promised to take him to football training in the park. Sean had been thrilled.' Their boy had loved nothing more than kicking a football around. 'Then he'd promised to take him to see the latest *Toy Story* film. He loved Woody the cowboy, it was one of his favourites, and he'd seen the films a dozen times or more but could never get enough.'

'Sounds like a nice kid,' Ben said encouragingly.

'He was,' Zoe enthused, wanting the world to see her son the way she did. 'He was a wonderful kid, and I know every parent says that, but Sean was so loving. That morning, the day he died, before he left for school, he had flung his arms around my neck and told me I was the best mum in the world. It was something he did every day and I had laughed as I smelled the top of his head and held his warm body in my arms. He was growing fast, his head almost coming up to my chest. I knew he wouldn't want to cuddle me like that forever. I hugged him tighter as I thought that, wanting to drink in the essence of him while I could.'

Ben smiled as he rested his chin on his hands. 'That sounds very wise.'

Zoe held his gaze. 'I'd always wanted kids. When I found out Sean was on the way I was overjoyed. It's true what they say, there really is no love like it. The power of it as you hold that squealing little tot in your arms and realise this little baby you created is all yours. Sean was my world. And as he grew up, he became the perfect little boy, my best friend, which probably doesn't sound that healthy but it's true. I would have died for him.'

Ben nodded, wanting her to keep talking.

'After Sean hugged me goodbye, David kissed my cheek, and promised to cook steaks on the grill that night when I got home from work. I was looking forward to it. I'd been working hard as I'd just had a promotion at the city hospital. David being off for a few days had definitely lightened my load and it was nice, being able to spend some proper time together.'

Zoe took another deep breath, the next part less comfortable to recall. 'Then I went to work across town. At about four, just as I was getting ready to finish, a call came through to the nurses' desk. It was David, calling from the public hospital near our house. He was crying so hard I could hardly hear him, but I managed to understand Sean had been hit by a car. I hung up, got my car keys and raced across town. I'll never forget that feeling of running into the hospital, my stomach turning over as I reached the admissions desk, demanding to see Sean. The moment I said his name I caught the look of pity that passed across the nurse's face and knew he was gone.'

'I know that look,' Ben said gently, 'that careful flicker of pain that passes across even the hardiest of nurse's faces when a child dies.'

'The nurse immediately understood. She took me straight to the emergency room where the trauma team had just called time of death. I think I screamed, but I pushed past the medics, crawled onto the bed and held my son in my arms, his little body still warm as I sobbed into his hair and begged him to wake up.'

'Oh, Zoe,' Ben said, laying his hand on top of hers. 'I can't imagine how painful that must have been.'

The warmth from Ben's palm soothed Zoe and she felt steady enough to carry on.

'I don't remember what happened next. I was led away at some point. The nurses were kind and let me have a bit longer with him because I was a nurse, you know? They respected that.'

'Where was David?'

'He was outside,' Zoe said bitterly. 'He couldn't bear to be with our boy once he'd died – he was terrified of seeing his body. We left the hospital at some point, but before we did, the nurse that had taken care of Sean came to find me and pressed a note in my hands.'

'This note?' Ben echoed, a look of understanding passing across his face as he slid the lined piece of paper across the table.

Zoe nodded and put it back into her handbag.

'These were Sean's final words,' Zoe said, her face wet with tears. 'The nurse had captured the very essence of my boy. That note told me that he hadn't been scared in those final moments, that all he was thinking about was living out his dreams.'

'That's why the notes mean so much?' Ben said carefully.

'David explained he and Sean had been playing football in the park. David had hit the ball too hard and it had gone in the road. Before David could stop him, Sean had run to get the ball. That was when he was knocked down, by some hoon of a driver going too fast. The car never stopped.'

'Did they ever catch the guy?' Ben asked in disbelief.

'No, and that was something else David blamed himself for,' Zoe recalled. 'Even at the funeral he kept going on about how he ought to have run into the road for the ball, how he should have stopped Sean, how he should have gone after the car. He said it was his fault over and over again and I agreed with him. One night I screamed at him that a real father would never have let Sean play close to the road or hit the ball so hard. A couple of days after the funeral, I left. I didn't know I was going to do it. I'd been doing the ironing, getting ready to go to work. Then I saw Sean's T-shirt in the basket and broke down. I couldn't stay in that house, be with David or even be in Australia any more.'

'You flew to the UK?'

Zoe swallowed. 'And I never once looked back.'

'And you never spoke to your husband again?'

'Not on the phone. He tried at first, of course. Now he sends me emails, texts and direct messages. He sent me a picture of Sean's grave, when it was put up eighteen months ago. I think he was trying to remind me I still had ties in Australia but I never said a word. I came to realise I would never forgive him for what he did.'

'Wow, Zoe.' Ben let out a low whistle. 'I can't say I blame you. I think I'd probably feel the same.'

Zoe looked up at him in surprise. 'Really? You don't think I ought to try?'

'I think even though it was a horrible accident, you have so many feelings about David it's going to be hard to untangle. You'll both be different people now.'

Relief washed over her. She had worried that once the story came tumbling out, Ben would think her irrational.

'Well then,' Ben said determinedly. 'I think we've got to carry on with the notes.'

'What changed your mind?'

'You.' Ben's eyes were filled with warmth. 'Knowing you still carry the last note from your child, I can't ignore how much they mean to loved ones. These notes are too important for me to give up at the first try.'

Chapter Sixteen

By sharing the horrific story of what had happened to her son, Zoe felt she and Ben had reached a quiet understanding. She found that Ben sought her advice about patient management, as well as new ideas and plans for the hospice.

Crucially, he hadn't pressed Zoe about her divorce or Sean and she found herself looking forward to her shifts when Ben would be on the floor. As if to further cement their new relationship, Ben had asked Zoe to deliver another note with him the following Sunday because she was off work. Zoe had agreed and suggested they meet in a cafe at the top of the city where she and Sarah planned to have breakfast.

Now, as Zoe nursed a flat white in the cafe at the top of town and waited for Ben, she looked at Sarah stuffing a sausage sandwich smothered in brown sauce into her mouth. Zoe felt envious. She had only ordered a round of toast, which remained on her plate uneaten. She was oddly nervous again.

'Seems like you and your new boss are finally getting on,' Sarah ventured, dropping a bit of sausage onto her lap, causing Zoe and Lottie to smile as she scooped it up.

'Yeah, I like him,' Zoe said, offering Sarah a serviette. 'He's more than I thought he was.'

'What did you think he was?' Sarah asked.

'An arsehole,' Zoe quipped. 'But I'm beginning to realise Ben's layered. He's achieved so much.'

'You've achieved so much,' Sarah said loyally. 'Not only are you a fantastic nurse but look at the way you started a new life far away from home.'

Zoe made a face. 'Never quite escaped my past, though, did I? I told Ben all about Sean.'

Sarah dropped her sandwich in surprise, this time the sausage staying on her plate. 'Wow. When?'

'A few days ago,' Zoe admitted. 'It felt right somehow.'

'That's great,' Sarah exclaimed. 'You should open up more – it's the only way to heal, Zoe.'

About to reply, Zoe was saved from doing so when she peered through the window and saw Candice walking towards them.

'Lovely to see you girls again,' Candice said, arms outstretched in welcome. 'Ben said he was meeting you here and I couldn't resist popping in to say hello before I went shopping.'

'And you too,' Zoe said, with a beam. 'I love your top; I've never been able to wear jewel colours.'

'Oh, this old thing?' Candice grinned as she gestured to the paisley silk kimono that floated effortlessly over her jeans. Her hair was swept up in a bright yellow and black scarf this time, and she smelt of Jo Malone's Pomegranate Noir. The effect was both expensive and down-to-earth. Despite borrowing a pretty black broderie anglaise top from Sarah, Zoe felt dowdy by comparison. Running a hand over her greying blonde hair, she wished she had made more of an effort.

'Where's Ben?' Sarah asked, sensing Zoe's discomfort.

Candice rolled her eyes. 'Parking his precious car. Couldn't find a space outside so he's looking for the perfect spot.'

At that Zoe realised she hadn't thought to ask what sort of car Ben drove. She was just about to when the roar of an expensive sports car echoed down the road.

'Flash git,' Sarah grumbled, as a sleek graphite Porsche 911 pulled into a space outside the cafe.

'What a beaut,' Zoe marvelled, her mouth gaping open at the shiny bonnet and iconic fly line. Thanks to David she had come to appreciate cars in her later years. He had introduced her to the power and freedom a car could give and before Sean was born the two of them often spent weekends rally driving or attending classic car shows. Now, as the driver door opened, Zoe let out a bark of surprise at the tall but familiar, long-limbed man stepping from the vehicle.

'Ben!'

'Ben drives a car that costs a hundred grand.' Sarah gasped, following Zoe's gaze.

'It's his pride and joy,' Candice moaned, her eyes never leaving the menu, although she had said she wasn't staying.

Stepping inside the cafe, Ben's eyes landed on Zoe and he flashed her a wide smile.

'I think it's you with the nice wheels,' Zoe said admiringly, gesturing for him to sit down. 'You remember Sarah, and this is Lottie.'

'Hi again.' Sarah smiled, giving her daughter a nudge to look up from her pancakes.

'Hello,' Lottie said, looking briefly at Ben and Candice before returning to her breakfast.

'Sorry.' Sarah shrugged.

Candice waved her apology away. 'Out of a choice between saying hello to us and pancakes, I know which I'd find more interesting.'

'What's the story with the car?' Zoe asked, tilting her head towards the Porsche. 'You kept that quiet.'

Ben pulled out a chair and swiftly ordered two lattes from a passing waitress in one fluid move. 'I don't reveal everything straight away.'

'But how on earth can you afford that and your posh flat?' Sarah asked, aware she was being rude but curiosity getting the better of her. 'You're a nurse.'

'He wasn't always a nurse,' Candice put in. 'Before he got all do-goodery he was a hedge fund manager. In fact, he encouraged me to get into banking, even though I never went to uni like Brains here.'

Sarah looked impressed while Zoe stared at Ben, bemused.

'I thought you were joking,' she said.

'Afraid not.' Ben looked slightly embarrassed. 'After uni I wanted to make money and a mate of a mate set me up in his dad's company in London. I enjoyed it for a while but knew it wasn't where my heart lay.'

'Judging by that car and your flat at the top of town, you must have done all right,' Sarah remarked, as the waitress placed two coffees in front of Candice and Ben.

'Yeah. Made a few solid investments, which paid for nursing school.'

'How do you afford to keep it all going?' Zoe asked. 'If you don't mind me asking.'

Candice giggled. 'Like I said, I'm still in banking!'

'You pay for nothing, C!' Ben snapped.

From his tone, Zoe sensed this was a sensitive subject and moved the conversation on. 'How long have you had your flat?'

'About seven years,' Candice said.

'We always wanted to live there.' Ben took a sip of his coffee. 'When we saw a flat was up for sale that needed renovating, we jumped at it.'

'I'll bet,' Sarah marvelled. 'Are you from that part of town originally?'

At the question, Candice and Ben let out identical cackles. The sound was loud, but comforting. Zoe watched them laugh, mirror images of each other. She glanced at Lottie, who looked equally as entranced as she did.

'Oh dear,' Ben said, tears running down his cheeks as he finally brought his laughter under control. 'Can you imagine, C? We've finally done all right for ourselves. People actually think we're from the posh bit of town.'

Candice clapped her hands together and whooped with laughter. 'We're actually from the other side, near the old gasworks. Do you know it?'

'Vaguely,' Zoe said. 'I think I might have delivered a note around there once.'

'Well, that's where we're from. We were brought up by our mother after our father buggered off and left us when we were one,' Ben explained.

'We lived in a one-bedroom flat that was riddled with damp and our mama had to fight tooth and nail to get the council to do something about it,' Candice said with a grimace. 'It's why we wanted to do something with our lives.'

'And banking gave me a chance to make some money so I could do something proper with my life and still make enough from that to keep the fun in life going.'

'That's what I want when I grow up, to have lots of fun,' Lottie said so abruptly Zoe jumped.

'Is that right, young lady?' Sarah laughed.

'You've got the right idea, Lottie.' Candice leaned forward across the table to meet the little girl's eyes. 'But to have a lot of fun, you have to work really hard at school. Do you work really hard?'

'Yes!' the little girl shouted, her face serious.

'Not hard enough if your last report card is anything to go by,' Sarah said wryly.

Ben looked as if he was about to add something when he unexpectedly let out such a loud belch, Lottie dropped her fork and giggled.

'Easy!' Candice admonished. 'You're not at home now.'

'Sorry,' Ben said, looking sheepish.

'It's fine,' Zoe assured him over the sound of Lottie's giggles.

'It's not fine,' Candice put in. 'He's been doing that for weeks and complaining of belly ache.'

'Oh yes, you had some tummy trouble last week, didn't you?' Zoe said, remembering how Ben had hunted down some milk of magnesium. 'You should see a doctor.'

'Thank you!' Candice called, giving Ben a pointed glance. 'I've been saying that for ages.'

Ben rolled his eyes. 'How many times? It's just gas.'

'Gas.' Lottie continued to giggle. 'Gas, gas, gas.'

'Oh yeah,' Candice said, smiling at Lottie before turning back to Ben. 'That explains why your stomach's like a balloon these days.'

'Erm, actually, yes,' Zoe said, feeling slightly sorry for Ben. She knew from experience that the one way you could guarantee someone wouldn't go to the doctor was to nag them. 'Could be irritable bowel syndrome.'

'More than likely,' Ben said with a sigh. 'I've run out of indigestion medicine.'

Zoe thought back to the three bottles she had seen in his office a few weeks ago. Things were bad if he could get through all that. She reached into her bag, fished out a small bottle and placed it on the table. 'As a fellow IBS sufferer, I never travel without it. Here, present.'

'Ever the Girl Scout,' Sarah said fondly.

Zoe shrugged and Ben looked at her gratefully. 'Well, I'm pleased you're a Girl Scout. Without it we might have had to cut the fun short.'

Sarah checked her watch and gave her daughter a nudge. 'Speaking of fun, we'd better get going. We've new school shoes to buy.'

'Oh, if you're shoe shopping, I'll come with you. I've got a date tonight,' Candice said, draining the last of her drink and setting the cup down. 'If you don't mind, that is?'

'Course not.' Sarah grinned as she got to her feet and helped Lottie out of her chair. 'And if you can persuade this one to at least try on a pair of lace-ups, I might even throw in another coffee. It was nice to see you again, Ben.'

'Likewise,' Ben replied.

With that the trio left the cafe, their thoughts firmly on shoes.

Once they had gone, Zoe turned to Ben and smiled encouragingly. 'Come on, let's hope this delivery's more successful than the last.'

Chapter Seventeen

As Zoe sat in the passenger seat of the Porsche, she let out a whistle of admiration. The leather interior was shiny, the dash sparkled and as for the sheer number of gadgets, her mind felt blown just looking at them.

She wailed. 'It's still got that new car smell.'

'Yeah, I like it,' Ben said, as he started the engine. The car pulled smoothly away and all Zoe could hear was the car purr like a contented kitten.

'What's the horsepower? Six hundred and thirty-five?' Zoe asked as Ben drove out onto the road towards the villages south of the city.

'How do you know about horsepower?' Ben asked, his voice incredulous.

Zoe rolled her eyes. 'Don't tell me, because I'm female I'm not supposed to know that this 911 S goes from zero to sixty-two in two-point-seven seconds and that its top speed is over two hundred miles per hour.'

'Who the hell are you?' Ben exclaimed.

Laughing, Zoe found herself enjoying the fact she was surprising Ben with her car knowledge.

'Just because I drive a Yaris doesn't mean I don't know about sports cars and this one is incredible.'

'It is.' Ben nodded. 'I only got her this year. If you're good, I'll let you have a go.'

'No way,' Zoe gasped. 'I'd be devastated if I crashed it. I haven't driven a car like this in a long time.'

'Well, the offer's there,' Ben said, signalling right and pulling into a small lane.

'Where are we going?'

'Not far, little village up the road.'

'And who are we seeing this time?' Zoe asked, enjoying the feel of the road beneath her as Ben pulled out onto the dual carriageway.

'Hopefully Mrs Bell, a wonderful woman who lost her husband after sixty years of marriage.'

'Wow!' Zoe marvelled. 'That's an achievement.'

'It is. They were both fabulous, full of sense and fun. They were great together.' There was a hint of wistfulness to his voice.

'You sound almost jealous,' Zoe remarked.

'I guess I am,' Ben admitted. 'I know what I said before about Jess, but honestly, I do believe that if the right person is out there for me, I'll drop everything.'

'I don't believe you,' Zoe scoffed, assuming Ben was and always would be married to his job.

'It's true! Which is why I haven't found her and probably never will,' Ben quipped, taking the first exit off the dual carriageway.

A short time later they pulled up into a smart, tree-lined street full of creamy traditional cottages and identical black doors.

Zoe clambered out of the car once they'd come to a stop. 'This is pretty.'

'It is, isn't it?' Ben said, looking around him and smiling at a pair of community police officers who rode past on bikes. 'Good morning, officers.'

'Morning,' they said, each shooting him and Zoe a curious look.

'Do you know them?' she asked, puzzled.

'Nope,' Ben replied. 'But I find that when you have the skin colour I do, it usually helps if you're polite to the police, especially when you're driving a Porsche.'

'Really?'

As she watched the officers turn around and look at them with interest, she saw how Ben continued to smile politely.

'I've already lost count of the times I've been stopped in this car. And I always carry my registration and insurance with me to prove I'm the legal owner. It saves a lot of time answering questions, or being shoved into the back of a police car because of the colour of my skin.'

'That's never happened!' Zoe gasped, aghast.

Ben gave a hollow laugh. 'I'm afraid to say it has. Welcome to my world, Zoe. Anyway, we're not here as part of a Black Lives Matter protest; we've got a job to do.'

'Okay,' Zoe agreed, although her thoughts were still wrapped up in what Ben had just said. She supposed race was something she tried to forget about, like most white people did. But she was aware that in itself was a privilege and exchanges like the one Ben had just been a part of brought back the cruel realities of living outside of that privilege.

'Oi, wake up!' Ben called. 'I haven't got all day, even if you have.'

'All right, sarky,' she said, snapping herself from her thoughts.

Together they walked up the street and found Mrs Bell's house easily. Ben pushed open the iron gate and rapped on the front door, and Zoe was pleased when it opened almost straight away.

'Ben!' A tall, willowy lady with grey hair and a warm, open face beamed. 'What on earth are you doing here? And who's this with you?' she asked, catching sight of Zoe, who gave a polite wave.

'This is Zoe, my colleague, and the reason I'm here after so long is that I've got something of Eric's I should have passed on to you a while ago.'

A flicker of confusion passed across Mrs Bell's face as she welcomed them inside. 'Well, I've just made some tea. Come on in.'

Stepping into the bright hallway, Zoe couldn't miss the wall of family photos that lined the corridor. Smiling faces throughout the years beamed down at her. There was Mrs Bell and she guessed her husband, Eric, contentment etched across their faces as they cradled babies in black and white photos. Later, their arms were wrapped around older children as they gathered around caravans, picnicked on sands or graduated, all in full colour. Next, weddings were celebrated, and then more babies, this time with Mrs Bell and her husband sporting more grey hair and lines around their faces, but still the same warm smiles beaming out from each shot.

'Ben love,' Mrs Bell said, gesturing for them to take a seat at the table in the kitchen. 'What is it of Eric's you've got for me? I thought I'd picked everything up from the hospice when he died.'

'It's nothing serious,' Ben said, with a reassuring smile. 'I like to give all my patients a chance to say a few words before they pass, as it were. When Eric was admitted to the hospice, I spoke to him a day or two before he passed away and asked if there was anything he wanted to say, in case he didn't get a chance.'

Mrs Bell frowned as she set down a pot of tea in the centre of the table. 'I don't understand. Eric and I did all our talking before he went into the hospice. We wanted to make sure there was nothing left unsaid, you know...'

At that, something caught in Mrs Bell's throat as she took in the loss of her husband. 'Sorry. I came to terms with losing Eric when he was diagnosed with heart disease years ago. Or at least that was what I hoped. But of course, you can never prepare, can you? Sixty years of marriage is a lifetime.'

Ben leaned forward and squeezed Mrs Bell's hand, while Zoe discreetly poured the tea.

'Loss does funny things to people. You deal with it how you can,' Ben said softly.

The widow quickly wiped her eyes with the backs of her hands. Zoe could tell she came from the generation that thought emotions were best off bottled up.

'You're very kind, dear,' she said with a smile, slowly removing her hand from Ben's. 'But all this is rather a surprise. It's been, what, four years?'

At the mention of time, Zoe saw Ben flinch and gave his forearm a reassuring squeeze.

'I'm sorry,' Ben said. 'I didn't mean to rake things up; I should have come a lot earlier.'

Mrs Bell waved away his apology. 'You young people are busy, I understand that. But what are these last few words?'

Zoe watched Ben reach for the note. She felt nervous on his behalf. Usually, relatives were elated to discover their loved one had something extra to say, but there had been occasions when the reaction hadn't been as Zoe expected.

'He said to tell you that it was Carbis Bay and it always would be,' Ben said, reading the note aloud.

As Ben delivered the words, Mrs Bell's hands flew to her mouth. 'Oh, I knew it. Oh Eric, my wonderful Eric.'

Mrs Bell seemed to collapse into herself. Chin down, arms wrapped around her body and shoulders heaving up and down, she sobbed with all the abandon of a grieving widow. Zoe reached out an arm and draped it carefully around her shoulders.

'Are you all right?' she asked. 'This must all be a bit of a shock.'

Mrs Bell patted her eyes dry with a tissue from a box that stood on the table, then smiled at Zoe as she looked up. 'Yes, I'm fine, thank you. May I?' she asked, turning to Ben, hand outstretched, waiting for the note.

As he pressed it into Mrs Bell's palm, she took the paper gratefully and in a gesture Zoe more than understood, clasped it against her heart.

'I always knew, but Eric continually denied it. Carbis Bay was where we fell in love. Eric was married at the time we met. I lived nearby and was out walking my dog across the sands. He was on holiday with his first wife, Larissa. I could only have been about eighteen at the time. Eric was a good ten years older than me. Anyway, our eyes met and I felt this pull towards him. I had never experienced something like that before. I could tell he felt it too. A year later when we finally met in London, me as a secretary for a partner of the law firm he worked in, he said he had the strangest idea that he knew me from somewhere. I told him about our encounter in Carbis Bay a couple of years earlier. I had never forgotten it. But he said it was nonsense, he hadn't been in Carbis Bay then. It was something he maintained throughout our marriage, that we had never met before. But I knew Carbis Bay was where we had fallen in love, and I knew it was the catalyst for the end of his marriage to Larissa. Now, hearing Eric say that makes everything seem even more real, our love, our relationship…'

As her voice trailed off, Mrs Bell turned to Ben, with joy in her eyes. 'I can't thank you enough for bringing this to me.'

'You're very welcome,' Ben said. 'I'm just sorry it took me so long.'

Once again Mrs Bell waved away his apology. 'It doesn't matter, dear. You've made me happy. I feel as though the final piece of the jigsaw Eric and I shared has been put in its place.'

Zoe knew it was time to leave. The message had been delivered. Mrs Bell had the ending she needed.

Outside the sun continued to beam down and Ben turned to Zoe. 'That went well, didn't it?'

'It did. I can't believe she finally found out the truth about her husband after all this time.'

'You were right, though,' Ben added as they walked back to the car. 'These notes are important. Thanks for helping.'

Zoe flushed with colour at the praise. 'It's my pleasure.'

There was a pause as Ben regarded her carefully. 'I think it's time you had some fun, Zoe.'

'How do you mean?'

Ben reached into his pocket, glanced at the car and tossed her his keys. 'You're driving us back.'

Chapter Eighteen

As Zoe pressed her foot on the accelerator, she felt her body move with the car. It was as though she and this lump of metal were one, soaring across the earth with all the energy of a cheetah.

'This is wild!'

Ben laughed at Zoe's enthusiasm. 'Knew you'd like it. But you might like it a bit more if you go above forty; this is a dual carriageway.'

She scowled. Zoe wasn't usually this hesitant in a car, but it felt strange to be in charge of such an expensive car that belonged to her boss. Her confidence wasn't what it used to be. She took a deep breath. This Porsche was itching to be let loose and Zoe began to gain speed, remembering the sheer joy of what it felt like to drive a car like this.

As the city she now called home came into view, Zoe gave in to her sense of adventure. Before Ben could object, she signalled right and drove straight through the park, pulling up near the bandstand.

'What's going on?' Ben looked at her, aghast.

'There's something I've always wanted to do but never had the money or courage,' Zoe said, in a determined tone. 'But I've learned something today.'

'Oh yeah?'

'I'm beginning to realise that this is all there is,' Zoe said, pointing to the trees and grass. 'This is literally all the time we have. None of us know if there's something on the other end of this so maybe I need to start living a bit more.'

'I agree. Why are we here?'

'I thought that after it went so well with Mrs Bell, we could have a late lunch over there,' Zoe suggested, gesturing through the trees towards the hotel that stood in front of them.

Ben's eyes lit up with glee. 'Now *that's* what I call living.'

They walked into the grand hotel that stood in the centre of the Royal Crescent. Much to Zoe's surprise, they were welcomed straight away and shown to a table outside. As the waiter handed her a menu, Zoe paused for a moment to drink in the winding lavender paths that framed the verdant green lawns, the sweet sound of birdsong providing the perfect soundtrack to this very unexpected lunch.

'I feel like a movie star.' Zoe laughed, ordering the Cornish halibut.

'You need to get out more,' Ben replied, settling on the Wagyu steak and ordering two glasses of shiraz.

'Maybe you're right,' Zoe admitted. 'Did you see all those framed photos of Mrs Bell and her husband through the years?'

'A happy family on steroids,' Ben ventured as the waiter set down two glasses.

'I suppose they were.' Zoe tipped her head in thought. 'It was good, though. I mean, for her to know now that her story was complete. That's what your note gave her today, Ben, the final piece of what looked like a very happy love story. In my book that's something for your bucket list.'

Wrinkling his nose, Ben thought for a moment as he leaned back in the rattan chair, the sunshine making his skin glow as he considered Zoe's question. 'I think I've already done most things on my bucket list.'

Zoe gaped in surprise. 'Really? Like what?'

'I've travelled the world, bungee jumped in Argentina, parachuted out of a plane, driven around Silverstone, been part of a Formula One Team at Monaco—'

'You were part of an F-One team?' Zoe exclaimed.

'I was the tea boy for a couple of days when I was at uni.' Ben winked. 'Mate did me a favour, but it was still exciting.'

Zoe shook her head in disbelief. 'What else?'

'Erm, I've been to the Olympics, ridden a horse across a beach—'

'In Australia everyone does that,' Zoe said with an eye-roll as she reached for her glass of wine.

'But not everyone in Australia runs the London Marathon or treks the Inca Trail, or even spends the night in a Las Vegas bar getting hammered with The Rock.'

'The movie star?'

'Yeah.' Ben shrugged as if it was no big deal. 'Before he was as famous as he is now, of course. He was with some mates.'

'Come on, dish,' Zoe urged, surprised to find she was genuinely excited by a bit of celebrity tittle-tattle.

Ben tapped the side of his nose. 'You know the saying, what happens in Vegas stays in Vegas. Let's just say he was best man at my wedding.'

Now Zoe's eyes were out on stalks. 'Really?'

'No!' Ben threw his head back with laughter. 'But you should see your face.'

'Who was best man at your wedding?' Zoe asked, feeling affronted.

'Nobody,' Ben said, fiddling with his napkin. 'It was quiet, just the two of us and a couple of witnesses we dragged in off the street. Neither one of us wanted a fuss and seeing as we split a couple of years later it was probably for the best.'

Zoe said nothing; the mood was souring and she wanted to turn it around.

'There must be something left?' she pressed. 'On your bucket list, I mean. I've hardly started on mine.'

Ben shook his head. 'Why doesn't that surprise me?'

At that statement, Zoe felt uncomfortable. A bucket list hadn't been something she'd given much thought to. In truth, she had been too busy concentrating on simply getting through life since Sean died.

'Never mind all that,' Zoe said impatiently. 'This is about you.'

'All right, let's see.' Ben bit his lip in thought. 'Tell you what, I've been all over the world but I've never been to the edge of the country. I want to go the Lizard, be surrounded by all that nature, the sea, the birds, the cliffs, the coastline, lose myself in it all.'

'So you've been to the other side of the world, bungee jumped in Argentina, but you've never been to the edge of this country?' Zoe exclaimed. 'Why not?'

'I dunno,' Ben said, running a hand across his head as he usually did. Zoe had come to notice he did it when he was perplexed. 'Time. That feeling of it's only down the road, I'll get around to it. Who knows? I'm sure I will at some point.'

'You should. The Lizard's beautiful,' Zoe remarked as their food arrived.

Ben nodded his thanks at the waiter and picked up his cutlery. 'When did you go?'

'When I first arrived here from Oz. I went there, Bath of course, Snowdonia, the Highlands, the Lake District.'

Ben raised an eyebrow. 'You packed a lot in.'

'Britain's not big. You can get to most places in a couple of hours by car, train or plane,' Zoe said. 'And Europe's on your doorstep. All those countries a short plane ride away.'

'You make it sound as though the best thing about living in Britain is the fact it's close to other places.' Ben laughed as he speared a new potato with his fork.

Zoe shrugged. 'Would you judge me if I said it was?'

Ben laughed again, and as Zoe listened to the noise reverberating through his body, she thought there was no nicer sound.

'Maybe you could come with me?' Ben said lightly. 'You know, to the Lizard? Show me around if you know the place so well.'

Zoe looked at him in surprise. 'I wouldn't say I know it well; I only went once.'

Ben's eyes flared with embarrassment. 'No worries,' he said, spearing another potato into his mouth. 'It was a silly idea, forget it.'

Watching him eat, she felt guilty that she had upset him. 'You know, maybe it would be nice to do that together.'

'Really?' Ben's eyes filled with optimism.

'Yeah.' Zoe realised she meant it. 'Really.'

As they smiled shyly at one another, Zoe felt another flash of pleasure unfurl through her body. This time, however, it had nothing to do with a car.

Chapter Nineteen

Since their lunch at the hotel, Ben and Zoe's relationship had changed. Now, Ben would think nothing of buying her a flat white when he bought his own cappuccino from the cafe opposite the hospice. In return, she offered him the eggs from her Niçoise salad at lunchtimes and they frequently took it in turns to pick each other up and drop each other home if their shifts began and ended at the same time.

Nothing had been said, but things were different – a *nice* different, Zoe thought, as she sat at the nurses' desk surveying the floor. The only trouble was, she wasn't sure where she stood with him and, perhaps more pressingly, she didn't know where she wanted to stand. Had Ben asked her to Cornwall as a friend? Had he intended them to go away as part of a big group? Or had he asked her with something more in mind, something she knew she wasn't ready for?

Zoe was sick of thinking about it. Sarah had told her it was obvious, that of course Ben had asked her to go away as more than friends. She had seen the way they looked at each other in the cafe that Sunday and witnessed pure chemistry. But Zoe hoped Sarah was wrong; romance was the last thing on her mind.

After Sean died and she had walked out on her marriage, Zoe felt as if she had been stripped of the ability to feel love. It floored her to discover the stirring of something warm in her heart towards Ben, something she hadn't felt since she first met David, and it frightened her.

Shaking her head free of the direction her life had suddenly taken, Zoe reached for the admissions list. There were two today. Mrs Harper was back for a couple of days, which made Zoe smile. She hadn't seen the hospice owner's mother for a while. The other admission she noticed was Ricky Pagett. This admission made her stomach turn over. Ricky was only four years old and suffering from neuroblastoma. He had been a day patient for a year, the hospice giving his mum, Ella, occasional respite. Zoe had known Ricky would need to be admitted full-time one day, but she had hoped it wouldn't be for a little while yet.

'Ricky Pagett,' Ben murmured behind her. She glanced up and saw his eyes scanning the list. 'I spoke to his mum yesterday. She was incredibly matter-of-fact.'

'She'll be devastated inside,' Zoe said bluntly. 'Efficiency is her way of coping, I expect. I was the same when Sean died. I planned every detail of his funeral. I thought it would keep me going, but the truth is nothing can prepare you for the death of your child.'

Ben squeezed Zoe's shoulder, his large biscuit-brown eyes brimming with concern. 'Would you like me to cover the admissions today or ask Miles to do it?'

Zoe looked at him in horror. 'God, no! It's important to me that Ricky has a good death. Besides, you have that budget meeting this morning.'

'If you're sure?'

'I'm more than sure.' She smiled at him. 'But thanks for thinking of me.'

'Okay. Let me know if you need help.'

With that he walked away and up ahead she saw Mrs Harper being wheeled through the hospice doors by her son. She got up from her chair to welcome them.

'Nice to see you again,' she said warmly.

'I wish I could say the same,' Mrs Harper barked, before her expression softened. 'Though I will say you look a bit more *together* since the last time I saw you. Have you brushed your hair?'

'Mother!' Mr Harper exclaimed.

Zoe gave a half-laugh. She wasn't offended. 'Actually, Mrs H, I haven't just brushed my hair, I've had it cut too. Nothing fancy.' She touched the loose curls that framed her face. She had been persuaded to visit the salon with Sarah last week. Usually, she trimmed her own fringe when it got too long but Sarah had insisted enough was enough and booked her in for a trim. Zoe had been reluctant, initially thinking it a waste of time. Yet as the stylist chopped away the split ends and the uneven lengths into something more face-framing, Zoe had smiled as she took in the sight of her reflection. She looked like a girl she used to know, almost like an old friend.

Mrs Harper sniffed as she appraised Zoe. 'It suits you. Life is too short to go around looking like a bedraggled cat.'

Zoe laughed while Mrs Harper's son cringed, his face glowing as red as a tomato. She was about to agree when the sight of two paramedics wheeling a tiny, withered boy through the hospice doors caught her attention. Ricky Pagett had arrived.

She exchanged a small smile with one of the paramedics working today but the expression didn't meet either of their eyes. It was almost a private code for the sadness of the situation. Each of them knew how tough it was when a child was admitted, their life about to end before it had begun.

'Would you excuse me?' she said to Mrs Harper.

She went to walk away, only as she did so, Mrs Harper gripped her arm. 'Is that a child?' she asked, her voice a gruff whisper.

Zoe nodded. 'Four years old. Neuroblastoma.'

'And that's the mother?' Mrs Harper gestured in the direction of Ella. Zoe could see she looked ashen as she walked alongside the hospital bed, her hand never leaving Ricky's.

'Yes,' Zoe said simply.

'Make sure she gets *everything* she needs, won't you, Zoe?' Mrs Harper whispered vehemently, her eyes never leaving Ella. 'If I can help, please tell me. Nothing is too much trouble.'

Turning in surprise, Zoe was astonished to see the older woman fighting back tears.

'Of course.'

At that Mrs Harper gave a small smile and released her grip.

'Come on, Mother, let's get you settled with a cup of tea in the day room,' Mr Harper said, giving Zoe a brief nod before he wheeled his mother away.

Watching the two of them disappear down the corridor, Zoe had a feeling there was more to the exchange than Mrs Harper simply wanting the best for a young mother. She tried to work it out but there wasn't the time. Her place was with Ella and Ricky now.

'Hi,' she said, walking towards the young woman and giving Ricky a warm smile. 'How are you both doing?'

Ella smiled, through eyes that were red raw from crying. 'We're all right, aren't we, sweetheart?' she said, turning to Ricky, who was fast asleep. Zoe felt glad. Ricky was too young to have to suffer like this and for his sake and Ella's, who at twenty-four was too young herself to have to face something this painful, Zoe hoped Ricky's end would be quick and as painless as possible.

'He's been in such terrible pain the last few days,' Ella croaked. 'I've been giving him morphine but nothing seems to help.'

'We're here now,' Zoe said kindly. 'We'll make sure everything goes as smoothly as it can for you both.'

Ella nodded and Zoe could see that this was not only a time for Ricky needing his mum; Ella desperately needed her family around too.

'Is there anyone we can call?'

'No,' Ella said in a small voice. 'Mum's on a cruise. I thought Ricky would have more time and I told her to go. She's been good looking after us all; I don't want to ruin her holiday. It's the first one she's had for years.'

Zoe frowned. 'I think she would want to be here for you, Ella.'

But Ella shook her head. 'I don't want to trouble her.'

It was then the nurse saw the quiet set of Ella's jaw and the steely determination in her hazel eyes. She wanted this on her own terms, a private moment between mother and son.

Zoe thought back to those empty, vacant days between Sean's death and his funeral. She had wanted Sean's death dealt with her way and she saw the same resolve in Ella now. Zoe would help her however she could. Her son's death was something Ella would carry with her for the rest of her life and Zoe didn't want the young woman to have any regrets.

'We've got you a lovely room made up in the children's ward,' Zoe said brightly. 'Miles sorted it this morning.'

At the mention of Miles, Ella's face briefly lit up. 'Oh, Ricky love, Miles is here today.'

For a moment, Zoe gave a start of surprise. Miles didn't usually connect with patients, at least not on a level where they asked for him.

'I'll make sure we find him, okay?'

Zoe turned to the paramedic and told him where to take Ricky. Watching them walk away, Zoe already knew she couldn't leave the hospital until Ella did. This was where their journey as mother and son would end, and Zoe wanted to make sure it was both beautiful and peaceful.

Chapter Twenty

The sun came out from behind the clouds shortly after Ricky Pagett passed away. Zoe took the bright ball of yellow that beamed down while Ella nursed a cup of tea, teeth chattering with shock, as a sign of brighter tomorrows.

Peering through the window of the door leading to the small but comforting family room, she saw Miles with his arm around Ella. She felt a flash of affection for her colleague and thought of the card she had written earlier for Ella resting in her pocket.

Ricky was too young and hooked up to too many machines to give any message to his mother. Yet Zoe hadn't wanted the young mum to leave without something to cling to during the dark moments that Zoe knew would fill the days ahead. And so, after Ricky died, Zoe had thought carefully about the kind of note she wanted to give Ella. She knew that the worst had happened and when it did you needed to know you would survive.

Pushing the heavy fire door open, she smiled at Ella and Miles as they looked first at her and then the tea tray in her hands.

'Here you go,' Zoe said gently. 'I thought you could both do with something warm inside you. I imagine that's gone stone cold by now.'

Miles looked up at her gratefully. 'Thanks, Zoe.'

'You all right?' she mouthed, catching his eye.

Miles gestured for her to sit opposite him and Ella. Taking the mug from Ella's hands, he replaced it with a warm, fresh one. 'Come on, sweetheart.'

But Ella said nothing as she took the mug and continued to gaze listlessly at the floor.

'You can stay here as long as you need,' Zoe offered. 'There's no rush for you to do anything or go anywhere.'

'Thanks,' Ella said, her voice flat.

'And are you still sure we can't call your mum?' Zoe asked. 'I think she would want to be here for you now.'

At this, Ella lifted her gaze and met Zoe's eyes. 'Yes, please.'

Zoe looked at Miles, who immediately got to his feet. 'I'll make that call.'

Zoe smiled at him. He had been sitting with Ella for almost two hours. He would need a break so he could return and care for her.

'I don't think I can stand it,' Ella whispered when Miles shut the door. 'Ricky was my everything. Who am I without him? Ricky is – *was*,' she said, catching herself, 'such a good boy. Why has this happened? Mum kept telling me in the days leading up to this moment that he would always be with me, that he would go to heaven, but I don't know if that's true. What do you think?'

Zoe said nothing for a moment. Over the years she had wondered many times if there was an afterlife and if there was, what that meant for Sean. Zoe had no idea. For a long time after Sean's death, she had clung to the idea that he was with her and David in spirit, as if he could pop up as and when he felt like, or perhaps more selfishly, whenever Zoe needed him. But as time passed Zoe hoped that wasn't the case. Even though the idea of Sean being around her was wonderful, that wasn't what she wanted for her son. Zoe wanted for Sean in death what she had wanted for him in life – to be happy.

'I think wherever he is, he's out of pain and he's free from a life of drugs, machines and heartache,' Zoe said honestly. 'I think that what's left are some beautiful memories for you to hold on to, and those can never be taken from you.'

'I don't think I can.' Ella shook her head fiercely. 'I don't think I'll ever be able to remember Ricky without thinking of the pain he was in.'

Zoe leaned forward and squeezed Ella's knee. 'I promise you won't always feel like that. Ricky was only ill for a short part of his life. Before that, there was laughter, cuddles, bedtime stories, screams of joy as he whooshed down slides or giggles of excitement as he took his first steps. You will remember those special times fondly one day, I promise, and the thing is, you'll *want* to remember.'

Ella looked earnestly at Zoe. 'You sound as if you know.'

'I do. My son died over two years ago. He was just seven.'

'But you cope?' Ella asked, a note of incredulity creeping into her voice.

'I did and I do,' Zoe said, slowly, setting her cup of tea on the table. 'It's been a tough path for me. Sometimes the pain still catches me out, and I can't believe my son has died. A whole week can go by sometimes where it doesn't hurt and then just like that' – Zoe clicked her fingers – 'it hits me as if I'd been in the ring with Anthony Joshua that he's gone. The grief I felt right at the beginning is with me all over again.'

Ella shook her head at Zoe. 'I haven't got your strength. I can't do this.'

With that the young mum hugged herself into a small ball and rocked backwards and forward on the small sofa.

Zoe moved to sit beside her and held the woman in her arms. 'You will get through this, Ella. There will be days when you think you can't go on but you will. You must keep Ricky's memory alive and live for him. Trust me, Ella, one day you will remember Ricky with nothing but love and it's that love that will get you through what's next.'

Ella broke into sobs against her shoulder. Zoe knew that there were no words that could lessen the grief Ella felt now. The best Ella could hope for was that she could learn to live with it.

After a few moments, Ella stopped crying and lifted her head. She moved towards her cup of tea, only as she did so, Ella's eyes strayed to the small square envelope addressed to her, lying on the tea tray.

'Who's this from?'

'Me. It's nothing.' Zoe felt embarrassed. She didn't like explaining why she wrote the notes she did. 'A little something to help you with whatever comes next.'

Ella turned back to the envelope and carefully opened it to reveal a small white card, blank apart from an image of a pair of hands intertwined.

Ella flipped the card open and Zoe watched her read the words she had thought so carefully about.

> *Sometimes there are no words, there is no escape from the pain, but there is and always will be love.*

Ella seemed to reread the note a few times before she set the card down and started to cry again. Alarmed, Zoe reached out to hold her, but Ella shook her head.

'That's the most beautiful thing anyone has said about all of this. Thank you, Zoe.'

And as Ella continued to cry, Zoe turned her gaze towards the window and saw the sun shine even brighter. Despite her uncertainty about the afterlife, in that moment she felt as if Sean was with her, encouraging her to go forward, to live out her own dreams as well as his. Zoe held Ella tightly in her arms. This had been her once. She had experienced something so devastating she had allowed grief to take over her life. But perhaps now was the time to let hope flood through her body like the gentle kiss of the sun shining through the window.

Chapter Twenty-One

Once Ella had finally gone home, safe in the company of her best friend, Zoe found herself desperately needing a drink. She invited Ben to join her in the pub across the road, as well as Miles, but the nurse claimed exhaustion and Zoe could see that Ella's dependency on him that day had taken its toll.

Zoe, however, felt strangely energised. Ella was a reminder of how far she had come and how much progress she had made since those early days of grief.

Picking up the chilled glass of white wine Ben had thoughtfully bought her, she gave it a sniff and found the wine lacking. Back in Australia the wine smelled more fragrant, fresher somehow.

'You look deep in thought,' Ben said as she took a sip, wrinkling her nose.

Zoe raised her glass in thanks. 'I'm fine. Been a tough day.'

'If you ever want to talk—'

'I don't,' Zoe said, cutting him off before he had the chance to say anything else.

'Okay. Then how do you feel about making another letter delivery?'

Zoe rolled her eyes. 'Right now, I'm going with no.'

'Not now.' Ben grinned. 'But you've got a day off next Friday, haven't you?'

'Maybe,' Zoe said in a non-committal tone.

'I know you have; I drew up the roster,' Ben said, with a wink. 'I've got the day off too. Thought we could go to Wales.'

'Which part?'

'Near Cardiff.' Ben took a pull on his pint. 'You'll like this delivery, it's different.'

'Different how?' Zoe asked.

A smile played on Ben's lips. 'I've got some last words for a horse.'

Zoe almost choked on her wine. 'You want to go to Wales to deliver a note to a horse?'

'I know it's out there,' Ben said, trying to keep his face straight, 'but hear me out.'

'This I can't wait for.' She took off her cardigan and readied herself for whatever was about to come next.

'About two years ago I was with a very sweet girl named Hannah. She was only twelve when she died of leukaemia,' Ben explained.

'Poor kid,' Zoe whispered.

'It was horrible; Hannah was so full of life.'

'Children always are,' Zoe replied, images of when she first met a laughing, cheeky Ricky flooding her mind. 'Where does the horse come in?'

'She had a horse named April who was her best friend by all accounts. Her parents had recently divorced and I think April helped her get over it.' Ben shrugged, and Zoe was reminded that he was also from a 'broken' home. 'Just before Hannah passed, she begged me to keep an eye on April. She was worried that her horse wouldn't cope without her and her little brother Josh wouldn't look after her so I promised to visit when she died.'

'But you didn't.'

A flame of colour crept up Ben's cheeks as he shook his head. 'I meant the promise at the time, but you know how it is, life and work, yada, yada.'

Shaking her hair free from her ponytail, Zoe felt the tension headache that had plagued her all day begin to ease. 'Why now?'

'Because you, Zoe Evans, are the perfect nurse and have made me realise how important it is to keep your promises to the dying.'

Zoe laughed. 'What's your plan? Turn up at the house and say you're here to see a horse?'

'Maybe.' Ben looked uncomfortable. 'What's wrong with that?'

'Nothing.' Zoe giggled as she reached for her wine. 'But won't that upset the family?'

'Why do you think I want you to come?' Ben said with an eye-roll. 'Regardless, Hannah asked me to tell the horse how much she was loved so that's what I'm going to do.'

'Fair enough.' Zoe took a sip of her wine, grateful that the taste had improved. 'What time?'

'Pick you up at eight?' Ben suggested as he reached into his pocket and pulled out a bag of pork scratchings. She frowned. That would do his IBS no good at all and she was about to say as much when she saw Miles at the bar and instead waved him over.

'Thought you were too tired,' she said, spotting two drinks in his hands.

Miles shot her a weary smile. 'It's been a bugger of a day. I thought I might join you instead.'

'I'm glad you did.' Zoe smiled, then spotted Sarah coming out of the ladies. She glanced from Sarah and back to Miles.

'Zoe, there you are.' Sarah beamed as she walked towards Zoe. 'I came to find you at work to see if you fancied a drink, but Miles here told me you already had company.'

'Thought I'd escort her,' Miles explained.

'How gentlemanly of you,' Zoe remarked, looking at the two of them in surprise.

'I thought so.' Miles ignored Zoe's look of concern and pulled out a chair for Sarah.

'Why did you come looking for me?' Zoe asked, turning to her friend.

'Miles told me about the young boy who came in today so thought I'd check on you,' Sarah said, her eyes saying what they were both thinking, that this would have been tough for Zoe in more ways than one.

Zoe smiled fondly at her friend. 'I'm fine, but thank you.'

'In fact, Zoe's so fine, she has agreed to help me deliver a message to a horse,' Ben put in cheerfully.

'Come again?' Sarah said, looking bemused.

As Ben briefly outlined the story to Miles and Sarah, Zoe giggled as she saw disbelief pass across their faces.

'I don't know what to say!' Sarah exclaimed. 'I don't think I've ever known you to deliver a note to a horse before.'

'In fairness, it's not a note, it's a message,' Ben pointed out. 'I know it sounds weird but I made a promise to a little girl.'

'Fair go, mate,' Miles said, taking a large gulp of his own pint. 'Tell you what, if it goes all right we can put it on the hospice's Instagram page.'

'Oh, for goodness' sake! Shouldn't we stick to pictures of nurses in scrubs doing charity walks or something?' Zoe grumbled.

'Don't be so old and grumpy. It's good for the hospice, raises its profile and the kids love it. Look.' Miles pulled his phone out and with one meaty finger tapped on the app's icon and brought up the page for Ben and Zoe.

'You've posted a picture here of Ella and Ricky!' Zoe exclaimed.

'I know.' Miles grinned. 'It's all right before you start. I got her permission. But look at the comments and likes. Over fifty shares, almost one thousand likes and I can't even get through all the messages for Ella.'

Zoe snatched the phone from Miles's hand and began to scroll through the comments. He was right, there were hundreds of messages of love and support. Zoe knew this would be a huge comfort to the young woman. When Zoe lost Sean, all she wanted to do was talk about him with anyone who would listen; here Ella could do just that with all these willing souls ready to sympathise and commiserate.

'I had no idea,' she said at last. 'This is lovely.'

Miles grinned. 'I got the idea a while back – patients seem to love it.'

'Bit like a more up-to-date version of your note-keeping, Zoe,' Sarah said wryly.

'Haha. Anyone for another drink?' Zoe asked, standing up.

Sarah and Miles shook their heads and Ben frowned as he checked the large steel watch resting on his wrist. 'Thanks, but I have to go.'

Miles arched an eyebrow. 'It's still early.'

'I know, I've got a date and I'm already running late,' Ben said with a nervous laugh. 'Great first impression, eh?'

Miles raised his full pint glass towards Ben's. 'Been there, mate. You'd better arrive with flowers if you want things to improve.'

'Good idea.' Ben gave Miles a grateful grin, setting his empty glass down and reaching for his jacket from the back of his chair.

Zoe felt a stab of disappointment. Ben had a date? So, what did that make the two of them? Then she checked herself. She and Ben were just friends and colleagues. Besides, he hadn't even said he liked her; she had been a fool to think otherwise. She glanced at Ben and did her best to smile as she caught his eye.

'Hope it goes well,' she managed. 'Give us all the gory details in the morning,'

As Ben left the pub, Zoe felt Sarah's eyes boring into her.

'What?'

'Nothing,' Sarah said quickly, before turning to Miles. 'Go to the bar, get her another drink.'

'But it's not my round,' Miles protested.

Sarah glowered at him. 'Just do it.'

Miles scuttled off, leaving Zoe and Sarah alone.

'A date, then?' Sarah said.

Zoe nodded, fiddling with a strand of her hair. 'Looks like it.'

'I'm sorry,' Sarah said with a rueful grin. 'I got it wrong.'

'It doesn't matter. We work together; it would be foolish to take things further and besides I'm nowhere near ready for a relationship.'

'As long as you're all right,' Sarah pressed.

There was a pause as Zoe thought for a moment. Was she all right? She thought about Ella and Ricky. Then Sean, David and Ben. She thought of all the heartache in the world when you cared too much and allowed yourself to get in too deep. This, she decided, as Miles returned with a fresh drink, had been a lucky escape.

'I'm fine,' she said, almost convincing herself that she meant it.

Chapter Twenty-Two

The news of Ben's date had shaken Zoe more than she cared to admit. When she got home, she had gone straight to bed but hadn't slept. Instead, she had lain in her bed feeling hot and irritated with herself for getting things so wrong.

By the time she managed to drift off it was almost time to get up, the alarm sounding in her ear only moments after she'd got to sleep, telling her it was time to face the day. With eyes as heavy as lead, Zoe silenced the noise with her hand, swung her legs out of bed and made her way to the kitchen. It was still early, just after five in the morning – too early for breakfast. Instead, she started the coffee machine and heard her phone vibrate on the worktop above the din of the grinding beans. Eyes still glazed, Zoe reached for it and felt dread build in the pit of her stomach as she saw an Instagram alert letting her know David had tagged her in a post.

Warily, she clicked the colourful icon. Taking in the image staring back at her, her stomach dropped. It was Sean. He was beaming up at her with his familiar toothy grin and mussed-up hair. Gazing at his face in the half-light, she ran her forefinger across the screen and glanced down at the accompanying message – *My son, my world, my family.*

Scrolling across to the next picture, she saw it was a photo of the three of them taken shortly before Sean had died. They were on holiday in the Gold Coast and David had managed to take a selfie as the sun set. They all looked happy. Zoe had one arm clamped around Sean's shoulders, while her other arm was wrapped around David's waist. Sean was giggling for the camera, covered in sand, eyes alive with excitement as Zoe had promised him he could choose where they went for dinner that night. She'd hoped he would pick one of the fancy restaurants that lined the beachfront but of course her son had wanted sticky ribs and fortune cookies.

Shucking off the memory, Zoe swiped again to the next picture. This time it was of Sean blowing out the candles on his birthday cake when he was seven – his last birthday. Underneath, David had written: *Our boy, always here and never forgotten. Happy birthday Sean, love Mum and Dad xxx*

Zoe threw the phone back on the table and took a step back as if the device was on fire. Today was Sean's birthday. He would have been ten. Double figures! As dawn started to break, lighting the room around her, she wasn't sure which hurt more. The knowledge her precious boy would be fast on his way to becoming a man or that she hadn't remembered today was his birthday. Zoe paled. How could she have forgotten?

It was then she saw her phone glow with a message from David. Cautiously, Zoe picked it back up.

Happy birthday to our beautiful boy. What a fine young man I know he would have grown up to become. He is always with me. David xx

When Zoe finished reading, she pressed the phone to her heart, closed her eyes and tried to catch her breath. Sean's birthday always sent her off-kilter, her mind full of what-ifs. She opened her eyes and clicked into the Instagram post once more. As she scanned the beach photograph, she remembered the smell of the salt in the air and the way the waves had crashed against the shore, tickling their legs as she and Sean squealed with pleasure, begging David to hurry up and take the picture before the waves soaked them through. David had been laughing, teasing them with his inability to get it right, and pleading for just one more.

Zoe had known what he was doing – he was eking out this bubble of happiness. He had never wanted it to end and neither had she.

Six months later, Sean was dead and the memories of this trip were one of the few things she had clung to in the very dark days that lay ahead.

Now, as she reread David's message, she felt something stir. She wasn't sure if it was the guilt, the earliness of the hour or even the fact that she was feeling sorry for herself after what had happened with Ben the night before, but she found herself typing a reply.

And always in mine. Zoe x

At lunchtime, Zoe found herself in the cafe across the road picking at a tuna sandwich, berating herself for not remembering her only child's birthday. She was so engrossed in feeling guilty she didn't notice Ben until he tapped her on the shoulder.

She jumped and pressed her hand to her chest. 'Jeez. You frightened the life out of me.'

Ben grinned and gestured to the hard plastic seat opposite. Zoe pushed her food away.

'You not eating?' he said.

'Not hungry,' Zoe replied.

'Me neither,' Ben said, taking a sip of the milky coffee he had just ordered.

'That's not like you.'

Ben shrugged. 'Yeah, not been feeling good lately. Lots on my mind.'

Glancing across at him, Zoe saw Ben looked worried and tired.

'Is this something to do with your date last night?' she blurted.

'My date?' he echoed in surprise.

'Yeah.' Zoe felt uncomfortable now she had brought it up. 'I wondered if it hadn't gone well or something.'

At the question, Ben laughed and Zoe added 'embarrassed' to the list of things she felt. It was none of her business.

'It was all right.' He gave a small shrug and sipped his coffee. 'She was a nice girl but looked nothing like her photo.'

'Oh, it was a Tinder date,' Zoe said knowingly.

Ben caught the judgement in her tone. 'And what's wrong with that?'

'Nothing. I didn't expect it to be your thing to find a date that way. My mistake.'

'It's not really. Candice made me go. She reckons she always finds good dates on there,' Ben admitted.

Zoe frowned. 'I didn't realise Candice was dating. Thought she was too busy.'

'She is.' Ben raised an eyebrow. 'But she'll tell you herself life shouldn't be all work and no play, so she makes time to date girls as well as boys.'

'I take it she hasn't found Mr or Mrs Right yet?' Zoe joked.

Ben smiled and shook his head. 'To be fair I don't think that's what she's after. My sister likes being single. That said, she thought I was spending far too much time working, which is why she found me a date, but she was boring as hell. We won't be going out again.'

Zoe smiled. 'Least you gave something new a try.'

'I guess. I've told Candice I haven't got time to date but she never listens.'

'I know that feeling,' Zoe said as Ben looked at the remnants of her sandwich.

'Here, have it if you want it.' She pushed the plate towards him, hoping it would go some way to making up for her nosiness.

Ben shook his head, then suddenly came out with, 'Do you date?'

The question caught her off guard. 'What? No, of course not, I'm married.'

'Except you're not,' Ben reasoned.

Zoe blanched. 'I'm not divorced either.'

'You've never had a date since you got to the UK?'

'I'm not interested,' she said firmly. 'Work's my focus.'

'Cheers to that,' Ben said, holding his coffee cup aloft.

Smiling, Zoe touched her half-empty mug to his. 'If it's not a bad date, what's up?'

For a moment Ben said nothing and Zoe tried to read him from across the table. He looked guilty, she thought, and conflicted.

'It's nothing,' he said at last. 'Tell me about you. You don't look all right.'

Morosely, Zoe shook her head, before saying in a small voice, 'I forgot Sean's birthday when I woke up this morning.'

'What do you mean?'

Zoe told him about David's Instagram post and how she felt upset and guilty at forgetting her son's special day.

By the time she had finished, Ben was looking at her in wide-eyed dismay. 'Zoe, sweetheart, that's a lot.'

'I know, I thought I was over all this.'

'Why would you be over it?' Ben exclaimed. 'I'm still not over my mum's death. I miss her every single day. I can't imagine what sort of complicated feelings are going through your mind. Grief is such a horrible, complex beast – it's ever-changing. All those feelings you're experiencing right now don't mean you loved your boy any less or that you've forgotten about him. It's part of a journey. You need to forgive yourself for that.'

Zoe nodded, grateful her friend understood. 'How do you know all the right things to say?'

'Because I'm a master of emotion,' Ben said, a small smile playing on his lips. 'And besides, just because you didn't remember Sean's birthday when you woke up doesn't mean you might not have remembered in the shower moments later.

It's luck that David got there first, and let's consider the time difference. He'd have had all day to come up with that message; you were dealing with it at the crack of dawn. You need to look at the positive side.'

'Oh yeah, what's that?'

'You woke up and saw a lovely photo of your son that has great memories attached to it.'

Zoe realised Ben was right and she felt as if a physical weight had been lifted from her chest. 'Thank you.'

'You're welcome.'

'Are you sure you don't want to tell me what's up with you?'

He shook his head as he checked his watch. 'I have to get back to work.'

'Are you sure?' Zoe tried again.

'Yeah, I'm fine. Another time.'

-

It had been a relief to hear Ben say he wasn't interested in dating. And deep down when Zoe had said she was married, she had meant it. She was, however, concerned about Ben. He had been kind enough to offer her advice whenever she needed it and Zoe wanted to repay the favour. Spotting him the following Tuesday in the staff room, shoving files into his bag after their shift, she ventured towards him.

'Have you got time for a drink across the road?' she said.

Ben looked hesitant. Then, running a hand across his bald head, he gave a brief nod. 'Yeah, go on then.'

'Great.' Zoe beamed, putting her rucksack on her shoulder. 'My treat.'

And with that she led them out of the hospital and towards the pub before Ben could change his mind.

'So what's all this in aid of?' Ben asked, as he looked suspiciously at the pint Zoe set in front of him.

'What?' Zoe asked as she took her own seat across from Ben in one of the booths towards the back of the bar. She had been delighted when she had seen it, hoping a bit of privacy might encourage Ben to open up. 'Can't two friends have a drink together?'

'Yes,' Ben said, shucking off his jacket. 'But I have a feeling you want something and given we're taking my car to Wales on Friday, I'm wondering if you've got your eye on my Porsche.'

'I don't want anything,' she said firmly. 'But I drive that car a lot better than you do!'

Ben let out a peal of laughter. 'If you say so.'

Smiling, Zoe said in a soft voice, 'I just wanted to see if you were all right. Give you a chance to talk if you wanted to. You haven't seemed yourself the last few days.'

'I'm fine,' Ben said quickly.

'If you're sure.' Zoe had already decided she wasn't going to force him to talk to her. 'It's just that we're friends and friends help each other.'

Sitting back in his chair, Ben pinched the bridge of his nose, then said in a woeful tone, 'I've done something awful.'

Zoe's eyes widened in alarm. 'It can't be that bad.'

Ben looked morosely into his pint. 'It is. I've opened Mrs Myerson's letter.'

Zoe didn't know whether to feel relieved or annoyed at Ben's admission. Opening other people's letters was far from ideal, but she thought it was something a lot worse.

'Ben, why?'

The troubleshooter thought for a moment. 'After we couldn't find Mrs Myerson's husband, I felt guilty. I wanted to see how important her words were, if I had missed something vital he needed to know.'

'And did you?' Zoe asked.

Wordlessly, Ben reached into his bag and pulled out a familiar-looking envelope. As he slid it across the beer-stained table, Zoe saw it was the opened letter to Mr Myerson. She looked at Ben hesitantly, only for him to push it further towards her.

Reluctantly, Zoe pulled the letter out and began to read.

Dear Michael,

These are just a few words, my darling. I haven't got the energy to write much. We both know the end isn't far, but in case I don't have time, I want to do it here. Michael, I love you and I'm sorry.

If I had done as you asked, gone to the GP earlier, perhaps I would still be here, and we would still be together. The sad truth is I didn't. I thought it was nothing, I was too busy with work. Now of course I wish I had done things differently. Knowing it's time to leave you breaks my heart. Of all the things I've done, the awards I've won, the research I've been a part of, spending forty years as your wife has been my biggest achievement.

Forgive me, my darling,
Your Heidi

When Zoe finished reading the letter, she noticed rain was beginning to fall outside the window. Lifting her chin, she felt a lump form in her throat. It must have cost Mrs Myerson dearly to write something like this when she was in the final stages of such a horrific disease. Zoe felt a stab of guilt. These words belonged with Mrs Myerson's husband; they could change everything for him.

'We have to do more to find him. Someone must know where he is,' she said.

'They do. I rang my old hospital department shortly after we tried delivering this letter. They told me Mr Myerson had died a year after his wife,' Ben said flatly.

'Oh no,' Zoe exclaimed. 'I'm sorry, Ben, but you weren't to know, and I'm sure just the act of writing a note would have been hugely comforting for Mrs Myerson.'

Ben hung his head and let out a small snort of laughter. 'That note's been plaguing me for the last couple of weeks, Zoe, but it's not because I didn't deliver it.'

'Then why?'

'Because it triggered something inside me,' Ben said gruffly.

'What do you mean?'

'Mrs Myerson got me thinking about my own health. I've had this problem with my stomach for months and done nothing about it, thinking I'm just going to get better. I kept reading her letter, and thinking maybe I ought to get *myself* checked out, if only so I can stop buying sodding indigestion medicine.'

Zoe smiled at his feeble attempt at a joke and looked at him encouragingly.

'I made an appointment with my doctor a few days ago, expecting him to tell me it was a simple matter of irritable bowel syndrome.'

'And he didn't?' Zoe pressed.

Ben shook his head. 'He referred me to hospital for tests. I've got to see a colorectal specialist next Monday for the results.'

'Oh, Ben.' Zoe's eyes widened in horror and she caught herself just in time as Ben looked at her, the terror in his own eyes clearly visible for a moment.

'I'm scared, Zoe,' he admitted in a low voice. 'I've faced some frightening stuff but this is the scariest.'

At the admission, Zoe leapt to her feet and walked around to Ben's side of the table. She didn't wait for an invitation as she wrapped her arms around him.

'You're going to be fine; there is absolutely nothing to worry about.'

But as she made the promise, she was acutely aware she had no idea if it was true.

Chapter Twenty-Three

By the time Friday rolled around, Zoe was exhausted. After Ben's admission on Tuesday night, he had released himself from Zoe's arms, thanked her for the pint then abruptly headed home. She had been tempted to chase after him, but stopped herself. Twenty years as a nurse told her that people usually needed time to themselves when faced with worrying news, so she let him go. They would have plenty of time to talk during their trip to Wales, assuming Ben still wanted to go.

Checking her phone when she got up, Zoe was relived to find a message from Ben earlier that morning, seemingly his usual upbeat self.

> See you soon, Zo! I'm bringing bacon butties and coffee so don't waste time with breakfast. B x

As Zoe waited outside her house, she found herself hoping this trip would help take his mind off things. She didn't usually advocate for opening other people's letters, but if there was something wrong with Ben, perhaps it was a good thing Mrs Myerson's note had pushed him on to get checked out.

Pulling up outside, Ben beamed at her as he got out of the car.

'Top of the morning to you,' he said, giving her a mock bow.

She eyed him suspiciously. 'What's with the Irish?'

Ben reached for her rucksack and stuck it in the boot. 'Just a bit of fun.'

'Oh-kay,' she said, feeling bemused as she opened the door and clambered into the passenger seat.

The moment she had clipped in her seatbelt, Ben roared down the street and Zoe clutched the sides of her bucket seat, fearful they were about to take off.

'What's the rush?' she asked as Ben took a corner at speed.

'Sorry,' he said with a rueful grin. 'I'm excited about our trip.'

'Are you sure there isn't anything else on your mind?' Zoe asked doubtfully.

Ben hunched his shoulders. 'Look, about the other night. I shouldn't have said anything. I'm sorry.'

'Of course you should,' Zoe insisted. 'If you're worried you should always talk about things.'

'I'm not worried, not any more,' Ben said, his eyes never leaving the road. 'It was a shock, my GP referring me for tests, that's all. But I've thought about it since then. I'm a health professional. I know I'm young and healthy. This is most likely routine and it's pointless worrying about something that hasn't happened yet.'

'Really?' Zoe tried again. 'Because you seemed upset the other night.'

Ben indicated left and shook his head. 'I'm sorry. Truly, Zo, it was good of you to be there for me, but I was being silly.'

She turned to look out of the window as they began to cross the Severn Bridge, determined to shake the bad mood that was threatening to cloud her day. If she was honest, it wasn't only Ben that was troubling her, it was Sarah too. Shortly before Ben had picked her up, Sarah mentioned Miles had asked her out on a date.

Zoe had been appalled, the displeasure clearly evident across her face, but Sarah had merely laughed.

'I think Miles could show me how to have fun with a bloke again and I think that's just what I need,' she'd said. 'After all, that's what you're doing with Ben and I think it's a good idea.'

Zoe had arched an eyebrow at that. 'What do you mean, fun is what I'm having with Ben?'

'You're going on dates—' Sarah began to point out, only for Zoe to cut her off.

'We're not going on dates! He had a date with someone else, remember? We're friends. Neither one of us is interested. I'm just helping him out with a work project.'

Now it was Sarah's turn to raise an eyebrow, a look that gave her a slightly comic edge given the state of her mussed-up bed hair, which was sticking up at right angles. 'Look, Zoe, you've had lunch in a fancy hotel, he invited you to the Lizard and you're off to Wales together. Despite the fact he might be dating and even though you claim you're not interested, I think there's more to this friendship, and there's nothing wrong with that. You've spent years cooped up with me and Lottie watching telly and going to work. Now you're beginning to fly, and I'm thrilled for you.'

Zoe felt a flash of fury at Sarah's words. 'I've been a burden to you and Lottie all this time?'

A look of incredulity had spread across Sarah's face. 'No! What are you talking about? I'm only saying you're the happiest I've ever known you and I think some of that is down to Ben. I'm taking a leaf out of your book and having fun with Miles. It's all good, Zoe; we're moving on.'

But the last thing Zoe felt was good. 'I'm not moving on and I had no idea I was getting in the way of you doing that. Miles is definitely a laugh but he'll chew you up and spit you out once he's had his way with you.'

'Had his way with me?' Sarah cried. 'It's a date in the twenty-first century and last time I checked I was a grown woman capable of making her own decisions. You need to get out more.'

'Is that right?' Zoe fired back.

'Yes, that's right,' Sarah shot back, face red. 'Putting your life on hold because Sean's dead isn't going to bring him back, you know. You're a nurse; I thought you would have realised that.'

The pain of Sarah's words tore through her as keenly as if she had been slashed with a knife. To her credit, Sarah looked appalled, eyes wide and hands clamped over her mouth as she realised what she had said. She had of course tried to apologise but Zoe hadn't wanted to hear it. She had fled from the house, rucksack in hand, preferring to wait for Ben outside. She knew Sarah had said the words in anger, but they hurt nonetheless.

Now, as Ben continued to skilfully drive his car towards their destination, Zoe pushed the row from her mind and focused on the fact that it was a perfect summer's day. The sun was shining, the company was good and, as well as the bacon sarnie, Ben had even packed coffee and biscuits. She took a sip from the travel cup he had prepared, and the warmth of the liquid coursed down her throat and soothed her soul.

'Have you got your speech ready?' Zoe asked as the signs for Cardiff appeared in English and Welsh now they were across the border.

'Speech?' Ben looked at her, alarmed, as he briefly took his eyes off the road. 'I haven't got a speech! Should I have done a speech?'

In spite of her mood, Zoe giggled. 'I'm not sure you could give a horse a speech. I meant more what are you going to say to the family?'

'Oh right,' Ben replied, a look of relief sweeping across his face. 'I thought I might wing it. I spoke to Hannah's dad the other day and he was pleased to hear from me.'

'That's a good start,' Zoe said. 'And the chatting to the horse thing?'

'He was fine about it.'

Zoe said nothing. She wasn't sure she had ever winged anything in her life but this wasn't her rodeo. At the unintended pun, she mentally giggled. It had been a tough day and she already felt her emotions beginning to lift.

'You think it's a bad idea, don't you?' Ben ventured.

'Not at all. It's not my way, but I'm quickly realising my way isn't the only way, or even the best way,' she muttered darkly.

'Woah, what was that?' Ben asked, turning the car into a narrow country lane.

'Nothing.' Zoe sighed. 'Me and Sarah had a row this morning, that's all. Ignore me; I'll perk up soon.'

'Anything you want to talk about?' Ben asked.

'No – yes!' Zoe wailed, remembering how she'd advised Ben that it was important to talk a little over an hour ago.

Ben laughed. 'If it helps, we've got a while until we arrive, so feel free.'

Zoe told him all about Miles dating Sarah, how she had said it was a terrible idea, and finally she told him about Sarah's last shot – how Zoe had been putting her life on hold since Sean had died and that nothing would bring him back.

Ben visibly winced. 'We've all said things we don't mean.'

'Yeah, I know,' Zoe admitted. 'It just hurt.'

'Perhaps you hurt her. She's only going on one date with Miles and he's all right, if a little immature. Maybe he needs to find the right woman. A date doesn't necessarily mean it's serious,' Ben reasoned.

'I guess,' Zoe said. 'Perhaps we both said some stuff. But for her to come out with something like that about Sean—'

Her voice broke off at the sound of her phone ringing. Reaching for it in the footwell of the car, Zoe finally managed to locate it. Checking her screen, she grimaced.

'It's Sarah.'

'You going to answer it?'

'No,' Zoe said firmly, putting the phone back in the footwell. 'I'm not ready to talk to her yet. I need to calm down.'

'Then put it on silent and let's have a good day,' Ben suggested, his gaze fixed on the road. 'Perhaps afterwards we could go for dinner, enjoy this beautiful countryside, or we could take a detour to the Gower?'

Zoe looked at him, perplexed. 'Where's the Gower?'

Ben's eyes flashed with delight. 'Aha, you've never been! Rhossili Bay will give your Bondi Beach a run for its money.'

'You reckon?' Zoe said teasingly. 'Bondi's pretty special.'

'Yeah, so is the Gower.'

Laughing, Zoe was about to protest. She had no beach stuff, no shoes for sand and certainly not enough food or water; plus they were both on the mid-morning shift at the hospice tomorrow.

But then she remembered Sarah's words to her that morning. Maybe she should allow herself a little fun.

'Go on,' she said, wondering as she did so where her words might take her.

Chapter Twenty-Four

They had stopped for a long lunch at a little pub outside the city centre, arriving at the paddocks just after school closing time. Getting out of the car, Zoe saw a short, stocky man walking towards them, wearing a grin almost as wide as his frame.

'You must be Ben and Zoe,' he said, extending his hand. 'I'm Jack, and this is Josh.' He pushed a young lad, who was hiding behind him, to the front. 'Say hello.'

A rangy boy with shiny dark hair, who hadn't grown into himself, looked briefly up at them, before his eyes darted back down to the floor, cheeks as red as fire engines.

'Hello,' he managed.

Zoe's heart went out to him. Being a kid was hard enough without being forced to talk to daft strangers that wanted to whisper stuff to your dead sister's horse.

'Hi, Josh,' Zoe said kindly. 'It's good of you to let us visit April today.'

Ben nodded. 'Yes, and I'm sorry it's taken so long.'

Jack shook his head. 'To be honest, if you'd come sooner we'd probably have thought you were mad.'

'Finally, my tardiness has paid off,' Ben said with a half laugh.

'Tea or coffee before we get started?' Jack asked in his lilting Welsh accent.

Ben and Zoe shook their heads politely.

'We had one on the way up,' Zoe explained.

'I think we should get along and meet April if that's all right?' Ben said.

'Fair enough. Show them the way, Josh,' Jack instructed his boy.

As Josh led them across the field towards the stables in the corner, the boy's whole demeanour changed – his head lifted and his gait became lighter.

'Here she is,' he said, almost reverently, as they reached a small brown horse with a thick black mane. April was munching on a bale of hay, but at the sight of Josh she stopped what she was doing and gave him a welcoming whinny. Josh responded in kind by stroking the horse's nose and ears.

'She's gorgeous,' Zoe said, stepping forward to pat April, who leaned in towards Zoe.

'She likes you,' Josh said, giving Zoe a shy smile.

Zoe beamed and continued to pat April. 'And I like her. You're a beaut,' she murmured in the horse's ear. 'Do you ride April much?' she asked, looking to Josh. 'You two seem to have a real bond.'

Josh shook his head, his long fringe falling into his eyes. 'No, I fell off last time I took her out.'

'Josh isn't much of one for taking risks,' Jack explained, 'especially since Hannah died.'

Zoe continued to stroke April. Horse riding was pretty much a rite of passage for every Aussie, in case they found themselves in the bush one day. At the realisation, Zoe recalled with a jolt that the week Sean had died, he had been due to start his first riding lesson. He had been filled with excitement at the idea and Zoe had already been looking forward to taking pictures of him trotting round the arena.

She gazed back at Josh, who wrapped his arms around April's neck. She was his best friend, Zoe realised with a pang of sadness. It was a shame he was too frightened to ride her because of one accident. She thought about what she might have said to Sean if he fell off a horse during a riding lesson. No doubt it would be what her mother always said – 'Get back on the bloody thing and get going.' Even as an adult she missed her mother's sage wisdom. Gazing around the stable, Zoe felt a wave of homesickness. In that moment she would have loved to ask Ruth what she thought about Ben and this whole situation.

'Is it okay to give April some mints?' Zoe asked, pulling herself back to the present and smiling as April's ears pricked up at the word.

Jack laughed. 'Course. We always do, don't we, Josh?'

She reached into her pocket and placed a few Polos she had bought especially into her hand. Then, with an outstretched palm and thumb tucked neatly in so April didn't bite it, Zoe offered the treats to the horse, who devoured them in a heart-beat. At the feel of April's wet tongue against her skin, Zoe giggled.

'I know this is a bit of a cheek but I don't suppose I could take April for a quick ride round the paddock, could I?'

Ben looked at her in alarm. 'Zoe's just joking.'

'No, it's fine,' Jack said amiably. 'April would be delighted, I'm sure. One of the girls from the village usually comes up and rides her but she's been poorly the last few days so April's not had much exercise. You do ride, then?'

'Oh yes. It's been a few years, though,' Zoe said honestly.

'If you haven't ridden for years, I'm not sure you want to start now. Don't you want to do it in an arena where there are staff and instructors nearby?' Josh asked, his tone filled with alarm.

'Yes, maybe Josh is right, Zoe,' Ben put in, looking uneasy. 'You're not a kid any more – breaks hurt more now.'

Zoe shook her head. 'Guys, live a little, eh? I'm sure April will be kind to me.'

'I'm sure she will. She's a lovely horse,' Jack said fondly. 'She and Hannah won so many competitions. She's very gentle.'

'Great.' Zoe beamed and turned to Josh expectantly. 'Do you want to help me sort out her tack, mate?'

Wordlessly, Josh nodded and Zoe gave Ben a wink. 'Maybe now's the time to have that word with April you wanted?'

Jack clapped his hands together in delight. 'Ah yes. We promise not to eavesdrop.'

Ben looked at Zoe in alarm, then almost hesitantly walked towards April and stood next to her ear.

'Go on,' she coaxed as Ben seemed stuck for what to say.

Then she watched as Ben whispered something that seemed to last about two long minutes. When he stepped back, April gave a little whinny and pushed her nose into Ben's chest.

'She's happy,' Josh said with an excited laugh. 'She liked what you said.'

'We won't embarrass you by asking you what it was.' Jack grinned before his face fell. 'Though we would love to know.' His eyes grew misty for a moment, and he said, 'Knowing Hannah, I bet it was something mushy.'

Ben gave Jack a warm smile. 'That's exactly what it was.'

Jack said nothing, merely put his hands in his pockets, satisfied with the answer. His gaze turned towards his son, who seemed very excited as he walked towards a little room by April's stable, returning moments later with a saddle, riding hat, bridle and reins. Together with Josh, Zoe tacked April up and, climbing into the saddle, felt as if she were back in that arena as a child, Ruth in the stands cheering her on.

Feeling everyone's gaze on her, instinctively Zoe gave April a quick and gentle nudge in the ribs and together they began trotting around the field. Almost immediately Zoe allowed herself to enjoy the feel of the wind against her cheeks as she and April moved as one. It took her back to a time when she was a child with no responsibility other than what she was going to buy with her pocket money. How life changed.

Before long, she found herself back in reality, and returned to the waiting group, who were looking at her with something like awe and astonishment in their eyes. Smiling, she brought April to a halt and slowly climbed off before handing the reins back to Josh, who continued to gawp in amazement.

'You did all that?' he said.

'I sure did,' Zoe said, patting April's neck and beaming at Josh. 'You know, I didn't say this before I rode April, but the last time I got on a horse I broke my arm.'

'And you got on now?' Josh gaped in wonder.

'Yep. Because I knew April would look after me. She'll take care of anyone who rides her.'

Josh said nothing, simply looking at his father and back at Zoe for confirmation. 'Is that true?'

'Course it's true,' Ben said, recognising Zoe was trying to encourage Josh. 'In fact, that was one of the things Hannah asked me to say to April when I got here. She wanted me to thank her for always taking care of her and she told me to say she would never forget her.'

Jack nodded at that. 'She and Josh always loved April, didn't you? Even though April was Hannah's horse, she always let you look after her and ride her.'

'We used to go on hacks together in the woods up the road.' Josh gestured around the corner.

'I think she'd still look after you,' Zoe said carefully. 'Look how she took care of me and she hadn't even met me before.'

Josh looked at her with doubt across his blue-green eyes. 'Do you think?'

'I'm sure of it,' Ben said firmly, before looking across at Jack for reassurance, who nodded eagerly.

There was a pause and Zoe could see the boy thinking it over in his mind.

'All right. Maybe I could take her for a walk around the paddock and if I fall you'll all be here to help me because you're nurses.'

'Exactly,' Zoe said, handing him the riding hat. 'But I promise you won't. Trust April; she'll look out for you.'

Josh somewhat nervously climbed on top of April, and after whispering something in her ear set off rather slowly around the paddock.

As his confidence grew, so did the pleasure across his face and Zoe, Ben and Jack watched in delight as he went from a walk to a trot around the field.

'He hasn't shown any interest in riding April since that day he fell a week after Hannah died. I've even wondered about selling her. I thought it was doing him no good at all burying himself in the past, the poor animal not being ridden, but now look at him,' Jack marvelled. 'He seems happy. I can't thank you two enough.'

Their work was done, Zoe thought. Ben had nursed one little girl into a good death and today they had brought her brother back to life. Zoe fished out her phone to take a photo for the hospice Instagram page. This was a happy ending and one that should be shared.

Grief was, after all, a funny thing, Zoe mused. It could take you to places you could never anticipate. As she continued to snap the beams of pride and happiness on Ben, Jack and Josh's faces, Zoe understood that whilst the grief of losing her boy had crippled her, it had made her see, try and do things in life she would never otherwise have done. There were times life could break your heart, she thought, but there were times it could be very much worth living.

Chapter Twenty-Five

After saying a warm but short goodbye to Jack and Josh, and with promises to keep in touch, Zoe and Ben had got back in the car and made their way out across the top road towards the beach.

'You were incredible!' Ben exclaimed, once they were a couple of miles away from the paddocks. 'How did you know riding April would reach Josh?'

'I didn't.' Zoe shrugged. 'I could see he was lost, and his best friend was April. He wasn't scared of riding her; he was just scared of taking a chance.'

'Something you recognised?' Ben enquired.

'I think so. Maybe you and Sarah were right, I have been afraid to move on. I thought in some way it was disloyal to Sean, and it felt safer to stay stuck in the same place. I saw something similar in Josh.'

'I would never have thought of that,' Ben said admiringly, 'but I don't come from a cattle farm in the outback.'

Zoe laughed. 'Oh yeah, you're all about the mean streets of Bath!'

'You know it,' Ben quipped, before his expression changed. 'Seriously, Zoe, it was amazing watching you help Josh like that. I stupidly thought carrying out Hannah's request, talking to the horse, was going to be job done. But Josh was who this was really all about. You managed to get to him in a way I would never have thought of. You've got a gift.'

'Come on,' Zoe protested, feeling abashed. 'I just did what anyone else would do. And it's only because I've been through a similar loss. I know how devastating it can be to lose your world and how tough it can be to find your place in it again. It takes time and you need to have the right key. Josh just needed the key.'

'I think you're being too modest,' Ben said firmly. 'You've got a knack with people, Zoe. I never really appreciated that before. You're an inspiration and make me want to be a better nurse every day.'

Zoe looked at Ben in surprise. She wasn't sure anyone had ever said anything so complimentary about her nursing. Yet Zoe didn't consider she had done anything different to any other nurse. But the way Ben was looking at her, his gaze temporarily taken from the road and fixed on her face, made her feel awkward.

'What did you say to April?' she asked lightly.

Ben laughed. 'I sang her "My Lovely Horse" from *Father Ted*. Do you know it?'

Remembering the legendary sitcom featuring three Irish priests, Zoe roared with laughter. The lyrics and melody became like an earworm to her whenever she heard the song.

'You sang that to April?' she said.

'Yup! What else could I do? Hannah gave me no instructions and in fairness April is a lovely horse.'

Zoe had to agree with that. She was about to say as much when Ben turned right and her eyes fell on the sweeping expanse of golden yellow sand and the ocean that stretched as far as her eye could see. Letting out a gasp of delight, she opened her window and marvelled at the noise of the waves crashing against the shore.

'I'm in heaven,' she exclaimed as Ben found a parking space.

He switched off the engine and grinned at her. 'Me too.'

-

After that, the rest of the day seemed to unravel before them. Zoe forgot about time as she enjoyed the simple beauty of the beach with Ben by her side, the two walking barefoot across the sands, the sun warming their bodies, providing the perfect backdrop for swapping stories about their lives.

'I can't believe you got away with throwing your teacher's shoes on the roof, and his diary!' Zoe laughed as they sat on the sand, gulls crying noisily around them.

'Why not? I wasn't always Mr Nice Guy.'

'I think there are a few guys at work who might say you're not Mr Nice Guy now. Didn't you cut overtime last week?' Zoe put in.

Ben grimaced as he wriggled on the beach, trying to get comfortable. 'Yeah, perks of being the troubleshooter.'

'I think you might be known as the troubleshitter after that,' Zoe said with a wry grin.

'Imaginative.' Ben kicked a clump of sand with his bare toe.

'People don't mean it,' Zoe offered. 'You're the boss; you're going to get stick. It's half the reason I never wanted to be in charge. Anyway, let's not talk about work.'

As silence descended across the pair, the only noise was the sound of two children shrieking as they played in the waves.

'You know, Zoe, I've actually got a bit of a problem I wanted to talk to you about,' Ben said, his voice hesitant.

'Oh?' Zoe turned to look at him in surprise, only to see worry etched across his face.

'The thing is, I've done something I swore I'd never do and I hoped you might help.'

'Do you want to talk about your hospital trip? You know, Ben, I'm here for you anytime.'

At the question, Ben shook his head and laughed. 'No, Zo, it's nothing to do with that. In a way I almost wish it was; that would probably be easier.'

'Then what on earth is it?'

Ben gazed down at the sand, carving out circles with his finger, clearly stalling for time.

'I've fallen for someone at work and I'm not sure what I should do about it,' he blurted.

Zoe's heart sped up. 'Miles is into women, I'm sorry to tell you,' she said, hoping a joke would bring them back onto safer ground.

'Don't do that,' Ben said, his tone gentle. 'I think you know how I feel about you, Zo. Surely you do?'

He lifted his gaze and slowly reached out. When she didn't move away, he stroked her cheek with his forefinger.

At the feel of his touch against her skin, Zoe shivered with pleasure. She might have told herself that she hadn't developed feelings for Ben, but she had been kidding herself. The way she had responded to his touch told them both that.

'I thought you didn't date people at work,' she whispered.

'I don't,' Ben replied. 'That's why this is hard for me. It's why Candice sent me on a Tinder date, to try and make me get over my feelings for you.'

'Candice knew?'

'She knew from the moment she saw us together. She said the chemistry between us was obvious.' Ben laughed. 'But Candice is a romantic at heart.'

'And you're not?' Zoe said, trying to ignore the ripple of excitement coursing through her body.

'I've tried not to be. Falling in love with a work colleague you admire, I can't see how that's got a happy ending. But on the other hand, I can't keep being around you without telling you how I feel. All I wanted when I was on that date the other week was to be with you,' Ben continued, his voice almost pleading. 'It's why I ended it early and went home feeling guilty. I've tried to talk myself out of my feelings, Zoe, but I can't.'

'Why are you saying something now?' she asked, sure Ben could hear the pounding of her heart over the crashing of the waves.

'I don't know,' Ben wailed. 'Because I can't keep hiding my feelings. Because I have to know if there's any chance you might feel the same way. I know you probably don't, I know you're probably not ready, but I guess since I saw my doctor, I've begun to think about what's important. Maybe life isn't all work and achievements and if there's a chance I've found someone who might feel the same way about me, then screw work and what all of that means. This is far more important.'

As Ben brought his speech to a close, the hope in his eyes sent Zoe reeling. She thought she had done such a good job of burying her emotions and telling herself it was a good job Ben wasn't interested, not when she was still married and not when she was still so broken over Sean. But now it felt as if the air had been sucked out of her lungs and she realised she couldn't deny her feelings for Ben any longer.

'Are you sure you want me?' she managed. 'I'm a mess, Ben.'

'You don't have the monopoly on mess,' Ben said, reaching for her hand and pressing it to his heart. 'And if you are a mess, it doesn't stop you deserving to be loved.'

His touch anchored her and as Zoe looked at their fingers intertwined, she thought how natural it seemed. She closed her eyes and took a deep breath to steady herself. If life had taught her anything it was that there was no such thing as perfect timing, and you could be knocked off course when you least expected it.

Ben kissed the back of her hand and Zoe's eyes flew open.

'I want to make you happy,' he said. 'I want to make your heart sing and fill your life with joy. I want to give you my world, Zoe Evans.'

As Zoe's blue eyes met Ben's brown ones, the ground beneath her seemed to shift. Without even thinking about it, Zoe leaned forward, placed her lips on Ben's and gave in to the feelings she had been trying to deny ever since she had got closer to Ben Tasker.

Chapter Twenty-Six

As the sun streamed through the windows, Zoe blinked her eyes open and saw a steaming cup of coffee on the bedside table. Sleepily she reached for it, silently thanking her housemate for not bearing a grudge. Only, as Zoe took a tentative first sip, panic set in. This wasn't her usual mug, these weren't her bedsheets, this wasn't her bed and it wasn't her room. She sat bolt upright, slopping brown liquid all over the pristine white sheets, and took in her surroundings whilst simultaneously realising she was naked. The king-size bed, the high ceilings, the single-pane sash windows with views that overlooked the lush green fields around Bath. The Mark Rothko framed prints on the wall and Bose sound system that was playing something classical and calming, if she wasn't mistaken.

Where the hell was she? Then, at the sound of footsteps on the floor below, she realised – she was at Ben's. Memories of the previous day flooded back. The trip to Wales, the ride on April, Josh and his father, the walks on the beach, the confession of feelings and the kiss. The sweet, tender kiss that made Zoe feel as if she had found her way home.

And then there had been after. The drive back to Bath, the burgers from the oldest hamburger bar in the city and Zoe laughing about onion breath as they strolled through Vicky Park, as Ben called it, both knowing but not saying they were going back to his home. There had been the key in the door followed by the walk upstairs towards his bedroom. And there had been no hesitation or awkwardness as he guided her inside.

Zoe felt her cheeks flame with colour as she sank back onto the soft pillows, reliving the memory. She hadn't been with another man since David but Ben had instinctively read her.

'Trust me,' he had said.

And she had.

The way they had kissed and fallen into each other's arms, desperate for more, yet holding back, eager to make the most of the first time they would see each other, touch each other. Then there had been greed. Hands roaming one another's bodies, exploring contours as if they were undiscovered lands. It had been beautiful. In fact, it had been one of the most beautiful and tender nights of Zoe's life. She felt a sudden thrill as she recalled every kiss, every gasp of pleasure. And then the door opened.

Feeling suddenly awkward, she turned her neck and came face to face with a grinning Ben.

'Morning.'

Carrying an overladen tray filled with toast and breakfast pastries, he walked towards her. 'Thought you might be hungry.'

Zoe met his gaze and sat up in bed, duvet clutched under her chin, as he perched on the bed opposite her and slid the tray towards her.

'You thought right.' She grinned, awkwardness forgotten as she helped herself to a piece of toast and took a large bite. 'Mmmm, Vegemite.'

Ben laughed. 'I've always loved it, ever since I backpacked. Better than Marmite.'

Zoe grinned. 'Don't say that to Sarah. She's a Marmite girl all the way.'

After rubbing a finger across her cheek, Ben licked it. 'Vegemite. Couldn't have you going to work looking like that.'

At the mention of work, Zoe let out a loud groan. 'Why did you mention work? What's the time?'

He glanced at his mobile on the bedside table. 'Almost nine and I'm working a double in a few hours. Are you on the ten o'clock shift?'

'I am,' Zoe grumbled. 'I'm going to be late and my boss'll kill me. He's a right bastard.'

'That a fact?' Ben chuckled. 'I have a feeling he'll be very understanding if you're not on time.'

As Ben leaned in to kiss her, all thoughts of work and being late were forgotten as Zoe gave in to the deliciousness of his touch.

-

The fact that she was only thirty minutes late for work seemed like a miracle to Zoe as she sneaked through the hospice main entrance, head low. Keeping her eyes firmly on the floor, she hurried to the staff room, but as she laid a hand on the door, she heard the sound of Miles's guffaws.

'My eyes have gotta be deceiving me! Zoe Evans late for work, and not even in her uniform yet!'

Zoe lifted her chin and felt her cheeks burn red for the second time that morning. 'Yeah, all right. Doesn't happen very often, though, does it?'

Miles grinned. 'Fair go. Just wish you could've warned me; I might have stayed round at your place with Sarah last night if I'd have known you weren't coming back.'

Now it was Zoe's turn to look incredulous. She hadn't realised Miles and Sarah would be going on a date quite so soon.

'I'm kidding.' Miles laughed again. 'I was the perfect gentleman.'

At the admission, Zoe had to admit her curiosity was piqued. 'It went well?'

'I know it pains you to believe it, Zoe, but I can behave myself and I don't see every woman as a notch on my bedpost. I told you before, I really like Sarah.'

Shifting her rucksack to the other shoulder, Zoe nodded. 'Just go careful. She's got a kid and I know you like her but there's more than Sarah to think of.'

The sound of patient chatter washed over them as they looked at each other, guarded. Miles cleared his throat and stood up straighter, his eyes never leaving Zoe's. 'I know that, so stop lecturing me and keep your beak in your own business, eh?'

With that he pushed past her and stalked off down the corridor. Zoe felt wounded. She was just looking out for her friend. She groaned. Falling out with Sarah didn't feel good. They were best mates and she resolved to make it up with her when she got home that night. Maybe she'd order a pizza with some extra dough balls for Lottie. Together they could watch a movie, drink wine and, when Sarah's daughter was in bed, gossip about their dates.

Rattling off a quick text to Sarah suggesting just that, Zoe shoved her phone in her pocket and tried not to worry when she didn't hear from her friend all day.

But when Zoe got home that night, her best-laid plans were forgotten as she heard the sound of raucous laughter coming from the living room. She walked towards the noise and saw Miles, Sarah and Lottie sprawled on the sofa together watching a daft comedy on the TV.

'Hi,' she said warily, feeling like an outsider.

'Hi,' Sarah said with a smile, but her tone was formal. 'Come on in, then.'

'Zoe!' Lottie exclaimed. 'Mum said you were getting my favourite tea.'

Lottie wriggled herself upright and looked at Zoe with her heart-stompingly beautiful eyes radiating pure affection. Sarah laughed. Lottie had perfected the art of looking like the cat from *Shrek* when she was after something.

'I did,' Zoe said. 'Pizza and dough balls are on their way.'

'Hope there's enough for me,' Miles ventured as the doorbell rang. Getting straight up to answer it, he returned moments later with three pizza boxes and a smaller carton of garlic bread.

'I almost didn't bother with the bread but it's a good job I did with an extra guest,' Zoe said with a grin – only a little bit forced – as she took the pizzas from Miles's hands and set them on the table.

The moment the words were out of her mouth, she regretted them as she saw Miles and Sarah exchange a look that made Zoe feel like an outsider again. She pushed the negative feelings away as Sarah opened a box and reached for a slice of pizza.

'Thought we could watch a film,' Sarah said carefully. 'Fancy it?'

'Okay,' Zoe said, helping herself to a large slice. Taking several hurried bites, she perched on the chair instead of in her usual spot on the sofa that was taken by Miles and tried not to feel annoyed. But even with a belly full of pizza she couldn't shake her bad mood, resenting Miles for intruding on the time she had earmarked to sort things out with Sarah. It wasn't until later, when Lottie was in bed and Miles had gone home, that Zoe felt as if she could relax.

'Things look like they're going well with you and Miles,' Zoe said at last when she and Sarah were alone.

Sarah reached for a bottle of wine from the fridge. Pouring two glasses, she pushed one across the table to Zoe. 'It's good.'

'I'm glad.'

Sarah made a face. 'Are you?'

For a second, Zoe wondered. Was she? 'Of course I am.'

There was another silence as Sarah gazed down at the table and back up to Zoe. 'Look, I'm really sorry about what I said. It was stupid.'

'Don't worry about it.' Zoe took a sip of her wine and tried to calm her heart rate.

Sarah laid a hand on Zoe's forearm, the grip so intense Zoe almost writhed in pain. 'No, honestly, I think I've just been a bit overwhelmed with what's going on with Miles and I didn't think.'

'Forget it.' Zoe waved her apology away. 'These things happen. Maybe I'm wrong about Miles. He seems incredibly keen.'

'He surprised me,' Sarah admitted.

'He's surprised me too.' Zoe set her almost full wine glass on the table and pushed it away. She stood up, stretching her arms overhead. 'I'm pleased everything's okay, but I think I'll go to bed. I'm knackered after last night and today.'

'But we haven't talked about your trip to Wales!'

'Another time,' Zoe said. 'I'm bushed. See you in the morning.'

And before Sarah could protest further, Zoe made her way to bed, all the while telling herself how wonderful it was that Sarah was getting on well with Miles. It was only as she snapped off her bedside light and closed her eyes that she realised there was a tiny, horrible part of her that felt scared things were changing and what that might mean.

Chapter Twenty-Seven

By the time Zoe arrived at work on Monday morning, she thought she had experienced every single emotion possible. She had spent Sunday catching up on housework, and while she washed, ironed, pressed and folded, Zoe lost herself in thought. She felt so guilty about her uncharitable thoughts towards Sarah, she had made her and Lottie breakfast in bed, then cleaned the living room and bathroom even though it was Sarah's week to do it. It hadn't made up for the unkindness and Sarah had been baffled as to why Zoe was going to so much effort but it made Zoe feel better.

Then there was Ben – incredible, gorgeous Ben. Every time Zoe thought about him, she smiled like a lovestruck teenager. Reliving some of the highlights of Friday night made her blush, and she knew that no matter how much Sarah pressed her, that was an evening Zoe would keep private.

Shaking herself back to reality, Zoe dumped her stuff in her locker then made her way to the nurses' desk to check the rota. As she peered through the diary, she felt a stab of guilt as she looked at the top entry – *Ben off*.

How could she not have remembered that Ben was in hospital today? She had been so caught up in her own emotion, his appointment had slipped her mind. Guilt ate away at her, but Zoe knew that would get her nowhere. Instead she pulled out her phone and texted him, wishing him luck at his appointment. She stared at her phone for a few moments hoping for a reply, but when none came, she knew it was time to focus on her job rather than her personal life. Whatever news Ben's specialist had, they would deal with it together.

A tinkling laugh caught her attention. Looking up, Zoe saw the noise belonged to Mrs Harper, who was sitting in the bay window, sharing a joke with her son. The mother and son seemed more contented in each other's company than before and Zoe felt pleased.

'Mrs Harper.' She beamed, walking towards her. 'Mr Harper, lovely to see you both.'

'Hello, Zoe.' Mr Harper returned her smile. 'How are you?'

'I was about to ask you the same question. I'm good thanks. And you?' she asked, turning to Mrs Harper.

The older woman shook her head. 'I'm fine. Simon's brought me in because I've been feeling tired.'

Zoe frowned. 'How tired?'

'No more tired than anyone else,' Mrs Harper replied.

'Has the doctor seen you?'

'Not yet,' Mr Harper said, a flash of worry evident in his pale grey eyes. 'I've asked him to make Mum his first port of call.'

'And I've told you I don't want any special treatment,' Mrs Harper said firmly.

Sensing this was not an argument to get involved in, Zoe changed the subject. 'I came to see if there was anything either of you needed. More tea maybe?'

But at the request, both Harpers shook their heads and the new hospice owner got to his feet. 'I must be going. Far too many meetings today.'

'If you're sure. I didn't mean to interrupt,' Zoe said as she watched Mr Harper pull on his coat.

'You didn't; I'm late anyway.'

He bent down to kiss his mother's cheek and squeezed her shoulder. 'I'll see you later.'

'Bye,' Mrs Harper called as her son walked down the corridor towards the exit, then she turned to Zoe. 'I'll have that tea if you don't mind; maybe you can join me?'

Zoe checked her watch. 'Technically I'm not on duty for another half an hour so let me go and sort out some drinks.'

Moments later, Zoe returned with a steaming cup of hot tea for Mrs Harper and a mug of instant coffee for herself.

'You and your son seemed to be getting on well,' she remarked, setting the cups on the table by the window.

'Yes.' Mrs Harper smiled. 'I think the joy of dying is you know you can be completely yourself because it doesn't matter any more.'

To anyone else the words Mrs Harper spoke may have sounded flippant but Zoe knew that was the last thing the older woman was being. In fact, she knew she was being what everyone should be more often – honest.

'You've found a new understanding.'

'That's it. I no longer feel the need to meddle. That's what all mums do, isn't it, meddle? And Simon, I think, is beginning to realise my health is out of his control.'

'Even though he's brought you here?'

There was a brief pause as Mrs Harper looked out of the window, the morning sunshine making the gardens look fresh and full of life.

'Yes, even though he's brought me here,' Mrs Harper admitted. 'In a way, I'm thankful. Coming back has given me an opportunity to make peace with my past.'

'Really?' Zoe asked in disbelief. 'Isn't the past best left?'

'Not long ago I would have agreed with you, but lately, I don't know.' Mrs Harper's eyes rested on the lake. 'I feel as if I've been given an opportunity to remember the good I experienced here as well as the bad.'

Zoe nodded, her eyes following Mrs Harper's gaze out towards the grounds. She turned to watch the older woman look out at the place that used to be her home, the peace evident across her face.

From nowhere, Zoe caught herself thinking about Sydney. She remembered the home she had shared with David and

Sean and realised Mrs Harper was right. There were some good times, in even the very darkest of places.

-

It wasn't until later that Zoe heard from Ben, or rather saw him as the doorbell rang just after seven that night.

'I'll go,' Zoe called.

Opening the front door, she couldn't immediately see who it was because of a huge stuffed unicorn obscuring her view.

'Er, Ben?' She laughed, finally spotting a gleaming black head peeping out above a mass of pink and white fur.

'What gave it away?' Ben set the unicorn on the floor so he could lean in to kiss her. She savoured the softness of his lips until eventually Ben pulled away and they locked eyes, each lost in the simple pleasure of being with one another.

She stared at him and the unicorn, unsure for a moment whether she should ask about the stuffed animal or his hospital appointment first.

'How did it go?' she asked, unable to cope with the suspense any longer.

Ben smiled. 'It's all fine. I'll tell you properly later.'

Pushing past her, he walked into the living room where Sarah, Lottie and Miles were waiting.

'Oh, Ben, what's this?' Sarah said, taking in the unicorn.

'Yeah, mate, you're making the rest of us look bad,' Miles teased as he slipped a cold bottle of beer straight from the fridge into Ben's hand.

'Cheers, buddy,' Ben said, raising his bottle in gratitude and turning to Lottie, who was looking at him expectantly.

'Is that for me?' she asked eagerly.

Ben laughed and placed the unicorn in her lap. Zoe stifled a giggle; it was almost twice the size of Sarah's daughter. 'To show you that hard work means you can have lots of fun. All for you.'

Lottie gasped in delight as she threw her arms around the unicorn, only for Sarah to shoot her a warning look.

'I think there's something you've forgotten to say, young lady,' she admonished.

The little girl immediately looked up from the toy and stared at Ben with her best Puss in Boots eyes. 'Sorry,' she said meekly. 'Thank you, Mr Ben.'

Ben crouched down and rewarded the child with a big smile. 'You're welcome. And if you like unicorns so much I could draw you one later if you like.'

Lottie's eyes lit up at the prospect. 'You would?'

'Sure.' Ben grinned. 'It won't even cost you one of those fish fingers you've almost finished eating.'

'You can have one, Mr Ben,' Lottie said earnestly, pushing a piece of breaded fish towards him.

Ben thought about it then dived in, dipping a small piece in the large puddle of ketchup that had accumulated on her plate. 'Thanks. You can have some of my chow mein, if you like.'

He stood back and reached into the bag of Chinese takeaway boxes he had brought for everyone to share.

Lottie wrinkled her nose. 'I don't like chow mein, Mr Ben.'

'All the more for me,' Ben said, looking pleased. 'Oh, and another thing.'

'What?'

'Just Ben is fine. You don't need to call me "Mr"; I feel like a cartoon character off of the eighties.'

Taking a final bite of her fish finger, Lottie looked nonplussed. 'Okay, Just Ben.'

Ben looked at the group expectantly. 'I asked for that, didn't I?'

'I'd say you pretty much walked into it.' Sarah laughed. 'I'll get us all some plates.'

A couple of hours later and the little group were sitting in the living room, a Spotify playlist Miles had found on in the background. With the breeze streaming through the windows, the evening felt very relaxed. Zoe glanced at Ben; he seemed happy enough after tucking into his Chinese. Perhaps everything had gone well at the hospital after all.

'Any plans for tomorrow? I've got the rest of the week off,' Sarah asked, once the last of the Chinese had been devoured and Lottie carried to bed by Ben.

'I'm working a split shift,' Miles said, frowning.

Sarah's face fell. 'That's a shame, I was hoping we could do something.'

Miles smiled. 'Yeah? Maybe after my first shift? I get off at three.'

It was impossible not to miss the way Sarah's face lit up and Zoe couldn't help feeling pleased. Turning to look at Ben, she locked eyes with him once more and they exchanged a smile.

'Have you got plans tomorrow?' he asked.

'My shift is over by twelve,' Zoe said.

'I've got my last message to deliver. I hoped you could help me with it.'

'Where is it?' Zoe scratched head, clearly considering the request.

'At my house. It's a video call,' Ben explained.

'Why?' Sarah quizzed.

'There's no other way,' Ben said. 'It's a lady named Irene who lost her mum a couple of years ago. She lives in your old neck of the woods, Zo.'

'London?'

Ben shook his head. 'Sydney.'

'It'll be like going home, Zoe,' Sarah said, clapping her hands together and turning to look at Ben. 'Have you spoken to Irene yet?'

'We've exchanged emails,' Ben said. 'I've told her I like to deliver notes in person but Australia is a bit far.'

At the thought of being in contact with someone from her homeland, Zoe felt unsettled. Lately Australia had been playing on her mind and this latest request of Ben's gave Zoe the feeling her past was taunting her.

'All right. There'd better not be any horses involved this time.'

'I promise.' Ben grinned. 'It's arranged for nine in the evening our time, so do you want to come over for dinner? Candice is going out.' Ben threw the remark in casually but Zoe knew what he was getting at. Her heart raced at the thought of another night with Ben.

'Sounds great,' she said casually.

'You bring the wine, I'll do steak. Make it the perfect Aussie meal.'

Miles and Zoe instinctively rolled their eyes.

'Bonza, mate,' Miles said, in an over-exaggerated Aussie accent.

Ben laughed as Sarah stretched her arms overhead and yawned. 'I'm off to bed. I'm exhausted.'

Miles set his beer down. 'Yeah, I'd better go too; I've an early start tomorrow.'

Ben wagged his finger at him. 'And no being late. You're the most senior nurse on the floor tomorrow morning.'

At the announcement, Miles looked shocked, but Zoe noticed a flash of delight pass across his face.

'Righto, boss,' he said nonchalantly, but Zoe could see how much the responsibility meant to him.

Waving goodbye and good nights, Zoe and Ben were finally alone and Zoe could stand the suspense no more.

'Well? How did you get on at the hospital? I've been so worried!'

Ben leaned across the sofa to tuck a stray strand of hair behind Zoe's ear. 'There's nothing to worry about; I'm going to be fine.'

Decades as a nurse meant Zoe's ears pricked up. 'What do you mean, *going* to be?'

There was a pause, before Ben blurted, 'I've got bowel cancer.'

For a moment Zoe thought she hadn't heard him properly. Then the words began to sink in.

'But you said everything was okay?'

'And it will be,' Ben insisted. 'The specialist is hopeful he can remove the lump with a very simple operation. He thinks we've caught it early. I'm going in next week.'

Zoe stared at him for a moment. She felt as if the world was rushing past her and she was struggling to keep up.

'I'll need a few days off to recover, then that's it, I'm good as new,' Ben continued with forced brightness.

As Ben leaned forward to kiss her, Zoe tried to push her fears away. But if life had taught her anything, it was that after a crisis, you were rarely as good as new.

Chapter Twenty-Eight

The smell of freshly cut grass and the warmth in the July air made Zoe smile as she walked towards Ben's house the following evening. It was a far cry from what would be happening in Australia, where everyone would be hunkering down for chillier days.

Much to her astonishment, Zoe had begun to feel homesick. She supposed it shouldn't be that much of a surprise. After all, she had spent well over forty years in the country; it was embedded in her soul. She only felt a pang of nostalgia for her homeland when she spoke to her mother or combed through Facebook and saw photos of her old friends with their kids. Zoe would scan their faces, looking in greedy amazement at the boys Sean had gone to school with, each one looking more manly as they headed into their futures. Zoe still heard from some of these women through social media. Casual messages that always said the same thing. *Can't believe how long it's been. We must catch up.* And finally, the cheery but empty *We all miss you so much.* Zoe didn't often reply. These women weren't really her friends. When Sean died, they had been mysteriously absent, as though the death of a child was catching. In a way, Zoe understood. What had happened to Sean had been a tragedy and she knew these women were thinking, *Thank God it wasn't my child.* Because as terrible as it sounded, she too would be thinking the same if it had been someone else's kid that had been killed.

She wondered what these women would say if she told them about Ben. That she was faced with the prospect of losing someone else she was close to. Would they find this more palatable because it was an adult dealing with a well-known disease? Or would they distance themselves from this too?

Zoe chastised herself. Ben wasn't dying. He was facing something terrible but the prognosis was good. As a nurse she knew the key to successfully recovering from cancer often lay in early diagnosis. Thankfully that was something Ben would benefit from.

Now, as she stood on Ben's doorstep, she was greeted by a beaming Candice.

'Am I glad to see you! Ben is doing my head in.' She let out a loud groan, simultaneously hugging Zoe and pulling her inside in one fluid movement.

'Why?' Zoe giggled, handing her a bottle of red she had stopped off to buy on the way over. 'Will this help?'

Candice kissed the wine and then Zoe. 'I hope so. I'm supposed to be off out but of course, Ben can't get Zoom to work. My brother's a very intelligent man but when it comes to technology, he makes Homer Simpson look bright.'

Sure enough, the filthiest of swear words echoed through the flat. Candice raised an eyebrow, as if to say, *I told you so*.

'Ben,' she shouted. 'Zoe's here, and she doesn't want to hear you effing and jeffing while your relationship's quite this new. At least let the poor girl keep the notion of romance alive for a bit longer, eh?'

'All right, all right,' Ben shouted through the floorboards while Candice gave Zoe a knowing look and a quick wave goodbye. It was all Zoe could do to contain her laughter as she walked into the lounge and saw Ben hunched over his laptop, tapping at the keyboard like a man possessed. There were wires everywhere and bits of paper littering the parquet flooring.

'What is going on?' she asked, taking in the chaos around her.

Ben looked up, a mournful expression on his face. 'I can't get the internet to work. I've got to make this call in a few minutes and I can't without a working sodding laptop!'

'Have you tried resetting the router and switching it off and on again?'

Ben shot her a look so withering Zoe felt as if she had suggested kicking a puppy.

'All right! Have you typed in the diagnostic IP address and logged in to your account?'

The withering look was replaced with one of admiration. 'What language are you speaking, woman?'

Zoe laughed and held her hands out for Ben's laptop. 'I'm saying give it here.'

Within a few taps Zoe had logged in to Ben's Wi-Fi, diagnosed the problem and reset the internet with what appeared, at least to Ben, to be relative ease.

'How did I not know you're an IT genius?' He gasped, gazing at the fully functioning Wi-Fi and back at Zoe.

'There are some things I keep close to my chest.' Zoe leaned back against the sofa. 'You can show your appreciation by getting me a drink.'

Ben got her a drink and joined her. 'I can think of another way of showing you how grateful I am.'

He started kissing her and Zoe reciprocated, feeling hungry for more when Ben sprang back abruptly, a pained expression on his face.

'We've got to make that call,' he said, slightly breathless.

Zoe flashed him a lazy grin. 'Well, I want to finish this conversation later.'

A ripple of shock froze her in place. Never in her life had she felt confident enough to say something like that to a man but Ben was different. He made her feel capable, confident and as though she could be anything she wanted. She leaned over him as he set up the laptop, a sense of satisfaction coursing through her that she had been the one to fix his problems.

'How old is this note?' Zoe asked, as Ben positioned the screen correctly so they could both be seen in the frame.

'Only six months. It was from my last place, but I didn't catch Irene before she left to return home.'

Zoe nodded. That didn't sound too bad. 'And then that's the last of your letters?'

'Aside from the one I can't deliver to Mr Myerson, yes.' Ben rubbed his hands together in glee. 'Then my conscience is clear and it's all down to you.'

Soon a woman about Zoe's age with long blonde hair, tanned skin and a kind smile filled the screen.

'Hi, Irene.' Ben smiled, giving the woman a wave. 'This is my girlfriend, Zoe.'

There wasn't time for Zoe to register surprise at Ben's use of the word 'girlfriend' as Irene started speaking.

'Hi, Ben,' Irene said, returning Ben's wave. 'Great to meet you, Zoe. I hear you come from around here.'

'Sure do. I lived in Mosman for a while, and before that I had a little place not far from the beach.'

Irene clapped her hands together in delight. 'I live near Manly now.'

Zoe looked at the backdrop of the all too familiar coastline behind her. The clouds might have been thick and grey but the beauty of the beach didn't change, no matter the season.

'Wow, that view is incredible,' she said wistfully.

Irene glanced at the window behind her. 'I moved out here a few years ago. Got myself a little place. Beautiful, eh?'

'I used to love it over there,' Zoe said admiringly.

'Mum did too. I was amazed when she said she wanted to go back to England,' Irene said, reaching for a glass of water. 'She moved to Australia in her teens but wanted to see out her days in the UK. I couldn't understand it.'

'It has a certain charm,' Zoe said, her gaze straying between Irene's face and the sight of the beach behind her. The image was so real Zoe could almost smell the tang of the sea air. 'I was sorry to hear about your mum. Breast cancer, right?'

'Yeah, she'd had it years earlier and beaten it. Then the bastard came back.' Zoe saw tears prick Irene's eyes before she plastered on a false smile. 'What's this letter?'

'Straight to the point, eh?' Ben ventured.

'No point being anything else.'

Murmuring his agreement, Ben reached for the envelope and showed it to Irene before gently slitting it open. He pulled out a folded sheet of paper and began to read.

'*Dear Irene*,' he began. '*If you're reading this now then I've passed away and I'm a gutless fool.*'

Ben paused, and Irene and Zoe exchanged a grin. Irene's mother might have been a pom but she was as blunt as a born and bred Aussie.

'*I've been wanting to tell you this for a long time. But the truth of the matter is I was a bloody coward, so I saved it for my deathbed. The fact is your father is not who you thought he was. This will come as a shock, love, but your father is actually Dave McGraw. He knows what I'm doing. He thought it wasn't right I told you like this, but there you go.*'

As Ben read on, Zoe looked at Irene intently. She seemed to be handling the news well. Her face was composed and her breathing steady. Zoe herself had given a letter like this soon after arriving in the UK. However, the news hadn't gone down well as the lad, who was much younger than Irene, had thrown Zoe out of the house.

'Well, thank Buckley's for that,' she said, once Ben finished reading the letter. 'My dad was an old bastard; we never got on.'

'Are you sure you're all right, Irene?' asked Ben gently.

Irene took in a deep breath, her blonde hair blowing across her face thanks to the sea breeze wafting through her window. 'I always knew deep down. Dad left us when we were small but because he kept footing the bill while Mum raised me and my three brothers, I suppose she thought it best to keep quiet.' Irene shook her head and smiled. 'So good old Dave's my dad, eh? Well I never.'

Zoe felt a flash of concern. 'This Dave fella's all right, is he?'

'He's a diamond. Looked in on us after Mum passed. I suppose he's been waiting for me to say something but Ben here took his sweet time about it.'

The flash of guilt that passed across Ben's features wasn't lost on Zoe and she squeezed his hand in support.

'I'm really sorry, Irene,' he said. 'Zoe's been helping me deliver all my late letters.'

Irene waved away his concerns and flashed him a grin. 'You're all right, Ben, I'm teasing. The truth is, I'm stoked. Mum's given me the very best present she could in death.'

With that, Zoe, Ben and Irene exchanged a few more pleasantries before the call ended. As Ben shut the lid of his laptop, he shook his head.

'Do you really think she was all right? She seemed remarkably calm for someone who's just discovered a family friend is actually their father.'

'I think she's fine. I reckon Irene would have said if she wasn't.'

'But she seemed so calm,' Ben reasoned, as he rubbed his chin in thought.

'A bit like someone else I know.'

Ben looked puzzled. 'What do you mean?'

'I mean you told me yesterday you have cancer,' Zoe pointed out gently, 'but you're acting like nothing's happened. Does Candice know?'

'Not yet,' Ben said gruffly. 'I'm just getting my head around it all.'

Rubbing his hands over his face and scalp, he met Zoe's gaze and she saw the determination in his eyes.

'I need to handle this my way. My specialist says I'm going to be fine, the operation should sort it, and I want to leave it at that. I just need space, okay?'

'Okay.' Zoe understood that perhaps the spell from earlier had been broken. 'Perhaps I'll go home tonight, give you a bit of peace.'

When Ben didn't argue, Zoe knew she had said what he wanted to hear. Twenty minutes later she was in the back of a cab, head lolling against the seat. She closed her eyes and thought of the view from Irene's window, the memory of it giving her some unexpected comfort.

Chapter Twenty-Nine

Over the following week, Zoe found she hardly saw Ben. The hospice diary told her he was in and out of meetings or spending much of his time at St Mary's so she tried not to worry. He had also been clear that he wanted space and Zoe knew she needed to respect that. But the notekeeper inside Zoe still wanted Ben to know she was there, so she began to leave letters in his locker.

Last night Lottie asked if I wanted to sleep with the unicorn you gave her because she said I looked like I needed a hug. I miss you but I get why you need to do this your way. Zo x

And later, Ben had replied.

I'm a fool but a fool that's mad about you. xxx

The notes anchored Zoe and a part of her enjoyed the old-fashioned courtship playing out between them. But as well as worrying about Ben, Zoe had found herself thinking a lot about her native Australia since the call to Irene. She found herself recalling happier times, which occasionally meant she thought of David. They had met at Manly Beach when she was twenty. She and her friend Amanda had called in for a drink after their nursing shifts and David had stridden in, all tanned skin and wide smiles. They had locked eyes and the next thing Zoe knew he had set a pint of beer in front of her, making her smile. He was the first guy she had ever known who had correctly guessed what drink she wanted, and all without talking to her.

Most guys assumed she would be a cold white wine sort of girl but David had read her, something he had continued to do throughout their married life until the day everything changed.

It had been over ten days since Sean's birthday and she hadn't heard anything else from David. To her surprise she found herself hoping he was okay and happy. She even wondered if he was dating anyone. The thought was uncomfortable but that wasn't the only reason she was feeling reflective. Today was her forty-fifth birthday and so far she was doing a good job of ignoring it. She'd never been one for celebrations, and now every birthday was a reminder that although she had the luxury of getting older, Sean never would.

After she stuffed her belongings into her rucksack, she swung her bag onto her shoulder, intending to head home and treat herself to a bath, when Ben walked in. She smiled in surprise; it had felt like a lifetime since she had seen him.

Ben grinned. 'You off?'

Nodding, Zoe raked her fingers through her hair. 'It's been a long day.'

'Time for a quick drink?' he asked.

At the question, Zoe paused. She was tired, but she ached to spend time with her boyfriend.

'Just a quick one,' she suggested.

'That's good enough for me.'

Ben reached for her hand and together they walked out of the hospice and into the pub across the road.

The moment Zoe stepped inside, she saw what appeared to be a party in full flow and much to her surprise, several people she knew appeared to have been invited. Sarah was sitting by the bi-folds that opened out onto the beer garden, along with all her friends from work, including hospice director Karen and Indira. Even Candice had joined in, sipping elegantly on a glass of champagne.

'What's all this?' she asked in astonishment.

Ben gave her another of his broad smiles, then broke into song. From behind him, Miles joined in and together the unforgiving strains of 'Happy Birthday' poured through the pub.

'Thank you,' Zoe gasped, when they'd finished. 'How did you know?'

Ben wrapped her in his arms. 'I asked Sarah.'

Zoe looked up at him, aghast. 'You did *what*?'

'Sorry,' he said hurriedly. 'I knew it was sometime in July and I wanted to make the day special for you.'

'You put my best friend on the spot?'

Zoe fixed Ben with what she hoped was her coldest glare, while Miles gazed at the floor, muttering what she thought sounded like, 'Told you not to bother, mate.'

As Ben looked at her with eyes that would rival Lottie's Puss in Boots from *Shrek* impersonation, she turned her gaze towards the mound of cake that stood in the centre of the bar. Lamingtons – her favourite, and judging by the number of them, Ben and Miles had organised several different flavours.

'You did all this?'

'We made them yesterday,' Ben explained. 'Miles helped with the recipe.'

'Wanted to make sure they were authentic,' Miles added gruffly.

Zoe pulled herself free from Ben's grasp and helped herself to one – it was delicious. 'I'm sorry,' she said through a mouthful of cake. 'I don't like making a big deal of my birthday.'

'I wanted to spoil you,' Ben said eagerly.

'And I'm grateful,' Zoe replied, reaching for another cake.

'You sharing those cakes, Zo?' Miles asked hopefully.

'No,' she said hotly, casting her gaze between Ben and Miles. 'They are the only reason I'm forgiving you both for such a gross intrusion into my privacy.'

'Righto.' Miles grinned. 'I'm getting a round in. You want a beer?'

'Shiraz please. Large,' she called to his retreating back. 'I can't believe you did all this.'

'I wanted to see you smile,' Ben said sheepishly. 'You do so much for everyone else. Now it's our turn.'

He leaned forward to kiss her gently on the lips and Zoe felt a fire begin to burn in the pit of her stomach. She had a feeling the real celebrations would be with Ben later when she could truly lose herself in his arms.

Aware she was being rude, she reluctantly freed herself from Ben's embrace and walked towards the table where Miles had thoughtfully placed her wine. As she took a seat next to Sarah, her friend raised her own glass in welcome.

'Can't believe we're actually celebrating your birthday this year.'

'I can't believe you don't bother,' Candice added, overhearing the conversation. 'What's wrong with you, girl? You should celebrate every moment you can on this earth.'

'Something you do without trouble, eh?' Ben remarked drily as he watched his twin help herself to another glass of champagne from the bottle he had bought and left on the table.

Candice gave him a nudge and took a sip. 'What's the point in living if you don't enjoy it while you can?'

With that she poured Zoe a glass of fizz and clinked her own against the rim. 'Now drink up; we're partying.'

For the next couple of hours, Zoe lost herself in the heady laughter of her friends. It wasn't until she was a couple of drinks in and nearly knocked Ben's pint over that she realised she might have had one too many.

Ben reached for her hand and squeezed it. 'I've got a present for you.'

'You mean the party isn't my present?' Zoe asked incredulously.

Shaking his head, Ben reached into the top pocket of his jacket, pulled out a white envelope and handed it to Zoe. She looked at Ben and down at the envelope. There was nothing written on it. Frowning, she sliced the top open, pulled out a sheet of A4 and began to read a booking form for a remote cottage at the peak of the Lizard. The reservation was for a weekend away in three weeks' time.

'You've bought me a weekend away?' Zoe gasped.

'Yes, but I'm hoping you're going to take me!'

'And how did you know I wasn't working or if I had plans?'

'Because I made sure that nobody changed the staffing schedules and I also told Sarah not to rope you into doing anything over that particular weekend.'

Zoe laughed and turned to Sarah.

'Guilty as charged,' her friend admitted.

She turned back to the reservation sheet once more. 'The Lizard, eh?'

'Thought I might kill two birds with one stone,' Ben said casually. 'The Lizard's on my bucket list after all.'

At the mention of the phrase 'bucket list', Zoe tried to push the worries she had about Ben's upcoming operation from her mind. It was in two days' time but she didn't want to spoil tonight by mentioning it. Hopefully by the time they went away Ben would be on the road to recovery and they could look to the future.

'You old romantic.' Zoe gave him a wide smile. 'It sounds gorgeous, and oh my God, it's right by the sea.'

'I do my best,' Ben said, looking embarrassed.

'This is way more than your best; you've nailed it,' Zoe cried, wrapping her arms around him. 'Thank you, honestly, you've made this the best birthday ever.'

Ben tipped his forehead to meet hers. 'Good. Because, Zoe, all I want is to make this birthday and every other perfect for you. I love you.'

The moment those three little words were out in the open, Zoe knew these were the words her heart had been dancing around for weeks. Now here he was bringing them out into the open and she finally felt able to do the same.

'I love you too,' she whispered.

Chapter Thirty

'Zoe, come on, you're going to be late,' Ben called, his voice echoing up the stairs of his flat.

'Coming,' she called, hearing the stomp of footsteps on the stairs.

Whirling around, she saw Ben wearing a nervous but eager smile as he pressed a cup of takeaway coffee into her hand.

'What's this?' she asked, taking the cup.

'Just because I'm nil-by-mouth doesn't mean you should be,' he said. 'Besides, you're going to need your energy if you're covering for me over the next couple of weeks.'

Zoe rolled her eyes at the thought. 'Just when I thought I'd got rid of the pesky job.'

Ben laughed and slid his arms around her waist. 'You love it. But don't get too comfortable.'

'No chance,' she replied. 'Remind me what I'm telling people about your absence.'

'I'm away on a conference. Simon and Karen know the truth but that's it. You know what it's like, the moment you tell someone you've got cancer they look at you differently.'

Ben was right; Zoe had seen it a million times before. Standing on her tiptoes, she kissed him and felt the warmth of his lips flood through her body. This man had changed her life. Zoe wanted to be there for him when his world was temporarily uprooted.

'Are you sure you don't want me to come with you today?' she asked, pulling away.

Ben shook his head and dropped a kiss on her forehead. 'We've been through this. Come see me tomorrow when it's all over. I can't deal with worrying about you too. I just have to get myself through this. You and I are still so new, let's not spoil things with me needing your help just to get to the loo.'

'I want to be there for you…' Her voice trailed off. They had been through this argument regularly in the two days since her birthday.

'You're helping by taking on my job so I don't have much to deal with when I get back,' Ben said firmly.

'All right, but you'll let me know, won't you?' she pressed. 'How it goes.'

'Zoe, Candice will ring you if there's anything urgent, otherwise, I'll see you tomorrow.'

Sensing this was another argument she wasn't going to win, Zoe checked her watch. 'I'm going to be late. What sort of an impression will that make?'

'Not a good one,' Ben said easily. 'See you soon.'

Nodding, she kissed him one final time on the cheek, savouring the familiar scent of aftershave, then walked away. As she reached the doorway, she turned around to look at him one last time. Dressed in tracksuit bottoms and a grey University of Oxford sweatshirt, he looked the picture of health. It was hard to believe he was going to face such a brutal operation and even harder to believe she wasn't going to help him through it.

By the time Zoe arrived at work, she had almost driven herself mad with worry, so it was almost a relief to be distracted by Miles, who was frantically waving at her from the hospice entrance.

'What are you doing?' Zoe asked.

'Looking for you,' he barked. 'I've been running in and out of this doorway for the past ten minutes hoping to find you. People think I've lost my mind.'

'They think that anyway,' she quipped. 'What's the problem?'

'Mrs Harper,' he said, leading her inside. 'She's been asking for you.'

Zoe looked at Miles with concern. 'Why?'

'She was admitted as a permanent resident last night. She's in a bad way.'

Miles handed Zoe Mrs Harper's file and she scanned through the notes of the previous night's shift. Eyesight deterioration, moments of delusion and weakness. The end was coming and Mrs Harper and her son would need to be strong for what lay ahead.

'Right,' she sighed, handing the file back to Miles and scraping her hair back into a ponytail. 'What is it she wants?'

'She says she needs help with something only you can provide,' Miles said as she walked towards Mrs Harper's room.

Feeling bemused, Zoe found the older woman sitting up in bed, stabbing at a sudoku puzzle.

'What's that puzzle ever done to you?' she called cheerfully.

At the sound of Zoe's voice, Mrs Harper looked up and beamed. 'Not so much what this puzzle has done but more what I can do to this puzzle in my brief moment of clarity.'

Zoe smiled supportively. She understood the mildly manic cycle Mrs Harper could be expected to experience.

'Are you comfortable? Anything you need?' Zoe asked, pulling up a chair to sit beside her.

Mrs Harper raised her eyebrows. 'That depends. Have you got a miracle cure up your sleeve?'

'Sorry.' Zoe let out an apologetic sigh. 'Wish I did.'

'I do too, dear,' Mrs Harper said, 'but this isn't your fault, it's this bloody tumour's fault and my own daft body's for not being able to shift it. It's life, or in my case death, I suppose.'

'I'm still sorry I can't do more,' Zoe said, reaching forward to clasp her own hand around the older woman's.

Mrs Harper cleared her throat and put down the magazine. 'Zoe dear, I want to talk to you properly. I know all about your notes. I've even heard you occasionally make videos.'

Zoe laughed as she recalled how a younger patient had asked her to make a TikTok video last week. 'You have to move with the times.'

'Well, don't worry, I don't want anything too technical,' Mrs Harper said. 'I want you to help me write a note.'

Feeling a flush of understanding, Zoe reached for her notepad. 'Of course.'

But as Zoe's pen hovered over her pad, she saw something in Mrs Harper's eyes that told her this note was something different. 'This isn't just a few words for a loved one, is it?'

Mrs Harper shook her head, reached into her bag, which stood on her bedside table, and pulled out a photograph. 'That's my first husband, Alfred, and our son, Nathaniel.'

Zoe stared at the black and white picture of a very tall man holding the hand of an equally tall toddler. Both were standing on a beach, the waves behind them as they beamed into the camera. But there was something about the way the man was looking down at the child as though nothing else mattered. The bond between them was obvious.

'We both adored Nathaniel, from the moment he was born. He was all we could talk about,' Mrs Harper whispered.

'It's a beautiful photo.' Zoe couldn't tear her eyes away from it. She had a similar one of David and Sean when he was about a year old. She had taken it during a family outing to the beach. Zoe had been so keen to capture the moment of David holding Sean, who was gazing adoringly into his father's eyes. The love that radiated between them both had been accidentally, rather than intentionally, captured by Zoe that day. Yet the photo was proof of the happy event between father and son, connected by love, trust and everything in between. Zoe recognised that look between Nathaniel and Alfred. It was priceless and would mean the world to Mrs Harper.

'Nathaniel was five when he died. Drowned with his father in that lake over there.'

Zoe followed Mrs Harper's gaze out of the window towards the calm waters. It was hard to believe the scene held such tragedy.

'There was a boating accident. People used to do that then. Father used to invite friends and family over and they'd mess about in the lake,' Mrs Harper explained. 'Zoe, when I came here, I told you that I used to live in this old house and I hated it. The reason I hated it was because the two people that meant the world to me were killed in a horrible accident.'

Zoe looked at the woman sympathetically. 'I'm so sorry. Does your son know?'

Mrs Harper gave her a watery smile. 'He knows the scant facts. I told him that was why I didn't want to come here.'

'What did he say?' Zoe asked.

'He was sorry,' Mrs Harper said. 'As was I. I should have told him earlier but I couldn't. But coming back here stirred up so many emotions, I had to tell him.'

'I'm sorry.'

'I'm not,' Mrs Harper said. 'I thought being here would be awful but actually it's been the best thing that could have happened. I never made my peace with what happened to Nathaniel and Al, and I've realised being here, living through those memories again, that there is still so much left unsaid.'

'You have some loose ends?' Zoe clarified.

'I suppose I do.'

As Mrs Harper turned to face her, Zoe saw an expression she recognised in herself – one of quiet sufferance, a sense of having to do whatever it took to get through the days ahead.

'I hear your son died, Zoe,' Mrs Harper put in, her tone wary but gentle.

'Where did you hear that?' Zoe asked, more sharply than she had intended.

'One of the nurses mentioned it, I think. Then again, I wasn't sure if it was my tumour playing up again.' She gave a rueful smile. 'I'm sorry if I overstepped.'

'No, it's all right,' Zoe said, her racing pulse beginning to steady. It was true after all. She had lost a child – a child she had loved, adored and been proud to call her son. She looked at Mrs Harper, and a moment of shared understanding passed between them.

Zoe's throat swelled with emotion. 'It's just hard to talk about. It never seems to get any easier.'

'No,' Mrs Harper said sadly. 'It doesn't. How did your son die, if you don't mind me asking?'

'Sean,' Zoe clarified, wanting Mrs Harper to know her son's name. 'He was seven. A hit-and-run.'

'How awful.' A look of regret passed across Mrs Harper's face. 'And your husband?'

Zoe shook her head in a bid to answer Mrs Harper and also to try to stop the tears that were threatening to spill down her face. 'We're not together any longer. It was sort of his fault. He wasn't watching properly.'

Mrs Harper nodded. 'I think I might have felt the same if Alfred hadn't died at the same time. But being here again, I've come to realise all that anger doesn't help. It doesn't do anything for the poor souls you've loved and lost and it certainly doesn't do anything for you, still living with this nightmare. In fact, the only person you're hurting is yourself. That's why I need your help.'

'Of course,' Zoe said.

Mrs Harper took a deep breath. 'My time is almost at an end. I've had a good life. I found love again, went on to have another child, but I always carried that very private pain with me. Now, I want to write a letter to the son I lost. I feel as if I need to let him know that although I carried on living, I never forgot him, that he has always had a place in my heart. Can you help?'

Chapter Thirty-One

The following day, Zoe walked along the stark corridors of Bath's main hospital, wondering why hospitals the world over looked and felt the same. Why was that? Why didn't each hospital celebrate its difference? Probably because personality was the last thing you needed in a place where the focus was dedicated to healing and you certainly didn't want medics distracted.

Reaching Ben's ward, Zoe took a deep breath and composed herself. Although Ben had told her no news was good news, that hadn't stopped her frantically checking her phone every five minutes since the moment she had wished him well. Consequently, she had barely slept the previous night and spent most of the day full of nervous energy. Zoe wouldn't rest until she knew Ben was all right, and the moment it was lunchtime she had rushed to get to the hospital to be by Ben's side. It was only as she saw Candice sitting on a chair in the corridor and took in how broken Ben's twin looked that she paused.

'Candice, are you all right?' she asked cautiously, taking in Candice's appearance. Her usual vibrant self seemed grey and wan. She was dressed in black leggings and a shapeless jumper, and her eyes looked puffy and red raw.

Candice flashed Zoe a thin smile. 'I'm fine. It's been a long twenty-four hours.'

'How is he?' Zoe ventured.

'Fine.' Candice nodded. 'The surgeon said it went well.'

'Oh, thank goodness!'

Zoe knew she had been on edge but had no idea how much until she felt the trickle of relief course through her veins at Candice's words.

'Apparently, they managed to get it all and will assess the margins over the coming days. Hopefully no further treatment will be needed but we'll see.'

'And how's Ben doing in recovery?'

Candice made a face. 'You know my brother. He wants to get home and is making the medical staff miserable, demanding they discharge him.'

'You're not serious.'

'I bloody am,' Candice replied, stifling a yawn. 'And I wouldn't mind but I've been here all night and I really need some sleep. Do you mind if I go?'

'Course not.'

'Thank you.' Candice smiled at her gratefully. 'If I don't go now, I think I'll fall down. See you soon, Zoe.'

After watching Candice stumble down the hallway, Zoe made her way to Ben's bedside. Dressed in the uniform hospital gown, head lying serenely on the pillow, Ben looked as if he were sleeping and Zoe resolved not to stay too long. He needed his rest. Bending down to kiss his forehead, she felt him stir.

'Hello, you,' Ben whispered, trying to open his eyes.

'How are you doing?' she asked, perching on the edge of his bed and slipping her hands around his.

'All right,' Ben said, trying to sit up in bed only for Zoe to press gently on his shoulders to stop him.

'Candice says everything went well.'

Ben nodded sleepily. 'The surgeon's confident.'

Zoe squeezed his hands, relief rippling through her. 'I'm so pleased.'

'Me too,' he murmured. 'I'm just focusing on recovery now.'

'Quite right.' Zoe patted his hand. She couldn't explain how relieved she felt that this nightmare had been short-lived. She was about to say as much when she saw a surgeon walking purposefully towards Ben.

'Is this your specialist?' she said.

Ben nodded again, and silently urged Zoe to help him sit up.

'Do you want me to stay? Candice has gone,' Zoe asked.

'No thanks, Zo, why don't you get on?' Ben said.

Zoe looked at him, perplexed. 'Are you sure? I'm happy to help, ask questions you might not think of, that sort of thing.'

She pulled the sheets up around him and became aware of Ben glaring at her.

'Zoe, don't fuss,' he said gruffly, properly awake. 'It's been lovely to see you but I can handle this. Maybe I'll see you tomorrow.'

Stung, Zoe was about to say something but with the surgeon in spitting distance knew now wasn't the time.

'Sure,' she said instead, kissing him on the cheek.

She walked away. But back in the car as she drove back to work, Zoe had mixed feelings. Naturally, she was thrilled Ben was on track to make a good recovery but equally she felt as if he were pushing her away. She knew he felt their relationship was still so new he didn't want to put extra pressure on it, but she wanted to be there for him. She cared about him; she loved him. That was what made relationships work, wasn't it?

Frustrated, Zoe pulled into a space in the hospice car park, just as her phone began to ring. As she went to answer it, the phone went to voicemail – it was Sarah.

Hi. Can you ring me when you get this?

Pressing dial, Zoe rang Sarah's phone but this time it was her turn to leave a message.

'Hi, Sarah, it's only Zoe returning your call. Try me at work, okay?'

Hanging up, Zoe walked through reception, nodding good afternoon, and exchanging how-are-yous, and went into the staff room. She was just about to get changed when Miles appeared, his eyes brimming with concern.

'You all right?' she asked, shucking off her trainers.

'Fine.'

'You might want to tell your face,' she suggested, not unkindly.

Miles managed a rueful smile. 'That bad, eh?' He ran a hand through his brown locks. 'I guess I've got a couple of things on my mind.'

'Oh?'

'I've been thinking about Sarah. Do you think she might like to come to Oz with me for Christmas? I'm thinking of going home and seeing my folks. Thought it might be nice for her and Lottie to meet the family.'

'Wow. Are things really that serious between you two?' Zoe asked in astonishment.

Miles's expression softened. 'I really like her, Zoe.'

Zoe exhaled. 'I've never known you to be serious with anyone.'

'She's what I want,' Miles said firmly.

'But Christmas is ages away,' Zoe pointed out.

'Not that long if I want to get us some cheaper tickets,' Miles said. 'I was hoping to surprise her with them.'

Zoe frowned. 'But aren't you intending to go back to Oz permanently when your visa runs out?'

'Yes—' Miles began only for Zoe to cut him off.

'Don't you think taking Sarah to Australia is a bit pointless? Sarah's life is in the UK. I don't think she'll want to live in Australia,' Zoe reasoned.

Miles looked at her sulkily. 'Things change. Who knows what the future holds?'

'Well, she's the happiest I've seen her in a long time. Maybe I'm wrong.'

At the statement, Miles's face lit up. 'I hope so.' And then, as an afterthought, he said, 'Oh, almost forgot. There's a bloke looking for you. Says he won't leave till he sees you, seems a bit shirty.'

As she gazed at Miles in surprise, Zoe's phone rang again. Pressing the green button to accept, she said, 'Hang on a minute, Sarah,' down the phone.

'Zoe, wait,' she heard Sarah hiss.

Zoe looked at Miles. 'What bloke? Is he a patient?'

But as the words left her mouth, a tanned, tall man suddenly appeared in the doorway and Zoe felt her blood run dry. It was a man she knew as well as she knew herself and despite the passing of the years, he hadn't changed a bit. Still the same build, still the same lazy smile and still the same ability to make her stomach do cartwheels.

'Zoe,' came Sarah's voice again. 'I've been trying to tell you. David is looking for you.'

As Zoe's eyes met her ex-husband's, she felt shock ripple through her, but eventually managed to say, 'Thanks, Sarah, he's just found me.'

Chapter Thirty-Two

The years seemed to melt away as Zoe gazed at a man who was a perfect stranger and yet as familiar as a favourite pair of shoes. He looked the same as he always had. A little more worn perhaps. Tired, beaten up by life if the lines around his face and the salt and pepper around his temples were anything to go by. But the sparkle in his olive eyes, the way his lips turned up at the corners as he drank her in and the way he carried himself – upright and proud as if the world were still at his feet – that was all the same.

Zoe had a strange compulsion to run and hug him tight, but stopped herself. Instinct could be powerful. But David had been her best friend and confidante for so long, it felt unnatural not to hold him as she had done for over twenty years.

'David,' she managed. 'What a surprise.'

'Yeah, I'll bet,' David said with a grin before tuning to Miles, who was looking at the pair of them, agog. 'Clear out a minute would you, mate?'

Miles needed no further encouragement. 'Righto.'

He scuttled out of the room and shut the door firmly behind him. Zoe smiled. Miles hated domestic arguments and despite his love of gossip, the relief of not being a part of something this awkward would outweigh that desire.

'Shit, Zo, you haven't changed a bit,' David said with an appreciative sigh as he set his bag on the floor and looked her up and down.

Zoe felt wrong-footed, the memory of how she had just left Ben's hospital bedside distorting her feelings.

'Why are you here?' she asked, ignoring the compliment.

David rubbed his face. The days-old stubble made him look even more tired, she thought, wondering when he had arrived.

'I needed to see you,' David said, taking a step towards her. 'After I sent you that letter about filing for divorce, I felt it wouldn't be right to finish things without seeing you in person so I've brought details of the proposed settlement with me.'

Zoe gaped at him. David had always been a decent man, but she didn't think that extended to flying across to the other side of the world to draw a line under things. What was he really here for?

'I'm not here to cause trouble, if that's what you think,' David put in. 'I thought it best to sort this out in person. I figured we at least owed each other a proper chat.'

'Right.' Zoe took a seat on the wooden bench that stood in the middle of the room and gathered her thoughts. 'When did you get here?'

'Last night,' he said, in his broad Antipodean accent. 'Got the train from Heathrow and went round to your place first thing this morning but your housemate said you'd left for work.'

'Where are you staying?'

'Got a place in Bristol. Bath was a rip-off,' David replied, sitting on the bench beside her.

The familiarity of his scent, a hint of gasoline mixed with washing powder, caught her off guard. Zoe closed her eyes, transported back to a time and a place when she thought life was mapped out.

'You always did like to watch the cents,' she said, opening her eyes.

'Nothing wrong with that,' David said, with a good-natured shrug.

'Which is why it's a bit of a surprise you've flown all this way,' Zoe said, trying to steady her jangling nerves. 'If I'm honest I'd been expecting you to start proceedings a lot earlier.'

David nodded. 'Why didn't you do it?'

'I dunno. Guess I couldn't quite bring myself to. It's hard to say goodbye after we spent so long together, shared a life, a family...'

Her voice trailed off as she thought of Sean and her gaze rested on the floor.

'We were happy, weren't we?' David ventured hesitantly. 'Once upon a time.'

Zoe felt uncomfortable. David had no right to show up like this unannounced. Her work was her safe place and she didn't want it invaded by her past. Getting to her feet, she gave David a tight smile that didn't reach her eyes.

'I really must get to work. I'm already late.'

David stood up, his six-foot frame towering over her. 'Yeah, all right. I only wanted to let you know I was here. What time do you finish? I'll wait for you.'

Panic began to rise. She wasn't ready for this. 'I'm working a double tonight,' Zoe lied. 'How about I call you tomorrow?'

'Yeah, okay,' David said agreeably. 'I'll see you, Zo.'

And with that he picked up his bag and walked out of the door, whistling as he went, leaving Zoe feeling as if she had just stepped off a roller coaster.

-

For the first time in almost all her working life, Zoe's mind wasn't on the job that day. She spent much of her time staring at the computer screen pretending to deal with admin but her mind was fixed on David. Her ex turning up at work had merely brought home the truth that it wasn't possible to ever really escape your past and that she had been running on borrowed time.

'Earth to Zoe,' boomed a gravelly voice, causing her to jerk her head upright in surprise.

Seeing Miles leaning over the nurses' desk, she clutched her chest, heart pounding. 'Jesus, you nearly gave me a heart attack.'

Miles laughed and Zoe noticed that he had shaved off his beard. 'When did you do that?' she asked, gesturing at his chin.

'Last week,' he said, stroking his smooth cheekbones.

'Last week,' she echoed with a shake of her head. She had been so wrapped up in herself she hadn't even noticed.

'Only just realised, hey?' he said in a gentle voice.

'No, I...' she began, then stopped. She didn't want to tell more lies. 'It suits you, makes you look more together.'

Miles nodded, a small blush creeping up his neck. 'Yeah well, Sarah prefers the smooth look.'

'That right?' Zoe said with a smile. 'All this for Sarah, huh?'

'Not all,' Miles said quickly, his brows furrowing in earnestness. 'I mean, some...'

As his voice trailed off, Zoe shook her head affectionately. 'I think it's great.'

'Yeah?' There was a hint of unease in Miles's voice.

'Yes.' Zoe looked at him properly. Miles wasn't bad looking, she realised. In fact, she might even go as far as to say he was handsome. 'Anyway, I'm sure you didn't want to talk about your beard or lack of,' she said.

'No, but it's nice to get a compliment instead of the usual stick you give me.' He chuckled briefly before his expression became grave. 'I wanted to see if you were okay, after earlier.'

'Oh, David,' Zoe muttered in a low voice as Indira scuttled past, giving them both a sideways look. 'Yeah, I'm fine. I mean, it was a surprise.'

'I'll bet. Can't say I'd be too stoked about an ex flying thousands of miles to track me down.'

That uncomfortable feeling returned. Zoe didn't want to talk about this here. 'No, it's a surprise but I'm getting my head around it.'

Miles looked at her doubtfully. 'You sure?'

'I'm sure,' Zoe said a little more forcefully than she might have intended. 'Now, did you want me for something else?'

At the question Miles looked blank for a second before he remembered. 'Oh yeah. We've got a new admit coming. Youngish woman in her late forties. Terminal cancer. Can you get her settled? It's delicate because she's got no family.'

Zoe raised an eyebrow. 'Nobody?'

'That's what St Mary's told me,' Miles said as he handed over the file. 'She's been going there as a day patient but they're too full with permanent admits. Now we're all one big happy family...'

'She's coming here instead,' Zoe finished, as she opened the file.

Rebecca Nyborg, forty-one, the file read. A former Danish ballet dancer with end-stage bone cancer. She had been through the rigours of chemo and radiotherapy but the cancer had advanced regardless.

Zoe continued to read the additional notes St Mary's had included. No husband or wife, no children and estranged from a mother who lived in London. She had a friend that occasionally dropped in, the file continued, but since Rebecca's health had deteriorated, she had asked them to stop coming.

Sorrow built like cement in the pit of Zoe's stomach. This was terrible. Every patient that came through those doors deserved to have the best end possible, and she found it hard to believe that self-imposed isolation was the best option.

'When is Ms Nyborg due in?' Zoe asked, snapping the file shut.

'Anytime now.'

Zoe nodded, already feeling fired up with a desire to do what she did best. 'I'll get everything in order, thanks, Miles.'

Miles smiled in reply. 'I knew you would. Thanks, Zoe.'

As Miles walked away, Zoe heard the familiar rumble of the ambulance pulling into the car park. She wasn't sure why this admission was different to any other, but the idea of this woman cutting herself off from everyone she loved and having nobody around her at the end troubled Zoe for reasons she didn't care to admit.

Chapter Thirty-Three

'I think that's everything,' Zoe said, as she finished helping settle Rebecca into her room. 'Can I get you anything else, Ms Nyborg? A cup of tea maybe?'

At the suggestion, the former ballet dancer brightened. 'That's the best offer I've had all day. And please, not Ms Nyborg, I feel like my mother. I'm Rebecca. If I'm dying here, I want to be on a first-name basis with you at least.'

Zoe felt a stab of affection for her patient and smiled. 'Give me five minutes and I'll be right back.'

'Before you do, can I give you something?'

As Zoe looked at Rebecca propped up against the pillows, she could see the effort of the day beginning to take its toll. When Rebecca had first emerged from the ambulance, Zoe had been surprised at how well she looked. Rebecca had been smiling and joking with paramedics as they brought her inside and had gushed over the beauty of the gardens. Now, as she looked at her new patient, Zoe saw a woman who was genuinely frightened of whatever lay ahead.

'Okay.'

Rebecca handed her a small sheet of paper.

'What's this?'

'A list of people to contact when I die,' Rebecca said brusquely.

Zoe fixed her eyes on the list. There were five names written down in a careful hand, each with a phone number and address next to it. One stood out – Pernille Nyborg, with a London address. Could this be Rebecca's mother?

'Would you like me to contact any of them and let them know you're here?'

Rebecca gave a brief shake of her head. 'No, they're mainly all ballet friends, busy at the moment touring. They haven't got time to come and see me.'

'I'm sure they would if they knew you were here,' Zoe tried again.

The dancer's face hardened. 'No. I mean it. Nobody on that list is to be contacted until I die.'

The last thing Zoe wanted was to upset Rebecca and so she simply nodded and put the note in Rebecca's file. 'Of course. Now relax, and I'll be right back with that tea.'

But as Zoe left the room, her mind was whirring. She didn't want Rebecca to die alone, and she couldn't believe Rebecca truly wanted that either. As she waited for the kettle to boil, she thought about the pack of notecards in her bag. Rebecca might not want anyone to know she was dying, but Zoe was sure she could be encouraged to at least leave a few final words for those she was leaving behind.

-

Back at home after her shift, Zoe walked into the little terrace exhausted. Thoughts of David and Rebecca had been swirling around her mind all day. Now, as she entered the living room, she saw that as well as the TV for company, Sarah also had Miles beside her. Zoe's heart sank; she had hoped to have Sarah to herself for the night. She smiled at them both, about to beat a hasty retreat when Sarah caught sight of her.

'Zoe! Are you all right?' She got to her feet and rushed towards Zoe, arms outstretched.

Zoe sank gratefully into her friend's arms as Miles slipped out of the room and into the kitchen, and she felt a flash of love for her friend's consideration. She needed Sarah's counsel.

'I'm fine,' Zoe murmured into her friend's shoulder. In this moment with her friend's arms around her, Zoe felt as if she could relax for the first time all day.

'It's been a bit of a day.'

'I'll say,' Sarah said, pulling back to look at Zoe. 'I'm so sorry I couldn't reach you before David turned up at the hospice. I was trying hard to warn you.'

'It's fine.' Zoe smiled miserably. 'It's all just come as a surprise.'

'Tell me everything,' Sarah insisted, pulling her onto the sofa. 'Why is David here?'

'He says he wants to sort out the details of our divorce settlement. Thought it best to do it in person and wants to say goodbye I suppose, closure or something.'

'Makes sense.'

'I feel unprepared. He was the last thing I was expecting, especially after…'

Zoe's voice trailed off as she gazed at the floor. She had promised she wouldn't say a word to anyone about Ben's condition but after the day she had endured it felt like too much of a burden to keep it to herself any longer.

Sarah leaned forward and rested her warm hand on Zoe's knee. 'Especially after what?'

Lifting her chin, Zoe met Sarah's eyes, which were brimming with concern. 'If I tell you something, can you keep it to yourself?'

'Of course.'

'You can't tell anyone. Especially not Miles.'

'Okay,' Sarah said slowly. 'Zoe, what is this? You're scaring me.'

'It's Ben,' Zoe admitted, in a whisper. 'He's got bowel cancer.'

Sarah's hands flew to her mouth. 'Oh Zoe! I'm sorry. Is he going to be all right?'

'I don't know, I hope so,' Zoe cried, voicing her fears for the first time since Ben's diagnosis. 'He went into hospital yesterday for an operation. They think they've got it early.'

Sarah rested a hand on her heart and exhaled. 'Oh, thank goodness. Poor Ben, he kept that quiet.'

'He doesn't want anyone to know, especially at work, so please don't say anything.' Zoe repeated her warning.

Sarah made a zipping gesture across her lips. 'Don't worry, I won't say anything. Did Ben have anyone with him?'

'Candice. He thought it best that way,' Zoe replied, doing her best to keep the hurt out of her voice.

'Have you seen him since?'

'Lunchtime. He seemed all right but I wasn't there for long,' Zoe said flatly.

'I expect he was tired,' Sarah assured her. 'Having an op really takes it out of you.'

'No, it was more that he didn't want me to talk to his surgeon,' Zoe explained, feeling like a sullen teenager as she curled her legs up beneath her.

'I'm sure that wasn't it,' Sarah admonished.

'It felt like he didn't want me there, Sarah,' Zoe wailed. 'He said he didn't want me to be his nurse, that our relationship was still so new it wasn't right for me to get bogged down in something like this so quickly.'

'I agree,' Sarah said matter-of-factly as she leaned back against the sofa. 'You've only been together five minutes and he probably knows how fragile you are after Sean.'

Zoe's nostrils flared. 'I'm not fragile.'

'I think anyone who's lost a child has a right to be fragile,' Sarah said gently. 'Ben's obviously trying to keep you from any more hurt.'

'But I wouldn't be hurt!'

'Zoe, Ben doesn't want his cancer to define your relationship, which is what will happen if you take over and start nursing him. He doesn't want a nurse, he wants a girlfriend, so respect that.' Sarah was uncharacteristically sharp and for a moment Zoe struggled to think.

First Ben, then Rebecca. All Zoe wanted to was help them, but she hadn't pushed Rebecca to do something the moment she said no and she shouldn't treat Ben any differently.

'You're right.' Zoe groaned. 'I ought to be happy; this is good news. Ben's going to be all right.'

'And I imagine you might be feeling a bit happier than you do now if your ex hadn't suddenly turned up,' Sarah ventured.

'It's totally thrown me. This day has been a nightmare.'

'Some days are like that,' Sarah said. 'But it's probably a good thing David's here.'

'How do you work that out?'

'Like he says, this is finally a chance for you to have closure. Shut one door before you open another.'

'It's a long way to come just for that. Why couldn't he have video-called me?'

'Probably because he knew you wouldn't pick up,' Sarah countered and Zoe winced at the truth in that statement. 'Look, this is hard and you're going to have all sorts of weird feelings about this. But you and David, whether you like it or not, have a lot to talk about. You need to forgive him for what happened to Sean—'

'I will never forgive him,' Zoe said firmly.

Sarah raised an eyebrow. The sounds of Lottie and Miles talking in the kitchen were clearly audible. Zoe cocked an ear; it was long past the child's bedtime. It sounded like she wanted a glass of water and Miles was pretending to hand her a gin and tonic. Despite her tiredness, she laughed.

'Miles has got a way with kids, hasn't he?'

Sarah laughed. 'For a single bloke he's surprised me. Lottie seems to have really taken to him.'

'I'm pleased.'

'And I would be pleased if you could forgive David. Let's face it, as parents we've all taken our eye off the ball for a couple of seconds, and I know,' Sarah continued hurriedly, sensing Zoe was about to protest, 'that this is different. That this isn't letting your child have one too many ice creams, that the mistake he made cost Sean his life, but Zoe, all this hate you're carrying around is only hurting you.'

'I want to forgive him but I can't,' Zoe said quietly. 'Every time I try, I remember Sean lying dead in the hospital and this need to blame David consumes me.'

There was a silence between them and Zoe's gaze turned to the window. The sky was that lovely bluey-ink colour, as if a fountain pen had spilled its contents across the sky. Another day over with, another day without her child survived.

'I think you need to talk to David about Sean once and for all,' Sarah said, wrenching Zoe from her thoughts. 'It's only by facing those demons from your past that you'll be able to find the love and happiness I know is in your future.'

Chapter Thirty-Four

Sarah's words continued to whirl around Zoe's mind during her shift the following day. Was facing the past the only way to find a happy future? Was that even what she truly deserved? Zoe was no closer to answers when her phone rang. Reaching into the pocket of her scrubs to silence the vibrating mobile, she saw a name flash across the screen – David.

'You'd better get it,' said Miles, who was helping with the routine drug count. 'The sooner you get this sorted, the better.'

As Miles walked away to give Zoe some privacy, she felt a fresh wave of irritation towards her ex-husband.

'Hi,' she said after picking up the phone.

'Hi, Zo.' His voice sounded familiar. 'I wondered if we could talk today?'

Zoe sighed. She had so much to do. She wanted to chat to Rebecca about the idea of leaving a note. And then there was Ben. She had hoped to go and visit him later on. But Miles's parting words echoed in her mind and she knew he was right as she said, 'I'm doing a half day, so could meet you just after noon?'

'Great,' David said and Zoe could hear the cheeriness in his voice. 'Shall I come to you? We could grab a bite at the pub across the road from the hospice.'

The last thing she wanted was hospice gossip flying around.

'No, how about I come over to Bristol after work? I can probably get to you for about one if we meet by the harbour,' Zoe suggested.

'That works,' David said, the warmth in his voice never wavering. 'Message me when you're nearby. Looking forward to it.'

'Yes, see you then,' Zoe said, unable to echo her ex-husband's sentiments.

-

It didn't take long to reach Bristol. In fact, Zoe thought, as she stepped off the bus, she could have done with it taking a bit longer as it felt like an aviary had set up residence in her stomach. Trying to distract herself from the fluttering sensation, Zoe instead focused on the city's architecture. She didn't get a chance to visit as much as she liked but it was a perfect spot for a visitor and she had a feeling Bristol, with its mix of bohemian culture, history and business savvy, would be just the right city to catch David's interest. As she walked down towards the belly of the harbour, she took in his familiar shape. David was peering at the sign that proudly told visitors that during the global race protests, this was where protestors had thrown the statue of the city's notorious slave trader, Edward Colston, into the water. David had always been interested in history and Zoe knew he would find this particular spot at the water's edge fascinating. As if sensing her presence, David picked that moment to swing around and face her. He smiled and gave her a wave, and Zoe was amazed at the effect his smile still had on her as she found herself unwillingly returning it.

'You been waiting long?' she asked, walking towards him.

'Nah, only got here a couple of minutes ago. I've been sightseeing all morning. It's incredible, the history here; you just don't get that at home, do you?'

'It's certainly different,' Zoe said, conscious not to forget her native homeland's aboriginal roots, 'but I suppose our culture is so wound up in English history sometimes it seems as though we're forever bound.'

David laughed. 'You said "our". That means you're still an Aussie true blue at heart, eh?'

Zoe ignored him and instead gestured for David to follow her to the nearby pub she had picked out.

'What are you having?' Zoe asked as they went inside, only for David to shake his head.

'I'll get these,' he said firmly before addressing the barman. 'I'll have a lime and soda water, mate. Zoe?'

Zoe looked at him in surprise. He usually always ordered a beer, no matter where they were or what time of day it was. A soft drink was unheard of. She shook her head, aware that David was looking at her expectantly. 'I'll have an orange juice, thanks,' she said, keen to keep a clean head.

'Expected me to have a cold one, eh?' David said as they found a table near the window.

Zoe nodded as she pulled up a chair.

'Gave up drinking soon after you left,' David said. 'Realised it wasn't doing me any good, drinking for the wrong reasons, you know, especially after Sean...'

As his voice trailed off, Zoe recognised where he was going with that sentence. She too recognised the pain of just saying the words aloud that their son was dead. They may be only words, but they could wound as brutally as the collision that took Sean's life.

The thought of the person behind the wheel of that car never failed to make the anger inside her swell. The worst part of it all had been that whoever had killed her son had never faced justice. It seemed remarkable in this day and age with social media, cameras and smartphones that the BMW who hit Sean was never found.

An awkward silence was forming across the table. 'I know,' she said, feeling clumsy that there was nothing better to say.

'Do you think if they'd caught the bastard that did it, you'd have forgiven me?'

Zoe let out a breath she hadn't realised she'd been holding. She had asked herself that question many times and each time her answer had always been the same.

'No,' she replied, watching David's face fall.

'Will you ever forgive me?' he asked quietly.

'I don't think so.' Zoe's voice was quiet but firm. 'It's not that I don't want to. But I think too much has happened. After we lost Sean, I would think how I trusted you to look after the most precious person in my life and how you broke that trust.'

'It was an accident, Zoe, a horrible, horrible accident.' David leaned across the table, tears forming in his eyes. He wiped them away hurriedly with his palms and gave her a weak smile. 'You made it clear in the weeks that followed Sean's death you couldn't forgive me, but you do know I've never forgiven myself, right?'

Despite Sarah's insistence that Zoe needed to face her demons, she wasn't sure she had the stomach for it now. 'Naturally.'

David gave a watery grin and she looked at him in confusion. 'What?'

'You sound so English,' he said, taking a long sip of his drink. 'I never would have thought you would have become such a refined Englishwoman. What happened to the Aussie girl I knew and loved?'

Despite the situation, Zoe found herself laughing. 'People change; I feel at home here. England understands me in a way Australia didn't. That said, the English winters aren't for everyone.'

David shuddered at the thought. 'I couldn't stick it; I dunno how you can.'

'You get used to it,' she lied, stirring her drink with a straw. An image of the winters back in Sydney came to mind. The climate had always been fairly Mediterranean and spring-like. When the weather got a bit chilly, she would think nothing of reaching for a light jacket back in her hometown or snuggling around a lit fire you didn't really need.

And there, just like that, was that feeling of homesickness once again. Zoe was about to say as much when her stomach gave out a loud rumble. She hadn't eaten anything before she left work. Her eyes roamed over the paper menu in front of her and she licked her lips as she caught the immortal words *fish and chips* – a classic English dish and the perfect antidote to any feelings of longing for her homeland.

'Hungry?' David asked, catching the gesture. 'I'm starving but didn't know if you had to get back.'

Where was the harm in sharing a meal with her ex?

'Yeah, all right,' she said. 'What do you want? My treat.'

'I'll take the superfood salad,' David said. Zoe's jaw dropped open in shock only for him to cackle with laughter. 'Just kidding. I might not drink any more, Zoe, but that's the only thing that's changed. I'll have a burger – bloody!'

Zoe scooped up the menus and ordered at the bar. Her eyes caught the rows of wine bottles that lined the shelves behind the barman. Just because David wasn't drinking didn't mean she couldn't; besides, she needed something to calm her nerves.

Returning to the table with a large glass of pinot for her and another lime and soda for David, she set a bowl of peanuts on the table just as he finished a call.

'Sorry, I didn't mean to interrupt,' Zoe said, setting the glasses down, taking care not to spill her unfinished orange juice.

David waved her apology away. 'You didn't. It was only a work call, nothing important.'

'How is the garage?'

'Fine. We've opened another branch on the other side of the city.'

'Wow.' Zoe smiled with pleasure for him. 'I had no idea.'

'Why should you? We haven't spoken in over two years,' David said bluntly, raising his glass aloft. 'But enough of that; here's to the future.'

Zoe clinked her own glass against his. Perhaps Sarah was right, maybe David being here was a good thing.

'I can't believe Ed's a father now,' Zoe exclaimed, taking a slug of her second glass of wine.

David gave a proud smile. 'Yep, my nephew is a dad and all before he's twenty.'

'What did your mum say? Bet she wasn't pleased.'

At the mention of David's mother, Elizabeth, they both raised a knowing smile. Elizabeth had strongly objected to Zoe and David living with one another before they got married, saying it showed a lack of morals. She had come around eventually, but had refused to visit them in their tiny Sydney apartment for at least a year, which Zoe had considered an unexpected bonus.

'She took it in her stride,' David said with a smirk, before adding, 'She misses you, you know. Always asks if I've heard from you.'

Zoe twirled her finger around the stem of her wine glass. Mumford and Sons was echoing across the bar. 'I never thought I'd say this but I miss her too. I miss everyone actually,' she said, and to her surprise found that she meant it.

A flash of hope sparked in David's eyes. 'Does that mean you'll come back one day?'

'No,' she said firmly. 'My life is here now.'

'Not even for a visit?'

'It's such a long way…' Then Zoe laughed as she realised David had only days ago made the trip.

'It's the other side of the world, not another planet,' David said softly. He reached for her hand and Zoe went to pull away but David held on to it, his calloused hand warm against her skin. 'I didn't come all this way just to sort our divorce, Zoe, I came to see if you'd think about coming home and giving our life together another shot. I know we've been through hell and back, but we were together before Sean came along and we loved each other. Surely we can do that again?'

The blood pumped furiously around her veins and for a moment she imagined what it would be like if she said yes. Her mum would be delighted, and so would Elizabeth. But what about Zoe? Could she return to her nursing job? Go back to the same house, see Sean's old bedroom turned into a gym?

And that was the undoing. The moment her son entered her head, she knew going back to David and her old life wasn't an option.

She shook her head. 'It's over, David. You and I are different people now. We share a history and it's time to leave that in the past.'

'Is that why you won't come back, Zo? Because of Sean?' David blurted, furious tears pooling in his eyes. 'You know how much I wish I could change things. It broke me when Sean died, but when you left, I felt as if I'd died right along with our son. Do you know the hell I've been through since you went? My entire family gone in less than a month.'

Zoe looked at him, her hand still resting in his. His face was puce as tears spilled down his cheeks and he wiped them away angrily with his free hand. For the first time since she'd left, Zoe felt a stab of guilt. She had never once thought about what her departure would mean for David. She had been too busy hating him.

'I'm sorry,' she whispered. 'I was devastated when Sean died; I wasn't thinking. I didn't handle it well.'

David took his hand away and rested it underneath his other forearm. 'No, Zoe, I'm sorry. I shouldn't have said all that.'

'You were right to say it.' Zoe took a deep breath. She wanted to be strong for this conversation; it had been coming for a long time. 'I couldn't forgive you but I should have at least told you I was leaving. I should perhaps have at least tried to forgive you.'

At the last few words, David looked up, that spark of hope in his eyes again. 'Do you think there's any way you could forgive me now?'

Slowly she shook her head. 'I'm sorry.'

There was another silence before David spoke; this time his voice was almost timid. 'And all this has got nothing to do with that bloke you've been hanging about with? That nurse or whatever from your Instagram posts you're always tagging each other in?'

Another wave of guilt washed over Zoe. Ben wasn't the only reason she couldn't go back to David, but he was a compelling reason to stay in Britain. She looked at her ex-husband. They had once meant the world to one another and she didn't want to hurt him any more than she had to, but equally she didn't want to lie.

'No,' she said truthfully. 'He's been a great support to me recently but he's not the reason I won't come back. We're over, David, I'm sorry.'

As Zoe finished speaking, David took another slug of his drink and winced. 'Christ, I wish that was beer.'

Zoe laughed. David had always known how to break the tension. At the sound, he set his glass down on the table and smiled. Then, he reached into his backpack and pulled out a large white envelope. When he slid it across the table, she saw her name emblazoned across the top in a thick black typeface. The butterflies in her stomach returned.

'Are those the settlement papers?'

David nodded. 'Go through them properly. I hope I've been fair but in all honesty, Zoe, nothing in here really matters. Have whatever you like; all I want is for you to be happy.'

Zoe reached for the envelope. It was thicker than she'd expected. 'Thank you.'

David drained his drink. 'I guess I'll get going.'

'Oh.' Zoe felt a jolt of surprise. 'Already?'

'Yeah, I booked a tour of one of the museums. Plus, I'm sure you need to recover if you worked a double last night.'

'Right,' Zoe said, feeling off balance. 'When do you want me to get these back to you? When are you leaving?'

'Not until Wednesday,' David said. 'I couldn't stay away too long; the business needs me.'

'Of course.'

'You can mail those back to me or my solicitor, it's fine,' David said, getting to his feet. He reached for his bag, slung it over his shoulder and smiled. 'I'm glad you're getting your life together, Zoe.'

There was a silence as it hit her this was probably the last time she would ever see David again. This was really it.

'What will you do now?' she asked at last.

David shrugged. 'Do a bit of sightseeing and go home. Start again, like you have.'

He leaned in to kiss her cheek and as she caught that familiar scent that was uniquely David, she felt a tug at her heart. He pulled away and said goodbye, and Zoe watched him walk out of the pub. Once he had gone, Zoe sat for a moment and began to flick through the settlement documents. On the last page, she saw a handwritten note stuck to the top.

Zoe, sign this and make this new start official. It's time but know I'll always love you. David xx

The tears she had tried to keep at bay coursed down her face as she thought of her ex and the sadness he had endured after she left. She thought of Ben lying in a hospital bed recuperating, of Sarah and Miles at the beginning of something very special. She thought of Rebecca, getting ready to say goodbye. Change, whether good or bad, was inevitable. Gazing down at the papers, she saw the space left for her to sign her name and ran her finger across it. Her demons felt as if they had been laid halfway to rest; perhaps that was good enough for her to start again.

Chapter Thirty-Five

Despite the fact it had rained almost constantly in the four days since Zoe had met up with David, she was, to her surprise, beginning to feel more hopeful about life.

It helped that Ben seemed to be getting on well in hospital too. He had taken to pestering doctors with constant questions and Zoe took it as a sign he was firmly on the mend.

She had promised him and Candice that she would visit after her shift. Poor old Candice had taken on a huge amount, looking after him the way she had, sitting by his bedside day after day. It would be a lot for her to deal with both physically and emotionally going forward. And despite Ben's continued protests that his sister was great at compartmentalising, Zoe could see that Candice was exhausted.

As she dumped her bag in the staff room and began sorting through the stuff she needed for the day ahead, Zoe resolved to try to take more of the strain when Ben was discharged.

'You look deep in thought,' a gravelly voice boomed.

'Miles, hey.' She beamed. 'How are you going?'

'All right,' he said, rubbing at his chin, seeming surprised his beard still wasn't there. 'Had a rough shift. I need a kip.'

Zoe frowned. 'Anything I need to know?'

Shucking his trainers off, Miles thought for a moment. 'Mr Henshall passed away, you know, the old guy with Alzheimer's. And that new girl Rebecca's deteriorating pretty fast.'

At the news, Zoe's face crumpled. 'Oh no. How is she?'

Miles grimaced. 'Not good. I don't know how much longer she's got, to be honest. She had a difficult couple of hours at about one this morning. She's zonked out on morphine.'

'Was she still insisting she doesn't need anyone?'

'That's the size of it,' Miles said, stifling a yawn as he reached into his locker for a jacket. 'Dunno if you can work your magic when she wakes; it might be too late.'

'I guess there's only one way to find out.'

Saying goodbye to Miles, Zoe walked towards Rebecca's room and heard the sound of someone quietly moaning. Gingerly, she pushed the door open and saw the woman lying in bed crying. Zoe's heart went out to her as she padded to Rebecca's bedside.

'Are you all right?'

'Ffffine,' the woman whispered.

'Are you in pain?'

'No more than usual.'

Zoe glanced carefully at the woman. Her eyes were red and swollen from crying, making her pale skin appear even more thin and translucent than it was when she had been admitted. She reached for Rebecca's hand, noticing straight away how cold it was.

'What can I do for you?' Zoe asked carefully.

At the question, Rebecca closed her eyes, almost as if the effort of having to answer would break her. For a split second, Zoe wondered if she had gone, but the rasping, shallow breaths told her Rebecca was still holding on.

'My mum,' she croaked. 'I want my mum.'

Zoe's mind went straight to the list of names Rebecca had given her on her arrival.

'Do you want me to ring her?'

'Yes,' Rebecca whispered, the effort clearly costing her.

'Okay, I'll phone her.' Zoe laid her hand on Rebecca's for a moment, wanting to reassure her that she wasn't alone.

'She might not come,' Rebecca rasped, her eyes filling with a fresh round of tears. 'The last time we spoke... things... not nice things...'

Zoe squeezed her hand again. 'You rest and don't worry about that. We all say things to our families we don't mean.'

'But I haven't spoken to Mum in ten years,' Rebecca said with a sudden burst of energy. 'She doesn't know I'm sick.'

Zoe thought for a moment. What would she want to say to Sean? If, heaven forbid, they'd had ever fallen out, would it matter in this moment? Zoe knew that it wouldn't.

'She's your mum; she loves you. All she'll want is to be by your side.'

'She might not.' Rebecca sobbed, as if she were no more than a child who had banged their knee after a playground fall.

'Rebecca, I'm a mum,' Zoe said gently, 'and I can tell you that if you were my child there would be nothing you could have said to me that would keep me from being with you. Let me call her.'

The emotional effort of asking for what she wanted seemed to have taken a toll on Rebecca and she slipped into a quiet but deep sleep. Zoe watched her chest rise and fall, glad that the young woman was no longer in distress. She squeezed Rebecca's hand again, then reached for the extra blanket at the foot of the bed, carefully tucking it around Rebecca's tiny frame.

Zoe felt pleased she could help. All she had wanted to do since Rebecca had arrived at the hospice was help this woman have a good death, a death with love at the very heart of it. But having dialled the number Rebecca had listed for her mother, she let out a groan of frustration when the answering machine kicked in.

'This is Pernille Nyborg. You know what to do,' the sing-song voice answered.

After the beep, Zoe left the message she never liked to leave. 'Mrs Nyborg, my name is Zoe Evans, senior staff nurse at The Oaks hospice in Bath. Your daughter Rebecca is with us and she's asking for you. I wonder if you could call me back as soon as you can. Many thanks.'

Rattling off the hospice's phone number before she hung up, Zoe walked back to Rebecca's room and found the woman slipping in and out of sleep.

'Is she coming?' Rebecca murmured.

Zoe crouched beside her and stroked the soft hair away from her head. 'Yes, Rebecca, don't worry, she's coming.'

At the news, Rebecca blinked her eyes open and the delight that shone in them was unmistakeable. 'Is she really?'

'Yes, she's getting the first train she can.'

While Zoe hated lying to her patients, she knew that if she told Rebecca her mother hadn't answered the phone that would only lead to more distress.

Standing up, Zoe felt the familiar rustle of the notepad she kept in her trouser pocket. Walking around to the foot of Rebecca's bed, she reached for the chart that was attached to it. The notes made for distressing reading. Rebecca really didn't have long left and Zoe wasn't entirely sure that Mrs Nyborg would arrive in time. Thinking of her notepad, she knew with a heavy heart there was only one thing to do.

'Rebecca,' Zoe said carefully as she replaced the clipboard. 'Would you like to leave a note for your mum? Just in case...'

As Zoe's voice trailed off, Rebecca nodded, knowing precisely what the nurse meant and saving Zoe from carrying on the conversation.

'Yes. I'd like that,' she said.

Perching on the edge of the bed, Zoe reached for her notepad and pen.

'Don't worry about any of it making sense. You just speak from the heart, okay?' Zoe offered.

Nodding again, Rebecca's eyes filled with tears, and she began to whisper a few words. Zoe began to write as she had a thousand times before, but as she committed the words that were in Rebecca's heart to paper, Zoe knew these few sentences would set the dancer free.

Chapter Thirty-Six

It never failed to amaze Zoe how ironic the world could be. The leaves on the trees were thick and green, flowers bloomed in the hedgerows and the fields were full of vibrant reds and yellows. The magic of the English countryside was a riot of colour, thriving with life, yet here inside the tiny relatives' room of the hospice, Zoe sat beside Pernille Nyborg, who was grieving bitterly over the daughter she hadn't seen or spoken to in over a decade.

Pernille had arrived three hours after Zoe's message. She hadn't bothered to return Zoe's call, merely looked up the address of the hospice and driven straight down. Sadly, it had been too late. Because despite Zoe's best attempts to give Rebecca the end she wanted, the dancer had passed away shortly after giving Zoe her final words.

Zoe had never left Rebecca's side. She had stroked her hair and held her hand, offering words of comfort whenever she could. Rebecca had drifted in and out of consciousness, occasionally thinking Zoe was her mother. Zoe didn't correct her. The only requirement of any nurse in that given moment was to be there. And she had been, right up until Rebecca had drawn her final breath. Something that seemed to be of little comfort to Pernille now.

'I should have been here,' she sobbed. 'I would have dropped everything to be with her. I let her down.'

Zoe looped an arm around the woman's shoulders. With her long face, blue eyes and striking dark hair, she looked so much like Rebecca, Zoe had done a double take when she first saw Pernille walk through the hospice doors.

'You didn't let anyone down,' Zoe said kindly. 'Rebecca wanted you here; that has to count for something.'

Pernille wiped her eyes with a tissue. 'Did Rebecca tell you why she fell out with everyone?'

Zoe shook her head. 'I didn't want to pry.'

'She fell in love with this awful woman – Bella.' Pernille's face twisted with fury as she recalled the story. 'She was a nasty piece of work. Selfish and unkind. She was always mean to Rebecca, calling her fat and untalented. Bella was a choreographer, a big deal, you might say, in the world of ballet. But to me she was pure poison.'

Pouring them both a second cup of coffee, Zoe handed a cup to Pernille and encouraged her to continue with her story.

'One day I told Rebecca that she deserved better than Bella. Rebecca was furious. She told me that she and Bella were in love and if I couldn't support their relationship, she wanted nothing to do with me. I never heard from her again.'

As Pernille brought her story to a close, Zoe's eyes widened in dismay. It must have broken Pernille's heart to have lost her daughter like that. She thought of Sean, and wondered if there would ever have been anything he could have done or said that would cause such a rift to form between them. She hoped not. Sean had been her world, but children grew up and took on personalities of their own. You couldn't predict the future, any more easily than you could go back and correct the past. Who knew what would have been in store for her, Sean or David? This wasn't the first time Zoe had heard of such a sad family dispute and she was sure it wouldn't be the last. It was, however, the first time she'd cared for a patient who had been entirely alone.

'I'm guessing things didn't work out with Bella?' Zoe ventured.

Pernille let out a bitter laugh. 'No, they didn't. I learned in the dancing press that Bella left her for another ballerina.'

'And her friends?'

'Rebecca fell out with them, too, shortly after our row,' Pernille said with a sigh. 'She told them what I had said about Bella, expecting them to side with her, but they didn't. She was furious and told them that if that was what they thought, they were no friends of hers.'

'Oh, Pernille,' Zoe said, struggling for something to say. She looked at the older woman, who was gazing out of the window, her mind clearly on her daughter. It was all so sad, and could easily have been prevented if they had only talked to each other.

'She didn't come to me when she split up with Bella,' Pernille said, her voice breaking with emotion. 'My poor little girl was lonely and all because of pride. Her father was the same.'

'Where is he?' Zoe asked, wondering if he was about to pop up.

'We divorced when Rebecca was a baby. To my knowledge, she hasn't seen him since.' And her eyes widened in wonder. 'Or do you think she found him? Turned to him instead of me?'

Zoe shook her head. 'She never mentioned him. But, Pernille, before Rebecca died, she did leave you a few words.'

Pernille's mouth opened in surprise. 'What did she say?'

Zoe pulled the folded sheet of blue paper from her trouser pocket. As she did so, she found herself hoping that the few words Rebecca had managed would mean the world to Pernille in the way her own note from Sean did now. Gingerly, Pernille began to read aloud.

> *Mum, I should have listened. I'm sorry life came between us but I've always loved you and always will.*

At the few words, Pernille's eyes scrunched together like the tissue in her hands and she wept for the loss of her estranged daughter. As Zoe moved closer to her on the tiny sofa, she held her convulsing body, knowing they would stay like that, mother to mother, as long as Pernille needed to.

It was well past visiting hours when Zoe arrived at the hospital to visit Ben, but she was hoping that one of the kindly staff nurses might allow her a few minutes inside. After all, she had been known to admit a struggling relative in the past and hoped she could rely on a little bit of kindness now. She was in luck, and Zoe smiled at the team leader on duty that night, who mouthed, 'Go on then.'

Hurrying towards Ben's ward, she was surprised to see her boyfriend sitting up in bed and chatting to the man in the bed next him.

'Hello,' she called brightly.

At the sound of her voice, both men stopped talking and smiled. Ben, she was pleased to note, looked delighted to see her.

'I got your text,' he cried, holding out his arms to hug her. 'Sounded like a rough day.'

'It was a bit,' she said, allowing herself to be pulled into the safety of Ben's arms. With his stubble grazing her cheek, she felt as if she were home. Pulling away, she looked expectantly at Ben, waiting for him to introduce her.

'Zoe, sorry,' he said, picking up on her curiosity. 'This is Nico. Nico, this is Zoe.'

She smiled at Nico, who looked to be a similar age to Ben. 'Hello.'

'I've heard a lot about you,' Nico said, with a hint of an Italian accent. 'Your boyfriend's good company.'

'He has his moments,' Zoe said drily.

'He has plenty of moments,' Nico said seriously. 'He's kept me sane today.'

Ben waved away the compliment. 'Like you haven't done the same for me.'

Nico smiled. 'Think I'll take a walk down the corridor. Give you two a bit of privacy.'

As Zoe watched Nico get out of bed with all the grace of a man twice his age, she reflexively sprang into nurse mode. 'Would you like some help?'

Nico rewarded her with a huge smile that lit up his face. Despite the bald head and non-existent eyebrows and lashes, he was still a very handsome man.

'No, it's good for me to do these things for myself. But thank you, Zoe, that's very kind.'

Respecting his wishes, she watched him walk slowly past her and out into the corridor. Once Nico had gone, Zoe looked at Ben. As always, she found herself searching his face for clues about his health. But his skin was bright and clear, his eyes tired but refreshed.

'He seems a nice guy.'

'He is. He was only admitted yesterday.'

'I detected an accent,' Zoe put in.

'He's from Naples originally but lives here with his wife and kids. He's got colon cancer now, though. The last of his surgeries was a few days ago and he's recuperating.'

'He needed more than one surgery?' Zoe asked, doubt about Ben's recovery creeping swiftly through her veins.

Picking up on her concerns, Ben stroked her forearm with his thumb. 'Zoe, that's Nico's story, not mine. Two different people, two different cancers.'

As usual, he was right. 'You're out of here tomorrow, huh?'

A smile spread across Ben's face. 'I certainly am. I can't wait.'

'How does Candice feel about that?' Zoe tried to smile.

Ben sighed. 'Yes, she's not as good at compartmentalising as I thought. I've caught her in tears a couple of times and I know it's been a lot for her, juggling work and coming here.'

Guilt coursed through Zoe again. She should have done more to help.

'You have done more than enough,' Ben said, catching sight of Zoe's face. 'I know it's been hard for you to give me the space I've needed but it meant a lot that you listened.'

'This was never about me,' she countered.

'And I'm grateful you understood.' Ben squeezed her hand. 'But things will soon be back to normal and the moment I'm out of here and have my life back, all I want is to start living – with you.'

Happiness flooded Zoe's heart and she bent down to cover his face with kisses. 'I've been so worried.'

'I know,' he whispered. 'But there's no need to worry any more. It's over.'

Zoe rested her face in Ben's neck, simply enjoying the very essence of him in her arms. She could have stayed like that for hours but, hearing Nico shuffle back along the corridor, Zoe forced herself upright.

'Time for me to go,' she said. 'Don't want to upset the nurses after they were kind enough to let me in.'

A look of regret passed across Ben's face and Zoe wished she had arrived earlier.

'I'm sorry.'

'Nothing to be sorry for,' Ben replied firmly. 'You were with a mum and daughter who needed you. I'll be seeing you at home all the time soon; you'll be sick of me.'

Waving goodbye, Zoe left the hospital. Today had been a tough day but a good one. She was pleased she had been able to pass on a note to Pernille, but that didn't stop Zoe wishing she could have persuaded Rebecca to contact her mother earlier so they could have said a proper goodbye. The parental bond was precious and as Zoe wandered back towards her car she thought about her own mother, Ruth, and found herself reaching for her phone. Searching for the familiar name in her contacts list, Zoe pressed call. After just a few rings the phone was answered, and Zoe felt a lump form in her throat as she said the words she realised she had wanted to say all day.

'Hi, Mum, it's me.'

Chapter Thirty-Seven

It was two long weeks after the operation before Ben was finally declared fit enough to return to work and, for both Candice and Zoe, the day couldn't come quickly enough. On the morning of Ben's return, Zoe was as excited as a new puppy as she laced into a pair of trainers, ready for her shift.

She was just debating whether to slip a welcome note into Ben's locker when the staff room door opened and in walked the man himself.

'Hello,' he said with a shy grin.

But Zoe wasn't one for standing on ceremony and she rushed towards him, throwing her arms around his neck, not caring who walked in.

'I'm pleased you're back.'

'And I'm pleased to be back,' he said, his voice muffled as he kissed the top of her head. Pulling away, he held Zoe by her shoulders and met her gaze.

'There were times in that hospital bed when I dreamed of a normal day like this one. Going to work, meetings, patients and you.'

At the admission, Zoe let out a gasp of delight. 'You're back where you belong.'

Nodding, Ben's eyes shone like the sun but as he sat down on the bench behind him, Zoe noticed how frail he seemed. Whilst she had done a good job of keeping Ben's illness a secret, Zoe had a feeling the rumour mill would be working overtime once people saw how thin he had become.

However, Zoe knew this wasn't the moment to say anything and instead she sat beside him and looped an arm around his shoulders.

'I still can't believe you're here.'

'Well, believe it,' Ben said, nudging himself closer towards her. 'Because all that extra responsibility you've been shouldering is firmly back with me.'

Zoe let out an audible sigh of relief. 'I promise that's not the only reason I'm glad you're back.'

He laughed. 'Good. Then why don't you come over to my place tonight? I want to cook you dinner to say thank you for all you've done whilst I've been ill.'

'I think that might be a bit much after a first day back,' Zoe ventured. 'I like the sentiment but let's not go too fast too soon.'

'All right,' he agreed with a hint of reluctance. 'A takeaway then, my treat. Candice will be there, though; is that all right?'

'Of course.' Zoe beamed. 'You know how much I love Candice.'

'Ben!' Miles exclaimed as he burst into the staff room. 'Where've you been, buddy?'

The troubleshooter rolled his eyes. 'You know how it is. Work, meetings.'

Nodding as if he understood, Miles grinned. 'It's great to have you back. I'd forgotten what a rotten manager Zoe can be.'

'Oi!' Zoe admonished. 'I can still stick you on a month of nights if you keep it up!'

'Yeah, yeah.' Miles threw her a wink before changing the subject. 'Oh, Mrs Harper's asking for you, Zoe.'

'Is she all right?' Zoe stood up, feeling concerned, her bag and coat still strewn across the bench.

'I think so, but she seems keen to see you sooner rather than later.'

'You go; I'll put this in your locker for you,' Ben offered.

'You're a lifesaver,' she said, following Miles out into the corridor.

Entering Mrs Harper's room, Zoe smiled brightly at the older woman. 'You wanted to see me?'

Mrs Harper beamed. 'I did. I wondered if we could talk about that little matter we spoke about recently.'

Remembering how Mrs Harper had asked for her help with a letter to her son, Zoe said, 'Of course. Have you come up with anything?'

Mrs Harper let out a little cough to clear her throat. 'I think so. I've been up most of the last few nights thinking back to when Al and I were new parents with a little mewling infant who had so many needs.'

Zoe smiled knowingly. 'I remember that. Me and my ex-husband would look at each other and back at Sean, begging him to tell us what he needed.'

'We tried everything,' Mrs Harper said fondly. 'Me more than Al perhaps. It was always more of a woman's job to deal with the children in my day and despite protests and marches I don't think an awful lot has changed.'

Zoe managed a wry grin; how wise Mrs Harper was.

'But there's something special about being a mother,' Zoe replied. 'The way you carry that child in your belly from the moment they're a collection of cells. Then as if by magic they're a human being, out in the world, once a part of you, but still connected by love, biology and everything in between.'

'You sound as if you enjoyed being pregnant,' Mrs Harper observed.

'I did,' Zoe said, remembering the joy she had felt at feeling her son growing inside of her. And when he was born, the sheer wonder of just looking at him and loving him.

'I bet you were a wonderful mother.'

Zoe shrugged. 'I don't know about that. I hope I was a loving mother.'

Mrs Harper reached across the bedside table and pulled out a slip of paper. 'It's all I ever wanted myself. I wrote this, for Nathaniel. Do you think it's enough?'

Zoe took the impressive sheet of thick, creamy white paper and unfolded it.

> *The greatest gift in life was being your mother. The greatest gift you ever gave me was you. Being your mum was all I ever wanted to be – thank you, my greatest love.*

The last sentence chimed with her. It was so similar in sentiment to Sean's last few words before he slipped away. All Mrs Harper wanted to be was a mum; all her son wanted to be was a cowboy – it was funny how the human spirit could focus on what really mattered when the time came. She folded the paper and beamed affectionately at Mrs Harper.

'It's perfect. You didn't need my help at all.'

Mrs Harper patted Zoe's hand. 'You've helped more than you know. You made me realise that all I had to be to my boy was a mum.'

After Mrs Harper had given Zoe her letter, she told the nurse to send it into the sky somewhere wonderful once she had passed. Zoe knew the best place and she knew that Mrs Harper's darling boy would get it.

The strength of Mrs Harper's letter stayed with Zoe for the rest of her shift. The older woman's words could so easily have been her own. If she were only able to say one last thing to Sean, it would have been this.

Back in the relative safety of her car after a long shift, she leant against the headrest and closed her eyes. An image of Sean came to mind. It was the day before he had been killed. He had been full of excitement about trying out for a junior football team and couldn't wait to get started. He had been practising scoring goals all afternoon, shouts of 'Mum, Mum, look at me,' pouring through the windows.

She recalled the joy on Sean's face as he fired the ball right past his dad and into the makeshift goal. The cries and cheers as he raced around in circles in the backyard. Zoe hated to admit it but she had got fed up of watching after a while. Instead, she had tackled the laundry. As ever, the endless round of punishing questions took hold. What if she hadn't been busy? What sort of mother was she if she got fed up watching her boy kick a ball? Zoe had often felt, certainly during the early days of Sean's death, that if she had been a better mother Sean would never have died.

Feeling the onset of tears, Zoe pushed the memories of her past life away. It was time to look forward, and that began with Ben. He was her happy place, she thought, as she drove towards his home.

It didn't take long to reach the familiar crescent and, knocking on the door, she was grateful Ben let her in almost straight away.

Walking behind Ben up the stairs, Zoe bit back the temptation to offer to slip her arm through his and help. He had been so busy in meetings all day she hadn't had a chance to assess how he was coping. She shook her head; she knew Ben wouldn't want her thinking like that so instead she asked, 'Is Candice here?'

'No,' Ben said shortly, as they reached the flat. 'I asked her to go out tonight.'

A wide smile stretched across Zoe's face as she walked into the large kitchen. 'Is that right?'

But Ben didn't return her grin; instead, he leaned against the fridge door, arms folded.

Zoe thought she saw a trace of anger. 'Is everything all right?'

'I don't know, Zoe. You tell me?'

Zoe felt uneasy. 'Yes?'

'Sure?' Ben asked again, his jaw clenched, eyes giving nothing away.

'If you've got something to say, will you just spit it out?' she blurted.

'All right,' Ben said, unfolding his arms. 'Why didn't you tell me you saw your husband while I was in hospital?'

At the question, Zoe was aghast. How had he found out about David? 'Because I didn't want to worry you.'

'Worry me?' Ben echoed. 'Why would I be worried? The fact you didn't tell me makes me worry.'

'You can't be serious,' Zoe gasped. 'You were in *hospital*. Getting over a very serious operation. The last thing I wanted to do was burden you with my problems.'

'But you could have dropped it into conversation, instead of letting me hear about it from Miles. Fool I am, he assumed I knew all about it,' Ben pointed out.

At the mention of Miles, Zoe felt a flash of anger towards him. Then again, she realised, it wasn't as if she had asked him to keep David's visit to himself.

'I didn't know he was coming,' Zoe reasoned. 'He came to talk through our divorce settlement.'

'It's fairly big news if someone flies around the world to the wife they haven't seen in over two years,' Ben growled. 'And don't tell me he didn't ask you to get back together while he was here. No bloke flies ten thousand miles to drop off a bit of paperwork.'

Zoe's jaw dropped open in surprise. 'I told him there was no future for us.'

At this, Ben's face twisted in fury. 'Yeah? Then why haven't you signed the settlement agreement?'

'What?' She faltered.

'The papers fell out of your bag when I put your stuff away this morning,' he explained. 'I wasn't snooping; I just happened to see.'

'And did you just happen to see that I hadn't signed the papers yet?' she said angrily. 'Did the pages just happen to fall that way?'

Ben looked away and Zoe had her answer. Why couldn't he see that there was nothing to this?

'I'm sorry,' she said at last. 'I should have said something about David's visit but I didn't want to add anything else to your plate.'

'I know.' Ben pinched the bridge of his nose. 'But the thing is, you didn't. Lately, I've been wondering if we've been rushing into things. Maybe we don't know each other as well as we thought.'

Zoe felt as if the air had been sucked out of her lungs. 'What?'

'You said it yourself,' Ben continued as if she hadn't spoken. 'I have to concentrate on my health and work, and you have baggage, Zoe. Look, I can understand why you didn't tell me about David but I can't understand why you haven't signed the papers. He delivered them over a week ago.'

'I was getting around to it,' she said quietly.

'What stopped you?' Ben asked, not unreasonably. 'You want to keep a last link to David? I get it, but if you do, that means you're not ready to be with me.'

Zoe thought for a moment. What had stopped her? She had been about to sign back in the pub after David left. But she thought she ought to go through things properly. Check there weren't any surprises – and so she had shoved the papers in her bag and that's where they had stayed ever since.

'I just wanted to take time to go through the document.'

'Makes sense.' Ben nodded. 'But when I put it all together, I wonder if the world is trying to tell us something. What with my illness and your issues, maybe we've both got stuff we need to deal with before we enter into a relationship.'

The world beneath Zoe's feet started to shift. 'But, Ben, that's crazy. We love each other.'

'I know,' Ben said softly. 'But sometimes love isn't enough.'

Chapter Thirty-Eight

The morning after Ben dumped her (there was no other way of putting it, Zoe had tried), she found herself sitting at her kitchen table feeling bereft. After their disastrous evening, Zoe had driven home to an empty house where she had sat staring at the television watching something on Netflix but not taking in whatever it was supposed to be. Eventually, exhaustion had taken over and she fell asleep on the sofa, waking briefly to find Sarah pulling a blanket over her.

Zoe had properly woken at the crack of dawn with a stiff neck and a chill in her bones. After trudging to the kitchen, she had made herself a cup of tea and gazed listlessly at the New York poster that hung in the kitchen. Now, splashing cold milk over her breakfast cereal, she didn't realise the liquid had spilled all over the table until Lottie let out a squeal of delight.

'You're making a mess, Auntie Zoe!'

At the sound of the little girl's giggles, Zoe came to. Spotting the milk lake she had created, she reached for the tea towel hanging on the back of the oven, only for Sarah to come to her aid.

'Blimey, where were you?' she asked, helping clear the mess while Lottie continued to giggle, grateful that for once it wasn't her who had created the chaos.

'Sorry, I've got a lot on my mind.'

'I've noticed.' Sarah took a seat between Zoe and her daughter. Taking a bite of toast, she observed Zoe carefully. 'Busy at work?'

'A bit.'

'But it must help that Ben is back,' Sarah tried again.

Zoe shrugged. 'I guess.'

Sarah sighed in exasperation. 'Zoe, what is *wrong* with you?'

At the question, Zoe knew she would have to confess. 'Ben broke up with me last night.'

'What?' Sarah gasped, her lips forming a perfect circle as she dropped her toast.

'Yup, said the timing wasn't right,' she croaked, trying to hold back tears.

Sarah gasped again. 'Timing? You've been there for him while he's had cancer and now he treats you like this when he's well.'

'It's not like that,' Zoe whispered.

'Then what is it like?'

Zoe's eyes turned towards Lottie and the mum of one immediately understood.

'Lottie, go and brush your teeth,' Sarah barked.

'But I haven't finished,' Lottie protested, pushing a small amount of toast around her plate, sensing adult gossip was about to take place.

'You have now,' Sarah said, snatching the toast from Lottie's plate and shoving it into her own mouth.

'Mu-um!'

'Go!' Sarah ordered.

As Lottie reluctantly got to her feet, Zoe giggled despite her misery. 'Wow!'

'Yeah, I know, crack parenting, right?' Sarah said with a sigh. 'But enough of all that. What's happened?'

Zoe told her how Ben had found out about David's visit, the unsigned settlement papers and what he had said about her baggage. As she moved through the story, Zoe could see Sarah's face shift from dismay to despair then irritation.

'Bloody hell,' she said when Zoe had finally finished.

'Yup.'

'Do you think he might have a point?' Sarah asked, as she topped up Zoe's coffee mug from the cafetière that stood on the table.

'What?'

'I'm just saying, as an innocent bystander,' Sarah said quickly, 'that he might have a point. I get why you didn't tell Ben about David, but he's right, you could have read through the settlement by now and got the papers signed. I also think you could have mentioned it to him. It didn't have to be a big thing, but you could have said something.'

'I was concentrating on *Ben*,' Zoe said hotly.

Sarah blew across the top of her coffee cup to cool the liquid down. 'And I get it. But equally I think perhaps Ben might be right too. Either way it won't do you any harm to have some time apart, see how you feel, sort your shit out, get that paperwork in order.'

Zoe let out a loud sigh. 'You've got to be joking.'

'Look,' Sarah began as she got to her feet. 'I know how much this hurts but I do think it was all a bit much too soon. Look at it this way: Ben still loves you and you still love him. You just need a bit of space.'

'You think?' Zoe asked, visibly brightening at the idea.

'I do.' Sarah kissed her on the cheek. 'Let's get drinks tonight and moan about relationships.'

'Sounds good.' Zoe laughed. 'And seeing as I have to face Ben today, I think I'll be in need of several of them.'

-

But luckily for Zoe, Ben was away in Bristol all day. She wondered if he had deliberately arranged it but chastised herself. Ben wasn't like that; he was a professional. Yet that was the last thing Zoe felt as she constantly checked her phone for messages from him, telling her he had made a mistake and couldn't live without her.

She hated herself for behaving like such a teenager and by lunchtime resolved to get back to what she did best – note-writing. There was one lady who Zoe felt deserved some words of comfort: her new friend Mrs Harper. Over a coffee in the cafe across the road, Zoe pulled out a card with a picture of a setting sun. It was one of Zoe's favourite images, taken over Lulworth Cove in Dorset, the familiar rocky arch looking picture-perfect in the blue sea. Turning the card over, she pressed her pen to the paper and wrote.

Dear Mrs Harper,

I saw this and thought of you. I wanted you to know that your precious note will be more than safe with me. I will treasure it, as if it were a letter to my own boy.

Love,

Zoe x

Sealing the letter shut and stuffing it into her bag, her eyes strayed to the divorce settlement still in its envelope. The mere sight of it now irritated her. Why hadn't she dealt with her past so she could move on with her future? Feeling fired up, Zoe pulled out the documents and read through the proposed financial agreement. David really had been very generous. He was suggesting they sell the house and she take seventy per cent of the profit to reflect the fact she had put down almost all the deposit. David, the documents said, would handle everything. She felt a flash of affection for her ex-husband as she signed her name, agreeing to the proposed terms.

Yet there was a part of her that felt nostalgic for the past. David's regular messages had stopped since this visit, and before she could stop herself, Zoe reached for her phone and began scrolling through David's Instagram page. There were no entries today but yesterday he had posted a selfie standing outside a large building on what she recognised to be the outskirts of Mosman. His arms were spread wide and the caption underneath read *New premises! Next stop Melbourne!*

Zoe laughed as she saw how happy he looked. It was nice to see life working out for one of them. She tapped out a comment underneath his photo.

Huge congratulations! Looks like your quest for world domination is well underway.

She was about to put the phone away when it buzzed in her hand with a notification. She saw to her surprise that David had replied. She frowned. It was the middle of the night in Australia.

What do you mean underway? Watch out, Evans! We'll be setting up a garage in the UK next.

Smiling, she put her phone in her pocket, surprised to find that a tiny part of her wouldn't mind if her ex did expand his business over to her neck of the woods. In the moments since she had signed the papers, Zoe had felt something shift. Perhaps she could consider forgiving David after all. He was many things, but perhaps going forward he could also be her friend.

-

Any newfound hopes Zoe had for the future were dashed when she returned to the hospice and saw Miles looking forlorn at the nurses' station.

'Everything all right?' she said.

Miles shook his head. 'I'm sorry, Zoe, but Mrs Harper died while you were out.'

Zoe's face fell. 'What? Were you with her?'

'No, Ben was,' Miles said.

'Ben?' she echoed. 'I thought he was out all day.'

'He got back early.'

'Where's Mrs Harper now?' Zoe demanded, not wanting to dwell on Ben any further.

'The funeral directors have just taken her,' Ben said.

Zoe whirled around, about to charge off and talk to the funeral home, when she came face to face with Ben.

'Was she all right?' Zoe asked him, all thoughts of their past temporarily forgotten. 'At the end, I mean.'

Ben nodded, his biscuit-coloured eyes filled with sadness. 'It all happened very quickly. I made sure she was comfortable.'

Zoe felt a stab of frustration. A good end was more than being comfortable and Ben knew it. 'But did she have everything she needed? Was her son there?'

'He was,' Ben said gently. 'I got him just in time.'

Relief flooded through her. 'I can't believe she's gone,' she murmured.

'She really got under your skin, didn't she?' Ben ventured.

To her surprise, Zoe felt tears prick her eyes. 'Yes. I wrote her this note.'

She fished inside her bag and pulled out the envelope, waving it morosely around for Ben and Miles to see.

'I'm sure she would have appreciated it,' Miles offered. 'She was grateful for everything you did.'

'But it wasn't enough,' Zoe said sadly.

'It never is,' Ben replied.

At that, their eyes locked and Zoe felt a moment of understanding pass between them. Sometimes her job seemed futile. No matter what she did, people always died; it was the natural order of things. She blinked and the moment was gone, the awkwardness between her and Ben returning. She checked her watch, about to make up an excuse to walk away when Ben beat her to it.

'I'd better get on.'

'Course. See you later.'

Ben turned and disappeared down the corridor. Zoe could do nothing but stand there and watch, until she felt Miles's hand on her shoulder.

'Are you all right?' he asked.

Lifting her head, she met her friend's eyes. 'Why?'

Miles looked sheepish. 'Sarah told me to keep an eye on you today.'

'She told you we'd split up?' Zoe managed.

'She might have mentioned something,' he mumbled, looking embarrassed. 'She also said he didn't know David had visited. I'm sorry, Zoe, I didn't mean to drop you in it.'

Zoe hung her head, ashamed that she was apparently the talk of the hospice.

'You didn't,' she said eventually. 'It was my fault for keeping it from him.'

'Well, don't worry because I haven't said a word about to anyone else at work about all this and I won't,' Miles promised. 'Listen, forget about babysitting Lottie tonight. I'm sure you and Sarah will need some time together.'

A blank look passed across her face before Zoe remembered how she had agreed to collect Lottie from school and then babysit.

'No, no, I'm fine,' Zoe promised. 'You two go and have fun.'

'Are you sure?' Miles looked at her doubtfully. 'We can go another time.'

Zoe shook her head. 'Just because my love life has hit the skids doesn't mean yours should. I'm fine, honestly.'

-

Later that night, after Lottie had gone to bed, Zoe curled up on the sofa with a cup of herbal tea for company. She had been tempted to open the wine but felt there was a strong chance a glass might become a bottle and she didn't want to tread that particular path. Today had been a terrible day. She was pleased Mrs Harper had resolved the issues from her past and had been given a good death, but that didn't stop her feeling sad over the loss. She and Mrs Harper had shared a special bond. They were part of a club no parent wants to find themselves in, but together they had bonded, and without her Zoe felt alone yet again.

Her eyes strayed to the large yearly calendar they had pinned onto the kitchen wall with various dates and occasions. She saw, written in big black letters for the following weekend: *ZOE AWAY WITH BEN – CORNWALL!!!!*

It seemed like a lifetime ago Zoe had excitedly scrawled those words and the familiar threat of tears didn't seem far away. She bristled. She wasn't feeling sorry for herself any more. Yes, she was hurt that things between her and Ben hadn't worked out, but the important thing was he had shown her what it was to feel love again, and that was something she had never anticipated when she made that long journey from Australia to start a new life.

Just after ten, Sarah and Miles returned home. Zoe couldn't miss the blissful expressions on their faces as Sarah perched on the sofa and Miles magically produced a bottle of champagne and three flutes.

'Good night?' Zoe asked, bemused, as Miles set a glass of champagne in front of her.

'Magical,' Sarah said. 'Miles took me out in a hot-air balloon.'

Zoe raised an eyebrow. 'How did you swing that?'

Miles tapped his nose and sat next to Sarah opposite Zoe, who was occupying the easy chair nearest the telly. He wrapped an arm tightly around his new girlfriend and grinned.

'I know a guy who knows a guy.'

'Course you do.' Zoe giggled. Even when he was trying to be flash it didn't suit Miles.

Zoe took a minute to observe the two of them. Sarah looked gorgeous in a red dress but there was a glow about her. A certain something that her own mother would describe as 'a quality'.

'What's going on?' she asked, suspicions raised.

Miles and Sarah exchanged knowing glances, the happy bubble they were both in clearly evident.

'We're getting married,' they shouted in joyful unison.

'What?' Zoe gasped, champagne spilling across her hands in shock.

'Miles proposed on the balloon tonight. It was so romantic!'

Zoe stared at them in disbelief before turning to Miles. 'I thought you were just taking her to Australia?'

Miles laughed. 'I know. But after talking to you, Zoe, I realised that wasn't enough.' He looked at Sarah with love in his eyes and kissed her gently as though she were a precious Ming vase. 'I want to be with this woman for the rest of my life.'

'And I realised I felt the same way. I've felt the same way ever since I laid eyes on him,' Sarah said softly as they broke apart.

Zoe felt momentarily speechless. Wasn't this all a bit soon? They had been together for less time than she and Ben and look what had happened to them. And what about Lottie? Was Miles really ready to become a stepfather to a little girl?

But as she looked at Sarah and saw the delight in her eyes, Zoe kept her mouth shut. Her friend was an adult and if she thought marrying Miles was the best thing for her then who was she to say otherwise? She was, after all, hardly an expert on life or relationships.

'Congratulations.' Reaching for her flute of champagne, Zoe lifted it in the direction of the newly engaged couple. 'I'm delighted for you both.'

'Thank you.' Sarah grinned. Then she thrust her left hand out and Zoe let out another gasp as she saw a sparkler the size of Uluru.

Zoe looked at Miles in open-mouthed shock. 'You're a nurse! How did you afford that?'

Sarah let out a peal of laughter. 'It's not real and do you really think I'd wear something as gaudy as this?'

'I dunno, it kind of suits you.'

Miles looked at Zoe pointedly. 'We're going to go into town to pick something out. This was just symbolic really. One day, when I'm a rich and famous nursing god, I'll be able to treat Sarah like the princess she deserves to be.'

'You already do,' Sarah pointed out loyally. 'Anyway, I'm looking forward to showing off this bit of bling at the party.'

'Party?' Zoe echoed, feeling as if she were in some sort of parallel universe where she was slow to catch on.

'Yes, we're having an engagement party on the first of October,' Sarah said.

'Wow! You've booked it already?'

Zoe's face must have registered confusion because Sarah was nodding like a woman possessed. 'Yes, Miles organised it last week.'

'I was really hoping she would say yes otherwise it would have been a very different party.' Miles finished his champagne then topped up all their glasses.

'You really have thought of everything,' Zoe said admiringly.

'He has,' Sarah whispered.

At that, Sarah looked into Miles's eyes and Zoe felt like an intruder in her own home.

'I'll leave you to it,' she said, getting to her feet.

But they were so lost in their own world they barely even noticed. As Zoe padded out of the lounge and up towards her room, a feeling of emptiness washed over her. Climbing into bed and pulling the covers over her head, all Zoe wanted to do was give in to the bitterness that had been threatening to take over from the moment Sarah and Miles had broken their news. It was all so unfair, she thought, wallowing in the feelings of resentment. Sarah was getting engaged after just a few weeks and she had ended up with a man facing a difficult cancer battle who had dumped her. Zoe knew she was being childish but, as the sounds of Miles and Sarah's happy laughter rang out from the living room, Zoe really didn't care.

Chapter Thirty-Nine

Over the course of the following ten days, the bad mood that had taken hold when Sarah got engaged had left her feeling so disagreeable Zoe knew she wasn't fit to be around people. Consequently, she buried herself in admin and volunteered to work night shifts all so she could avoid the happiness that had otherwise flooded through her home. It was something akin to sod's law that the first person she bumped straight into the morning after two night shifts was Ben.

'Hello,' he said warmly as Zoe entered the staff room. 'How are you doing?'

Zoe felt wrong-footed. Why was he being welcoming? Then a wave of awkwardness crashed over her. Did he feel sorry for her now Miles and Sarah were engaged? She tried to smile. The last thing she needed was Ben's pity.

'I'm good. You?'

The moment she asked, she realised she genuinely did want to know how Ben was.

'I'm fine, doing really well.'

'That's great.' She nodded. 'I bet Candice is pleased.'

Ben raised an eyebrow. 'What, now she doesn't have to play nurse? Yeah, I should say so. Let's just say only one of us siblings was blessed with a good bedside manner.'

Zoe tried a laugh. 'I'm sure she did her best.'

'I suppose you could call it that,' Ben mused as he unlaced his trainers. 'Do you know that towards the end of my recovery she was serving me cold soup and told me that if I didn't like it, I could shove it up my arse?'

'Wow!' Zoe was laughing properly as she pictured Candice saying that very thing. 'Can you imagine if we said that to our patients?'

'Should we try it, do you think?' Ben asked, laughing along with her. 'It certainly made me want to get well a lot sooner.'

'Let's get Miles to give it a go first,' Zoe suggested. 'He's got a thick skin.'

'He'll need it if he's getting married,' Ben quipped.

Zoe stopped, the easiness that had briefly flowed between them gone. 'You know they're engaged?'

Ben looked uncomfortable. 'Yes, he told me last week over a beer.'

'It's wonderful news.'

'It is,' Ben agreed readily. 'To find love like that, I always think it's a miracle.'

'Let's hope it doesn't end in divorce like mine did,' Zoe said, then, realising the tastelessness of her remark, shook her head. She decided to try being truthful rather than brazen. 'Sorry. I feel a bit awkward.'

'Me too. Tell you what, let's accept this is difficult for both of us and try to be friends.'

'I'd like that.' Zoe gave him a small smile. 'Why don't you tell me how you are really?'

'I'm genuinely fine. My latest tests show the op was a success, the surgeon was pleased with the margins and I'm free to get on with my life.'

'That's great,' Zoe said, feeling genuinely pleased at the news.

'And you?' Ben asked.

'I'm fine. I've mailed my settlement papers.'

Surprise registered on Ben's face. 'Wow, didn't think you would.'

'Why?'

'I thought it was something you needed, to keep you connected to Sean,' Ben said, scratching his bald head.

For the first time, Zoe understood how he would have reached that conclusion. 'There might have been a bit of that. Not telling you about any of it was stupid – it was well-intentioned but stupid.'

'And how was it really, seeing David?' Ben asked gently.

Zoe thought for a moment. How had it been?

'It was good,' she said at last. 'It gave me closure and made me realise there was nothing left between us.'

'You weren't tempted to go back to him?'

Zoe couldn't help laughing at the question. Then, seeing Ben's hurt look, rearranged her features.

'No. David is my past. Once I signed the papers, I realised I could even one day think about forgiving him. It was as if something had been released. I can't explain it.' Zoe shook her head, still trying to work it out. 'I think I would like for me and David to try and be friends, though. We've been through a lot together – only we understand the pain of losing the child we shared.'

'You don't blame him any more?'

'Not like I used to,' Zoe said slowly. 'There's no denying what happened to Sean was terrible but David has to live with the fact he was there when it happened, not me. When I fled Australia, I was desperate to get away from the pain I was in. What I don't think I realised is that the pain we carry stays with us regardless of where we go.'

There was a pause and Zoe could see Ben thinking before he spoke again. 'And what about Australia?'

Now it was Zoe's turn to look surprised. 'Australia? What's that got to do with anything?'

'You left in difficult circumstances. Maybe you ought to go back and make your peace with the place now you've realised you can start to forgive David. After all, you haven't seen your family, your friends, you haven't even seen Sean's grave.' As Ben trailed off, Zoe could see the worry in his eyes as he wondered if he had gone too far with the last remark. She wanted to reassure him.

'No, but I did speak to Mum recently.'

Ben raised another eyebrow. 'Really? Thought you only managed birthdays, Christmas and the odd email.'

The sounds of Miles and Karen arguing about rotas echoed through the staff room. 'Yes, but something in me wanted to talk to Mum. I've missed her.'

'Wow!' Ben said, over Karen's raised voice. 'Maybe Australia's not as bad as you thought?'

Zoe shrugged. 'Maybe. But the UK, that's still home for me.'

'Is it?' Ben ventured. 'When I was talking to Nico in hospital, he was quick to assure me that even though he's spent twenty years in Britain, his heart will always belong in Naples.'

As Ben tapped his heart, Zoe smiled.

'I don't feel like that. I don't hate Australia like I used to, but I don't carry it in my heart. Everything I loved about the place – my friends, my family, my son – is all right here.' She tapped her own heart now.

She smiled at Ben and walked towards the nurses' desk, only to run straight into Mr Harper. She couldn't miss the haunted look on his face.

'Mr Harper,' she said gently. 'Are you all right?'

'I'm okay,' Mr Harper replied with a smile that didn't reach his eyes. 'Me and the family have been going through Mum's things, getting everything sorted out. It's hard; we thought we had more time.'

'People always do,' Zoe said sympathetically. 'But those memories you have of your mum, they'll never go away.'

'It's hard to believe she's gone, even here.' He looked around the corridors wistfully. 'The place is still so full of her. She lived here, grew up here, but now I know how much she hated it here. I wonder if that's what made her go sooner than we expected.'

Zoe laid a comforting hand on his shoulder. 'Don't think like that. Your mum would hate for you to be this upset. She made her peace with this place and she knew how much you loved her. Often those we love the most hide how ill they are until the end, when it all becomes too much.'

Tears pooled in Mr Harper's eyes as she finished speaking and for a moment Zoe wondered if she ought to take him into the staff room so he could have a good cry. But as the thought crossed her mind, he regained his composure.

'Thank you,' he said, blinking the tears away. 'And thank you for all you did for Mum. I wondered if you were a little outspoken when we met at the party but I realised just how much you love your patients and I know how fond of you Mum became.'

'Your mum was very special,' she said softly.

'You took such good care of her, but you take good care of all your patients. I've seen that first-hand,' Mr Harper said.

Zoe smiled modestly. She wasn't quite sure what to say. It was the same when people suggested that doctors and nurses were angels in disguise. She and the majority of her colleagues didn't view it that way. They were professionals, doing a job to the very best of their ability because they were passionate about their vocation.

'Actually, I'm glad I've bumped into you,' Mr Harper continued. 'I wanted to invite you to Mum's funeral on Friday morning?'

'This Friday?' Zoe echoed in surprise.

'Yes, at ten in the crematorium. Ben and Miles have both said they're able to attend but if you're busy I completely understand,' Mr Harper said.

'Not at all, I would be honoured,' Zoe said.

Mr Harper nodded. 'Good. We'll see you then, Zoe, and thank you.'

Lifting her hand, Zoe gave him a little wave goodbye. Once Mr Harper disappeared, Zoe took a deep breath. Whilst she was more than accustomed to death, she hated funerals; they always reminded her of Sean. But Mrs Harper deserved to be honoured, and it would be good for Zoe to say goodbye.

Chapter Forty

The final notes of Frank Sinatra's classic 'My Way' rang through the crematorium. As the mourners filed outside into the sunshine, Zoe glanced at Ben and they exchanged a small smile.

Mrs Harper's funeral had been a beautiful service. Full of life-affirming stories from those that knew her and from some who apparently didn't know her quite so well but respected her, such as Miles and Ben.

'That was definitely one of the lovelier funerals I've been to,' Ben admitted as they made their way outside, into the warm August air.

'It was, wasn't it?' Zoe replied as she observed Ben, handsome in his black suit and tie. She was mildly annoyed that her pulse still raced at the sight of him.

'I thought it was great!' Miles tried to give Ben a fist bump, which he ignored.

'Miles, I don't think we can say that,' Zoe hissed, looking around to see if anyone had heard him.

'Why not?' Miles shrugged. 'It was bonza.'

Zoe shook her head in despair. 'Don't say that either; you'll have Aussies having a go for being too Australian.'

'Aren't all Australians too Australian?' Ben smirked.

Zoe wagged her finger at him in mock irritation. 'Don't you start, otherwise I'll insist Mr Harper plays nothing but Cold Chisel at the wake later. I'll say Mrs Harper told me on her deathbed it was her favourite band.'

Ben laughed. 'You wouldn't dare.'

'Try me,' Zoe said with a smirk.

'Are you both going to the wake?' Miles asked hopefully.

'I am; I've got the day off,' Zoe explained. 'We can get the bus together if you like.'

'I'm going too,' Ben said, 'and I drove.'

'Oh, the Porsche.' Miles's eyes lit up at the thought of a lift in the luxury car. 'Can you squeeze me in or are you still taking the bus, Zoe?'

'Er...' Zoe's voice trailed off.

'Zoe will be coming with us and she'll be sitting in the front,' Ben said, taking the decision out of her hands. 'You can squeeze into the back.'

She smiled at him and, following Ben and Miles towards the car park, she almost skipped with joy at the sight of the Porsche.

'Ah, how I've missed you,' she said, running her hand over the bonnet.

'If I didn't know you better, I'd think you only ever went out with me because of this car,' Ben said, unlocking the doors.

Miles got in the back and Zoe followed, breathing in the ever-present new car smell. 'To be fair, your personality only goes so far,' she teased. 'It was lucky for you the car sweetened the deal.'

'Like that, is it?' Ben expertly reversed out of the car park and headed onto the main road. 'Then what did you bring to the table?'

'You mean my stunning good looks and easy charm weren't enough for you?'

'I thought it was just because you were easy,' Miles quipped.

'Oi,' Ben and Zoe said in unison, their eyes meeting briefly as they did so.

'How are the wedding plans coming on?' Ben asked, changing the subject.

'Yeah, good,' Miles said. 'I think we might do it in Australia next year sometime.'

'Really?' Zoe turned around in her seat, her voice full of astonishment.

'Yeah, I think Sarah's into the idea of moving there once we're married.'

'You're kidding?' Now it was Ben that was surprised.

'Why are you both finding this shocking?' Miles asked with a laugh. 'She's suggested we extend our Christmas trip to see how she likes it. If she does, we'll look at spending our time here and in Oz.'

'Blimey, that's modern,' Ben said.

'And expensive,' Zoe threw in.

Miles shrugged. 'We'll work it out. The point is, we want to be together, that's all that matters.'

'Never thought I'd see the day,' Zoe murmured as Ben pulled into the pub car park.

'Comes to us all in the end. So,' he said, rubbing his hands together, 'shall we say a proper farewell to Mrs Harper?'

He marched straight into the pub as if he owned it, shaking hands with all of the Harpers and offering polite condolences before ordering two pints and a glass of pinot.

As Zoe had expected, the pub was overflowing with guests. And perhaps just as Mrs Harper would have wanted, everyone was smiling. With a pang, she thought of Sean's funeral. Nobody had been laughing then. It had been a horrific occasion, but it had been the funeral of a child, surely the most unnatural thing in the world. This, Zoe thought, watching Mr Harper giggle as he exchanged stories about his mother, was what a funeral should be like.

'Here you go,' Ben said, interrupting Zoe's thoughts and pressing a chilled glass of wine into her hands.

'Thank you,' she said, taking a sip. 'Good turnout, isn't it?'

Ben took a pull on the pint Miles had just bought for him. 'Certainly is. Though not enough people dressed in black in my opinion.'

Zoe laughed. 'Never had you down as a traditionalist.'

'I'm not, but someone's died; let's show some respect,' Ben said.

Running her tongue across her teeth, Zoe thought for a moment before she spoke. 'You're telling me that at your funeral you'd want everyone to be miserable as sin?'

Ben lifted his chin a little higher. 'Maybe. I just think you should be respectful. That said, I'm not averse to a bit of personality at a funeral.'

'Let me guess. You want "My Way" by Frank Sinatra?'

'More like "Bat Out of Hell"!' Ben shot back.

At that they both laughed and suddenly Zoe wanted nothing more than to roll around the floor giggling until she couldn't giggle any more.

'You know, you've got a lovely laugh,' Ben said, his statement bringing her laughter to a stop.

Glancing at him, Zoe noticed he was looking at her the way he used to. It was as if she was the only woman in the room and he had all the time in the world reserved just for her.

'I've been thinking about you and us a lot lately,' he began.

'Okay,' Zoe said. She felt nervous. Things were becoming easier between the two of them. She didn't want that to change.

'It's been hard, this break-up thing,' he continued.

Ben's brow was slick with sweat and his eyes kept darting to the floor.

'It has,' she agreed. 'But I'm glad we're friends. I'd hate to lose that.'

Neither of them said anything as they allowed the chatter and laughter of the guests to wash over them.

'The thing is, Zoe,' Ben tried again, 'I think I've made a huge mistake.'

Zoe's heart banged against her chest.

'What do you mean?'

'When I broke up with you, I think I might have been a bit hasty. I was hurt, and still recovering from surgery. I overreacted and rather than talk to you and try to understand, I ended things. I was stupid and I lashed out. It was only natural you would want to deal with something as momentous as your divorce settlement in your own time. I was stupid. Zoe, I miss you so much. I can't stand being without you any more.'

Zoe's heart was beating so loudly she was struggling to hear anything else over the roar of adrenaline in her ears.

She shook her head. 'You were right, Ben. I should have signed those papers earlier and I should have told you about David. I handled it badly.'

'We're a right pair, aren't we?' Ben moved towards her and reached for her hand. 'But ultimately life all boils down to this, doesn't it?' He gestured towards the crowd gathered around them, celebrating the life of Madeleine Harper. 'We all end up here one way or another – might as well enjoy the journey while we can. And, Zoe, I'm not enjoying my journey without you, so what I'm trying to say in this horribly crass way is would you come back to me?'

A part of Zoe wanted to grab this moment with both hands and allow Ben to sweep her into his arms. But another part of her recognised she had been on enough emotional roller coasters for one lifetime. She needed to take stock, slow down.

'Can I think about it?'

Ben's face fell. 'Yes. I'm sorry, didn't mean to ambush you.'

Ben let her hand go, and Zoe laid a hand on his forearm. 'You didn't. I just need some time.'

She set her glass down and walked out of the pub, unsure if she had just made the worst decision of her life.

Chapter Forty-One

'I cannot believe you said no,' Sarah said for the umpteenth time that morning.

Zoe sipped a mouthful of champagne as she perched on the chair of the posh bridal shop and glared at her. 'And I can't believe you're ruining my Saturday morning off by not only making me come wedding dress shopping with you but having a go at me too. I thought you'd be pleased at my restraint.'

'Pleased?' Sarah screeched. Her friend was dressed in a strapless white dress that Zoe thought made her look like Barbie – and not in a good way. 'Have you lost your mind? Why would I be pleased you and lover boy aren't back together?'

'Because I thought you would see it as evidence of the way I'm growing. How I don't need a man to define me or make me feel whole after Sean,' Zoe reasoned.

Sarah smiled at the shopkeeper, who was doing her best to look disinterested. Placing a delicate white veil on her head, Sarah admired her reflection. 'And I am pleased, but Zoe, it's Ben.'

'So?' She glanced at Sarah, their eyes meeting in the mirror.

'So you're surely not going to keep him hanging about forever? You guys are made for each other; any fool can see that.'

'That might be true, but my head feels as if it's been all over the place lately. If me and Ben get back together, I want it to be because we're both ready. He was right, I do have emotional baggage. I am technically still married and I do still have weird mixed-up feelings for David – he was the father of my child, after all.'

Sarah snatched the veil off and shook her head. 'Zoe, you really need to get on with it.'

'What do you mean?' Zoe asked with a frown.

'I mean Ben is hot; he won't hang about for long.' Sarah disappeared into the changing room with another white dress.

Zoe said nothing and instead smiled sympathetically at the shopkeeper, who was standing in the corner of the room doing her best to keep her expression blank. Zoe took another sip of champagne. When Sarah asked her to come wedding dress shopping with her last night Zoe had agreed, sure it would be fun. She had enjoyed hunting for her own gown with her girlfriends when she married David, but this morning, with Sarah's lack of support over her decision not to get back together with Ben, the day was fast losing its shine.

'How are you getting on?' Zoe called, trying to hurry her friend up.

'Fine,' Sarah replied as she emerged from the dressing rom.

At the sight of her friend in a cream spaghetti-strap gown, with tiny Swarovski crystals covering the bodice, Zoe gasped. 'Oh, Sarah, you look beautiful.'

Sarah's eyes were full of tears as she beamed at Zoe, her face flushed. 'I think this is the one.'

Zoe crouched down behind her friend to make little adjustments to the train. 'Definitely. It was made for you.'

Recognising that she might be near a sale, the shopkeeper took charge of the situation. 'It fits you like a glove,' she said authoritatively, but gently moving Zoe out of the way to expertly pull the gown this way and that. 'Are you planning on losing weight for the wedding?'

Sarah shook her head. 'He says I'm perfect just as I am and I don't want to change for him or anyone else.'

The shopkeeper beamed. 'Then it sounds to me like you've found a good man. I've served more brides than I care to remember and I always say, when you know, you know.'

At the statement, Sarah raised an eyebrow at Zoe. 'You hear that? When you know, you know.'

-

Later that day, as Zoe arrived at work that afternoon, Sarah and the shopkeeper's words were still ringing in her ears.

'Good morning then?' Miles asked from his position behind the nurses' desk.

She sank into the seat beside him. 'That depends on whether your idea of fun is drinking champagne and watching your best friend try on wedding dresses.'

At the mention of the words 'wedding dress', Miles lit up. 'Yeah? Did she find something?'

Zoe grinned. 'She did and she looks beautiful. You'll love it when you see it.'

'I can't wait.' Miles pressed his hands to his heart. 'I mean it, I just want to be married to this woman. I don't care how, when or where. She could turn up in a bin liner and I'd still say she was the most gorgeous bride in the world.'

'What happened to you?' Zoe marvelled, as she leaned over to ruffle his hair. 'My little Miles has grown up!'

'Get off,' Miles grumbled, moving away from her.

Zoe giggled. 'I'm serious. I think it's brilliant about you two. I couldn't see it before but you make a great couple.'

Miles looked at her in surprise. 'I think there's a compliment in there.'

'There is. I'm delighted for you both.' She grinned as she surveyed the peace of the day room.

'And what about you? You and Ben looked as if you were getting a little cosy at the funeral yesterday…' Miles ventured.

'Don't act like you don't know. I'm sure Sarah was straight on the phone to tell you Ben asked me to get back together.'

Miles looked sheepish. 'Actually, Ben told me after you left.'

At the admission, Zoe felt wrong-footed. 'Oh.'

'Listen, I think you're being smart,' Miles said, leaning forward in his chair as if to emphasise how seriously he was taking Zoe's situation.

'Now I am worried.'

'No, you've been through heaps; you ought to have a bit of time out, something I pointed out to Ben.'

'That was thoughtful,' Zoe mused.

'It's true. I think you and him make a good pair but it can't be all on his terms. It's got to work for you.'

'That's what I said to Sarah.'

'You take your time. No sense rushing things,' Miles advised. 'When you know, you know.'

And there it was, that expression again. Zoe groaned inwardly. It was all too much to think about. Right now, all she wanted to focus on was work.

'Anything I need to know about?' she asked, gesturing to the diary.

Miles shook his head. 'It's all been fairly run-of-the-mill but there's an official-looking package from Australia and Mr Harper dropped a letter off for you in your pigeonhole.'

Zoe frowned. 'For me? Did anyone else get one?'

Miles shook his head. 'Said he found it in Mrs Harper's things.'

Getting to her feet, Zoe reached for her post. Discarding her copy of the *Nursing Times* and various fliers, she soon saw the packet with the all too familiar Australian Registered Post logo. Puzzled, she ripped it open and let out a gasp of surprise as she did so.

'What is it?' Miles asked.

Zoe pulled out the official white papers and examined them. 'It's my decree absolute. I'm officially divorced. David must have arranged to have it sent here as he knows this is where I spend half my life these days.'

Miles rested a hand on her shoulder. 'You all right?'

Pausing for a moment, Zoe considered the question before she answered. 'You know what? I really am.'

'I think that's great, Zo,' Miles said softly. 'It can't have been easy.'

'No, but it was the right decision. It just took me a while to realise it,' Zoe admitted. 'That's it now, I'm free.'

Miles smiled. 'I guess you are. Ironic, you're getting divorced just as I'm planning on getting hitched.'

Zoe laughed. 'I'm sure yours will go better than mine did.'

'Oh, I dunno, it's just about finding the right person,' Miles observed. 'Relationships aren't about luck, they're about love.'

Zoe shook her head in astonishment at him. 'You have really changed.'

Miles nudged her playfully. 'Don't be a drongo, mate.'

'Okay, maybe there's still room to go.' She grinned as she reached for the next letter. Turning it over in her hands, she saw her name was written in thick, almost calligraphic handwriting on a square pale-blue envelope.

Dear Zoe,

For the notekeeper herself. I felt it only right I leave you a few words. You showed me a kindness and love I never expected to find at the end of my life and for that I want to thank you. I have always believed love to be in very short supply during our lifetime and so if you find it you should cherish it. We may not have known one another long, but I believe we shared a kinship, a uniqueness all of its own. Zoe, you deserve to find love in your life again. Go after it at every chance you get.

Yours affectionately,
Madeleine Harper

Zoe was filled with warmth at Mrs Harper's words. This lovely woman had known just how to reach her. Together they had found comfort in each other as they discussed their much-loved but lost sons, and their place in the world as mothers of children now departed. Theirs had been a special relationship and Zoe would always treasure it. Now, Zoe knew that Mrs Harper was right in her final words. Real, true, honest love was hard to come by. If you were lucky enough to find it, that love should be treasured.

Chapter Forty-Two

With the words of the bridal store shopkeeper, the note from Mrs Harper and now her divorce, Zoe was beginning to feel like the universe was trying to tell her to move on. As she lay in bed that Sunday morning, the light summer rain beating against her bedroom window, she couldn't stop thinking about Mrs Harper's note. Zoe had read and reread the note, each sentence striking a chord.

Her friend was right. Zoe did want to live a life filled with love, not just for herself but for Sean too. She had been living in limbo for far too long and it was time to stop. To live this way wasn't just a disservice to herself but also to the memory of Sean. He deserved to be honoured with a mother who could love and live life to the fullest. Now, she wanted nothing more than to put right the mistakes she knew she had made – before it was too late.

Swinging her legs out of bed, Zoe crossed the room to her wardrobe and cast her eyes over the three boxes of stationery that rested on the top shelf. Usually, she knew instinctively which card to write in or which notepaper to pick. Today, though, she wasn't sure. When her eyes lingered on the shooting star notepaper she had used to write to Arthur's widow, Audrey, Zoe felt drawn towards it. A shooting star signalled hope and wishes waiting to come true, and that was surely what was needed for this particular letter.

Tearing off a sheet of paper, she gazed at the blank canvas in front of her and pondered what to say. There was so much in her heart and in her head.

As Zoe chewed the end of her pen, the bridal shopkeeper's words the previous morning echoed in her head. *When you know, you know.* The statement swirled around her brain, berries in a smoothie blender, but it propelled her forward and Zoe finally found the few words she wanted to express. Putting pen to paper, she began to write.

-

Just over two hours later, Zoe found herself back at the top of town, rain hammering against her windscreen. Finding a parking space a little way from Ben's house, she clambered out of the car and walked quickly towards his home, rainwater quickly coating her hair and skin. The sky thundered ominously overhead but Zoe didn't care. Determinedly, she rapped on the door and waited for an answer, but this time there wasn't the familiar thud of footsteps. Undeterred, she tried again. By now the rain was trickling down the back of her neck and soaking her clothes, but she wasn't going anywhere, not until she had found him. Only banging against the door for the third time did Zoe realise she was probably going to have to give up, or at least go back to the car and decide what to do next.

Dejected, she turned away and began walking down the street. She had almost reached her car when she saw Ben coming around the corner, his hulking frame hunched under a large golf umbrella.

'Zoe! What are you doing here?' he exclaimed.

'I came to say I'm sorry,' she said, doing her best to wipe the rain from her face. 'And to give you this.'

She handed him the shooting star notepaper she had been labouring over that morning.

Smiling in spite of the rain, Ben tore the envelope open and Zoe watched his face as he took in every word.

Dear Ben,

I love you. Please come back to me. If for no other reason than: when you know, you know.

Zoe

As Ben finished reading the few scant lines, he looked up from the paper and smiled. 'Zoe, I've always known. I love you.'

And with that he pulled her under the umbrella and into his arms. As she felt his soft lips against hers, a feeling of warmth flooded her cold body – she was where she belonged.

-

They lay in each other's arms, legs tangled in sheets and one another. Zoe rested her head against Ben's chest, enjoying the sound of the strong and rhythmic beat echoing in her ear.

'You never told me what changed your mind, about us getting back together,' Ben said lazily, as he ran his hand through her hair.

'It was a couple of things,' Zoe admitted. 'I was so hurt when you ended things that I didn't want to rush into getting back together and making another mistake.'

Ben kissed the top of her head and whispered, 'I'm sorry.'

'No, don't be,' Zoe said. 'You did what you felt was right. But when I got a letter from Mrs Harper and my divorce came through all in one go yesterday it seemed like the universe was telling me to stop being a fool.'

'I was devastated when you said you wouldn't come back to me,' he said, his voice thick with emotion. 'This isn't a sentence I ever thought I would say, but I'm glad David divorced you and I'm glad you became friends with Mrs Harper.'

'So am I.' Zoe laughed. 'It was the letter from Mrs Harper that clinched it.'

'What did it say?' Ben blurted, before realising he was being impolite and hastily said, 'Not that you have to tell me if it's private.'

'It's not so much private, but special,' Zoe said, the words of the letter echoing in her mind. 'She reminded me how precious love is and how we should cherish it when we find it.'

'That sounds powerful,' Ben said, his fingers still threaded through Zoe's hair.

'It was,' Zoe agreed. 'That's the thing about these notes we write. You've seen for yourself the impact they can have on people's lives.'

Ben paused for a moment, and Zoe sat up to look at him. His face was surprisingly grave.

'Are you all right?' she asked.

'I'm fine now.' He cupped her chin with his hand, then leaned in to kiss her. As he pulled away, he fixed his eyes on her and smiled. 'Those notes we delivered to Irene, and April, and Mrs Bell of course – we helped get their lives in order. That's an incredible feeling.'

'You did it,' Zoe said softly, her eyes never leaving Ben's. 'You took the words down, you were there for them in their hour of need.'

'No, Zoe, *we* did it,' Ben said softly, leaning forward to kiss her again. 'Haven't you worked it out yet? You and me together are unstoppable.'

Chapter Forty-Three

Zoe had forgotten how long the journey to Cornwall could be. As she watched Ben patiently sit in their third jam of the day, she bit her tongue. Given it was the middle weekend of August, she wasn't surprised that families were flocking to the area.

Despite his assurances that he was fine, Zoe noticed in the week they had been back together that Ben tired easily. The nurse in her wanted to tell him to take it easy, but as his girlfriend, she knew all she could do was express her concern and leave Ben to make his own choices. Take this weekend, for example. Zoe had suggested they forget the trip to Cornwall but Ben had insisted on rearranging it, finding availability at short notice for the weekend ahead.

Much had changed since their reunion. Zoe no longer saw Ben as her rescuer; he was her partner, and in turn she was able to be more honest with him. Equally, Ben had promised to stop pretending he was Superman and could handle everything alone. They had a newfound respect for each other and, with Ben back in her life, Zoe felt as if the brightness had been turned up on her world.

She turned to him. 'You sure you're all right? Want me to take over?'

Ben shook his head, expertly driving through the winding lanes lined with lush purple rhododendrons. 'Now we're nearly there, you mean?'

'I didn't want to cramp your style,' she teased.

'And I'm grateful, but I've got it.'

Zoe didn't press the point, choosing instead to focus on the fact the traffic had vanished.

'It's beautiful, isn't it?' she said, gazing dreamily out of the window as a wisp of dark-blue sea came into view.

'It is,' Ben confirmed. 'I haven't been here since I was a boy and we went on holiday to Bude. Never been this far down, though.'

'I still can't believe this is your home country. You have all this beauty on your doorstep and you never made it further than Bude.'

Ben laughed, his throaty warm chuckle filling the car. 'I wanted to come back, I just never had the time.'

'Do you regret that?'

There was a pause as Ben turned left. 'No. That's who I was back then. Career focused, hungry to get ahead. Now I'm in my late forties that's not who I am, but I don't regret anything I did or didn't do. The operation has only reinforced that for me.'

'Honestly?' Zoe asked, looking at him for signs of doubt or worry.

'Yes. I'm happy with everything I've done, especially now you're back in my life.'

Zoe smiled. 'I'm not going anywhere.'

Ben raised an eyebrow. 'I'll hold you to that.'

-

Just over an hour later, they reached the cottage Ben had booked. Zoe didn't think she had seen anywhere so picture-postcard perfect in all her life. The photographs on the website didn't do the place justice. Perched at the most southerly point of the country stood a grand, whitewashed building that had once been an old signal station for ships crossing stormy Cornish seas. With only green fields and the striking blue of the Atlantic for company, Zoe felt as if she were the last person on earth.

Inside was just as beautiful. Bright, nautical-themed rooms with large sash windows made up the cottage, while the huge roof terrace looked out onto views right across the ocean.

'Like it?' Ben threaded his arms around her waist as she stood on the roof terrace gazing out at the sea, the gentle breeze ruffling her hair.

'I love it! I remember the Lizard being beautiful but never this beautiful. I can't believe you arranged all this for me.'

Ben pushed the hair from the nape of her neck and kissed her skin so gently she tingled all over. 'I'd do anything for you, Zoe. I want to give you the world.'

A warm flush of happiness passed through Zoe. She turned away from the sea and faced Ben, wrapping her arms around his neck, her forehead resting against his. But it was impossible to miss the gigantic yawn he was doing his best to contain.

'Tired?' she asked.

Ben paused, and she could tell he was half-thinking about putting a brave face on things before he relented and gave a brief nod of his head. 'A bit.'

She reached for his hand. 'Then let's take a nap. We've got all weekend to explore.'

Sometime later, Zoe woke to find herself in a sunshine-flooded bedroom, the seagulls circling overhead the only sound. She glanced across at the other side of the bed, wanting to share the moment with Ben, but to her surprise he wasn't there. Frowning, she wrapped herself in a brilliant white sheet and padded downstairs to find him in the kitchen, head bowed over his laptop.

'Hey,' she whispered, kissing his smooth skull. 'What are you doing?'

He snapped the lid shut then looked at Zoe, a flash of guilt across his features. 'Sorry. Work thing.'

Zoe frowned. She thought she had seen a map on his screen but didn't want to push it.

'Everything all right now?' she asked instead.

'Fine.' Ben grinned, getting to his feet and snaking his arms around her. 'Any thoughts on what you'd like to do now we've arrived?'

'I think we've done everything I wanted,' she whispered, leaning upwards to kiss him gently on the mouth.

'Is that so?' Ben asked, a smile spreading across his face. 'Well, in that case, I've got lots of things I want to do seeing as this place is on my bucket list.'

Zoe rolled her eyes playfully. 'And here's me thinking this weekend was all about me.'

Ben laughed and got to his feet. 'Yeah right! Get your boots, we're walking.'

As they headed outside and rambled along the dramatic landscape of the Cornish coastline, Zoe felt on top of the world. The green hills rolled on for miles while the dark, majestic blue of the sea contrasted starkly with the grey cliffs below. Zoe tried to imagine what life would have been like for the smugglers who had tried to make their living in those waters, importing goods that were never legal but always wanted.

'Hey, where have you gone?' Ben asked, reaching for her hand.

She turned to him and smiled. How different their relationship might have been in days gone by. Although most people didn't bat an eyelid now at the sight of an interracial couple holding hands, in the past Zoe imagined it was very different. But as she threaded her pale fingers through his dark ones, Zoe only felt relief she was living in this moment, here and now, which meant she and Ben could be together.

'I'm right here.'

He pulled her close to him and turned his gaze seawards. 'I've been thinking, Zoe, about us.'

'Sounds ominous.'

Ben turned back to face her and kissed the top of her head. 'Maybe we should get our own place.'

She looked at him in surprise. 'But we've only just got back together!'

'So?' Ben shrugged. 'Everything we've been through, the notes, the cancer, us breaking up, getting back together. We've already lived a life together, Zo, and when you know, you know. Isn't that what you said to me in your note? I *do* know. You asked me what I wanted from life and it's this. I want you and me to be together.'

She frowned. 'Has this got anything to do with that map I caught you looking at earlier?'

Ben's eyes slid away from hers. 'I swear, Zoe, I wouldn't do something without talking to you first, but yes, I've been looking at flats that might work for us. I've found a nice one in that little village near the centre.'

'Wow,' she exclaimed. The idea of living in the bohemian village just a short stroll away held immediate appeal.

'I thought we could look at it when we get home. Assuming that this is what you want.' He stroked her cheek. 'This might be moving a bit fast, I'm sorry. Candice says I'm a nightmare when I know what I want.'

'Does Candice know this has been on your mind?'

The waves crashed against the shore as Ben shook his head. 'I wanted to talk to you first before I did anything.'

'But you did arrange a flat viewing,' Zoe countered.

'Only because I fell in love with the place,' Ben protested. 'I can always cancel it if you decide this isn't something you want. I don't want to push you, and if you aren't ready I'm not going away. I just want you, any way I can have you.'

He leaned down to kiss her and Zoe felt her heart melt. After all the misery they had both endured, a happy ending seemed unthinkable. Yet now, Zoe felt as though a glorious future was being offered to her on a plate.

'But what about your flat?' she asked, suddenly remembering the fancy pad he and Candice shared.

Ben frowned. 'What about it?'

'It's your dream home, you said so yourself,' she pointed out. 'Why would you want to give that up?'

'And you're my dream girl, Zoe. A house doesn't mean anything to me without you in it to make a home.'

And there it was.

'All right,' she said, feeling as if she were throwing caution heavily into the wind. 'Let's move in together.'

Before she knew what was happening, Ben was sweeping her up in his arms and twirling her around the cliff path.

'Ben, put me down,' she shrieked, the swirling blue seas feeling perilously close. 'I mean it, you'll have us both in a watery grave if you carry on.'

But Ben refused. Instead, he kept whizzing her around as if she weighed no more than a sheet of notepaper.

'Zoe, I am going to make you happy; *we* are going to be so happy,' he said, finally setting her back on the ground. 'In all my life, I never thought I'd find someone that makes me as happy as you do.'

Zoe couldn't stop smiling. Ben was the man she wanted and she never wanted to let him go. She turned her gaze from his and back to the cliffs and the sea below. Once again, her thoughts turned to the smugglers. Yes, they had taken a chance without knowing what lay ahead, but when it worked the pay-off had been worth it.

Chapter Forty-Four

The subject of moving in together dominated the rest of Ben and Zoe's weekend. Arms entwined, they tramped around the Cornish coastline walking, talking and planning their future. Zoe insisted that she wanted takeaway nights, and domestic chores split fifty-fifty. Ben agreed but countered that he wanted lie-ins on Sundays and a night once a week where they didn't slump in front of the telly like an old married couple. Zoe was happy to agree, and as she drove them home, she couldn't take the smile off her face. She was finally, wholeheartedly happy.

Despite his best efforts to walk and stay up late, Zoe could see that the weekend had taken a toll on Ben. He had put on a bit of weight since his initial return to work, but was still nowhere near back to full strength. When she had suggested driving back and Ben agreed, Zoe was delighted they were working as a team.

'What time did you book the viewing for?' she asked, concentrating on the road.

Ben checked his watch as he leaned back in the passenger seat. 'Three. We've got plenty of time.'

Zoe nodded contentedly. 'Perfect. Might even be able to stop off for a quick celebratory sandwich before I start the night shift.'

'Forgot you were working tonight.'

'I hadn't.' Zoe sighed. 'Back to the real world with a very big bump.'

Ben smiled. 'All dreams have to come an end sometime.'

'But not in our dream home they won't,' Zoe said seriously. 'In our dream home, everything will be perfect.'

'You haven't seen the flat in real life yet. You might hate it,' Ben pointed out.

'Nah. I've seen the pictures. It will be perfect because you picked it.'

Ben grinned. 'I hope you're going to be this nice to me when we're living together.'

'Depends.' Zoe checked her door mirror as she changed lanes. 'If you leave your dirty pants all over the floor and put your used mugs on the side rather than in the dishwasher then we might fall out.'

'Hey!' Ben cried. 'It's endearing.'

'It's not,' Zoe said hotly.

'Stop nagging me, woman,' Ben said, with a laugh. 'We haven't even moved in together yet.'

Zoe grinned at the exasperation in Ben's tone. 'This is just a little sample of what life will be like in a few months' time.'

'Bring it on,' Ben said, his eyes crinkling with affection.

A couple of hours later and they had reached the flat with Zoe managing to find a space right outside. The estate agent, a cheerful woman in her twenties dressed in a sharp black suit, handed them the property details and welcomed them inside. The moment Zoe stepped into the hallway, she exhaled. There was something about the place that made it feel as if it had always been home. Glancing across at Ben, she saw he was just as enthused as she was, looking around at the flat and back at her in delight.

The pictures on the website hadn't lied; the place really was beautiful. The entire flat was painted white, making the place feel palatial. Tall ceilings and large sash windows allowed the light to flood in and the large living room had a surprisingly homely atmosphere thanks to the ornate tiled fireplace and open-plan kitchen, complete with walnut units and a granite island.

'We could have breakfast here every morning looking out onto that courtyard.' She walked over to Ben and linked her fingers through his.

'I like the sound of that.' Ben smiled, his gaze following hers as Zoe imagined potted purple and yellow lavender plants and a trellis filled with sweet-scented peonies lining the yard.

'The courtyard comes with the flat, of course,' the agent said, 'and it's totally private.'

'Totally private, eh?' Ben winked.

Zoe shook her head in despair. 'Easy, boy, we haven't signed on the dotted line yet.'

'But we're going to, aren't we?' Ben said, walking around the place with his hands expanded as if to take it all in.

The agent smiled. 'Do you want to see the rest of it?'

'Of course,' Zoe said. But even as she followed the agent upstairs to see the bedrooms and bathroom, she knew it was a done deal. There would have to be something seriously wrong with the place in order for her to say she didn't want to take it. Upstairs, the bedrooms didn't disappoint and as Zoe wandered around, more images of her wonderful new life with Ben flooded her brain. Thoughts of them waking up together, reading the Sunday papers and drinking endless cups of coffee made her shiver with pleasure.

'Like it?' Ben said as the agent left them upstairs to get a feel for the place.

Zoe snaked her arms around his neck and breathed in the by now familiar scent of Acqua di Parma. 'I love it.'

'Me too.'

'We're definitely doing this?'

'We are definitely doing this,' Ben agreed.

That familiar excitement that had built in the pit of her stomach burned bright once more.

'I take it you two want to take this flat, then?' the agent asked, interrupting them.

'We do,' Zoe assured her.

'Great.' The agent beamed again. 'It's available now so you can move in when you like, subject to references of course. Have you got time to come back to the office with me to fill out the paperwork?'

'I have,' Ben said, only for Zoe to shake her head as she checked her watch.

'I'm going to have to go or I'll be late for my shift.'

'That's okay. I can get going and you can fill in the blanks later, assuming that's okay?' Ben asked, turning to the agent, who nodded. 'Then that's settled. Are you all right getting to work?'

'The bus stop's nearby and takes me all the way in,' Zoe said, raising an eyebrow. 'It's almost as if someone thought of this.'

'Almost.' Ben nodded, his face the perfect expression of seriousness, apart from the crinkle of delight in his eyes.

Zoe swatted him playfully with her bag. He really had thought of everything. He leaned forward and kissed her goodbye.

'Look at that,' he whispered. 'Our first kiss in our new home.'

-

'This has got to be the last box,' Miles panted, as he heaved the crate of books from the back of the hired van and onto the steps. Zoe laughed when she saw the sweat pouring down his forehead. He had insisted it would be no big deal to help move Zoe's belongings. Looking at Miles, swearing and cursing under his breath, his new T-shirt crumpled and dirty, she had a feeling he was regretting his offer.

'You'll be pleased to know, that is the very last one. Thank you,' Zoe said gratefully.

Ben was sitting on the new sofa they had bought, and Zoe shot him a look urging him to get up. Her boyfriend might have already moved his own stuff but there was still a lot of heavy lifting to be done.

'All right, all right,' he grumbled, reluctantly getting to his feet.

As he helped Miles set the last box down, Zoe looked around her new home. There were boxes everywhere and she had no idea where the kettle was despite the fact that she knew she had packed it at the top of the box marked *kitchen*.

'Can we do anything else for you?' Sarah asked brightly, Lottie trailing after her, oohing and ahhing at all the rooms and the new nooks and crannies waiting to be explored. The little girl had been devastated at the idea of Zoe moving out, until the nurse explained she would have her very own room and could come and stay whenever she wanted. The first thing Lottie had done when she arrived was make a beeline for the box-room that would now be her room, excited about the idea of bedtime stories from Ben and Zoe whenever she stayed over.

'No, we're fine, thanks,' Zoe replied. 'We'll sort this.'

Sarah raised an eyebrow. 'Well, er, enjoy that!'

'We will,' Ben said, rubbing a hand over his head and joining Zoe in surveying the mess.

'Yeah, see you guys, and good luck.' Miles grinned, looking decidedly more chipper now he knew he didn't have to do any more work. 'I don't know about you, Ben mate, but I reckon I'm ready for a beer.'

'I think that might be my first job,' Ben said solemnly.

'I think it might be the first job for both of us,' Zoe said, leaning her head on Ben's shoulder.

'I should just get the essentials out for now,' Sarah advised, reaching for her daughter's hand. 'Everything else can wait until tomorrow.'

'Good idea,' Zoe said, stifling a yawn. Already all she wanted was to crawl into bed. 'Thank you so much for everything today. I appreciate it.'

'We both do,' Ben insisted. 'You'll have to come over for dinner soon, as a proper thank you.'

'Cheers, mate.' Miles patted Ben's shoulder as he made his way past them and out into the hallway.

Sarah kissed Ben on the cheek, then Zoe, and Lottie hugged their legs, clinging to them like a koala to a tree before Sarah gently dragged her away with promises they would be back very soon.

'Here we are,' Ben whispered once they were all alone. 'Our first home. What shall we christen first?'

Zoe laughed and sank onto the sofa. Her back ached and her feet were sore. 'How about we have a rest for a minute?'

'Typical.' Ben rolled his eyes as he sat beside her and looped an arm around her shoulders. 'They say all the passion goes the moment you move in together.'

Closing her eyes, Zoe allowed the tiredness to seep through her bones. It had been a long day and she didn't have the energy to rebut Ben's lame jokes.

'How about a glass of wine?' she suggested as she opened her eyes.

At the idea, Ben visibly brightened. 'Yes, though I'm not sure our glasses will have survived after the way Miles was lugging those boxes about.'

'We can use mugs,' Zoe suggested.

She soon found the wine and two mismatched but clean glasses and returned with a drink for each of them.

'Any regrets?' Zoe couldn't help asking as she handed him a glass.

'None at all,' Ben said firmly. 'This is all I've ever wanted.'

'All?' Zoe smirked. 'I may not have known you long, Ben Tasker, but I know you well enough to know you're always on the hunt for a new challenge. What's next?'

'Nothing.' Ben took a long slug of his drink and rested his arm on the back of the couch. 'I've got the dream career, dream girl and the dream flat. What else do I need?'

He leaned forward to kiss her on the lips and Zoe's stomach rumbled.

'I need dinner,' she said. 'What do you fancy?'

'Oh God, are we at that stage already?' Ben cried, his biscuit-coloured eyes filled with horror.

'What do you mean?'

'I mean please let's not turn into one of those couples where all we can talk about is what we're having for dinner and whose turn it is to put the bins out.'

'Never.' Zoe solemnly made a sign of the cross against her chest. 'How about some chips from the chippy across the road?'

'That's more like it,' Ben said, his tired eyes briefly lighting up at the prospect.

Later, after Zoe had wrapped up the leftover fish and chips and put them in the bin, she returned to what she already thought of as her place on the sofa beside Ben.

'That was quite a day,' he sighed. 'How often do you get to move in with the love of your life and enjoy a fish and chip supper?'

The words sounded casual. But looking into his eyes as she leaned forward and kissed him, Zoe knew she felt the same way. As she felt his lips against hers, Zoe remembered that lonely journey from Australia to England. She had never expected to find happiness again. Yet she had, and it was largely down to Ben. Like a shining star in the inky black sky, Zoe felt he had guided her towards him and she had felt his light shining on her ever since.

'Ben Tasker,' she whispered. 'Thank you for bringing me back to life.'

Chapter Forty-Five

It had been more than two weeks since Ben and Zoe had moved in together and the couple had surprised even themselves at how they had settled so quickly into a happy rhythm. Each day, whoever was up first made breakfast while the other made the bed. Then they usually drove to work before coming home and spending their evenings nestled on the sofa in contented bliss. The nights were becoming slightly longer now that August had turned into September and Zoe found herself looking forward to cold winter days and nights if it meant she and Ben could snuggle under blankets keeping each other warm.

The only thing that could improve life, Zoe thought, was if Miles stopped asking for a daily progress report on how it was all going. She turned away from the computer screen at the nurses' station to look up at him. His face was the picture of excitement as he waited for her answer on what Ben had cooked her for dinner the previous night.

'Miles, why all the interest?' she asked, bemused. 'Ever since me and Ben moved in together you've taken more interest in my love life than a teenage girl. What's going on?'

A flicker of guilt passed across Miles's features. 'Nothing. I'm just stoked you're happy.'

Zoe shook her head. 'I'm not buying it.'

Miles wrinkled his nose as if thinking about telling the truth, then spoke. 'I want to ask Sarah if I could move in, that's all. But I didn't want to jump straight in just in case.'

'Just in case?'

Miles looked awkward. 'Just in case things didn't work out with Ben again and you needed to go back to Sarah's.'

At the admission, Zoe threw her head back and cackled with laughter. 'Miles, you're hilarious.'

'No, you asked me to be honest,' Miles put in, sounding put-out.

As Zoe tried to compose herself, she saw Karen making a beeline for the nurses' desk.

'What's so comical first thing in the morning?' She frowned, peering first at Zoe and then Miles.

'Sorry, Karen,' Zoe said meekly.

'Yeah, sorry, Karen. We were only mucking about,' Miles added.

The director smiled as she set a thick stack of files on the desk. 'Don't apologise, it's nice to hear laughter like that. I just wanted to be let in on the joke.'

Zoe jerked her head towards Miles. 'This clown's worried I'm heading back to Sarah's.'

Karen raised an eyebrow. 'So soon? I thought you and Ben had just moved in together.'

'We have. Miles wants to get his feet under the table but is worried I might run back and ruin things.' Zoe smiled.

Leaning across the desk, Karen beckoned Miles towards her. 'Nurse Anderson, there's a saying in this country you might do well to consider and that is: would you be so quick to jump in your grandmother's grave?'

As Miles looked at her, perplexed, Karen let out a bark of laughter as she turned to Zoe. 'Could you come up to my office at ten? There's something important I wish to discuss.'

'Yes, of course,' Zoe said. 'Is everything all right?'

Karen gave Zoe a small smile she found impossible to read. 'Everything's fine. I'll explain everything then.'

Karen walked away and Zoe felt Miles lean over her left shoulder.

'I'd say you've got Buckley's chance of everything being fine!' he teased.

'Oh, shut up, Miles,' Zoe said, lightly tapping his head with one of Karen's files.

-

Despite Karen's assurances, by the time she made her way up to her director's office, Zoe felt concerned. What could be the problem? The paperwork was all up to date and patient care was going well. Could this be about her and Ben moving in together? Was Karen about to tell her the board had a problem with their relationship? Or worse, what if they wanted her to take over Ben's job? He was due to look after one of the Harpers' hospices in Gloucestershire soon. Cold dread coursed through her at the very idea of being in charge again.

As she reached Karen's office, she saw the door was slightly ajar and the sound of voices floated into the corridor. When she tapped lightly on the door, the voices stopped and she heard Karen say, 'Ah, that must be her,' before calling, 'Come in.'

Pushing the door fully open, Zoe saw Karen not sitting behind her desk as she expected, but at the far end of the room on an easy chair. Opposite her, each nursing a cup of tea, were two women Zoe recognised instantly.

'Ella! Mrs Pagett! How lovely to see you both!' she exclaimed, taking in the sight of Ricky's mother and grandmother.

'Hi, Zoe,' Ella said shyly.

'Zoe love, nice to see you,' Mrs Pagett said warmly.

'Come and join us.' Karen gestured for her to take the chair opposite hers. As Zoe did so, Karen poured her a cup of tea from the pot on the table and Zoe took it, recognising this wasn't the moment to ask if there was coffee instead.

'How are you both?' Zoe asked, taking in Ella's appearance. It had been three months since Ricky's death and Zoe had often found herself thinking about the young mum. Yet today it looked as though she was all right. True, the girl was thin and pale, but there was a resilience about her, in the straight line of her back and the way she met Zoe's gaze.

'We've been fine, haven't we, love?' Mrs Pagett replied, smiling brightly as she rubbed Ella's back.

Ella nodded. 'It's been difficult, like you said, but I've got up every morning and it's helped knowing Ricky's not suffering any more.'

'Good.' Zoe nodded approvingly. 'I know how tough it is, Ella, but honestly, it's a case of one day at a time. You'll get there.'

A tear rolled down Ella's cheek and Mrs Pagett squeezed Ella's hand and smiled at Zoe. 'That's what we wanted to talk to you about.'

Zoe frowned. 'How do you mean?'

'You were such a help to Ella when Ricky finally passed away.' Sorrow passed across Mrs Pagett's open features. 'I will never forget the kindness you showed; neither of us will.'

As her eyes strayed to her daughter's, Zoe couldn't miss the closeness between them. For a moment she ached for her own mother. Ruth had been a rock when Sean had passed, but Zoe had felt so tormented by her own feelings of loss she had resisted Ruth's insistence that she talk, preferring to bury her emotions. She hoped things would be different now. Since talking to Ruth a few weeks ago, Zoe had phoned her mum regularly and it felt as if they both wanted to find a new relationship for the future.

'You're very welcome. I'm glad I was there.'

'You made a huge difference,' Ella asserted, lifting her head and fixing her eyes on Zoe. 'Especially that letter you gave me. I read it every day. In those early days I clung to those words. It was as though you could see straight into my heart and knew what I needed.'

A wave of unease passed across Zoe. She wasn't looking for praise.

'I'm pleased to hear that,' she said softly. 'I know when I lost Sean, the note a nurse gave me with his last words meant the world. It still does.'

'And that's what we're here to discuss,' Karen said smoothly. 'Mrs Pagett and Ella contacted me last week with an idea.'

'Oh?'

'Yes, we were so moved by your letter, Zoe, it struck us both how important notes like the one you gave Ella can be,' Mrs Pagett explained. 'And we want to do something to honour Ricky's memory.'

Karen leaned forward in her seat and turned to Zoe. 'The Pagetts want to start a note-writing programme for parents who have lost a child. Just a short note to let them know they have support and love from another parent or someone else that understands their loss.'

'I went to a grief support group for parents a couple of weeks after Ricky's death and I told everyone about your letter,' Ella said earnestly. 'I said how even on my very darkest days your note made me believe that one day things would get better and I would wake up and the pain wouldn't be as bad. I'm not there yet, but your note helps me get up in the morning, Zoe, even when I think I can't.'

'What do you think?' Mrs Pagett asked.

'I think it's a beautiful idea,' Zoe whispered, overcome with emotion.

'Good,' Karen said with a smile. 'When Ella and her mother first came to Simon and me with the idea, we thought it was marvellous. Simon has volunteered the full support of the hospice as a way of honouring his late brother, Nathaniel, and has also agreed to help with funding.'

'Mrs Harper would have loved that,' Zoe said approvingly.

'Quite,' Karen said. 'But we were all very much hoping you would help Ella and Mrs Pagett set things up.'

Zoe let out a gasp of astonishment. 'You want me involved?'

'Who else?' Ella smiled at Zoe. 'We can't do it without you.'

Chapter Forty-Six

'Are you sure you're all right with this?' Ben asked her for what felt like the thousandth time.

Zoe frowned as they sat in the corner of the pub across the road from the hospice. It had been a week since Ella and her mother had discussed the note-writing programme and she had been rushed off her feet ever since.

It had been decided that the hospice would co-ordinate with other hospices, initially in the local area, to reach out to those recently bereaved. At first Ella and her mum wanted to concentrate solely on other parents but Zoe insisted that there were many people who would benefit from a note service such as this one and that they should widen their appeal. Ella and her mum didn't take much persuading and it was agreed that if the venture was a success they would expand the note service out regionally, with the hope one day of making it national. Ever since Zoe had been invited to spearhead the project, she had felt nothing but excitement. This was the challenge she had been looking for but hadn't known she needed.

The only fly in the ointment was Ben. When she'd told him about the idea, she had expected him to be thrilled. But to her surprise he had been concerned and Zoe couldn't understand why.

'Of course I'm all right with it,' she said a little crossly, taking a sip of her drink. She had opted for red wine now the nights were more autumnal, and was enjoying the rich grapey taste slipping down her throat. 'I don't know why you're not more supportive.'

Ben took a pull on his pint. 'It's not that. I'm just worried this will be a lot of work for you. I've hardly seen you the last few days.'

Zoe sighed. It was true there had been a lot to do. She had worked unpaid overtime all week getting an office ready on the top floor of the hospice so the three of them would have somewhere to deal with correspondence. She had also been putting out appeals to local companies to sponsor the stationery they would need and anything else that came with it. So far, they had received a good response, with one local stationer offering supplies and an accountant agreeing to cover postage. They had made an excellent start, but Zoe knew there was a lot more work ahead if they wanted to make the scheme a success.

'Is that what this is about? Our lack of time together?' she asked softly.

Ben looked sheepish. 'A bit of both.'

'You silly bugger,' Zoe said, leaning across the table to kiss him tenderly on the cheek. 'I've got plenty of time for you.'

'I know,' Ben whispered. 'But I worry this might drag you back into the past.'

Zoe pushed a stray lock of hair out of her eyes. She could see from his expression he wasn't being entirely selfish.

'You mean because of Sean,' she said quietly.

'You've made so much progress. And whilst I want you to remember Sean, I'm worried this will drag you back to a place of sadness again.'

She gave him an understanding smile. 'It won't, Ben. I know you're worried, but I know how lonely it can be as a parent when you lose a child. It can destroy your life, your relationships, your work and your sense of self. What better way for me to use my experiences than to work with Ella and her mum, and help others in my situation? It's through talking and sharing we can change things, and it means there was a point to Sean's death and all the heartache David and I went through.'

Ben's look of concern changed to one of affection. 'You're incredible, Zoe,' he whispered softly, the sound of Massive

Attack's 'Teardrop' playing quietly in the background. 'I'm sorry. I didn't understand how you felt. I thought this would make you unhappy again.'

'The thing is, Ben, the pain of loss never goes away, you just get better at living with it,' Zoe explained. 'I think about Sean every day; he's always with me, everywhere I go.'

'I'm sorry.'

'You don't need to be sorry,' Zoe said. 'But I need you to understand that, although Sean may not be alive, I will always be his mum. He will never be forgotten and I want others who have been through what I've been through to know you can do more than survive, you can live.'

'Is there anything I can do to help?'

'I would think so,' Zoe said. 'But don't ask me what – my head's swimming with it all.'

'Fair enough,' Ben said, offering a weak smile. He leaned back in his chair and closed his eyes for a moment. Zoe took a moment to observe him. He seemed quiet, and she worried that he had been the one working too hard.

Thankfully, Ben was beginning to put a bit more weight on, but he was still too thin. She and Candice had been trying to fatten him up, but he always claimed that since the operation he couldn't eat much, which was odd because his belly was starting to swell, something Zoe knew could happen post-operatively if there was an excess of scar tissue. She was making a mental note to remind him to talk to his specialist about it at his check-up next month when Candice appeared.

'Hello.' She grinned, sitting down, shrugging off her leather jacket.

'What time do you call this?' Ben asked, lifting his watch and tapping the face as if to make a point.

'Sorry.' Candice grimaced. 'Late train back from London.'

'That's all right, you're here now,' Zoe said smoothly.

Since she and Ben had moved in together, they had made sure they continued to spend lots of time with their friends, not wanting to be one of those couples who forgot their nearest and dearest the moment they found love. And so, particularly because Ben and Candice were twins and Zoe considered that a bond that should never be broken, she had taken care to ensure they always met for drinks every Tuesday, work commitments and of course any romantic entanglements Candice might have allowing. Ben always moaned about it, arguing his sister was over at their house enough, but Zoe knew the gesture meant a lot to them both.

'Good day?' Zoe asked Candice.

'Long.' Candice made a face. 'I need a drink – can I get you guys one?'

'I'll go, I need the loo anyway,' Ben offered, getting to his feet.

Once Ben was out of sight, Candice gave Zoe a wide grin and clapped her hands together in delight. 'I heard about your note-writing programme. It's brilliant! I've spoken to my manager and she reckons we can give you some funding.'

'Wow! Thank you!' Zoe exclaimed. 'I must admit I'm excited.'

'I can tell,' Candice said. 'I don't think I've ever seen you this thrilled, apart from maybe when you saw Ben's car the first time, but I figured that was more about Ben than the Porsche.'

'The Porsche is pretty impressive.' Zoe laughed. 'I had no idea my feelings for your brother were that transparent.'

Candice rolled her eyes. 'It was obvious to everyone apart from you two!'

Zoe reddened. 'Sorry.'

'No need to be.' Candice grinned. 'It was worth the wait. How is my little brother doing anyway?'

'He's tired,' Zoe said with a sigh. 'I keep telling him to slow down.'

'But he won't listen?'

'You got it,' Zoe said before a thought struck her. 'Any chance you could talk to him?'

Candice made a *tsk* sound between her teeth. 'Me? Forget it!'

'But you two are close, I'm sure he'll listen to you,' Zoe cried.

'Yeah right,' Candice said, with a snort.

'Seriously,' Zoe tried again. 'What about the twin thing you guys share? Can't you intuit something across to him?'

'Load of old bollocks,' Candice said bluntly, 'least it is for me and Ben. We're close, but he won't listen if I start telling him what to do, he'll only do the opposite.'

Zoe let out a sigh of frustration. 'Maybe I shouldn't have taken on this extra role. Ben is still fragile.'

Candice laid a reassuring hand on Zoe's arm. 'Don't even think about it. The moment Ben told me what you were doing, I knew this was the right path for you, Zoe. Besides,' she said hastily as Ben approached the table carrying a tray of drinks, 'last time I checked, my brother was a big boy and could take care of himself. You do you, Zoe Evans.'

Chapter Forty-Seven

At the end of September, the new note-writing programme was in full swing, with the first few notes hitting the post box. Watching Ella engage in the project reminded Zoe of herself when she began to find her feet in the UK. It was at times beautiful to watch the young woman find joy in something she felt passionately about, then heartbreaking when she remembered the sudden loss of Ricky.

Zoe had been much the same. The notes she had begun to take and distribute amongst patients provided her with a much-needed salve, but occasionally she would forget and be sent straight back to the abyss of losing her son. Yet as time passed Sean's loss became something she was more able to live with, a sentiment Ella had shared in the first note she sent from the programme.

'Do you think this is all right?' she had asked shyly, handing Zoe the slip of green notepaper she had chosen.

Zoe had taken the note and read it through. The note was brief, but the words beautiful.

> *Dear Mr and Mrs Peterson,*
>
> *When I lost my son, my heart shattered into a thousand pieces. I know those pieces will never be put back together again, but I am learning each day that those tiny pieces are still strong, they are still full of love and they remind me there is hope for the future even though it might look very different to the one I imagined when my son was born.*

Yours with sincerity,
Ella Pagett

'That's just what I would have wanted to hear,' she said, handing the letter back to Ella.

The relief on Ella's face was obvious. 'Really?'

'Really. You've got a talent for this.'

'I think it's you with the talent,' Ella said, a hint of admiration to her voice as she cast her gaze around the tiny office dedicated to the charity. 'Look at what you've done.'

'We're getting there,' Zoe said, stifling a yawn. 'Now word is getting out, we've seen a surge in requests for notes, and I also need to get my head around social media.'

'I could ask my brother Pete,' Ella suggested. 'He's been looking for something to do since we started all this.'

Zoe smiled. 'That would be fantastic. I'm crap at that sort of thing. I've had nothing to do with the hospice's Instagram page and have left all that to Miles now.'

'Consider it done,' Ella told her.

And Ella had done just that, freeing up Zoe's time in the process, something Ben couldn't resist commenting on as she recounted the story of her previous working day.

'Does this mean I get you to myself again?' he asked now, placing a steaming plate of scrambled eggs in front of Zoe one Saturday morning.

'Ha! You've always had me to yourself and you know it.' She speared a forkful of egg into her mouth.

'If only,' Ben said, taking a seat opposite her with his own breakfast. 'We've got to make the most of this honeymoon period, Zo; chances are before long you'll be sick of the sight of me.'

'Never,' she said tenderly, leaning over to kiss him.

'Why aren't Miles and Sarah here this morning?' Ben asked.

Since Zoe had assured Miles that she and Ben were together forever, he had moved in with Sarah and so far things were going well. Aside from the regular drinks with Candice, Sarah and Lottie – and occasionally Miles too – came over for breakfast every Saturday morning.

'Engagement party prep,' she explained. 'It's the big party tonight.'

Ben shuddered as he chewed his toast. 'Rather him than me.'

'Hey!' Zoe exclaimed. 'That's my friend you're talking about.'

Ben smirked. 'And I love her. But you have to admit she's got a bit crazy with this party.'

'I know.' Zoe grinned. 'But she's not our problem today, she's Miles's.'

'If I haven't said it before, he's a lucky guy.' Ben chuckled, earning a playful swipe from Zoe. 'Anyway, what time are we off this morning?' he asked, changing the subject.

Zoe glanced at the clock above the kitchen sink. 'In about half an hour.'

Ben wiped his mouth with a piece of kitchen roll. 'And you still won't tell me what this is about or where we're going?'

'Now we live together, I need to preserve a bit of mystery, keep the romance alive.'

'The romance will always be alive,' Ben promised. 'I'll get in the shower.'

'But you haven't finished your eggs.'

'I'm not that hungry. I'll put them in a sandwich and take them with me.'

An hour later and Ben was driving, complete with leftover egg sandwich, which Zoe thought smelled disgusting.

'Are you going to tell me exactly where we're going?' Ben asked.

'Wait and see,' she said, checking the sat-nav app on her phone. 'Not far, ten minutes.'

Before long their final destination came into view and as Ben parked the car in a bay right on the seafront, he looked at her incredulously. 'Weston-super-Mud? Why have you brought me here?'

Zoe wrinkled her nose at the unkind nickname for Weston-super-Mare. 'Don't be mean. Weston's very nice. It used to be posh.'

'Certain quarters would say it still is,' Ben replied diplomatically. 'Are you going to tell me why you've brought us here?'

'Once we've had a coffee and a little walk along the seafront.' Zoe got out of the car.

'Before it turns to mud?'

'Precisely.' Zoe grinned.

It didn't take them long to find a cafe serving delicious coffees. As she strolled hand in hand with Ben, the gentle autumn breeze whipping around her neck and the tang of salty air filling her nostrils, Zoe felt happy. She thought Weston had a lot of charm. The long stretch of coastline dotted with the odd Victorian building gave the front an almost majestic feel. As for the legendary Tropicana, which had apparently been a children's paradise in the eighties with its splash pools, wave machine, pineapple water flumes and roller coaster, it only added to the town's charm. She turned to Ben; he was doing a good job of concentrating on his coffee but it was time to put him out of his misery.

'Do you remember Mrs Harper?'

'Of course,' he said with a smile. 'But what's she got to do with Weston-super-Mare?'

'Before she died, she wrote a letter to her son Nathaniel, who drowned when he was a child,' Zoe explained. 'I've been trying to think of the right place to send her note, and it hit me last night – the coast. When we first talked about this note of hers, she showed me a picture of her, her first husband, Albert, and Nathaniel. It was taken right here.'

Ben looked around him. 'In Weston?'

'That's right.'

'I see.' A look of understanding passed across Ben's face. 'I take it you and Mrs H swapped stories about your experiences.'

Zoe nodded. She found it much easier to talk about Sean these days. Ella's writing programme had helped with that. Now there were times she could do it without wanting to cry.

'We did. I think she saw something in me that compelled her to share her story.'

'Or maybe she just thought you'd understand. Grief doesn't always have to define your place in the world, Zoe.'

'I know. But we shared a connection.'

'You chose to honour that connection by bringing her note here.' Ben grinned, expanding his arms wide to encompass the whole of Weston.

Zoe laughed. 'Yes. I have a feeling she would like it.'

'Me too,' Ben said, reaching for her hand. 'Let's do it.'

They removed their socks and shoes, the coolness of the coarse sand between their feet making them squirm.

'Oh, it's freezing!' Zoe screamed with delight.

Ben grinned and scrunched his toes, allowing the oozy squidginess to rush over his feet. 'Me and Candice had some great times on this beach when we were kids.'

'You did?' Zoe looked at him quizzically, keen to hear more about Ben's childhood.

'Yup.' Ben pointed to the Tropicana that was now an entertainment venue. 'I learned to swim when I was seven, in there. And it was also where I had my first kiss.'

'Not at the same time, I hope?' Zoe looked horrified.

'Nah, it was a few years later, behind the pineapple slide.' Ben chuckled at the memory. 'Tanesha Adams. She was gorgeous!'

'Come on, lover boy, enough trips down memory lane.' She chuckled. 'Let's deliver this note.'

'All right,' he agreed. 'Then we can get some chips.'

'Chips at this time?' Zoe exclaimed as she pulled away. 'It's not even eleven.'

Ben grinned. 'We're at the seaside – besides, you only live once.'

Zoe reached into her bag for the note, Nathaniel's name clearly visible on the front. She smiled before she frantically tore at the letter, ripping it into tiny shreds and throwing them into the air, the scraps falling like confetti across the sand. It felt like the perfect goodbye.

Chapter Forty-Eight

The familiar sound of 'Could It Be Magic' drifted out across the packed dance floor. Zoe looked across the room and saw Lottie dancing with her school friends, the little group full of joy as they held hands and jumped to the music. Elsewhere, a champagne tower had been set up in the centre and behind that, photos of Miles and Sarah were being beamed across a large screen.

It was all so romantic and Zoe grinned at the last image of Sarah and Miles, taken at home. Sarah was asleep on the sofa, Miles's arms around her as he beamed into the camera, posing for the selfie. Underneath he had written the caption *When you know, you know.*

How those words had come to mean so much. As her gaze drifted across to Ben, she felt that familiar pang of love herself. Even when she'd thought she hated him, she had been drawn to him. Her thoughts turned to Sean. He would have liked Ben, of that she was sure. She thought even David would like him if they ever met.

An image of her ex floated into her mind, and Zoe allowed herself a moment to think of him fondly. He had been as good as his word and dealt with the sale of the house and their possessions. He had forwarded her share of the money and she had a healthy lump sum in the bank to do whatever she wanted with. For perhaps the first time in her life Zoe finally felt free. The thought was both liberating and terrifying. She had tried to discuss it with Ben, but his advice had been to enjoy the moment. True freedom, he had told her, was hard to find.

As the sounds of Take That's hit came to a close, Zoe reached across the large round table for Ben's hand and he smiled.

'Shall I get us another drink?' she asked above the opening bars of a Fleetwood Mac song.

'I think someone's beaten you to it,' Ben replied, gesturing to somewhere over her shoulder. Zoe turned, spotting Miles, Sarah and Candice approaching them with a bottle of champagne and five glasses.

'Look what your sister's brought for us,' Sarah cried in delight as she held aloft a bottle of Veuve Clicquot.

'She's always keen to get the party started,' Ben remarked, pulling out a chair for Candice to sit down.

'And there was me expecting some sort of sarky comment,' Candice shot back as she kissed her brother and Zoe on the cheek.

'Thought we'd open it and share it between us,' Miles said, skilfully pouring the contents into five glasses.

'Because you haven't got enough champagne here tonight?' Zoe asked, taking the glass Miles handed her.

Miles laughed as he looked at the champagne tower behind them. 'What, that cheap crap? Nah, we'll enjoy the good stuff.'

With that he raised his glass aloft and the others did the same. 'Thanks, Candice, and here's to you all.'

'Here's to you,' Ben echoed, clinking his glass against the others. 'Wishing you a long and happy life together, guys.'

After everyone repeated the sentiment, Candice spoke. 'Have you set a wedding date?'

Miles and Sarah exchanged looks. 'We thought we might aim for next Christmas.'

'Ah, lovely.' Ben grinned. 'A Christmas wedding is special. Maybe snow with a bit of luck.'

'Not in Oz, mate.' Miles laughed.

'I thought you were going to wait until you'd visited before you committed to moving to the country?' Zoe said.

Sarah shrugged. 'Whatever. It's time for a new start. Australia has Miles's heart and Miles has mine.'

'That's not strictly true, love,' Miles said, looking sheepish. 'If you don't want to go, we don't have to. I'll stay here.'

'You'd stay in the UK?' Zoe asked in astonishment.

'I'd do anything for you, Sarah,' Miles said tenderly, his face a picture of sincerity.

'Please don't stay here,' Ben joked. 'Australia is much better.'

'You've been?' Sarah enquired, looking at Ben.

'When I was in my twenties. Loved it. Manly Beach is very special.'

'That's where we're planning on having the reception.' Sarah gasped, as she looked at Miles with love in her eyes. 'You'll have to make a holiday out of it when you and Zoe come over.'

Ben nodded. 'We will. I'd love to see Zoe back in her homeland. See if that accent comes out.'

'I've still got an Aussie accent,' Zoe protested.

At that the table laughed.

'You've totally lost it, Zoe, you sound practically Home Counties these days,' Sarah said.

'Good!' Zoe exclaimed. 'Though it comes out when I talk to my mum.'

'And when David was here,' Miles pointed out, picking up his drink.

'I bet it suited you,' Ben put in. 'You should be proud of your roots.'

Candice raised her now empty glass. 'Who's for another bottle?'

Candice went in search of more champagne and Zoe snuggled closer to Ben.

'Are you going to take me back to your hometown when we fly to Australia for your mates' wedding?' he asked.

Zoe looked up at him. 'Would you like that? To see where I grew up and stuff? Meet my mum?'

Ben lifted her chin with his finger and pressed his lips to hers. 'Of course! I want to know every single thing about you.'

For a moment Zoe paused. Could she really go back after the way she'd left? But as she gazed into Ben's eyes, she knew that with him by her side there was nothing she couldn't do.

-

By nine o'clock the party was in full swing. The sounds of The Killers pumped across the ballroom and Zoe sat back and watched Ben give it everything he had on the dancefloor. Zoe had danced the last three songs with him but now, feeling completely unfit, she had begged for mercy.

She was sitting on the banquette next to Candice, a fresh glass of champagne having magically appeared in front of her. She watched her boyfriend jump up and down with all the enthusiasm of a twenty-year-old.

'I don't know how he does it,' Zoe marvelled.

'He's always been the same,' Candice explained. 'He's spent every day squeezing every last drop out of life. It's exhausting watching him. You'd have thought after the op he might have slowed down a bit, but oh no, not my brother.'

Zoe smiled and watched Ben take the arm of Sarah's aunt and modestly swing her around. He looked breathless, Zoe thought, and tired too.

'I'm not sure he should be dancing so much. He hasn't eaten a lot; I ought to get him to rest,' Zoe said.

'Good luck.' Candice let out a snort of laughter.

But fortunately, Zoe didn't have to as the sound of Miles's voice echoed across the room.

'Everyone, can I have your attention please?'

Swinging around to face him, Zoe saw Miles clutching a microphone, looking nervous as he stood on the little raised platform at the front of the room.

'Oooh, this will be good,' Ben said, huffing and puffing as he took a seat next to her. 'I love a speech.'

Candice laughed. 'You love it when people muck it up, you mean.'

Grinning, Ben took a slug of his champagne. 'Same thing, isn't it?'

But there was no time to answer as Miles's Antipodean twang filled the room.

'I won't take up much of your time, ladies and gents, but I would like to say a few words. Firstly, thank you all for coming tonight. Sarah and I really appreciate having you all here with us.'

At that everyone broke into a round of applause and Miles seemed to relax. 'Mainly I want to say thanks to Sarah for agreeing to marry me. Sarah,' he said, turning to look at her, 'you're my soulmate, and I know everyone comes out with all that crap about how their partner completes them, and they can't imagine a life without them in it, but I know now why people say it because it's true. I love you, Sarah Rokeby.'

There was another round of applause and Zoe felt Ben nestle against her. She ran her hand against his freshly shaven cheek.

'I hope you'll all join me by raising your glasses in a toast to my beautiful Sarah, who I couldn't love any more than I do right now,' Miles finished.

There was another round of cheers and whistles and Zoe was delighted everything had worked out for her friend. Sarah caught Zoe's eye and lifted her glass in the direction of her friend. Zoe went to do the same, only as she did so she saw Sarah's look of love swiftly replaced with one of horror whilst she simultaneously heard a thud behind her. Turning around, Zoe saw Ben had fallen to the floor.

'Oh my God!' Candice cried, already on her knees as she crouched over her twin.

For a moment, Zoe felt nothing but blind panic before switching straight into nurse mode. Gently, she pushed Ben's sister out of the way and calmly assessed the situation. Her boyfriend was lying crumpled in a heap, and he looked as if he'd lost consciousness. 'Ben,' she said in a steady voice. 'Ben, can you hear me?'

Ben remained silent. Zoe rolled him into the recovery position, noticing as she did so that his eyes were glassy and his breathing rattly and constricted.

She looked around. The music had stopped and everyone was gazing at Ben as they would a motorway accident. Zoe felt a flash of annoyance at the rubberneckers but Miles came to her aid.

'Any response?' he asked, turning to Zoe.

She shook her head as Miles took his pulse. While he did so, she reached for her phone and called an ambulance, her eyes never leaving Ben.

Chapter Forty-Nine

The ambulance hadn't taken long to arrive at the hotel. As paramedics lumbered up the Georgian stone steps, dressed in dark green uniforms, the neon and white vehicle and crackling radios all seemed very much at odds with the elegant architecture of the street.

Miles and Zoe told them Ben's current heart rate and how long he had been unconscious along with any other information they thought important. Candice meanwhile had not taken things in her stride, shrieking as she followed the paramedics outside. Zoe had handled the situation, gently insisting Candice stay out of the way so the ambulance crew could do their job and summoning a taxi to take them to the hospital.

Now as they waited in the corridors of the casualty department, Zoe felt oddly calm, still dressed in her stylish green party dress and heels. She supposed it was because she was a nurse. She was trained to feel compassionately detached, a skill she was grateful for at the present moment. Candice, however, was a wreck. Her teeth were chattering and her legs jerking up and down. Zoe pressed cup after cup of lukewarm tea into Candice's hands and rubbed her shoulders, wanting to take care of her. She knew from experience it would be a while before they had any answers.

Eventually the sounds of footsteps caught Zoe's attention. Her head snapped up and she nudged Candice as Ben's doctor approached. She was a tall, young-looking woman with a neatly tied chignon and an authoritative air.

'We've admitted Ben,' the doctor revealed.

'What's wrong with him?' Candice begged.

The woman looked down at her notes. 'Is one of you Zoe Evans?'

Zoe nodded. 'Yes, me.'

'Ben has you listed you as his emergency contact. Can we talk privately?'

'Whatever you have to say, you can say in front of Candice,' Zoe explained. 'She's his twin sister.'

'Okay.' The doctor sat beside them. 'We believe Ben's cancer has returned.'

Candice's face crumpled. 'Oh no.'

'We can't confirm how advanced it is at this stage. We'll need to run more tests to be sure. It was fortunate you knew what to do and called us quickly,' she said to Zoe.

'She's a hospice nurse,' Candice said through tears. 'Like Ben.'

The doctor gave them a kindly smile. 'Ben will be with us for a few days. We've given him some medication to try and bring his breathing back to normal. He's responded well to the treatment so far.'

'Can we see him?' Candice asked, her teeth still chattering with shock.

'Not yet I'm afraid,' the doctor said gently. 'He's resting.'

'But he's all right?' Zoe asked, desperate for her to reveal just how serious Ben's condition was.

'He is for the moment,' the doctor confirmed. 'If he continues in this way, we're hopeful we can discharge him in a few days.'

With the mention of the word 'discharge', Zoe saw the hope flicker in Candice's eyes. She thought the doctor was giving them respite from this nightmare.

'That's wonderful,' Zoe said.

'I should warn you that this is not a reprieve,' the medic added. 'Ben's had quite an aggressive operation to remove a tumour already. Obviously, an oncologist will have to discuss a suitable treatment programme, but again, we need to run more tests before we can safely say what the situation is.'

'When will you know how serious Ben's cancer is?' Candice asked.

'Soon, we hope.' The doctor gave a thin smile. 'It's Saturday night so not the best time to run the tests we need, but we will work as quickly as we can.'

'When can we see him?' Zoe asked.

'I'd suggest you come back tomorrow,' the doctor said kindly. 'As I say, he's sleeping at the moment and if he does wake, we've given him so much medicine he'll feel disorientated.'

Candice nodded as the doctor gave a polite smile and got up, clearly signalling the conversation was over for now.

Once she had gone, Zoe turned to Candice. 'Are you okay?'

Candice let out a shuddering breath. 'I don't know how you do it, Zoe, you're so calm.'

Zoe sighed. 'Practice, I suppose. I'll fall apart later.'

–

It was late on Sunday afternoon when Zoe finally got home. She and Candice had taken a taxi back to her flat first, where Zoe had helped get her settled. Once she was sure Candice was okay, Zoe made her own way home. Letting herself inside, she heard the sounds of the television.

'Sarah?' she called, setting her keys in the bowl by the door and shucking off her coat. The familiarity of routine grounded her and she felt grateful for the minutiae of life. It was what kept you going when your world fell apart.

'Zoe!' Sarah exclaimed as Zoe walked into the living room. 'I let myself in with the spare key you gave me. Are you all right?'

Nodding, Zoe sank onto the sofa next to Sarah and allowed her friend to pull her into her arms. 'I'm okay.'

'And Ben?' Sarah asked. Zoe had rung her friend earlier to explain Ben was in hospital but she hadn't gone into the details about why, preferring to save them for a face-to-face conversation.

Lifting her head from Sarah's shoulder, Zoe felt all the strength she had been holding on to disappear.

'Ben's cancer's come back,' Zoe said, her shoulders heaving as she gave in to the tears she had staved off all night.

Sarah's jaw fell open in astonishment. 'But the operation was a success. Ben said the surgeon caught it all.'

'I know. But apparently, it's back. They don't know how advanced the cancer is yet; the doctors have got to run tests. Oh, Sarah, I can't go through this again. I can't lose anyone else.'

'I'm here, you won't be alone,' Sarah promised. 'I'm just sorry this is happening to you.'

Zoe lifted her head. 'It's me that should be sorry, your party was ruined.'

'You can't be serious! As if that matters now. And it wasn't ruined. We're all just worried about Ben.'

'I can't get my head around it,' Zoe whispered.

'I can't either,' Sarah said, shaking her head to try to make sense of it, her brown hair skimming her shoulders as she did so. 'He was full of life last night. Are you sure there wasn't a mistake?'

Zoe shook her head bitterly. 'There's been no mistake.'

'But cancer?' Sarah muted the television, asking, 'Are you really sure?'

Glancing at the television, Zoe found herself briefly fixated on the screen, the sight of a colourful period drama drawing her in, before she turned back to her friend. 'I'm sure.'

Sarah looked broken and Zoe reached out a hand to comfort her. 'I'm sorry to break this to you, not when this should be such a happy time for you.'

Sarah lifted her chin. 'Stop apologising. If anyone should be sorry it's me. I should have come to the hospital with you. I told Miles last night about Ben's cancer operation. I hope that was all right.'

'Of course,' Zoe said, with a sigh. 'I imagine he won't be able to hide it this time around anyway, not after such a public display.'

'Miles is in absolute bits. He feels so guilty he hasn't been there for him or you.'

'There's no need, there's nothing he could have done,' Zoe replied. 'Where is he?'

'He's back at home with Lottie.' Sarah eyed Zoe anxiously. 'Are you going to be all right?'

Zoe shrugged. 'I hope so.'

'Me too.' Sarah squeezed her knee. 'Because the thing is, Zoe, it's been a real pleasure watching you become the woman I always knew you could be. I would hate to see you go back to how you were.'

'What do you mean?' Confusion passed across Zoe's face.

'When I first met you, you were like a ghost. You kept yourself to yourself, wore clothes that meant you never stood out, took no time to care for yourself and didn't have any kind of life outside the hospital,' Sarah pointed out. 'But since you've met Ben, you've become more confident. Look at you at the party last night in your green dress and smoky eye make-up. You were confident, gorgeous and full of life. Whatever happens, don't lose that.'

Zoe felt her head spin at all Sarah was saying.

'I haven't known Ben very long,' Sarah continued. 'But what I do know I like, and I like how good he's been for you. He's one of those annoying people that has lived every day as if it were his last. Zoe, after so many years of heartache, you have finally started to do the same.'

Zoe thought back to those early days of her arrival in the UK. How lost and alone she had felt and how grateful she was simply to be away from the pain Australia held.

'When I got on that plane in Sydney, I didn't know what I was doing, not really,' Zoe said carefully. 'I didn't want a future; I didn't even want to be happy. The only thing I wanted was to survive, nothing more than that.'

'Oh, Zoe.' Sarah offered her a sympathetic smile.

'It's okay,' she said, swallowing a sob. 'The thing is, I've done more than survived since I got here. You helped put me back together, Sarah, and Ben has shown me the beauty there can be in life. Whatever the future holds, I'll always have that.'

Sarah reached out and stroked Zoe's cheek. 'Good. But let's not get carried away. We don't know yet what's wrong exactly.'

'We know he's got cancer, and whatever happens, he's got a fight on his hands,' Zoe said sadly.

'Ben's tough, and with you by his side he won't want to go anywhere. That love he has for you will get him through anything,' Sarah said firmly.

'Thank you.'

'And I'm here,' Sarah reminded her, 'whatever happens, good or bad, me, Miles and Lottie will always be here for you.'

At that, Zoe allowed herself to breathe out. She didn't know what the future had in store, but she knew she was lucky enough to be surrounded by love.

Chapter Fifty

Four days later and Zoe was doing her best to block out the rumble of the bin lorry as she got out of her car and strolled towards the hospital entrance. All around her people were going about their business as if every day was normal. For Zoe, normal was the last thing she felt. She wanted to scream at people when she saw them idly picking out a bottle of wine in the supermarket, making a cup of tea, collecting their kids from school, or even putting the rubbish out. The mundanity of it all was dull, but all Zoe wanted to do was shout, *Don't you know how lucky you are to be* bored *by life?*

But of course she didn't. Instead, she kept on walking until she reached the hospital, the tang of hospital bleach searing her nostrils and the perpetual purr of medical monitors, bleeping pagers and quickened footsteps providing the soundtrack to her daily life. In the days that followed Zoe had got into the rhythm of a routine keeping a vigil around Ben's bedside.

She hadn't yet spoken to Ben since he collapsed as he had been too full of drugs to even compute the fact she was there. That hadn't stopped Zoe visiting, where she sat by his bedside and wrote him letters. Nothing long, or fancy. Just words straight from her heart. She thought of the one she had written him earlier that lay folded in her bag ready to be left by his bedside.

Dearest B,

The sun is shining, but even when it rains it's warm in my heart whenever you are near.

I love you,
Zo xxxx

It wasn't exactly Shakespeare, but letter-writing had always given her comfort in the past. Why not now? Besides, it gave her a break from the blame she felt for not realising Ben was ill. She was a nurse. How could she not have seen his cancer was back? She berated herself for not paying more attention, just as she had when Sean had died.

As Zoe made her way to the ward, she was surprised to find Ben sitting up in bed, his gaze fixed on the window. At the sound of her footsteps, he turned around and, seeing it was Zoe, his face lit up.

'You're here,' he breathed.

Zoe rushed towards him. Taking his hands in hers, she kissed the back of each one. 'How are you?'

'Better for seeing you.'

'And I'm better now you're awake,' Zoe said, her eyes automatically straying to the chart at the bottom of his bed.

Instinctively, she went to reach for it, but Ben's grip around her fingers tightened. 'Don't.'

She relaxed. If Ben didn't want her looking at his medical notes, she wouldn't.

'Have Sarah and Miles forgiven me yet?' he joked.

'There's nothing to forgive you for. They are worried about you, though.'

Ben looked down, his hands still resting in Zoe's. 'There's nothing to worry about,' he said flatly.

'Isn't there?' Zoe asked gently.

They didn't say anything for a moment, the morning sunshine warming each of their faces.

'You know the cancer is back?' Ben said at last.

'I don't know how serious it is. The doctors told me they needed to run more tests.'

There was the sound of laughter and it took a moment for Zoe to register that it was coming from Ben. 'They've run the tests.'

'Okay.' Zoe swallowed the lump beginning to form in her throat.

'And the cancer has reappeared. In fact, it's quite advanced.'

'How advanced?' Zoe demanded, nerves building.

'Too advanced,' Ben admitted. 'There's nothing they can do. I've got a month at best.'

Zoe struggled to make sense of what Ben was telling her.

'What?' she managed. She felt as though someone had suddenly made off with her bag but there had been no sign of a thief. 'But you had the cancer removed. It can't have just come back like that.'

'It didn't just come back like that.' Ben propped himself up on his pillows. 'The operation was successful but the margins weren't as clear as the doctors hoped. They wanted me on chemotherapy after the op but I told them that I would take my chances, that statistics showed in cases like mine, with the margins they showed me, that surgery was usually enough.'

Zoe couldn't believe what she was hearing. 'Why didn't you talk to me? Why didn't you have chemo?'

'Because I didn't want to lose my hair.' He giggled, running his hand over his bald head.

Despite the bleakness she felt, Zoe laughed with him.

'Oh, Ben,' she said at last, 'why didn't you really have chemo?'

Ben sighed. 'Because I thought I didn't need it. Genuinely. I discussed it with my specialist and he said that whilst it was advisable for me to have chemo, the operation had been such a success it would more than likely be enough on its own.'

'But it wasn't,' Zoe finished.

'Correct.' Ben grimaced. 'I saw my specialist yesterday and he said that it was always a possibility the cancer would come back but even he couldn't have predicted it would be this aggressive.'

Ben was watching her, waiting for a reaction. This was not the time to fall apart. Zoe rested her head on his chest. The regular thrum of his heartbeat was loud and strong, ironically reminding her of the force of life still flowing through Ben's veins.

'Ben, whatever happens, I'm all in. You know that, right?'

'It's just not fair, Zoe,' he whispered into her hair.

'It's not,' she said, lifting her chin to look up at him. She smiled as she wiped his tears away with the pad of her thumb. 'And if there's one thing I know about life, it can be really fucking unfair.'

Ben laughed at her bluntness. 'You got that right.'

She kissed his face. 'What's next?'

'I get out of here,' Ben said firmly. 'I don't want to waste another minute in hospital.'

'I can understand that. Let me talk to the doctors, see what we can do.'

Zoe got up, grateful for the chance to compose herself before she completely broke down in front of her boyfriend.

-

After her hospital visit, Zoe went home, slumped on the sofa and allowed herself a moment to give in to her feelings of despair. This beautiful flat was supposed to have been a chance for them to have the future they'd dreamed of. It was a chance, for Zoe certainly, to move on from the past. She had vowed that in this new place she would think of Sean with love and tenderness rather than guilt and sadness that she hadn't been able to protect him. Instinctively she reached for the little wooden box where she kept Sean's last words. Pulling the well-worn note towards her, her eyes roamed greedily across the words, desperate for them to give her the strength they always offered.

I just want to be a cowboy

At the sight of those seven words Zoe felt a flicker of hope return. Even in moments of crisis, the power of the written word, the ability to hold and feel something physical from someone you cherished, offered her strength. As she continued to hold the note to her heart, Zoe vowed that this time love wouldn't break her – it would power her through whatever lay ahead.

–

Zoe walked through the aisle between the valley of hospital beds the following morning, finding Ben at the end. She paused for a moment and took in the scene. Back gently curved, wearing his favourite grey hoodie, he was sitting on the edge of the bed with his back to her, leaning his chin on a cane and gazing out at the houses beyond the window. Even from behind, Zoe thought he looked as if he had aged a hundred years. His frame was gaunt, which, given the amount of medicine he had been given, was no great surprise. But Ben was still gorgeous, beautiful both inside and out. She wanted to wrap her arms around him, but he looked as if he needed those few moments to himself and Zoe didn't want to deny him.

'I can see you standing there in the reflection, you know,' Ben said, his tone light. 'Are you going to say hello or are you going to keep standing there like some kind of weirdo?'

His voice sounded so normal, so typically Ben, that Zoe couldn't help laughing. She walked over to him and planted a kiss on his warm cheek, noting the smooth skin and the fact that he had found the strength to shave. *Or someone did it for him*, a dark voice echoed inside her head.

She pushed the unwelcome thought away and instead plastered on a smile. Zoe had been looking forward to taking Ben home ever since the consultant had agreed last night.

'Are you ready to split this joint?' she found herself asking in a faux American accent, which startled her as much as it did Ben.

'Er, yes,' he said. 'But if you keep talking like that I'm going to ask for an Uber.'

Zoe rolled her eyes. The forced jollity was perhaps a little too much for them both. She was just debating how to encourage Ben to use a wheelchair when one of the ward nurses came along. She was wearing a smile Zoe recognised as one of the battle-weary – a nurse who had been around the block a few times and got more than a handful of scrubs in the process.

'Right, time to get rid of you,' she said cheerfully, helping Ben into the wheelchair without complaint.

Zoe didn't pass comment. She had been expecting an argument but equally she knew Ben also had a lot of respect for his colleagues. It was entirely possible he simply didn't want to give a fellow nurse a hard time over a war he couldn't possibly hope to win.

Outside, Zoe thanked the nurse for her help and helped get Ben settled into the passenger seat of her car.

'I should have got you to pick me up in the Porsche,' he grumbled when Zoe slammed the driver door shut and started the engine. 'I'm dying, I should *only* be travelling in style.'

Zoe refused to rise to the bait. 'If you want to put me on your insurance and pay the bill then that's fine by me,' she said, nosing the Yaris smoothly out of the car park.

'Already done,' Ben said nonchalantly. 'The documents are on my laptop.'

'When did you become so organised?' Zoe demanded.

But even when Ben had been in hospital, he had surprised her. During those first couple of days when she and Candice had maintained a vigil around his bedside, Zoe had braced herself to have to organise things in Ben's life that she hadn't expected him to consider.

First of all had been the idea she would have to contact Ben's friends and let them know about his condition. To her surprise he had already broken the news with an online video chat from his hospital bed a couple of days earlier during a brief moment when he had been awake. She had next prepared to inform the hospice board that Ben had terminal cancer. Once again Zoe discovered Ben had beaten her to it, after speaking to Mr Harper.

'Didn't have him down as much of a note-taker, his organisation is usually terrible,' he had said in a mock grumble, 'but he emailed me a couple of days ago. It's devastating. Ben is so full of life and has so much potential to make change.'

Now, Zoe indicated left and pulled into a lay-by. Ben was prepared in a way she wasn't; she had to know what the next step was.

'What's going on?' Ben asked, looking surprised as she killed the engine.

'We need to talk.'

A flicker of wariness crossed Ben's face. 'What about?'

'You, this, us,' Zoe said, shrugging her shoulders and gesturing around her as much as the small interior of her hatchback would allow. 'And not the Yaris, before you start getting clever. I want to know if there's anything in particular you want to do with whatever time you've got left.'

Zoe prided herself on giving every one of her patients a good death. Just because this particular death was personal and would no doubt devastate her was no reason not to do the same.

Ben stared through the windscreen, the sun lighting his face. For a second, she wondered if he had heard her. But then he reached for her hand and held it. Neither spoke, and Zoe appreciated the warmth and love that flowed from his dark hand into her pale one.

'Zoe, I want to live as normally as I can. I want you and me to try and be a normal couple until I can't any more. It may be weeks or months, it may be days. I don't know. All I know is I just want it to be you and me. That's all that matters.'

His voice was so tender, so full of longing and regret it made Zoe's heart physically ache. She brought her mouth to his, kissing him with such passion – she wanted him to feel every ounce of love she had for him while he still could.

'We can do that,' she promised, as she pulled away. 'How about we go home?'

At the suggestion, Ben's whole body relaxed and Zoe knew she had said just what he wanted to hear.

'Yes please.' Then he closed his eyes and fell straight to sleep.

Chapter Fifty-One

When Ben had said that all he wanted to do was go home, Zoe's initial instinct was worry. Yes, Zoe had dealt with the deaths of hundreds of other people's loved ones before, but this was different. The knowledge that the bony fingers of the grim reaper were lurking nearby would surely cast a shadow over their relationship.

She didn't want Ben worrying that she thought of him differently now they were preparing to see out his final days, and so over the course of the following fortnight Zoe did her best to pretend everything was just the same.

Even now, as she brought Ben a cup of coffee and set it on his bedside table, knowing that it would be stone cold by the time he drank it, Zoe focused on trying to keep everything normal. Ben was sleeping so much more these days, waking only for a few hours of the day. But when he woke, she would tease him about being a sleepyhead and suggest they binge-watch the latest Scandi drama series on Netflix.

Tiptoeing across the carpet, she pulled back the blinds. It was past lunchtime and the room that had once looked full of promise and excitement when they first viewed the flat had taken on a bleak, dark edge with the blinds closed all the time. As if in defiance to the threat of death, Zoe threw the shutters open, exposing the room to a sweeping shaft of sunlight that enveloped the whole room like a warm hug. Already things seemed brighter. She perched on the edge of the bed, gazing out the window. The sky was a vivid blue, the sun high and not a cloud was in sight. Unusual for October, but all the more glorious for it.

'Hey,' Ben murmured.

Hearing the sound of rustling bedsheets, Zoe smiled as she watched her boyfriend come to.

'Hey, sleepyhead.'

She leaned over and kissed him softly on the lips. They were as dry as sandpaper. Reaching into his bedside drawer, she pulled out a lip balm and carefully applied some to his lips.

'That bad, eh?' he rasped.

She laughed. 'B&Q should market you as their newest invention. The human sander!' Ben smiled and the sight of it gladdened her heart. 'Anything you feel like doing today?'

'I thought we might go into London,' he croaked, his breath coming in great gulps. 'Lunch at the Wolseley? Stay overnight?'

'Sounds good to me.' She reached out a hand and stroked his head, enjoying the feel of his smooth, warm skin in her palm. 'Though I'm a bit tired. Do you mind if we stay home and chill?'

'We're not doing very well with this extra holiday,' Ben joked, referring to the fact he had left the hospice for good and Zoe had taken indefinite leave.

Zoe shrugged. 'True. But you know me, I'm not one for the high life. I'm happy just being with you.'

'All right,' Ben sighed, as he tried to reach for his coffee. She watched his hands shake, and Zoe leaned casually over and took the cup, pretending to take a sip of the coffee herself before handing it to him. It was a practised trick she had learned very early on in her hospice days – to make it look as though she wasn't doing everything for the patient.

Ben took the drink and Zoe smiled, with just a touch of sadness. This was the same dance they did every day. Pretending that nothing unusual was happening. That everything was fine, that they were just having a staycation.

Zoe had expected her heart to break, but in fact the only thing she felt was gratitude. To her it seemed like a miracle she had this extra time with Ben. It was a gift, to be able to say goodbye to someone in this way. She leaned forward to kiss him once more, when there was a rap at the door. Springing back, she looked at Ben in surprise.

'It's a bit late for the postie.'

'It's probably Miles,' Ben said softly. 'I invited him over.'

'Miles?'

Zoe's mind went blank. Although both Sarah and Miles called regularly to check how things were, she wasn't aware of Ben making direct contact with either of them. She had assumed he was too weak to do much more than text Candice, with whom he had a sibling shorthand. Candice was playing a huge role in keeping Zoe anchored through all this; she was a semi-permanent guest in their home and Zoe was grateful for her frequent presence – bringing much-needed life to the flat with her booming laugh and colourful dress.

'I will laugh in the face of death,' she had cried fiercely to Ben on the first day he arrived home, wearing a vivid yellow kimono over a wide-legged pair of green trousers.

'Fair enough,' he said. 'Just make sure you bring me my sunglasses on your next visit.'

And they had laughed, in that way they both did, mirroring each other's sound, though Ben was slightly quieter, less enthusiastic than usual.

These were all signs the end was on its way. Zoe knew that. But it seemed Ben still had the power to surprise her if he was inviting people over without telling her.

'I'd better let him in, then,' she said.

She hurried down the stairs and opened the door to a sombre-looking Miles. Hands shoved in pockets and eyes downcast, he seemed unable to look her in the eye.

'Blimey, he's not dead yet!' she exclaimed.

The poor excuse for a joke did the trick, as Miles shot Zoe a watery smile.

'Sorry, Zo. You'd think I'd be better at this, wouldn't you?'

'Why?'

Miles stood sheepishly in the doorway. 'I'm a hospice nurse.'

'And Ben is also a mate. Hospice nurse or not, this is tough,' Zoe pointed out as she pulled him inside.

'How is he?' Miles asked, keeping his voice low.

'He's okay,' Zoe said as brightly as she could. 'He's sleeping a lot.'

Miles nodded, understanding what she meant.

'When did he ask you to come round?' Zoe asked, unable to keep the curiosity at bay.

'This morning – said he wanted to talk to me about something.'

Zoe frowned, then led Miles into the kitchen and offered him a coffee, but he shook his head.

'I'll go straight on up if that's okay? He made out it was urgent.'

'Okay. You know where he is.'

Miles made his way upstairs. Zoe contented herself with cleaning the kitchen, something that had been sorely neglected of late. As she busied herself with washing down the surfaces and ensuring the sink sparkled, the hours slipped by like minutes and she saw it was dark by the time Miles emerged downstairs.

'Blimey! Can you pop round to ours?' he asked, surveying the kitchen.

Zoe smiled, pleased not only with her efforts but also because Miles seemed more at ease than he had when he first arrived.

'Everything all right?' Zoe jerked her head gently towards the stairs.

'We had a good chat. There were some things he needed to say. Ben's a good guy, you struck gold with him.'

Zoe felt the stab of tears pricking at the corners of her eyes. 'He is. I keep wishing we had more time, it's all so unfair.'

'Course it's unfair, Zo! I think the only bright spot about this whole thing is that you and Ben found each other when you did.'

Zoe allowed Miles to pull her into his arms and she simply enjoyed the feeling of being held for a few moments. Closing her eyes, she noticed he smelled of bonfires and autumn leaves. Healthy, seasonal scents of activities that she had hoped to have been enjoying with Ben. Instead, she was helping him have the good death he deserved. And, in that moment, she knew there was something she needed to ask, something she asked all her patients but so far had avoided because she was trying to be the one thing Ben didn't want her to be – a nurse.

Pulling herself away, she looked up at Miles and saw the kindness in his eyes.

'How could I ever have thought you were such a drongo?' she asked with a smile.

Miles laughed. 'Maybe because I was. You and Sarah got me to see the error of my ways.'

'I'm glad we did,' Zoe said with affection. 'I'd better get upstairs, see if he wants anything.'

'And I'd better be going too,' Miles replied. 'I promised Lottie we could watch *Frozen* one and two tonight.'

Once Miles had gone, Zoe shutting the door softly behind him, she allowed a genuine smile to spread across her face. She never thought she would be grateful for Miles but she had a feeling she wouldn't have got through the last few weeks without him.

She padded softly up the stairs and pushed open the bedroom door. Ben was lying on the bed, head on his pillows, eyes flickering open and closed.

'Hey,' she said, tiptoeing across the room and perching on the bed. 'How was Miles?'

Ben swivelled his head slowly to face her. 'Fine. It was good to see him.'

Zoe nodded. She would never ask what it was he needed Miles for but there was one thing on her mind.

'Ben, is there a note you would like to leave? Anything you would like to say…?'

She allowed her voice to trail off as Ben blinked his eyes firmly open and fixed his gaze on her.

'Zoe, no,' he rasped, his voice gentle but firm. 'You're with me, that's all I need.'

She could tell that the long day with Miles had cost him, and she stroked his cheek to show she appreciated the effort.

'Are you sure?' she whispered, not wanting to labour the point but wanting to make certain Ben had every opportunity to say anything he wanted.

'Sure. All I want is for you to lie beside me. Can you do that?'

'Of course.'

Zoe climbed onto the bed and wrapped her body around Ben's. As she laid her head in the familiar nook of his chest and listened to the rhythmic beating of his heart, all she wanted was for that sound to go on forever.

Chapter Fifty-Two

It was the sound of the rain sheeting against the glass that woke Zoe. Blinking her eyes open, she felt stiff and chilled and noticed the covers were tangled between her denim-clad legs. She glanced at Ben. He was still fast asleep, eyes firmly closed, mouth slightly open in that endearing way he had when he was in a deep sleep. She wasn't sure what time it was. Judging by the fact she could hear the dawn chorus, she guessed it was still early. There was no rush to do anything or go anywhere. She could relax, enjoy the chance to be with Ben. Reaching for the duvet, Zoe pulled it up high and tucked it around her boyfriend, not wanting him to get cold. Then she rested her head back against his chest and willed the deep fugue of sleep to claim her, wanting nothing more than to feel safe with Ben beside her, the two of them in their own private cocoon.

Only as she snuggled in, Zoe realised Ben wasn't just cold, he was freezing. She propped herself up, checked to see he was still asleep and wrapped an arm tightly around Ben's middle and rested her head back against his chest.

But as she did so, she noticed there was no rhythmic rise and fall of his chest as there had been when they fell asleep the previous night. In fact, there was no rise and fall at all and certainly no thrumming sound. She sat bolt upright, no longer caring if she disturbed her boyfriend.

'Ben,' she hissed, leaning towards his face. 'Ben, can you hear me?'

Nothing.

'Ben? Ben?'

There was still nothing. Gently she placed her hands on his chest and shook his body. When there was still no response, she shook him harder, but Ben still didn't stir.

'Oh no,' she gasped, her blood running cold. 'Not now, please not now. Ben. Ben.'

But no matter how much she pleaded, Ben didn't stir.

And in that moment Zoe knew the worst had happened. Her Ben, her precious, beautiful Ben had gone.

At the realisation, Zoe sat on her haunches and rocked back and forth on the bed beside him, crooning strange animal noises. Quiet at first and then louder, more guttural, the pain sweeping fast through her body, threatening to overpower her.

She wasn't sure when she stopped screaming. At some point the sun began to peep through the grey clouds and Zoe's throat, like her heart, felt ravaged by pain and grief.

Kneeling beside Ben, she ran her eyes properly over his body. She could see that it had been devastated by cancer. His body was thin, his cheeks hollow, but more than that, the very essence of her beautiful man had gone.

He had finally been released from the torment of the last few weeks. She wiped her tears away with her palms. Ben deserved the best and that was what she would give him. Tenderly, she took hold of his wrist and checked for a pulse, but of course there was none. She pressed her lips to the back of his hand, and gently dropped it by his side. Then she got to her feet and reached for her mobile, dialling the number of the on-call doctor at the hospice, who promised to be right over.

Putting the phone down, Zoe turned back to Ben, and before officialdom took over, she cared for him the only way she knew how. She rubbed the sleep from his eyes, ran a warm flannel across his face, rubbed some of his expensive moisturiser into his flesh and tucked the duvet around him. As she kissed his forehead, she relished the chance to bury herself in that sweet, unique scent that was all him one last time. Then she sat beside him and ran her eyes across his face. She wanted to commit every line, every pore, every feature to memory. But gazing at him, lying in the bed they had bought together, Zoe knew she wouldn't need to. She knew his face better than her own; she would never forget it. He would be forever imprinted on her mind and in her heart.

She held his hand one last time and remembered how struck she had been by his long dark fingers against her own stubbier pale ones the first time he had reached for her on that sun-drenched Welsh beach.

'Losing you will break my heart but I wouldn't change a thing. You're the love of my life.'

She kissed him, letting her lips linger on his forehead.

As if the universe was reminding her she couldn't hold on to this moment forever, there was a sharp rap at the door – the doctor. Her stomach flipped; this was the moment everything changed. Her Ben would no longer be her Ben. He would be taken from her to a place she couldn't go, at least not yet.

She kissed his cheek once more, his skin cool against her lips. The world they had created had gone. It was time to say goodbye.

Chapter Fifty-Three

'Zoe love, are you sure you should be here?' Miles asked as she sat at the nurses' station doing her best to go through the diary.

She lifted her head and gazed at him. 'Where else would I be?'

Miles shut the diary. 'At home. Coming to terms with your loss.'

'I'd rather be here,' Zoe said listlessly, her head bent, gaze still focused on the now closed diary. From what she had managed to glean so far, today was a big day. Three admissions and Karen was away on a team-building exercise. It was lucky she had come in to help, what with Ben no longer being available.

At the thought of Ben, she closed her eyes and felt her resolve crumble. It had been two days since his death. She knew it was far too soon to come back to work but she couldn't stand being at home. Everywhere she looked there were signs of her boyfriend. His scent was all over the unwashed pillowcases, his aftershave still stood in the bathroom cabinet, his handwriting was scrawled all over the wall calendar and his Porsche was still parked on the drive. The sight of it unravelled her every time she saw it.

She became aware of Miles squeezing her shoulder.

'Then take it easy. If you must be here, nothing difficult. No dealing with patients on their last legs, not today. Make coffees, tidy the hand sanitisers, order supplies.'

Zoe wasn't properly taking in any of what Miles was saying but knew it would make him worry less if he thought she was listening to him.

The high-pitched ring of the desk phone shattered the silence and Miles answered it. Zoe heard the sound of an ambulance pulling up outside and, getting to her feet, she raced outside to help the crew, aware of Miles's worried gaze following her as she did so.

As the paramedics began wheeling in their patient, Anita, one of the new paramedics, gave Zoe a sympathetic smile. Word of her loss had travelled fast.

'Nico Martelli,' Anita said, handing her the clipboard with the patient's details. 'End-stage colon cancer. Forty-nine years of age. Wife and kids following on later.'

Zoe's heart raced. Could this be the same Nico that had been in hospital with Ben? She glanced down at the man lying on the bed, oxygen mask attached to his face. She read through his notes and saw that it was. Her stomach flipped at the idea of this unexpected connection to Ben.

'It's Zoe, Nico. Do you remember me? Ben's girlfriend. We met at the hospital.'

At the mention of Ben, Nico's eyes lit up and he tried to take the oxygen mask off so he could talk. Zoe put a hand gently on the mask and shook her head.

'I need you to leave it on, Nico. We'll talk later, okay?'

Nico looked mollified and Zoe smiled gratefully at Anita as she handed over the final pieces of paperwork.

After Anita bade her goodbye, Zoe looked down at Nico. 'Let's get you settled.'

An hour later and Nico was comfortable in a bed that overlooked the gardens. It was in fact Mrs Harper's old room and Zoe was glad this one had been available as it was the nicest in the hospice. She looked at Ben's friend now. He had lost a lot of weight since she had seen him last, and his skin was sallow. According to his notes, he didn't have long left and she wanted to make him as comfortable as possible.

'How are you feeling?'

'All right,' Nico rasped, and turned back to face her. 'I heard about Ben. I'm sorry.'

'Thank you,' she managed.

'He was a good man,' Nico said wistfully. 'He wouldn't stop talking about you. He loved you so much.'

'And I loved him. I'll never stop.'

'He told me all about you,' Nico continued as if she hadn't spoken. 'Your notes… it's why I wanted to come here when my time came.'

She let out a small breath, relieved to be on familiar territory. 'Do you have a note you'd like me to take down?'

Eyes filling with tears, Nico nodded.

Zoe sat down on the edge of his bed and reached inside the pocket of her scrubs for her notepad. 'Okay, Nico, what would you like to say?'

There was a silence and Nico looked bereft for a moment. Zoe said nothing. She knew that sometimes people needed a minute or two to think.

'It's to my best friend, Ennio.' Nico looked down at his hands. 'I have made some mistakes, and it's too late to put them right. I need Ennio to do it for me.'

'I'm sorry.'

'Me too. We always think we have so much time but in the end there isn't. It runs away from us and I must ask someone else to do what I cannot.' Nico paused to gather his breath. 'He is the closest thing I have to a brother. We both left Naples together, upsetting our families in the process.' At that Nico managed a rueful grin. 'It brought us closer in the early days, knowing we both had difficulties with our parents. They came round in the end – not until we were both married and had children, though.'

Zoe smiled. 'It's often the way when children come along.'

'Yes, and Ennio and I are still close but we don't see as much of each other as we would like. He doesn't know I am ill. I couldn't face telling him. He is still like my brother, though, and the one person I trust with putting right a mistake I made.'

'What kind of mistake?' Zoe pressed gently.

Tears once again pooled in Nico's brown eyes. 'Last time I went to Naples, I went alone. Me and my wife Catherine were having some problems. I needed some time away.'

'Okay,' Zoe encouraged.

'Whilst I was there, I had relations with another woman.' At the admission, Nico's cheeks bloomed with colour.

'Oh, Nico.' Zoe sympathised, but it wasn't the first time she had heard deathbed confessions such as this one. 'I do think you're better off telling your wife, though. While you still can.'

Nico shook his head. 'She knows. She has forgiven me.'

'So what's the problem?' she asked gently.

'This woman fell pregnant. She has a son, Antonio – he is five.' Nico took a deep breath. 'When I discovered Antonio's existence, I was so ashamed, I told the woman he couldn't be mine. That we had only had one night together. She was angry. Insisted on DNA tests. They showed Antonio was mine but still I couldn't risk my family here and I told her I was not interested.'

Now the tears that had bloomed in Nico's eyes were cascading down his cheeks. Zoe put down her pad and pen and went to comfort him, taking hold of his hand and gripping it tightly.

'It is the greatest regret of my life. I have wasted all this time not getting to know my son, denying his existence. What sort of person does that make me? I am not an honourable man and now I cannot put right what I should.'

'I'm so sorry, Nico,' Zoe offered. 'What can I do?'

'I need you to talk to Ennio for me.'

'Does he know about Antonio?'

Nico shook his head. 'Only my wife. She has been trying to get me to have a relationship with him ever since we found out four years ago but I refused and she didn't push. She probably thought in time I would come round. We had no idea we would never have the time.'

'What is it you want to say? Do you know or do you need me to help?'

Nico shook his head. 'I know exactly what to say. Please say, "Ennio, I need you to help me. I have a son, Antonio. I need you to step in and be the father I was afraid to be. I know you have a family of your own, but I also know your heart is much bigger than mine. Please will you talk to Antonio, apologise for me for being stupid, tell him all about me, and over the years look out for him as if he were your own? It is too late for me to go home and make amends and I am begging you as your brother to do this for me. Your foolish friend, Nico."'

As she finished writing, Zoe caught Nico's worried gaze.

'Too much?' he asked.

'Perfect,' she said. 'Leave this with me. I'll make sure Ennio gets it when the time is right.'

The moment she said the words, she saw Nico visibly relax. As if all the fight and worry he had been holding on to had finally gone.

'Thank you, Zoe,' he said as he closed his eyes and sank his head back against the pillows. 'Ben was right. You're a lifesaver.'

Chapter Fifty-Four

As Zoe stared into the mirror examining her reflection, she felt sure she was trapped in a very bad dream. There could be no other reason for her to be wearing a black fitted dress, heels and a hat on a grey and drizzly Wednesday morning in November. She tried to wake herself by pinching the flesh on her right hand, but the only thing Zoe achieved was a bruise. Not that it mattered, she thought, as Sarah peered around the door.

'You all right?' Sarah asked, coming in and sitting on the edge of the bed. Zoe could hardly bring herself to look at it. This bed was supposed to signal the start of a new and happy life with Ben. But now Zoe would always view this particular piece of furniture as the place where Ben had died, wrapped in her arms. She shut her eyes, the memory of that awful moment when she had woken and thought Ben was still asleep never far away.

She gave Sarah a watery smile. Her friend looked lovely, Zoe noticed, dressed in a simple black sheath dress that was elegant and appropriate. That was Sarah all over, though – perfect in a crisis. She knew just what to wear, what to say, what to do. How would Zoe have managed without her?

'I'm fine,' Zoe said.

Sarah nodded. 'Candice is here.'

At the news, Zoe smiled. Candice had been a rock. After the way she had reacted to the news that Ben's cancer had returned, Zoe had worried she would fall apart. But in fact, Ben's big sister had been stoic. She had helped organise the funeral, checked in on Zoe regularly, and even brought over great big tubs full of jambalaya and lasagne to ensure she ate. Zoe had been grateful. In the aftermath of Ben's death, food hadn't been at the top of her list. If it had been down to Zoe, she would have been happy to subsist on the Haribos she kept in the sweet cupboard for Lottie's visits.

Therefore, it was no surprise Ben had made Candice executor of his will. Candice would ensure Ben's wishes were carried out to the letter. In fact, Candice had been incredibly generous in the three weeks since Ben had died, even insisting that Zoe ride to the crematorium in the family car. At the time Zoe had agreed, not wanting to cause trouble. Now the moment was here she wasn't sure if it was right, especially as she knew Ben's ex-wife would be paying her respects.

'This is what Ben wanted,' Sarah assured her, as if reading her mind. 'He viewed this flat, this life with you, as his home. You were his family just as much as Candice is.'

'I keep thinking,' Zoe began, swallowing back the awkwardness she felt at what she was about to say, 'that there's a chance Ben is looking after Sean. Or maybe after all this time, it's Sean who's looking after Ben. Do you think that's stupid?'

'No!' Sarah said fiercely. 'I don't think that's stupid at all.' Her voice was gentler now. 'I think that's exactly what's happened. I think Ben and Sean are watching us lot bawl our eyes out and laughing, wishing we'd just get bloody on with it.'

Zoe raised a smile. 'I can see them both doing that.'

'And I can see Ben worrying about you and Sean telling him he shouldn't because his mum's as tough as old boots and she's got this.'

'Have I?' Zoe asked.

But as Sarah went to reply, Candice appeared in the doorway and glanced at them apologetically. 'It's time to go.'

At the crematorium, Zoe sat beside Candice at the front. There was no 'My Way' and thankfully there was no 'Bat Out of Hell', but instead 'Ain't That a Kick in the Head' burst through the speakers. Despite her grief, the lyrics made her smile. *It was indeed a kick in the head to have had a life cut short so abruptly, but boy were you loved, Ben,* Zoe thought. She ran her eyes over the rows of people and was surprised to see Josh and his dad, Jack, at the back, who had travelled all the way from Wales. As she caught their eye, they gave a little wave and she managed a smile, delighted to see them despite the horrific circumstances.

You see, she said silently to the wooden coffin at the front of the room. *The care you gave, the letters you took, touched so many lives, Ben.*

She continued to cast her gaze across the room, noticing how everyone was dressed in black from head to toe. It struck her how outraged Ben had been at Mrs Harper's funeral that so many people had worn colour, and how he had said to her and Candice repeatedly that he wanted people turning up in black. 'Over my dead body will mourners turn up in pink,' he had said with a wink. 'It's my funeral and I want the aisles weeping.'

Zoe had doubled over with laughter when he said that. It was typical of his dark sense of humour and she loved him all the more for it.

The service was short and if Zoe was honest, there was much she tuned out. She couldn't tear her eyes away from the wooden coffin at the front of the room. Ben was in there, she kept thinking. *Any minute now he's going to jump out and laugh at the big joke he's played on us all.* But as the closing music of 'Always Look on the Bright Side of Life' began to play, Zoe realised that wasn't going to happen. She stood up, linked hands with Candice and filed through the room, leading everyone outside while Ben remained where he was – he and Zoe forever parted, but always in love.

-

'It was good of you to come,' Zoe heard Candice say for the umpteenth time as she handed around plates of sandwiches and made sure people's glasses were topped up. Zoe shot her a sympathetic smile from her position in the corner of the pub.

She was surrounded by colleagues, Ben's old uni mates and even pals from his banking days. All of them were kind enough to offer condolences but Zoe wasn't really listening. How could she? Her heart was in pieces.

Making her excuses, she headed outside into the empty pub garden. She thought of Josh and his dad. They had gone home straight after the funeral, claiming they had a long drive ahead of them. She wished she could have joined them – anything to be by herself and grieve for her loss. Instead, she took a seat on the damp wooden bench and inhaled deeply.

'Ben, what have you done to me?' she said aloud, as the sky rumbled ominously overhead.

'If you talk to yourself like that, people will stick you in the funny farm,' came a voice.

Zoe spun around and saw Miles standing behind her with a pint in his hand.

She offered him a weak smile. 'Maybe that's the best place for me. Anyway, we don't say "funny farm" any more, it's not PC.'

Miles smirked and sat beside Zoe. 'You've done brilliantly today, mate. In fact, you've done bloody well through all of this. Not sure I could have managed.'

'Bollocks,' Zoe said softly. 'If this was Sarah, you'd have been just the same.'

'But it's not Sarah.' Miles took a pull on his pint. 'It's Ben. The only person I've loved and had to bury was my granddad. Given he was like a surrogate dad to me after my old man cleared off, I was broken, so I can only imagine how hard today is for you.'

Zoe felt her insides turn over. She hadn't cried in over an hour and wanted to keep it that way.

'Please, Miles,' she pleaded. 'I can't take anyone being nice to me. Not right now.'

Miles nodded in understanding then pulled his scarf tight around his neck to keep out the chill. 'Have you thought about what you're going to do next?'

Zoe shook her head. 'Candice told me Ben put money aside for me to stay in the flat for at least two years if that's what I want, but I dunno. It feels wrong to stay there without him.'

'You know you're welcome to come and live with us anytime,' Miles said gently. 'Your old room is ready and waiting for you.'

'Thanks,' she managed, hoping Miles wouldn't take her one-word answer as rudeness. The truth was she didn't know what to think. 'I know I'm supposed to say that after losing so many people in my life, I'm aware how precious life is,' Zoe said cautiously, 'but actually life can be really shit.'

Miles laughed, a loud, roaring belly laugh that echoed around the pub garden. 'You're telling me. When I think of the mistakes I've made, along with all the bumps in the road, sometimes you wonder if life's actually worth it.'

'But then you meet someone like Sarah—'

'Or Ben,' Miles interrupted.

'Or Ben.' Zoe smiled.

'And they make life worthwhile,' Miles finished.

'Reminding you the sun will come up every morning,' Zoe said wistfully, catching a glimpse of brightness peeping through the clouds.

They were silent for a moment, each looking up at the rays of light casting a glow over the garden. And that was it, Zoe thought. That was how life was – amongst the darkness there was always a ray of hope, a glimmer of sunshine, and that was what made it all so very bearable in the very worst of moments.

'I've got something for you,' Miles said, cutting across her thoughts. He reached into the inside pocket of his jacket and pulled out a thick envelope. 'It's from Ben.'

Zoe felt a sob rise in her throat at the sight of his handwriting. She reached out to take the envelope, this last piece of the man she loved, and her fingers trembled. 'What is it?'

'I don't know,' Miles admitted. 'He gave it to me when he asked me over.'

'The day before he died,' Zoe said, remembering how Ben hadn't said what he and Miles had discussed.

'He told me to hang on to it until the right time and give it to you. He said I would know when.'

Zoe felt a ripple of excitement even as another part of her heart splintered apart. She ran her fingers across the envelope and thought of that afternoon when she had finally asked Ben if there was any note he wanted to leave but he had refused. She smiled. He had made his own arrangements there too. Knowing how much a note would mean, but wanting to make things easy for her. Now, looking at this letter, Zoe knew she would treasure whatever it said forever. It would live beside the note Sean had left, words to hold on to, words that would carry her through the rest of her life.

'I'll leave you to it,' Miles said, tactfully getting to his feet.

As Miles walked away, she pressed the note to her heart just as she had when she had been given Sean's last words. It felt as if Ben's arms were wrapped around her, holding her one last time. And then, she ripped open the envelope and began to read.

Chapter Fifty-Five

Dear Zoe,

Here we are, another note. But this time one intended just for you. I'm going to miss all our letters, though they were almost our undoing at the beginning when I banned you from notes altogether. I don't know how you didn't slap my self-righteous little face, but you didn't. Thanks to you, I came to understand how valuable words can be and how we can have an effect on those we love with what we say on paper.

And so, in my last message to you, Zoe, I want you to know I think you are the most incredible woman I have ever met. Out of everything I have ever experienced, meeting you, falling in love with you and sharing a life with you has been the best thing that has ever happened to me.

The love and energy you give other people, especially those in need, is nothing short of amazing. You are an inspiration, Zoe Evans, and I feel so privileged and lucky to have felt your love shine on me these last few months.

I've been thinking a lot about our relationship and I believe we met when we each needed each other. I like to think I had some small part in helping you come back to life, to rediscover yourself after the loss of Sean and to show you the joy there can be in life despite suffering such loss. In turn I think you were placed in my path to help me die. I don't mean that to sound morbid, but you've prided yourself on giving all your patients a good death, and that's exactly what you've done for me.

Zoe, you've given me the most loving end, and that's more than anyone has a right to hope for.

You'll know by now that the flat is paid up for the next couple of years, but I'm hoping you won't stay. The thing is, I want you to do a couple of things for me with the money I'm leaving you. This isn't for you to spend on more stationery but for you to find your real purpose and make a difference! I know you're going to go on and do incredible things with your life, Zoe. You have such a great gift for helping those in need. I know you can do something wonderful with this money.

The other thing I want you to do is return to Australia. Whether that's for good or for a visit is up to you, but you have some loose ends to tie up and I believe you need to deal with them so you can make the most of the rest of your life.

Candice will give you the details of the money I have left, and she also has a plane ticket back to Sydney. I want you to board that plane and when you arrive, I want you to spend some time with your mum, lay flowers at Sean's grave and work out why you fled in the first place. Then I want you to sprinkle my ashes along Manly Beach because I have a feeling you won't want to come back to the UK once you've made your peace with your past. I want to be near you, in this life and the next.

I'm going to go now. I'm tired and I'm struggling to hold on to my thoughts. But before I do, know this, Zoe: it's time to live your life. I wish I could be there to see what you do next, but if there is an afterlife then know that I'll be with you every chance I can, pushing you, encouraging you and loving you.

With all my love,

Your Ben xxx

Chapter Fifty-Six

'Mrs Stuart, are you sure this is what you want to say?' Zoe asked, looking at the wizened old woman in the hospital bed. She was one of Zoe's newer patients, having only been admitted the night before. However, with end-stage heart disease, Zoe knew that her death was more than likely to be hours rather than days away, and so she had wanted to ensure her patient had every chance to say whatever was on her mind.

'I'm sure,' Mrs Stuart croaked. 'Millie Newton's got it coming. She's been cheating me at bingo for years.'

Zoe peered down at the words in front of her.

> *When I meet my maker, I'm going to make sure I tell him that you go downstairs rather than up, you thieving little madam.*

Zoe swallowed the laughter that threatened to escape. She'd never had anyone say they would try to ensure a friend's passage was straight to hell before. It was the perfect end to her last day at the hospice so Zoe merely smiled and checked her patient's vitals, planning on discussing the note with her patient's daughter.

She turned out of the ward and walked down the corridor. Up ahead she saw a tall black man and for a second her pulse quickened – was it Ben? At the thought of her beautiful boyfriend, she felt the familiar return of sadness. It had been just over six weeks since Ben had died and she still couldn't quite believe he had gone.

It was a tragedy, of that Zoe was sure. But she knew what she was going to do with the eye-watering amount of money Ben had left her. That at least gave her some small amount of comfort, as had discussing the issue with Sarah.

'I've always thought you needed to go back to Australia,' Sarah had said over a coffee. 'Nobody flees a life like you did without mending fences at some point.'

Lifting her cup to her lips, Zoe had eyed Sarah cautiously. 'Then why didn't you say anything?'

Sarah shrugged. 'I thought it was something you'd come to terms with in your own time. But Ben's right. It's time to sort out the mess you left behind, see what's left for you back home now you're divorced.'

'And spread Ben's ashes across Manly Beach,' Zoe finished sadly.

'All of that and more,' Sarah had said encouragingly. 'What about this money he's left you?'

Zoe smiled shyly. 'I can't believe how much it is, Sarah. It feels wrong.'

'Of course it's not bloody wrong.'

Shrinking back a little, Zoe eyed Sarah warily. 'You sound like Candice.'

'Good,' Sarah replied, then a little more softly she said, 'So have you had any thoughts about the money?'

'I've got one idea. I think it's the sort of thing Ben would be excited about.'

'And it's a way you can make a difference?' Sarah enquired.

'It will be perfect, if I can pull it off.'

'You can do this, Zoe. And if it doesn't work out you know that you always have a home here.'

Sarah, like Ben, was right. And so she had gone back to see Candice shortly after Ben's funeral and said thank you very much to all he had offered.

'About time.' Candice smiled. 'I also need to email you your plane ticket.'

With just a few clicks, Candice had forwarded Zoe the documents for her journey to Sydney.

As Zoe opened the email, she gasped in astonishment. 'This is first-class.'

'It's a long way. You want to travel back in comfort. All Ben wanted, and in fact all I want, is for you to be happy. Time to live, Zoe.'

-

After Zoe had said goodbye to colleagues, patients and the hospice itself, she found herself jangling with nerves as she sat in the back of her old Yaris. She had gifted the car to Miles as a leaving present and he and Sarah had kindly offered to take her to the airport. Yet as the English countryside rushed past her, doubt took hold.

Her home was here, wasn't it? But the idea of staying in the UK without Ben didn't seem right, while the thought of going home and seeing her mum again, she had to admit, felt more natural. Was she ready to face the pain of stepping back into her homeland after the way she had left? She sank back in her seat, Lottie chattering excitedly beside her, and instead focused on her last note delivery.

Nico had died on the day of Ben's funeral, surrounded by his family. Zoe was glad Nico had been given a good end and that she had managed to speak to his wife, Catherine, about the letter Nico had asked her to deliver to Ennio.

'He felt anything you had to say to someone should be said in life, not death. I'm pleased he's putting things right with this letter,' Catherine had said, gesturing to the envelope in Zoe's hand. 'Are you really happy to deliver it? It's a long way.'

Zoe had smiled. 'Ealing is actually on my way home.'

Catherine had looked quizzical but hadn't pushed her.

Now, as Miles pulled into the cul-de-sac that was home to Nico's childhood friend, Zoe stroked the envelope nervously.

'Do you want us to come in with you?' Miles asked.

Zoe shook her head and stepped out of the car. Pulling her jacket up around her neck, she walked up the path, smiling as the rain began to fall. For her, the British winters would be a thing of the past in a few hours.

She rapped on the blue, wooden door and seconds later it was opened by a man with the same Mediterranean colouring as Nico.

'Can I help you?' he asked, without any trace of the Italian accent Nico had held.

Zoe cleared her throat. 'I hope so. I'm Zoe Evans, staff nurse at The Oaks. A hospice in Bath. Do you have a moment?'

Ennio frowned. 'What's this about?'

'Your friend Nico,' she said gently.

The moment she said Nico's name, Ennio's face fell and he welcomed her inside.

'What is it?' he asked, gesturing for her to take a seat in the neat but sparsely decorated living room. 'Catherine told me Nico had died… I still can't believe it.'

As his voice trailed off, Zoe perched on the edge of the cream sofa and faced Ennio, who sat down opposite.

'I think he kept quite a few things to himself,' Zoe explained.

'Yes, our friend Giulia has only recently told me that Nico was the father of her child.'

'You know Giulia?' Zoe gasped.

Ennio nodded. 'We have all been friends for years. I guessed when I went back to Naples last Christmas that Nico was Antonio's father, the two are so alike, but Giulia swore I was wrong.'

'Well, doing the right thing was obviously on his mind,' Zoe said as she reached into her bag and handed the small blue envelope to Ennio. She watched his hands tremble as he took the piece of paper and began to read. Moments later he got to his feet and threw the note across the room, shouting, 'Stupid! Stupid man!'

Then Ennio's knees buckled and he sank to the floor, weeping for the friend he had lost. Instinctively, Zoe wrapped an arm around his heaving shoulders.

'Nico, how could you leave it like this?' Ennio sobbed under his breath.

'These things happen,' Zoe consoled. 'It's up to you to help put it right if you can.'

'Of course. But Nico should have cleaned up his own mess.' He sat back on his heels and regarded Zoe with a sad smile. 'I'm sorry. I haven't even offered you a cup of tea.'

'Then it's lucky for you I don't drink tea.'

At that they both chuckled and Ennio wiped away his tears with the bottom of his T-shirt.

'When will you go back?' she asked, gesturing to the note that still lay by the fireplace.

'As soon as I can. I still don't understand why he didn't do this himself.'

'Maybe because going home, admitting he was wrong, seemed like too big a mountain to climb.'

'You sound as if you know something about this?' Ennio asked.

Zoe sighed. 'I guess I'm facing something similar myself.'

Ennio looked at her in surprise 'How so?'

'I fled my homeland of Australia over two years ago without a word to anyone. I'd lost my son in a terrible accident and needed to get away.'

'How did that work out?'

'I'm divorced,' Zoe said with a watery smile. 'And I still grieve for my son every day but I'm finally going back, ready to tie up loose ends. I'm on my way to the airport now.'

Ennio raised an eyebrow. 'Are you scared?'

'I'm terrified!' Zoe admitted.

'So why go back now?'

'Someone close to me made me realise I had to deal with my past to properly move on,' Zoe explained.

'And what will you do if it doesn't work out?'

'Come back, but at least I'll know I tried to set my world in order.'

-

By the time Zoe reached Heathrow Airport, her stomach was turning over with nerves, but this time, after her visit to Ennio, she felt more certain of her decision to return home. As she stood in the middle of the terminal, people were rushing past with their wheelie cases, talking into mobiles. Noisy tannoys were repeating final calls and departure announcements.

'Remember we'll see you in a few weeks,' Sarah pointed out. 'Miles is going to show me an Aussie Christmas.'

Zoe nodded. The fact that her friend would be joining her soon was reassuring.

'And if you really can't wait until then, you can easily get a flight back,' Sarah reminded her.

'Not first-class she can't,' Miles added as he bent down to tickle Lottie.

'Ahhh, stop it!' The little girl giggled.

Zoe beamed at them all. These wonderful friends of hers had become like family, but it was time to see what she was made of without them. She glanced up at one of the departure screens. Her flight check-in was closing.

Turning to Sarah, Zoe wrapped her arms around her friend. 'It's time.'

Sarah's voice was thick with emotion as she said, 'I'm going to miss you, but I'm proud of you.'

They buried themselves in each other until the sound of Lottie's shrieks became louder and Zoe knew that was her cue.

'I'll see you,' she said.

'You will,' Sarah promised. 'Text me when you land. I'll be tracking your flight.'

Zoe waved the little group goodbye as she walked through to departures. Once they were out of sight, she put her hand in her pocket and wrapped her fingers around her greatest treasures – her letters from Sean and Ben. On her flight to England all that time ago, the only thing that had anchored Zoe had been Sean's note. Now, as she walked towards security, that note together with Ben's would give Zoe strength to find her way home.

Chapter Fifty-Seven

Twelve months later

As Zoe stared out at the waves, she smiled. She would never tire of this view. There was something so magical about it that it had almost become a part of her, this living, breathing, azure-blue ocean that was much more than she would ever be.

'It's all going to be okay,' she muttered aloud.

There was no answer, of course, just the sound of waves crashing against the shore, but she knew that Ben was listening. He always was.

'I've gone for the caterers Mum recommended,' she told him. 'You know the ones that had those nice vegan options? I know you think vegans are wimps but times are changing. Oh, and if that's Sean rolling his eyes, tell him to stop it immediately!'

Mentioning Sean's name no longer brought the pain it used to. Since Ben's death, she had thought of her precious boys as at peace together.

When Zoe had stepped off the aircraft and into the bright Australian sunshine a year ago, she had felt the cracks in her heart starting to heal. The familiar Aussie accents, the passport control lady who smiled and welcomed her home. Home. She had mulled the word over. Because like it or not, she knew this place. Deep in her heart, this land, this way of being, was etched firmly into her soul. Outside in the heat, she hadn't been sure where to go, so she had got in a taxi and told the driver to take her to Manly Beach. There, she had got a coffee at one of the cafes that overlooked the beach and processed the events that had led her here.

Zoe had stayed there for hours. She had nowhere to be, no place to go and nobody waiting for her. She hadn't told Ruth or her sister, Jemma, she was coming home. They had both been incredibly supportive when she broke the news of Ben's death but she wasn't ready to start building bridges with family just yet. She needed time to just be.

But then a woman had come over and peered at her, hand shielding her eyes from the sun.

'Zoe?' she had called, uncertainly. 'Is that you? Ben Tasker's friend?'

Zoe had turned and gazed at the woman, struggling to place her, then realising in surprised delight that it was Irene – the woman she and Ben had video-called at her mother's bequest to reveal the truth about her biological father.

'Irene,' she had gasped. 'How are you?'

'I'm well. What are you doing here?' Irene had looked at her, an easy smile spreading across her face as she sat next to Zoe. 'Thought you were a fully grown pom now?'

Zoe had laughed. 'I'm back for a bit. Long story.'

Irene had signalled to a waiter, ordered herself and Zoe a smoothie each then said, 'I've got time.'

Zoe had told Irene about Ben's death, his generosity and his insistence that she return. Irene's hands had flown to her mouth in sorrow as Zoe delivered the news. And once condolences had been expressed, Zoe had revealed why she had left Australia in the first place with no intention of ever coming back. By the time she was finished, both women were spent.

'You came straight here from the airport?' Irene asked.

'I didn't know what else to do. I ought to phone my family but it feels a bit much.'

Irene had raised an eyebrow at that. 'As someone who recently connected with a long-lost relative, I can tell you that although it's rewarding it's also bloody exhausting. Come on, you look dead on your feet.'

Irene had got up and Zoe had looked at her questioningly. 'Where are we going?'

'My place.' Irene had gestured to a block of flats above a beach shop. 'I've got a spare room.'

'I couldn't impose,' Zoe had insisted.

Irene had let out a cackle of laughter. '*Impose?* You've been in the UK too long, Zoe. Let's go.'

And that had been that. Zoe had stayed with Irene for a month while she gradually got used to being in Australia again. It had been quite an adjustment, reconnecting with family, old friends and, of course, David. She had waited a couple of weeks before contacting him, worried what he might think her arrival would mean. But what Zoe had forgotten was just how much of a friend David had always been. One Sunday he had shown up at Irene's place, taken her out for lunch and let her talk about Ben, Sean, the notes that meant so much and her plans for the future without demanding anything. It had been, Zoe thought afterwards, wonderful.

But what Zoe had to get on with was the reason Ben had brought her here – her purpose. The first of those purposes had been to sprinkle his ashes along the coastline. She had stolen out of bed as dawn broke one morning ready to deliver an entire speech as she ceremoniously sprinkled Ben's remains along the shore. Yet it turned out a gust of wind had other ideas and just as she had taken the lid off the urn, Ben's ashes had been swept out into the ocean beyond.

A bubble of laughter inflated in Zoe's chest. 'You would have loved this. I can see you now, laughing and laughing.'

Then she had sunk onto the wet sand, all the pain she had endured over the past few years overwhelming her. After allowing herself a brief wallow, she had got up, literally dusted herself off, and thrown herself into the next part of Ben's plan.

The work had been hard, with days where she had done nothing but hit the phone, hiring people, finding office space and more. The only luxury she had allowed herself was arranging for Ben's Porsche to be shipped from the UK to Australia at great expense. She had nearly had a heart attack at the cost but she knew Ben wanted her to have fun in his car and she wanted to do something frivolous for him, to show him she was learning to enjoy her life.

Once Irene had found out about Zoe's charity work, she had generously insisted on donating her time – in exchange for a drive in the Porsche! Zoe hadn't liked to take advantage but Irene insisted, and Zoe had been grateful. Irene's skills as an accountant had proved invaluable, as had every volunteer and benefactor.

Then there was Ella. Once Zoe had settled in, she had got in touch with the young mum and told her how much she would like to extend the work she was doing at the hospice out internationally but with a twist. Ella had immediately thrown her support into Zoe's cause, telling her that Ricky's Wish, as the charity was known, would be delighted to help her from the UK with whatever she needed.

Now, as Zoe watched the large white banner unfurl above the restaurant on the cliffs, she knew it had all been worth it.

The Sean Ben Memorial Foundation. Zoe felt a sense of elation as she read the words. Today she was hosting a special lunch to launch the charity in honour of the two boys she had loved and lost. The foundation would be dedicated to ensuring those facing the end would have a good death and those left behind received the support they needed to find joy in their lives again.

'It's going to be brilliant,' a voice said beside her.

She turned and smiled at the sight of David, his dog, Loki, who gave an affectionate bark, and her mum, Ruth, just a few steps behind.

'You think?' she asked, a touch of anxiety to her voice.

'I know,' he said firmly. 'Think of all the families you'll help with this charity. Ben and Sean would be proud.'

At the mention of Ben's name, Zoe smiled. He had been right, she had needed to return to Australia. She had visited Sean's grave and forged an unlikely friendship with David, finally able to forgive him properly.

'I hope Candice will like it.'

'How could she not?' Ruth came to stand alongside Zoe, slipping her small hand into Zoe's. She felt relaxed in her mum's presence, the two having become closer since her return.

'What time is she coming down?' Ruth asked, pushing her sunglasses onto the top of her head, revealing sparkling blue eyes brimming with excitement.

'Just before the lunch to say hello and generally spread some Ben love,' she replied.

Despite the distance, the friendship between Candice and Zoe had blossomed. It was Candice who had championed Zoe's wish to create a charity honouring the dying. She had even flown over when she could take a holiday from her banking job, helping Zoe make phone calls and find premises around the corner from the tiny studio near Manly that Zoe found to rent. And it didn't hurt that Candice and Irene had developed a long-distance relationship either.

'What about Sarah and Miles?' David asked.

Zoe grinned. Sarah and Miles's wedding was in just a few weeks. Although her friend had found her dress back in Bath, Sarah had become something of a bridezilla in the run-up to her wedding, insisting everything was perfect. 'Sarah will be here after she's been to the caterers'.'

David raised an eyebrow and looked down at Loki, who was busy digging for bones in the sand. 'Is there anything I can do to help? Get Jemma?' he asked.

'Jemma's making her own way,' Ruth said. Zoe felt another rush of gratitude. Things had improved with her sister too now she was back home.

'Well then, we'll be off,' David said.

'Yes, me too,' added Ruth, who could see that Zoe was lost in her own thoughts.

Together the three of them walked back along the beach, but Zoe was too engrossed in making sure launch day was perfect to do much more than wave them goodbye. Zoe looked back up at the banner and felt a glimmer of hope beginning to unfurl. This charity would be the start of something wonderful, Zoe could feel it. But there was still one thing left to do. Perhaps the most important thing of all.

Pulling out a folded piece of paper, she smiled. She opened the note, a seagull crying above her head as she did so, and read the few words she wanted to share with those she loved.

Dear Sean and Ben,

Thank you for showing me how to love and thank you most of all for giving me hope.

With all my love forever,

Zoe xxx

Folding the note back up, Zoe ripped it into tiny pieces and threw it into the air. She turned her face to the sun and watched as the gentle breeze swept the words from her heart into the sea. Now she was ready to live.

Acknowledgements

I always think writing a book is a bit like raising a child, it takes a whole village and *The Notekeeper* is no exception. I have some truly phenomenal people to thank for helping make this book a reality, including my wonderful agent, Kate Burke, who worked overtime, helping me develop this novel from a kernel of an idea into something I could throw my heart and soul into. Likewise, I am indebted to my incredibly talented editor, Emily Bedford, who has truly helped make this book sparkle thanks to her wisdom.

I owe the idea of this book to a very old friend of mine, Ellie Winters. Not long after we first met, she enrolled in nursing training with a plan, if I remember rightly, to work in a hospice. At eighteen, I was outraged, convinced that would be nothing short of depressing. Ellie laughed at my reaction and told me that there was such a thing as a good death and that was what she wanted to do. Ellie's very wise words have always stayed with me and during lockdown when we were all faced with those terrible images of so many loved ones dying of Covid 19, I remember thinking about the nurses working overtime to ensure the dying had someone to hold their hand during their last moments. My mind strayed to Ellie's words and so, the idea of a nurse wanting to do everything for their dying patients was born. Naturally, I consulted Ellie, who does now work full-time in a hospice, about the possibility of a nurse who takes down the last words of the dying. I was on tenterhooks waiting for her answer, but Ellie assured me that doctors, paramedics, orderlies and many, many other hospice staff, all go above and beyond for their patients, not only taking down last words but also carrying out last requests where possible. Ellie, I'm so grateful to you for all the information, help and support, not to mention those words that stayed with me over twenty-five years ago – thank you a million times over.

Thanks, too, to Jean Fullerton for the proofread. As a keen author and former nurse, I felt reassured when Jean gave it a thumbs up. However, any mistakes made, particularly about anything medical, are entirely my own.

Special thanks must also go to my husband Chris, who has been encouraging me for years to write something I was passionate about. *The Notekeeper* is that book, and I want to thank you for believing in me and encouraging me to keep going even when I thought I shouldn't.

My fabulous author friends, Dany Atkins, Kate Thompson, Faith Bleasdale, Sasha Wagstaff and Rosie Hendry – the gossips, laughter and good dollops of advice and support are all so appreciated. I would be lost without you all – thanks for having my writing back! And of course my very special friends, Becki, Craig, Karen – where do the years go? Thanks for always being there, and thanks as well to Rebecca, Claire, Gemma, Kelly and Madi for always listening and generally being brilliant sources of support. Mum and Dad, last but certainly never least, your unwavering love and support is something I never take for granted – thank you for pretty much everything!

Finally, huge thanks must go to you lovely reader. There are so many books out there in the world but I'm delighted you took a chance on this one. If you'd like to follow me on social media or drop me a line I would love to hear from you. You can find me at facebook.com/fionafordauthor or Instagram/fionafordauthor.